Y031766

D0536649

THE OUTCAST GIRLS

THE OUTCAST GIRLS ✳

Alys Clare

severn
House

This first world edition published 2020
in Great Britain and the USA by
SEVERN HOUSE PUBLISHERS LTD of
Eardley House, 4 Uxbridge Street, London W8 7SY.
Trade paperback edition first published
in Great Britain and the USA 2021 by
SEVERN HOUSE PUBLISHERS LTD.

British Library Cataloguing in Publication Data
A CIP catalogue record for this title is available from the British Library.

ISBN-13: 978-0-7278-9045-0 (cased)
ISBN-13: 978-1-78029-733-0 (trade paper)
ISBN-13: 978-1-4483-0455-4 (e-book)

All Severn House titles are printed on acid-free paper.

Severn House Publishers support the Forest Stewardship Council™ [FSC™],
the leading international forest certification organisation.
All our titles that are printed on FSC certified paper carry the FSC logo.

MIX
Paper from
responsible sources
FSC® C013056

Typeset by Palimpsest Book Production Ltd.,
Falkirk, Stirlingshire, Scotland.
Printed and bound in Great Britain by
TJ International, Padstow, Cornwall.

In memory of my great-great-grandmother
Mary Leghorn Sutherland née Lea,
born Portsmouth, 13th July 1828,
who went to India.

PRELUDE

Lucknow, India, early autumn 1872

He lies back on the bank of pillows, inhaling the mixed smells, his heart hammering. After a few moments he gently peels his flesh free; sweat has made a temporary but fragile bond.

He hears her breathing deepen as she slips into sleep. It is a common occurrence, for she who is so elegant, detached and collected in everyday life gives way to gloriously enthusiastic abandon in bed and, in this heat, the expending of all that energy is utterly exhausting and wipes her out for a spell.

He turns his head fractionally, careful not to move too quickly and waken her, and looks down at her. Her thick strawberry blonde hair is spread across his chest, making him too hot. Her breasts crush against him, full and luxurious and his delight when he is full of desire and hungry for her. Now he is sated and her flesh on his is just one more source of heat.

Damnable heat. Blasted, bloody heat.

After the years he has spent in India he ought to be used to it. He knows he has the appearance of a confident, successful man who does not permit such minor irritations as the devastating climate of the subcontinent to disturb his English composure, but at times the illusion is difficult to maintain. At times such as this, he reflects sourly, when he wishes that, instead of a tumble of damp bedding in a room like an oven, he was lying in a shady patch of woodland in the cool green English countryside, a little stream bubbling close by and the soft cooing of wood pigeons in the trees, with the prospect of returning soon to some pleasant country house with well-tended flower borders, clipped hedges and emerald grass where there will be a discreet manservant awaiting his return to help him off with his boots and hand him a glass of straw-pale sherry at precisely the right temperature . . .

She stirs, mutters something incomprehensible, clutches at him with the hand that still rests deep down in his groin. He waits, barely breathing, but she sighs and sleeps again.

He has responded, despite his mood, to the brief clench of her hand, but as she relaxes back into sleep, he feels himself slacken again. And, in that instant, he experiences a stab of violent revulsion for the whole business. For the clamours of the flesh, for the grasping hands, the hungry mouths, the blind thrusting of his body that will not be denied, the desperate sucking-in of him and what spills out of him into that wet, dark, secret part of her . . .

I am exhausted, he tells himself soothingly. That is what is to blame for this despondency; that's all it is. I work far too hard, I am beset with worries and problems and anxieties that only I can resolve, and I must face up to decisions that I am loath to take.

His mind sheers away from one of those decisions, for he never allows himself to dwell upon it until he has had at least two drinks, and now it is mid-afternoon and the last alcohol he touched was late last night . . .

But he must not think about last night either.

He looks down at her again. She really is glorious, utterly his favourite type, and her beauty – her appearance in general – is a major factor in this delicate business. She—

But that, too, is not a thought for now.

He sighs, slowly, deeply, and her head rises on his chest with his ribs' expansion.

He realizes miserably that there is virtually nothing in his present situation that bears thinking about. And so he lets his mind turn back into the safer country of the past; specifically, to the knife-edge tension of that home leave when he first met Mary Featherwood. She was eighteen, coming into the flowering of her young beauty, he was eight years older and in need of a wife: indeed, a wife with prospects, for any other sort would only serve to exacerbate his . . . his challenges.

Even in the safety of his own thoughts, he will not use a stronger word.

He had been invited to a dinner party given by the very wealthy old lady who was Mary's grandmother. She had looked

at him with suspicious eyes as if she mistrusted flashily handsome men with shiny hair and well-trimmed moustaches on
sight. Mary had regarded him with very different eyes, and he
had wooed her with all the weapons in his considerable arsenal:
the little presents so tentatively given ('Oh, I do understand,
Miss Featherwood, that such a gift is not at all appropriate when
we have but recently met, but I could not help myself!'); the
careful advances ('I have shocked you, dearest Mary, and I
loathe myself for the insensitive rotter I am, but I could not
resist a tiny kiss on that peachy cheek!'); the steady advancing
of his suit ('Yes, India is indeed hot, but we Europeans have
found ways to cope with it, and many of us retreat to the hills
in summer'); the subtle implications that what is happening to
them is somehow inevitable ('I knew, my Mary, the moment I
set eyes on you, that fate had destined us for each other and I
would venture to say that it was the same for you?').

And what a triumph it was when she accepted his proposal!
The marriage hastily arranged, for home leave does not last
long. The splendid ceremony, his bride like an angel in her frills
and flounces of white, her late mother's veil upon her head and
her grandmother's diamond tiara holding it in place (taken
back, incidentally – the sour note intrudes on his reverie –
the following morning). The sumptuous wedding breakfast, the
sideboards groaning with extravagant presents, the delicious
food so discreetly presented, the vintage champagne.

His wedding night, and Mary the eager virgin bride of his
dreams, he the considerate, careful, tender husband . . .

And now, five years later, here I am, he thinks.

The reverie has worked too well, for it has taken him back
to a time when life was perfect. Coming back to reality is
consequently all the harder.

For life is very far from perfect now.

The woman lying across his chest stirs and quickly he soothes
her. 'Hush, Mary, sleep now,' he murmurs. How strange, he
thinks, that she too should be called Mary; how strange, how
convenient and how oddly prophetic.

He feels his mood slip further down from the comfort of
memory and the heights of his recent sexual delight, for in truth
the problems that beset him can never be held at bay for long.

He sighs, a long, slow exhalation. At least, he thinks, trying to cheer himself up, the infant clearly likes her nanny. Nanny Dora to the baby (no, not a baby, she will be four early next year), Nurse Tewk to him. Odd surname, odd-looking woman, with that tall, board-flat body under the severe navy uniform and those clear light-brown eyes that seem to see straight into him . . .

'Christ,' he murmurs very quietly, 'I bloody well hope they can't.'

He forces his mind away from dwelling on his little daughter's nanny, for he can hardly bear to think about his child. As for looking at her, listening to those awful, agonizing attempts to form comprehensible words, watching that stumbling progress as she tries again and again to walk and always fails—

No, he resolves, I cannot think about her now.

And there is a fresh anxiety, for Mary – the other one, his wife, the child's mother – is sick. Sick, and daily becoming weaker, and if the worst happens and she dies, then—

But that truly is unthinkable.

'*God,*' he says.

The woman stirs again, so before she wakes and starts on her pleadings and her cajolings, he slips out from under her, carefully lays her head on the pillow, kisses her lightly and mutters, 'Goodbye for now, my dearest. Until tomorrow.'

He creeps out of the room and firmly closes the door.

ONE

t is January, and the year is 1881. It is cold. Snow lies ankle-deep in Hob's Court, virtually undisturbed except for Felix Wilbraham's footprints, deposited as he arrived an hour ago and already frosting at the edges.

Felix is at his desk in the outer office. Lily Raynor, the proprietor of the World's End Bureau (*Private Enquiry Agency*, as it is described on the stationery), is in her inner sanctum. She is apparently absorbed in some papers she is reading. Felix shoots her the occasional glance, trying to determine if she is as cold as he is. She has a heavy black wool shawl around her shoulders, she wears fingerless mittens and her nose – bright red at the tip – appears to be running, to judge by the regular little sniffs, so he concludes that she probably is.

He stands up and positions himself in her open doorway.

'Lily?' he says after a few moments, during which she is either ignoring him or genuinely hasn't noticed him.

She looks up, frowning. 'Hm?'

'Is it all right if I fetch some more coal?' He nods towards the paltry little fires burning in the two hearths in their offices.

'Oh . . .' Her frown deepens.

Felix could have written out precisely what is running through her mind: it is very cold, the fires are giving out so little warmth that we may as well not bother, coal is terribly costly and, after a great flurry of new business following our successful solving of last autumn's multiple murder case, now everything has gone rather quiet.

She looks up, the frown clearing.

'Of course,' she says. 'But, Felix, I propose we build up just the one fire, and you move in here. If that is acceptable?' she adds.

He is grinning in relief. 'Yes, yes, good idea,' he says. Before she can change her mind, he grabs the coal scuttle from beside the hearth in the front office and hurries out through the office door, along the passage to the back of the house, through the kitchen and the scullery, into the yard and past the outside lavatory. The coal hole is at the rear of the yard, where – not nearly often enough – it is filled by men carrying heavy sacks on their shoulders from the narrow alley that runs behind the houses.

He fills the scuttle, balancing a particularly large lump of coal on the top, then hurries back inside.

It is colder than ever out in the still, blueish air.

'Where's Mrs Clapper?' Felix asks as he kneels before Lily's hearth, coaxing wonderfully warm flames from the newly mended fire.

Mrs Clapper, inherited, like the house, from Lily's grand-parents, comes in three times a week to do the heavy work. She is a small but powerful force of nature, and it has taken Felix some time to work out how to keep on her right side. Even now, after nine months of working at the World's End Bureau, he doesn't always manage it.

'Not coming in.' Lily, still enthralled, doesn't look up from her papers. 'According to her, Clapper's "bronicles" are misbehaving. He's bad with them.'

'She's deserted you to look after him?' Felix is surprised. 'I hadn't realized she was such a devoted wife.'

Lily smiles rather sadly. 'I don't think she is. But poor Mr Clapper coughs so hard that he stops breathing, and she has to thump him on the back until he brings up the gouts of phlegm that are obstructing his breathing, and then—'

'Yes, thank you, I understand,' Felix interrupts hastily. Lily, who before she opened a private enquiry agency used to be a nurse (she has packed quite a lot into her thirty-odd years upon Earth), is comfortable with the more repulsive aspects of the human body. Felix (four years her junior and experienced in very different ways) is not.

He was about to make a joke about Clapper's misbehaving bronicles sounding like a flock of unruly racing pigeons or a cage full of disobedient ferrets, but in the face of what sounds like a rather serious illness, he keeps quiet.

Lily returns to her absorbing papers. Felix, satisfied the fire is now as bright as he can make it, fetches his chair from the outer office and the books he is working on, and settles opposite Lily.

He is engaged upon the dispiriting task of writing up their current cases. Since there are only two, he realizes with a sinking of the spirits that the job will take him barely another quarter of an hour. The husband who went missing on New Year's Day, reported by his harassed wife (and her seven children) with a mixture of irritation, a sprinkle of anxiety and a very detectable hope that the bugger might never come back, thus sparing her any additions to the large family, turned up four days later in hospital in Deptford ('Bloody *Deptford*?' his wife shrieked. 'What the hell was he doing in *Deptford*?') with a broken leg, a black eye and concussion. The innocent expression he had presented to Felix as he swore blind he couldn't remember a thing after he set out at six in the evening for 'a swift half with me mates' was so patently false that Felix didn't even bother to say so, contenting himself with raising a sceptical eyebrow and turning away. The over-indulged young lady who arrived in a state of near hysteria two days after Boxing Day, claiming that the man she hoped to marry was involved in the running of an opium den, later confessed she had made it up; she had observed her fiancé kissing her sister under the mistletoe and wanted to give him a week or so's unease to punish him.

Now that, Felix reflects as he enters details of the young lady's payment in the big ledger, is unlikely to be a marriage made in heaven . . .

He completes the task, puts the heavy books back in their accustomed places and resumes his seat. Lily is still reading. After perhaps two or three minutes, he says quietly, 'Lily?'

She looks up. 'Yes?'

'I'm sorry to disturb you, but I have nothing to do.'

The brief and mildly spoken sentence has a disproportionate effect upon his employer, but then of course it says so much more.

Lily throws aside her papers, sighs heavily, glances wildly around the office and then, her light green eyes on Felix, says plaintively, 'I thought we would be *inundated* with work just now!'

He thinks he understands, but nevertheless says enquiringly, 'Yes?'

'*Yes!* Christmas, families all together, old tensions and rivalries resurfacing, arguments, suspicion, violence . . . Surely,' she goes on, 'fertile ground for our sort of work?'

Lily, Felix is well aware, is a good person. From his own experience of her, he knows she is honest, courageous, principled, kind. To think that she has been viewing the wonderful, warm, loving festival of Christmas as a source of new work for an enquiry agency makes him want to smile. He refrains from comment, aware that her remark would not have burst out of her but for the circumstances.

She is worried. And, because she is his employer and this is his work, he is worried too.

'And as if that was not bad enough,' she adds with a scowl, 'the Little Ballerina has gone off to Huddersfield without paying last month's rent.'

'Oh, dear,' Felix says.

The Little Ballerina is Lily's tenant. Her grandparents' house is large and costly to run. Letting the spacious rooms of the middle floor is a way for Lily to meet her expenses. Felix knows without being told that it is Lily's most fervent ambition to earn enough from the World's End Bureau that she may terminate the Little Ballerina's tenancy, for she is temperamental, smelly, chronically untidy and in a perpetual state of pending hostilities with Mrs Clapper. Added to her sins, it now appears she has become financially unreliable.

'I thought the production was doing well?' he says. The Little Ballerina's company is putting on an entertainment called *Christmas Delights*, which apparently contains elements of both classical ballet and pantomime and is designed to appeal to aficionados of both. 'There's clearly a call for it in Huddersfield,' he adds.

'Yes,' Lily agrees. 'And she's been promoted out of the chorus. She performs a solo where she dances with a clown.'

'I *hate* clowns,' Felix mutters, immediately hoping he has spoken too softly for Lily to hear: he was terrified by a white-faced clown holding what looked like a meat cleaver when he was four years old and still has the occasional nightmare, but this is not a weakness to admit to his employer. 'Oh, that must be encouraging for her!' he exclaims brightly. 'She's always moaning that she's far too good for the chorus and the director ought to realize and reward her talent, and the reason he doesn't is because she's Russian.'

'Rather than because she's lazy with an inflated opinion of herself?' Lily smiles wryly. 'She was only given the role because the girl who usually dances it has lost the nail on her big toe.'

'Eugh,' Felix mutters. He has been doodling on his pad of scrap paper as they talk, and now draws a little picture of a ballerina's elegantly pointed toe in its beribboned satin shoe, beside it a second image of a bloody, bruised, calloused, twisted and bunioned bare foot.

He hears Lily move her chair. Looking up, he observes that she is sitting up very straight, spectacles glinting, mittened hands folded before her on the desk, a determined expression on her face.

'Our funds are adequate for the time being,' she begins very formally, 'indeed, more than adequate, for I have been economizing rigidly in order to husband the resources we do have.'

Indeed you have, Felix thinks but does not say, reflecting on the meagre little fires.

'It is uneconomic for you to sit there with nothing to do,' she goes on, adding, 'and I too have no more urgent task than to go through the reports of some recent and rather interesting court cases.' She pauses.

That, Felix thinks, explains the reading matter.

'We have, I believe, two options,' Lily goes on. 'We could perhaps advertise – put a notice in the local papers, possibly. What do you think?'

'I think it's a good idea,' he says earnestly. He has been dreading that option one might be for his employer to lay off her sole employee, and his relief at finding it isn't is only marred by the fear that this could constitute option two. 'I could have a word with Marm, he has a nose for situations that require the sort of assistance we offer.'

Marmaduke Smithers is a journalist. He is also Felix's landlord; the two of them are sharing a modest first-floor apartment in a tall old house in Kinver Street, one of a maze of similar streets between the King's Road and Royal Hospital Road. The small room at the back has been a delight to Felix since he moved in three months ago, such an improvement is it on where he was living before, and sharing the digs with Marm is proving to be exciting and enjoyable, if exhausting at times and not a little damaging to the health; Marm likes to drink and Felix feels it is his duty as tenant not to let him do so alone.

'Good,' Lily says, 'please do.'

Felix waits. Lily is already glancing at her court reports, clearly eager to return to them, so, not without trepidation, he prompts her: 'What's the second option?'

She grimaces, then the expression turns into a rueful smile that does a great deal for her appearance. 'We could try praying.'

Some time later, Felix is trudging back from his errand to buy a loaf of bread and some cheese from the corner shop. There has been no further snowfall, but the temperature seems to have dropped considerably. Coat collar turned up around his ears and hat brim turned down, muffler wound several times round his face and neck to cover the gaps, he thinks of the merry fire in Lily's inner sanctum and increases his pace. Unwisely: barely able to see through the gap between hat brim and muffler, he takes the corner from World's End Passage into Hob's Court too fast, skids, throws out the hand not holding the bread and cheese to save himself and feels his hand encounter something soft that cries out '*Ouch!*'

And there is a thump as quite a heavy object falls to the ground.

Horrified, Felix stares down at the woman lying at his feet, surreptitiously trying to rub her buttocks and ease the pain of her fall.

'I'm so very sorry!' Felix exclaims, bending down to help her to her feet. 'I wasn't looking where I was going and I was walking too quickly for the prevailing conditions. Are you badly hurt?'

The woman is still holding on to her bottom, openly now. Felix surmises it really is painful. But she says, 'No, I am perfectly all right.'

It is a brave lie. She has tears in her round brown eyes.

Felix stares at her worriedly. She is perhaps in her mid-thirties, brown hair drawn back from a centre parting framing a face as round as her eyes. Her mouth is . . . kittenish, Felix thinks; small, prettily shaped with the suspicion of a rosebud upper lip. She is dressed modestly, not to say dowdily, in a felt hat with a misshapen brim and a heavy knee-length brown jacket over a skirt of a slightly darker fabric. A scarf in yet another shade of brown wound several times around her neck gives the illusion of several double chins.

'Have you far to go?' Felix asks. 'Perhaps you will allow me to see you to your destination?'

'I . . .' she begins. Not used to the city, Felix guesses, and not sure whether it is safe to accept the solicitude of a stranger.

Making up her mind, the woman says, 'This, I believe, is Hob's Court?'

'It is,' Felix confirms.

She smiles in relief. 'Ah, then I believe I need no assistance, thank you, for this is the place I seek.'

And Felix knows, even before she speaks, what she is going to say next.

'I am looking for number three, which is the address of the World's End Bureau,' the woman says.

And, as he jubilantly leads the way to the door, Felix reflects that he and Lily ought to try praying more often.

Lily hears the street door open and her stomach rumbles loudly at the prospect of fresh bread and cheese. There is a jar of Mrs Cropper's green tomato chutney on the larder shelf, which ought to—

But then she realizes Felix is not alone.

'. . . will inform Miss Raynor that you are here,' he is saying.

Lily stands up.

Felix hurries through the outer office, and Lily makes out a short, round shape in the hall behind him. He comes into the inner sanctum, and his light hazel eyes are bright with excitement.

'New client!' he hisses. 'Found her outside! Shall I bring her in?'

'*Yes!*' Lily hisses back. While Felix strides back to the hall, she draws forward another chair, placing it beside Felix's. She returns to her own side of the desk, a hand up to smooth her fair hair, then adopts an expression of guarded welcome. It wouldn't do to make this new client see how eager she is.

Eager? she thinks ruefully. Desperate is closer.

Felix ushers a dumpy woman dressed in brown into the office. The woman walks across the floor, limping slightly, accepting Lily's invitation to sit down with a brief inclination of her head.

Felix too, it appears, has noticed the limp. 'Oh, dear, you are indeed hurt!' he says, looking down at the woman in brown, his handsome face creased in distress.

'Hurt?' The word emerges like a pistol shot, and instantly Lily tries to mitigate the effect with a smile.

'I knocked her over,' Felix explains. 'I slipped coming round the corner and sent her flying. I really am so sorry,' he adds, turning back to the woman. Lily detects that it is not the first time he has apologized.

The woman is rapidly recovering her composure. 'I have suffered no more than a few bumps,' she says with dignity, 'and the limp is not caused by this or indeed any recent injury.' She does not explain. 'I accept your apology, Mr . . .'

'Wilbraham. Felix Wilbraham.'

'Mr Wilbraham. And you' – she turns to Lily – 'are Miss Lily Raynor?'

'I am,' Lily confirms.

'I am *most* relieved to have found you!' the woman says, her plump cheeks flushing. 'I—'

But, as Lily has observed often happens when a new client comes to the point where they must explain their business with the World's End Bureau, the woman is struck dumb.

Lily waits. Felix, lurking behind the woman and about to sit down, stands perfectly still. They have both discovered that client nervousness is not helped by imprecations to begin at the beginning, to take your time, to tell the story in your own words.

And, after a short pause, their visitor begins to speak.

TWO

'My name is Georgiana Long,' says the woman in brown, 'Miss Georgiana Long. I read about the World's End Bureau in the newspaper and' – she flushes slightly – 'I decided to seek you out because I believe I shall find it easier to speak to a woman.'

It is not the first time that Lily has been given this explanation. She is not sure how she feels about her Bureau being chosen because of the gender of its proprietor rather than the expertise of its two agents, but business is business. 'Please go on, Miss Long,' she says.

'I am a teacher, and I have a position at a girls' collegiate school in the Fens. I teach English to the senior girls. We have two Schools, Senior and Junior, the Seniors housed in Big School and the Juniors in New Wing,' she adds; you can hear the capital letters, Lily reflects, musing on how it is typical of people living within institutions to observe the minutiae of life within with such reverent formality. 'Miss Carmichael, our headmistress, is in charge of Senior School, and Miss Dickinson is responsible for Junior.' Miss Long pauses, looking up at Lily with a slightly apologetic expression as if aware that she must not waste time at this stage on the details.

'Our school, Shardlowes School, is funded by a philanthropic organization called the Band of Angels,' Miss Long continues, 'whose main aim is the alleviation of the conditions of the poorest of our capital city's inhabitants. The Band of Angels includes among its membership some of the most important and influential names in the land – the highest and most important of all, if you understand me – although they are *extremely* discreet. Perhaps you know of the organization?' she asks.

Lily shakes her head, glancing at Felix. He has been quietly writing with a small silver pencil in the notebook he always carries with him and he is undoubtedly now adding a memorandum to himself to ask Marmaduke Smithers about this Band of Angels that apparently includes British royalty in its ranks. The scandal of London's poor is a constant theme of Marm's writings, and it is highly likely he will have information to offer.

Miss Long is looking nervously at Lily.

'Before I continue,' she says, 'may I be assured of total confidentiality?'

Lily says, 'Of course.'

Miss Long nods. 'Thank you. Only a small number of our girls come from the ranks of the poor,' she goes on, 'if, as we surely do, we take the word to mean poor in its accustomed monetary sense.' She pauses, looking slightly uneasy. Then, gathering her courage, she continues. 'Now here I must, I fear, speak bluntly, for I have come to ask for your help, and circumlocution will be the ally of neither of us.' Lily risks a glance at Felix, who raises his eyebrows and silently mouths *circumlocution*? 'Almost all of our girls are, however, in some way or another disadvantaged, and a few come to us from orphanages,' she blurts out, flushing slightly, 'and it is for this reason that the Band of Angels supports our school.'

Disadvantaged. Lily's mind runs over several possible interpretations. Then, in the hope that Miss Long will explain in her own good time – probably when she is no longer feeling embarrassed by her own forthrightness – she observes mildly, 'The education of women is a laudable cause.'

'Indeed it is!' Miss Long agrees fervently. 'One of the Band of Angels' main tenets is that education paves the route out of poverty, and of course they fund schools for boys as well.' She waves a dismissive hand, as if to imply that boys are not her concern.

'So, Miss Long,' Lily prompts, 'how do you believe the World's End Bureau may be able to help you?'

Georgiana Long's round brown eyes stare intently into Lily's. 'Girls are going missing,' she says baldly. 'To elaborate: a girl ran away a few months ago, subsequently discovered to have been in the company of a haberdashery salesman in Brighton. We have no idea how she came to be there and we only learned of it because Miss Dickie – that's what we all call Miss Dickinson – grew up in Brighton and her widowed sister, who

still lives there, always sends her a copy of the local paper.'
She leans forward confidingly, lowering her voice. 'There was
some trouble, you see. The salesman could not pay his bill, and
Esme – that was the girl's name, Esme Sullivan – demanded
that the landlady give her the price of the rail fare back to
Shardlowes.' Miss Long pauses, frowning. 'A shoddy, disgraceful
business that aroused *much* gossip, or so Miss Dickie's sister
informed us. It was early in the autumn, the town was quiet
after the summer and there was, I imagine, a dearth of more
important news.' She gives a delicate shudder of distaste. 'Esme
is no longer with us.' Before Lily or Felix can ask where she is
now, Miss Long hurries on. 'But since then another, younger
girl has also disappeared, and we have found no trace of her.
Now, just this last week, it has happened again.'

'These girls' families must be distraught!' Felix exclaims.
'What did you tell them? How on earth did you break the news?'

Miss Long turns to him, and Lily spots a look of deep
discomfiture cross her face. 'As I said, Mr Wilbraham, some
of our girls are orphans. Esme Sullivan was a foundling, discovered in a church porch when only a few days old. Or so I
understand. The second girl's parents died some years ago in
Africa, where they were engaged upon missionary work, and
she has no other family. The third . . .' She stops.

'The third?' Lily prompts.

Miss Long drops her head. 'Miss Carmichael has written
to the girl's widower father. It is by no means certain the letter
will reach him, for he is an army officer stationed in the wilds
of Afghanistan.'

There is a pause while they all think about this.

Then Lily asks, as she always asks sooner or later, 'Have
the police been informed?'

For the first time, Miss Long's open, friendly face adopts a
different expression: she looks, thinks Lily, shifty.

'Er . . .' Miss Long prevaricates.

'Miss Long,' Lily says in a firm tone, 'you have told us of
Esme and the other two missing children. They were pupils
at your school, placed there in your care by their parents or
their guardians, and it is your responsibility to keep them safe.
It is imperative that you consult the police and—'

'I'm consulting *you!*' Miss Long says in a sort of suppressed wail.

'But—' Lily begins.

'Miss Raynor, let me make myself clear.' Miss Long seems to have recovered her equanimity. 'Our girls are—' She stops, takes a breath, starts again. 'Most of our girls have been at Shardlowes for a very long time. Many were brought to us when little more than infants and usually our pupils remain with us through the weeks of the school holidays in addition to term time. They are—' Again she stops.

Felix has looked up from his note-taking. 'They are the daughters, perhaps, of parents living in places unsuitable for the health and well-being of growing girls?' he suggests. 'Sent back to your school in England, Miss Long, for the education they are unlikely to receive in the far-flung corners of the Empire which are home to their parents?'

Miss Long flashes him a grateful smile. 'Precisely so, Mr Wilbraham.'

'I was educated at Marlborough College, Miss Long,' he replies with an answering smile. 'I had several friends in a similar position, whose fathers' work took them to Malaya, India, Ceylon, Africa and—'

'Quite so,' Lily interrupts. Miss Long, she detects, has more to offer. 'Miss Long?' she prompts.

'I— There are also—' Miss Long is looking flustered again. 'Oh, dear, it is difficult to explain, since of course you have not visited Shardlowes nor met any of our girls . . .'

Lily and Felix both wait in silence.

Miss Long takes a breath and says, 'I shall be frank, Miss Raynor.' She pauses, takes another breath and says in a rush of words, 'Truth to tell, many girls are sent to Shardlowes School because their families and society at large have little or no use for them.'

Lily and Felix are again silent, and Lily senses that he is as surprised as she is at this painfully honest admission.

'As I say, many are the daughters of men engaged in foreign service: the Army, the civil service, the ICS.' Indian civil service, Lily thinks automatically. 'In addition, we number among our pupils the daughters of foreign royalty who believe that a few years at an English boarding school will add to their daughters' value on the home marriage market.' A steely tone enters her voice as she says these words. 'These pupils spend years without even a brief return to their families and their faraway homes, and visits from parents home on leave are rare. Oh, some of them receive letters and parcels, and somebody who is probably a distant relative or an old family friend regularly leaves little presents of a cake or biscuits at the kitchen for one of our little crippled girls. These girls, however, the ones of whom I was just speaking, sooner or later are reclaimed; the daughters of foreign service families go out and get married, the little princesses and the maharajah's daughters have husbands found for them. They are not the ones to whom I just referred.' She glances anxiously at Felix, then returns her gaze to Lily and plunges on. 'Miss Raynor, we have many girls who are simply of the wrong intelligence: some are too stupid, some are too clever. We have disfigured girls, handicapped girls, the lame, the deaf, the dumb; in the past, even one who was blind. We have the grossly obese and the stick-thin. We have the perfectly ordinary whose sole misfortune is to be the sixth, fifth or even the fourth daughter of a man trying to make his way in a hard world who cannot afford yet another dowry. In short, we take the girls for whom there is little or no hope of the traditional route for a woman: marriage, children, the support of a man.'

The flow of words ceases. Lily, aware of the deepening silence – even the soft sound of Felix's busy pencil has stopped – is amazed at Miss Long's outspokenness. That such reservoirs of unwanted girls exist comes as no great surprise, but to hear one of these reservoirs described without the usual conscience-easing, fatuous remarks is surely unheard of.

The silence becomes awkward.

Recalling the question that opened the door to these outpourings, Lily says, 'And just why, Miss Long, should the nature of your pupils constitute a reason for not informing the police of the missing girls?'

'For several reasons, Miss Raynor,' comes the prompt reply; Miss Long, it seems, is on surer, less emotive ground now, and the hot magenta in her apple cheeks fades to soft rose. 'The first runaway, as I told you, left of her own accord, for her own disreputable reasons and in pursuit of satisfying the demands of her own base nature. It is not impossible that the same may prove to apply in the other cases.'

Felix makes a note, underlines it. Peering across the desk, Lily makes out *AGES: were they old enough to be seduced by travelling salesmen?*

'As I have said,' Miss Long continues, 'we are funded by the Band of Angels, and the august philanthropists who constitute its membership are strongly averse to publicity. They do good by stealth,' she adds primly.

'"Do good by stealth, and blush to find it fame",' Felix says softly. 'John Donne.'

'Alexander Pope,' Miss Long corrects him. Then, with a swift grin, 'I told you, Mr Wilbraham, I teach English. So, as you will deduce,' she says, turning back to Lily, 'for the Band of Angels' sake – and as I implied just now, they number senior politicians, lords, dukes and even princes among their membership – we must not risk any scandal, any notoriety, attaching itself to Shardlowes.'

'Scandal and notoriety wouldn't help your school's reputation, and therefore its ability to attract new pupils, either,' Felix observes.

Miss Long turns to him, her face flushing again and this time with indignation. 'Pray let me assure you, Mr Wilbraham, that such a consideration plays no part in Miss Carmichael's reluctance to involve the official authorities, no part *whatsoever*,' she says, her voice rising. 'Miss Carmichael is a good and honourable woman who has her pupils' best interests always to the forefront of her mind. She knows each girl by name, she gives them her time, she—' With a visible effort, Miss Long recovers herself. 'Miss Carmichael *cares*,' she concludes softly.

'And what has she done to try to locate the missing girls?' Lily asks coolly.

'She instructed Miss Dickie to send out search parties and Miss Dickie did a *very* good job, organizing the teachers and the other staff – groundsmen, caretaker, cook, cleaners and the like – into teams, and they left not a corner of the school and the grounds unexamined.'

'And how far did they venture into the surrounding area?' Lily persists.

'As far as was practicable,' Miss Long replies. The chill that has entered her voice suggests she is not going to elaborate.

'Miss Long,' Lily says after a short pause, 'how old are these girls?'

For some moments Miss Long does not seem to be able to bring herself to reply. Then she says, 'Esme is seventeen. The second girl was – *is* – thirteen. The most recent is eleven.'

This time the silence extends beyond awkward.

Breaking it, Lily says, 'If I judge aright, and the Bureau is indeed the only source of assistance to which you are prepared to appeal, what would you like us to do?'

Miss Long closes her eyes in evident relief. Then, leaning forward eagerly, she says, 'I believe that there are . . . *undercurrents* at Shardlowes, Miss Raynor. Oh, it is so hard to explain, to one who does not know us.'

Detecting a rather obvious hint, Lily says, 'Would you like me to visit the school?' Miss Long looks at her intently, eyes hungry for more. 'To stay there, perhaps in some guise that will not arouse suspicion as to my true purpose?'

'Yes, Miss Raynor, indeed I would,' Miss Long says firmly. 'There is a temporary vacancy in the ancillary staff: Matron's assistant has been called back to her home in North Wales to attend her dying mother. Is that a post that you could fill, Miss Raynor? Do you have the skills to assume with conviction the identity of a nurse?'

Nurse.

The word bangs around inside Lily's head like the incoming tide in a cave.

I gave up nursing. I was happy, fulfilled, and then came The Incident, and I turned my back for ever.

The horror of those terrible days in India flashes through her mind in a series of ghastly images: what happened, what might have happened, precisely what it was that made her flee . . .

Suppressing them with an effort that makes her heart beat faster, she says calmly, 'I trained as a nurse.'

And Miss Long sags with relief.

*   *   *

Lily and Felix are alone again. Georgiana Long, having achieved her purpose, ran through the arrangements for Lily's arrival and installation at Shardlowes School so efficiently and so quickly that it was perfectly obvious she had it all worked out beforehand. She agreed to the Bureau's charges and undertook to meet them herself: 'I earn my own money and I have my savings,' she said with quiet dignity as she got up to leave.

'She knew you'd take up the challenge,' Felix remarks as he pushes the door to Lily's office open with his bottom, widening the gap to accommodate the tea tray. He puts it down, pours the tea, hands Lily a plate containing bread, cheese, pickle and a large piece of Mrs Clapper's gingerbread (fortunately for Lily and Felix, Mrs Clapper embarked on a fury of baking before resigning herself to going home to nurse her ailing husband). Felix is quite determined that all the cakes, biscuits, pies and puddings will be consumed before they go stale; it would be a crime for Mrs Clapper's efforts to go to waste, and she is a *very* good cook.

Lily sips her tea. 'Yes, I agree,' she replies.

He looks at her, trying not to let her see. Difficult if not impossible, for his employer is very observant. Before she can speak, he says, 'So, assistant matron!' Lily makes no comment. 'Back to nursing, eh?'

It has come as no surprise today that Lily was a nurse before she opened the World's End Bureau; he learned this at their first encounter. He also suspects that the abandonment of her former profession was under unfortunate circumstances. There is something lodging in the edge of his memory . . . he brings it to mind.

Yes.

The first time he entered 3, Hob's Court, Lily had admitted reluctantly that the ground floor formerly housed an apothecary's shop, run by her grandparents and founded by an ancestor a hundred and fifty years ago. When he asked innocently if she hadn't wished to continue the tradition, she replied, with rather more asperity than was surely occasioned by the question, *No I did not.*

Felix has wolfed his bread and cheese and now takes a huge bite of gingerbread. It is as delicious as it looks and smells. He is very tempted to ask Lily here and now why she abandoned her calling; why the very mention of nurses and nursing pales her cheeks and puts that grim, determined and unflattering expression on her face. A mouthful of gingerbread is his way of preventing himself blurting out the questions, for he is as sure as he is that the month is January and there's snow outside that she won't tell him one single thing unless and until she wants to, if that day ever comes.

She still hasn't responded to his remark. Her gaze is inward; he suspects she is far away and perhaps didn't even hear him.

He bites off another hunk of gingerbread, giving himself a moment to come up with a different approach. He takes a sip of tea to wash it down and says, 'You will need a name, an identity. Any thoughts?'

She raised her bright green eyes and looks at him. 'I shall call myself Leonora Henry, and as regards my training, Leonora Henry has followed the same path as I: five years in a teaching hospital in London, midwifery and battlefield medicine with the St Walburga's Nursing Service, a spell abroad before a brush with cholera not only ended overseas service but imposed several months' convalescence. The opening at Shardlowes School is timely for Leonora, providing as it does a return to her profession that promises to be far less arduous than her previous posting.'

'What could be less demanding, harrowing or perilous than a girls' boarding school out in the Fens?' Felix says. 'And you're wise to make Leonora's experiences so close to yours. Keep as close to the truth as you can is the rule when it comes to lying.'

'Quite so,' Lily murmurs.

He detects a definite hint of irony.

And, gathering the last crumbs of gingerbread with his forefinger, he reflects that whatever brought his employer's nursing career to an end, it most certainly wasn't cholera.

Suddenly Lily sits up straight, draws her chair in closer to her desk and, with determined briskness, puts her empty plate, cup and saucer back on the tray. 'Now,' she says, 'what are we to make of Miss Georgiana Long's story?'

Felix has been prepared for this. Without the need to consult his notes, he says, 'She claimed there were several reasons why the school has not informed the police of the missing girls, yet she only mentioned one, which was to do with this Band of Angels and their dislike of publicity. She further implied that the specific type of publicity they really would not welcome is this sordid tale of a lusty young girl running away to Brighton with a haberdashery salesman.'

'Yes,' Lily agrees. 'You also suggested to Miss Long that Shardlowes School would not welcome . . . scandal and notoriety, I believe were the words you used. Even though Miss Long vehemently refuted such a base reason for not having involved the appropriate authorities, I believe her protest was a little too forceful – and swift – for us to afford it total credence.'

'"The lady doth protest too much",' Felix supplies. 'Alexander Pope,' he adds, grinning to indicate that it's a joke.

Lily smiles. 'Do you imagine Miss Long is a good teacher?' she asks. 'Good enough to impart fascination and meaning to a play as difficult as *Hamlet*?'

'None of my teachers managed that,' Felix says, 'but I'm not sure I gave the Shakespeare tragedies my full attention.'

'So,' Lily resumes, 'we may conclude that, despite Miss Long's denial, adverse publicity for the school is in fact one of the reasons for not reporting the missing girls to the police.'

'That's still only two, and two isn't really several, is it?'

'It is not. I'm wondering,' Lily goes on, 'whether it is to do with this business of the Shardlowes pupils being, to quote Miss Long, girls for whom there is *little or no hope of the traditional route for a woman*.' She looks at Felix enquiringly.

He knows what she is implying. It is harsh, cruel, and surely not right, but since they'll probably sit there staring at each other unless one of them voices it, he obliges. 'And you're wondering whether the school might be doing exactly what the parents want by not making much of a fuss,' he says softly. He stares steadily at Lily. 'That is monstrous,' he murmurs. Before she can speak, he adds, 'And, quite possibly, absolutely right.'

Lily looks anguished. 'I hope very much it is not,' she says sharply. 'But—' She does not go on.

'I have often wondered,' Felix muses into the silence, 'why

men and women choose to become parents when they know full well their children will become strangers before they reach adolescence. Boarding school does that. Mothers and, indeed, fathers may well begin by caring about, even loving, the baby, the infant, the toddler, although in many cases parental involvement ends soon after birth as the son or daughter is handed to the nurse. Often the only contact with Mother and Father is the regulation half-hour before bedtime. Then the nursery gives way to boarding school – I was six when that happened to me – and quite soon Mother and Father are mere dim shapes in the mist.' He hears the bitterness in his voice and collects himself. 'It is hard for closeness and love to survive between parents and their children. The child turns his back on the parents who have become strangers, and presumably the parents do the same.'

'So you're saying that you don't dismiss the concept of parents not wanting too much of a fuss made over a missing daughter?' she says sharply.

'Oh – no. It cannot be true.' It sounds so cruel when she puts it like that. 'Let us remember, however, that some of the girls are orphans or foundlings, and in their case there *are* no parents to ask awkward questions.'

Lily nods, making a note in her book.

Felix watches her writing. He has an idea as to what may constitute if not another reason for Shardlowes School shunning police involvement, then certainly a relevant factor. But it is a little delicate – and based upon instinct rather than hard fact – so he thinks before speaking. Then he says, 'Miss Long has a crush on Miss Carmichael and she is also rather in awe of her.'

Lily carries on writing. He is waiting for a few scathing words, but then she says mildly. 'Yes, I thought that too.' She puts her pen down. 'I sense also that she is in some distress, perhaps because the school is not making more effort to find these missing girls.' She pauses. 'And she's afraid,' she adds very softly.

'Afraid,' Felix echoes. He thinks about that. 'Hmm. I think Miss Long is battling with her conscience,' he goes on. 'She knows perfectly well that the matter is one for the authorities, but the paragon Miss Carmichael has ruled otherwise.' Something occurs to him. 'I would bet tonight's steak-pie supper that it was Miss Long's idea to come to us, and that Miss Carmichael only agreed because we were the lesser evil.'

Lily grins. 'I will not take your bet. I quite agree.'

'I wonder if Miss Carmichael even knew she was coming to see us?' Felix goes on. 'It's not as if Miss Carmichael is paying, after all, so there was really no need for Miss Long to tell her.'

'It is something I shall have to find out upon my arrival.' Lily writes another note.

'It's Miss Long's gift to her beloved,' Felix murmurs. 'Like a knight in a courtly romance, she is undertaking a trial to prove her devotion. She is going to try to solve the mystery of the lost girls by herself – well, with our help, of course – and lay the resolution at Miss Carmichael's feet like the Golden Fleece.'

Lily smiles. 'You are mixing the Arthurian Romances with Greek legends,' she points out. 'But I see what you mean.'

With a resolute gesture she closes her notebook. 'Today is Friday,' she says. 'The new assistant matron will present herself at Shardlowes School at the start of next week.'

Felix gets to his feet and picks up the tray. 'Tonight I'm going to ask Marm what he knows about the Band of Angels,' he announces.

He has just experienced a sudden, shuddering moment of fear, quickly dismissed, that has its roots in Lily going alone into a place where girls have gone missing and nobody except a modest but courageous little English teacher with a limp has seen fit to take action beyond an initial search. He would like to accompany Lily, to protect her, to watch out for her – she could easily have died in the course of their last major case – but he knows full well any such suggestion would infuriate her, and that's putting it mildly.

'Yes, please do,' Lily replies. 'You will be seeing him tonight? He's going to share that steak-pie supper?'

'Yes and yes,' Felix says. Then, with a rather forced cheerfulness – he can still feel the echoes of that cold fear – he adds, 'We'll discuss whatever I find out tomorrow morning, then in the afternoon I'll—'

'We will close the office tomorrow afternoon,' Lily puts in. She sends him a very swift glance, eyes as quickly averted. 'I'm going to – I shall not be here and, until we embark on the Shardlowes case, there is little for you to do.'

'An afternoon off!' Felix says brightly. 'Thank you, I shall make the most of it.'

Once again, his reaction is a little forced. He is all but sure what Lily plans to do tomorrow afternoon and, while it is not for him to object, the prospect makes him uneasy.

And he daren't even think about what could be the reason for that unease.

THREE

Felix decides to walk home. It is bitterly cold outside now that full darkness has fallen, and as he draws his muffler more closely round his throat, he wonders if he'll regret the decision. Walking – striding, in fact, as fast as he can – is, however, what he needs.

Because that moment of fear in Lily's inner sanctum is still lurking.

He tries to brighten himself out of the anxiety that won't go away by reflecting how much he prefers returning to his current lodgings than his former ones. Before last autumn's spectacular case, he was chronically short of money and could only afford a dark, dank and mould-stinking room where, despite the exterior season, it was always winter. The mean little window only opened a crack, so there was no ingress for fresh air; not that it would have been all that fresh, Felix's room being situated above the privy in the yard which, according to another equally disgruntled tenant, hadn't been cleaned since God was a lad.

The successful autumn case greatly improved the finances of the World's End Bureau, its proprietor and her sole employee. It also brought a suddenly increased demand for the writings and the opinions of Marmaduke Smithers, newspaper champion of the poor, thorn in the Establishment's side. Marm celebrated by taking rooms in the Kinver Street house and, there being a small and superfluous second bedroom, he offered it to Felix. Having decided already that he and Marm saw eye to eye, Felix accepted.

It is a well-run household. Mrs Horncastle, the landlady, is a fan of order and cleanliness; rather too much of a fan for Marm's liking, although Felix, still reeling with delight because he no longer sleeps in a mouldy box that stinks of raw sewage, reckons just now that it's impossible for a dwelling to be *too* clean.

* * *

Felix marches on. Shortly before the hospital, he turns off to the left, into the network of narrow roads between the river and the King's Road and on to Kinver Street. The front door of number 5 – gleaming black paint and a brilliantly shiny brass letter box – draws him on. He lets himself in, calls out a cheery good evening to Mrs Horncastle, undoubtedly lurking somewhere behind the door at the end of the hall and checking her residents off on a list as one by one they return to her fold, and bounds up the wide stairs to the first floor. He is careful not to brush against the wall, since the paint is flaking. The house may be clean but it is a little run-down; for Felix and Marm, however, this is more than offset by the high ceilings, the cornices and the plasterwork, the beautiful old wood of the elegant staircase's banister and the general old-fashioned charm of the place.

'Pie's in the oven and I'm by the fire with the whisky bottle.' Marm's greeting reaches Felix just as he is closing the door. Removing hat, coat, muffler and gloves, he hangs them on the hall stand and almost runs to join Marm, taking up his accustomed chair on the other side of the hearth. Silently Marm hands him a cut-glass tumbler with a good three fingers of whisky in it. Silently they toast one another. Silently Felix settles back against the cushions, letting the day seep out of him.

This has become their evening ritual, much appreciated by both of them.

Marm breaks the silence. 'How was your day, dear?' he says in a falsetto voice. 'It's very cold so I pray you have not taken chill?' It amuses him to adopt the role of fussing wife to Felix's manly husband, and Felix, not bothered, lets him. Felix is utterly sure of his own sexual preference and Marm's is his own affair.

'Hob's Court was perishing until we moved into one office and built up the fire,' he replies after another slow mouthful of whisky.

'Cosy,' Marm remarks. Fortunately he has abandoned the falsetto.

Felix looks up, meeting his eye. 'Something's come up: a new case concerning a girls' boarding school in the Fens.' Succinctly he relates the pertinent facts. 'There's the question

of the girl who ran away to Brighton with the travelling salesman
– we don't know what happened to her after Brighton – but
there's another aspect of the case I'd like to ask you about.'

Marm settles back in his chair, smiling in anticipation.
Felix has noticed that he blooms when someone – usually Felix
– seeks advice. It is a harmless pleasure, Felix reflects, and
Marm is right to be proud of his extensive knowledge and his
phenomenal memory.

'Ask away!' Marm prompts.

'The school is funded by a charitable organization called the
Band of Angels,' Felix responds, 'and I wondered if you—'

But he gets no further. Marm has put his whisky glass down
with a thump and is leaning forward, eagerness all over his
lean face, intelligent blue eyes bright with anticipation. 'The
Band of Angels!' he repeats.

Then he begins to talk.

Several hours, half a very good steak pie and rather more
shots of whisky than was wise later, Felix is lying in bed
trying to put his racing thoughts to rest so he can go to sleep.
His hand is numb with note-taking, his mind is full of facts
and speculations, and he senses that what he has heard tonight
is important.

His thoughts turn to Lily. 'I am afraid for her,' he admits
softly to the kindly darkness. While he is making admissions,
he murmurs another one: 'I wish she was going to spend
tomorrow afternoon and Sunday with me before she sets off
for Shardlowes.'

He knows the wish will not be fulfilled, for, as his old
nanny used to say with harsh repression every single time
the little boy Felix said 'I wish . . .', *if wishes were horses,
beggars would ride.*

'Bugger beggars and horses,' Felix mutters, turning over and
closing his eyes. 'Bugger Nanny, too.'

As he drifts off to sleep, the snow starts falling again.

Lily is down in her office early on Saturday morning. She has
been awake for some time, padding round the house in her
nightgown, shawl, socks and fingerless gloves, revelling in its

emptiness. Mrs Clapper is still nursing her husband, and last night sent round a note expressing distress at her continuing abandonment of her duties and fervently hoping Miss Lily is managing without her.

The very way she has written the words strongly indicates that she doubts this very much.

The Little Ballerina's rooms on the middle floor still smell of her even in her absence. Which would, Lily reflects, be lovely if the woman's habitual aroma was in any way pleasant. But the Little Ballerina smells of grease; of underarms, dirty hair and sweaty feet, with an underlying note of not very well washed clothes.

The day when the World's End Bureau earns enough for it to provide Lily's sole income is not, unfortunately, yet.

Now, washed, dressed, breakfasted, Lily sits at her desk, the fire burning well, the room, if not hot, then decidedly not too cold. Right on time, she hears the outer door open and Felix comes bursting in.

'Dear *God* but it's cold!' The words explode out of him even as he knocks the snow off his boots and hangs up his outer garments.

'Has there been more snow?' Lily enquires. 'I haven't really looked out this morning.'

'Yes,' he replies shortly. Then: 'Sorry about the blasphemy.'

'That's quite all right. I have a pot of tea here – come and sit down, I'll pour.'

She gives him a few minutes to warm his hands on the cup and take a few restorative gulps. Then she says, 'Had Marm anything to say about the Band of Angels?'

Felix puts down his cup and reaches for his notebook. 'Oh, yes,' he says with a grin. 'Ready?'

'Ready.'

'The Band of Angels constitutes a group of influential and affluent philanthropists who provide money for the education of the poor. They—'

'I keep thinking that the name is somehow familiar,' Lily interrupts. She thinks she can hear the words being sung.

If Felix is irritated by being stopped just as he is getting started, he manages to hide it. 'It's from a song called "Swing

Low, Sweet Chariot", which was written in Oklahoma in the 1860s and widely popularized by an outfit called the Fisk Jubilee Singers. You may well have heard it sung since the choir toured Europe a few years ago and did some concerts in London.' He looks down at his notes. *"'I looked over Jordan and what did I see, comin' for to carry me home? A band of angels comin' after me, comin' for to carry me home"*,' he sings.

'You are obviously more familiar with the ditty than I,' she says as the echoes of his rich baritone fade away.

'Not really,' Felix says. 'Marm told me how it goes.'

'I see. Please go on.'

'As Miss Long said, the Band includes some very well-known names among its numbers, from royalty and the aristocracy to the world of politics and the government,' he resumes, 'and although our prime minister is not actually a member, he is known among his inner circle to support the cause and approve of the Band's work.'

Yes, Lily muses, that is no surprise. William Ewart Gladstone makes no secret of his concern for the welfare of the disadvantaged, although his critics maintain it is exclusively prostitutes he agonizes over and only pretty ones at that.

'The Band was founded by two brothers, Mortimer and Cameron MacKilliver, who are twins. Their ancestral seat is in Scotland, on the southern shores of the Moray Firth. Mortimer has the public profile, while his brother lurks in the background. Mortimer is a widower, no offspring, but Cameron has never married and if he fathered a child or two, has kept the fact to himself.' Felix looks up suddenly. 'Sorry if that was inappropriate but I'm reading straight from my notes, and Marm speaks his mind.'

Lily smiles. 'That is perhaps the secret of his success,' she observes. 'Go on.'

'Each member of the Band of Angels pays a set sum per annum into a general fund, and the chairman and the committee decide how the money is to be spent. Chairman and committee members are elected annually, although until a couple of years ago Mortimer MacKilliver was chairman for almost a decade. A younger man has now taken over.'

'How old are the twin brothers?' she asks.

Felix flips back a few pages. 'Born 1820, so they'll be sixty-one some time this year.' He looks up, frowning. 'That seems young for Mortimer to give up a post he has obviously held successfully for years. Gladstone's much older, and so are most of his cronies.'

'Perhaps there was another reason, then,' Lily says absently. 'Did Marm have anything to say about Shardlowes School?'

'Not specifically, although he knew of a number of similar establishments that have received the Band's support.' Again he glances down at his notes. 'Almost exclusively girls' schools.'

'Probably because the members of the Band quite rightly believe that girls need more help than boys, especially in the matter of acquiring an education,' Lily says, and her words sound more censorious than she had intended. 'I didn't mean that it wasn't important to educate boys too, but—'

Felix smiles. 'I know what you mean. Boys get educated whether they want it or not, whether they appreciate it or not, whereas girls have to fight for the privilege. I am the first to admit,' he adds disarmingly, 'that I pretty much squandered what Marlborough College offered me.'

'That may be so, but nevertheless you do know some surprising things, more than a few of them very useful,' she says.

His smile widens. 'If they're useful then it's most likely I discovered them after I left. So, would you like to hear a list of other members of the Band?'

'Yes, please.'

For the next minute or so Felix reels off a list of names. Many are prefixed by Sir, quite a few by Lord, and there is a duke and a couple of foreign princes. Lily, trying to keep a tally in her head, reckons the total membership is around seventy.

'Seventy-one,' confirms Felix. 'They have stately homes and country houses all over Britain, most have a London address as well, and they all belong to a private club in Piccadilly known as Stirling's. And before you ask, I don't know the relevance of the name, if indeed it has any.'

'Is the club solely for the use of the Band of Angels?'

'I wondered that too. Marm isn't sure but he thinks not. It's lavishly appointed, apparently, and the claret is magnificent, and he thinks it wouldn't achieve such standards of luxury with only seventy-odd members, no matter how well-heeled.'

She nods. 'If they are spread all over the country then presumably they use Stirling's for their meetings.'

'They do.'

She leans back in her chair. 'You have done well,' she says.

Felix waves a modest hand. 'It's Marm's filing cabinet of a memory we have to thank,' he says. 'I just wrote it all down.'

She inclines her head in acknowledgement. 'Please thank him for me.'

'I will, but there's no need. He is quite an admirer of yours and happy to be of service. He refers to you as my Chief.'

She laughs. 'I like it.'

'Thought you might,' Felix mutters, not quite inaudibly.

Time has flown past. Looking at the small fob watch she wears pinned to her waistcoat, Lily sees that it is midday. She and Felix have been talking about the Band of Angels, Shardlowes School, the missing girls and whether or not Miss Carmichael really does know what her English teacher has done for two hours, and Lily feels there is nothing more to say.

She stands up, and Felix immediately does too. 'I will set out for Shardlowes first thing on Monday morning,' she announces, 'and, as we arranged with Miss Long, send a wire with the time of my train.'

'It still seems too soon,' Felix says, not for the first time. 'Is it really likely that Miss Long could find a relief assistant matron after one brief visit to London?'

Lily suppresses a sigh. 'We've been over this,' she replies. 'Miss Long will tell Miss Carmichael, Miss Dickinson and anyone else who asks that she had already written to me, having been given my name by an old friend. We must remember that the school is desperate for the post to be filled and can't afford to waste time by being too choosy.'

He doesn't look very reassured. 'Be careful,' he warns. 'I've been sensing—' He stops.

'What?'

'Oh, nothing.' He forces a smile. 'Good luck, keep your wits about you, and write to me as often as you can. I'll only be a train journey away, I can—' Again he stops.

You can come to my rescue, she finishes silently for him. 'Thank you, but I am going to a girls' boarding school, not a nest of thieves.' She smiles to take the sting out of the words.

She sees him to the door, waiting while he wraps himself up in layers of clothing. He hurries away, turning to give her a brief wave.

She closes the door.

It was decent of him to remind me he'd be nearby if I need him, she thinks as she walks slowly back to her office. But his help won't be necessary.

She looks again at her watch and, with a soft exclamation, diverts from the office and instead hurries up the stairs to her own apartment at the very top of the house. Here she changes out of her masculine-styled jacket, waistcoat and well-cut skirt and puts on a simple wool gown, a white bonnet, a worn wool cloak and a heavy knitted shawl. Hurrying back downstairs, she lets herself out through the back door and across the little yard to the shed built against the rear wall, unlocking the door to the lane on to which it opens then carefully locking up again. She turns left, towards the river, then right along the riverside path, following it until she reaches the basin where the river boatmen tie up.

She looks along the line of boats, not in the least anxious because he never lets her down. It was late last night that she came to the basin and asked another boatman if he could get a message to the master of *The Dawning of the Day*, and the man had nodded and said he would be seeing him presently, like as not. Lily's message was verbal, and merely asked Tamáz if he could be in the river basin today.

The Dawning of the Day is moored on the far side of the basin, last in a line of five. As she increases her pace and breaks into a trot – it really is cold outside – she is already looking forward to the warmth of the boat's little stove and a mug of piping-hot soup.

And the hugely reassuring presence of Tamáz Edey.

*   *   *

They are friends, she and Tamáz. They met a year ago when he came to her door seeking help for a woman in labour; a girl, really, panicking, desperate, and Tamáz had the care of her. The fact that Lily had gone to help that night – with extreme reluctance, for she had only just fled India and forsaken her profession, and attending a delivery was the very last thing she wanted – has aroused a strong response in Tamáz. His paternal kin all come from the Fens, although there is a powerful Irish matriarch among them. His mother was from Galicia. He is a big man, quiet, tall, strongly built. He is one of those people who are utterly content with who and what they are; rare, in Lily's experience. He travels in his beautiful old boat with a two-man crew and towed by a large black and white horse. In return for Lily's assistance and support that first terrible night, Tamáz has come to her aid in the past.

And now, considering where she will be going on Monday and what she is to do there – not to mention the shivery, fearful misgivings that lurk beneath the logical, sensible surface of her mind – she needs his help again. He is her friend, and she knows he will not turn her away.

Are we friends? Lily wonders as, trotting now, she covers the last few yards to *The Dawning of the Day*. If so, if that is what this extraordinary relationship is, then it's a friendship that will endure for ever.

She knows that, just as she knows her eyes are green and her hair is fair.

He is standing in the cockpit waiting for her. He stretches out a hand to help her aboard. His flesh is warm and strength flows out of him. He indicates for her to precede him down the little flight of steps into the cabin and he closes the hatch. The stove is burning well and it is wonderfully warm. There is no sign of the young men who form his crew.

'They will not return until tomorrow evening,' Tamáz says, noticing her quick glance. He puts a black iron kettle onto the stove, sets out mugs, tea, a little tin teapot. 'Sit down, cushla, and tell me how I can help you.'

FOUR

Felix arrives at 3, Hob's Court very early on Monday morning. Lily told him she would be setting out first thing and he does not want to miss her.

He almost does, for she is standing in the hall, thick coat on, small leather suitcase at her feet, about to leave.

They look at each other.

She has done her hair differently. It is drawn back ruthlessly from her face and fastened behind her head in such a severe manner that it is virtually invisible. Sensing his gaze, she reaches for a black bonnet with a deep brim and puts it on. Her gown too is black, with a stiff white collar that stands up around her neck. On the left-hand collar tip is a very small gold brooch made up of the letters SWNS.

'I thought I had better look like a nurse,' she mutters.

He senses that this is costing her a great deal. 'You *are* a nurse,' he says encouragingly, 'or, at least, you were.'

She nods. 'Yes, quite.'

The silence becomes difficult; heavy with what they are both holding back from saying. Then she says with an attempt at a smile, 'You're very early.'

'I wanted to wish you good luck,' he replies.

Silence again.

Wanting very much to break it, to normalize this strange encounter, he says, 'I've had an idea concerning the Band of Angels. One of the names Marm gave me was familiar, and—'

With an apologetic smile she stops him. 'I'm sorry, Felix, but if I am to catch my train I must go.'

'Of course.' He stands back and she walks out on to the street. Turning, she says, 'I'm pleased about your idea. Make your usual careful notes' – they both smile – 'and we shall report to each other when the chance presents itself.'

Everything in him wants to yell, *When? When will that be?*

But she doesn't know any more than he does, so he just gives
her a cheery wave, goes back inside and shuts the door.

Work, that's what I need, he tells himself as he prowls round
the outer office. Lily has left the door to the inner sanctum
open, and he can almost pretend to himself that she is there.

Almost.

I will make up my notes and form a plan for my next steps,
he decides. Lily has lit the fire in the outer office but it is
feeble, unenthusiastic, so before he settles down he fetches coal
and stokes it up. Then he makes himself a pot of tea and two
slices of toast with Mrs Clapper's lime and ginger marmalade,
and finally is ready to set to work.

He writes steadily for perhaps an hour. Then he turns his
mind to the idea he tried to tell Lily about.

As Marm dictated the list of Band of Angels members to
him on Friday night, one was familiar. And not familiar in the
sense of recognizing it from newspaper or magazine articles or
from London society gossip, but personally familiar: Felix
seemed to hear a voice uttering it in the sort of stage whisper
that carries further than the speaker intends.

Thinking about it directly did not lead to identifying the
owner of that penetrating whisper, so he had gone about it
obliquely, trying to prod his memory to provide the sights,
sounds and smells of wherever it was the incident had occurred.

And he had woken up this morning remembering.

He had been in a bawdy music hall in the Old Kent Road
called the Peeping Tom, in the next-door box to a beautiful,
mature, full-figured actress called Violetta da Rosa. They met
under unfortunate circumstances, despite which they had
recognized one another as kindred spirits, so that when Felix
said goodbye to her in her carriage outside the theatre where
she had just been performing, both of them seemed to know it
would not be for ever.

The moment when he heard the name had been in the interval
between the first and second halves of the music hall's entertainment. Violetta's companion had gone to fetch champagne
and, on his return, Violetta had hissed, 'Freddie Fanshawe-
Turnbull's up to his old tricks again.' The pointing hand indicated

an elderly man, bald but for a circlet of silvery hair that went all round his crown, brushed forward over the forehead in the style of a Roman emperor. He was expensively dressed and had his white-gloved hand down the bosom of an overdressed, over-made-up redhead's gown.

Violetta's companion muttered something about Old Turnip-Head getting too long in the tooth for groping tarts in music halls, and Violetta laughed and said she'd like to see the day when he gave up. Then she took a long draught of champagne, burped, and went on to speak of other matters.

Old Turnip-Head – the Honourable Frederick Alfred Fanshawe-Turnbull, to give him his full name – is, according to Marm who is rarely wrong, a member of the Band of Angels.

Felix leaps up and hurries out of the house. He composes a brief telegram and dispatches it to the Aphrodite Theatre, off the Strand, where Violetta is currently performing. He knows not to expect a reply before early evening, when Violetta arrives at the theatre: Monday is not a matinee day and she will probably sleep until noon.

Back in the office, Felix wonders what to do to fill in the time.

It is late. The Strand and the streets around it are full of theatre-goers: men in sweeping cloaks and collapsible top hats, women in glorious gowns, glittering jewellery and costly fur wraps. Felix is waiting at the Aphrodite's stage door.

Presently it is opened by an invisible minion and Violetta stands at the top of the steps, waving a hand to her fans as regal as that of the elderly queen. Not as many fans tonight as Felix has sometimes seen, but then it is very cold. Violetta spots him, gives an all but imperceptible nod, and then jerks her head to the right. Following her silent instruction, Felix walks over to where a narrow lane branches off the street and, as he expected, a carriage stands waiting. The driver, up on the box, seems to recognize him and mutters in a hoarse voice, 'You can get in.' What he actually says is *yer c'n ge'in*, the glottal stop so pronounced it almost strangles the final word.

Felix settles in the comfortable seat, spreading out the heavy fur-lined rug. Before very long, the carriage door opens again and Violetta clambers up beside him. 'Felix Wilbraham,' she says with a grin. 'Had a feeling we'd meet again.'

Felix knows Violetta to be an honest woman who appreciates that virtue in others. He says without preamble, 'I haven't come a-courting' – last time they had sat together like this she had kissed him and put her hand in his lap, laughing softly at his body's enthusiastic response, so it seems wise to get this out of the way at once – 'but to ask you about someone I believe you know.'

She studies him for a few moments. Then she leans out of the window to give a brief instruction to the driver, and the carriage jerks into movement. She tucks the fur more closely around them both, snuggles up against him – 'Just for warmth, you appreciate' – and waits. When he doesn't speak she says with a touch of asperity, 'Go on, then. Who is this person I'm meant to know?'

Felix tells her. She smiles indulgently, then chuckles. 'Old Turnip-Head,' she says. 'Yes, I do know him, in the sense that I've partied with him, been wined and dined by him, let him cry into my bosom when yet another young woman engaging in the oldest profession as a way of forging a way in a hard world makes it clear she was only playing him along for what she could get. Before you ask,' she adds, 'I've never bedded him. I'm far too old for his taste and I'm not a whore.' She makes the latter statement entirely without any sign of horror that anybody could have taken her for one. She pauses, then says, 'What's Freddie been up to, then?'

'Nothing, as far as I know,' Felix says hastily. 'I'm looking into a philanthropic organization called the Band of Angels and I'm told he's a member.'

Violetta is silent for so long that Felix wonders if she has nodded off. He wouldn't be surprise: it is warm under the thick rug, their two bodies are mutually comforting and she has been on stage all evening. But then she murmurs, 'I'm not asleep, you cheeky sod,' and he grins in the darkness.

'So?' he prompts eventually. 'What can you tell me?'

'Yes, Freddie's one of the Angels,' Violetta begins. 'You know who they are, of course?'

'I know something of them,' he says cautiously.

She touches his hand. 'Be careful, if you're having dealings with the Band of Angels.' There is a note in her voice that Felix hasn't heard before. 'There are princes among them, several ministers, and any number of dukes and earls and the like. They're rich, they wield power in virtually every field you can think of, they guard their privacy like a bulldog with a chop and they are notoriously averse to any sort of publicity.'

'I see.' Felix digests that. 'And Freddie's a member?'

'One of the founders, for he's a long-time friend of Mortimer MacKilliver and they are often seen in each other's company.'

'And Cameron, presumably.' She does not respond. 'Mortimer's twin.'

'I know who he is, silly!' Violetta says. She pauses, then goes on. 'You probably don't know, but Cameron MacKilliver is a recluse. He hides away in that great echoing ancestral home in Scotland and he rarely comes out.'

'What about his duties with the Band of Angels? I'm told they hold regular meetings, so surely as one of the founders he attends?'

'Yes, probably, although I don't imagine that bashful members are forced to turn out whether they want to or not, do you?'

'No,' he admits.

Again Violetta hesitates, as if reluctant to say what she is thinking. Felix waits. She sighs softly and says, 'I probably shouldn't be telling you this.'

Felix's heart does a cheerful little jig, for this is exactly what people say when they are just about to share a tasty piece of gossip that they really ought to keep to themselves. 'I am known for my discretion,' he says sententiously.

Violetta chuckles again. 'Get away! Very well, then,' she continues. 'Mortimer and Cameron are twins, like you say, but they're identical. They really are – I saw the pair of them together years ago, before Cameron shut himself away, and I know. It's rumoured that back then, when Cameron took an active role in life, there were times when Mortimer stood in for him. Pretended to be him, when there was a fete to be opened, a ribbon to be cut on the completion of a new building, a prize to be handed out to a scholarship schoolboy.'

'Why?' asks Felix.

Violetta glances sideways at him, light from a gas lamp they are passing reflecting in her large eyes. 'It's said – I can't vouch for the truth of it, mind – it's said that Cameron suffers from periodic bouts of insanity. Has done since childhood, apparently, and he managed to suppress the symptoms. He was cunning, so the story goes, and could behave like any other man even as he sensed a fit of madness coming on.'

'And now?'

Violetta shrugs. 'Who can say? Mortimer MacKilliver doesn't speak of the matter, and for all anyone knows, when Cameron does put in an appearance down here in London, it may be that it's really Mortimer.'

This is all very interesting, Felix thinks, but distant from the matter he has come to enquire about. 'And Freddie Fanshawe-Turnbull is a close associate of the twins,' he muses. 'Anything else you can tell me?'

'Hm.' Violetta is thinking. 'Freddie likes street women, as I said. But then that's hardly unusual, is it?'

'No.'

'Hmm.' The thinking goes on.

'What is it?' Felix prompts.

'Oh . . . I was just reflecting that, for all they try to keep their dealings private, the Band of Angels are widely rumoured to support the education of young women, and generously at that.'

'Yes, that's—'

But with a grin Violetta turns to look at him. 'That's why you're here, eh? Some troublesome little issue at one of the establishments funded by the Band?'

He has forgotten how bright she is. 'Something of the sort,' he admits.

'And that cool blonde boss of yours with the light in her eyes behind those prim spectacles has gone to see what she can find out.' She is still studying him. 'And you're worried about her.'

'She has gone in the guise of temporary assistant matron,' Felix says. He has realized suddenly that he can trust Violetta, and it is a relief to unburden himself. 'She will carry off the role with aplomb – that's not what I'm worried about.' Violetta waits, and he says, 'There's . . . I'm . . . It's just an instinctive reaction, but both of us sensed it when the little English teacher from the school came to seek our help. Something dark is going on there.'

For some time Violetta does not speak. Then she says, 'Instincts are there for a reason, young Felix. Trust them. The more you do so, the more faithfully they serve you.' She pauses. 'I spoke flippantly about your employer just now, but in truth I admire her. She's a woman in a man's world, and I wish her luck.' She pauses again. Then, apparently coming to a decision, she says, 'I will make some enquiries. Don't worry, I'll be subtle. If I discover anything useful or relevant, I'll tell you.'

'Thank you,' Felix says with warmth.

'Now, where do you want dropping?' Violetta is all at once brisk. 'I'm tired, I can't wait to get my stays off and my feet up, and Billy'll have a bottle chilled ready for me.'

Felix glances out of the window. The carriage seems to have gone east up the Strand and turned round again, so that they are pretty much back where they started. 'Here is fine.' Violetta raps on the roof and the carriage draws to a halt.

Felix opens the door. Turning back to her, he says, 'Still with Billy, then?'

'Always,' Violetta replies. But as he jumps down and prepares to close the door, she leans over and adds softly, 'Not, however, exclusively.'

Felix watches as the carriage draws away. As he trudges off towards the river and home, he distracts his mind from the biting cold and imagines himself wrapped up in a huge fur rug, naked beside the full, soft body of Violetta da Rosa.

The long walk passes in a flash.

Lily catches her train to Cambridge on Monday morning with ten minutes to spare and settles in a corner seat. There are half a dozen other people in the carriage. She is accustoming herself to wearing the SWNS uniform again; she had forgotten the way people recognize the black bonnet and the little gold badge on the collar, and the way they respond when they do: with a shy sort of smile, as if to say, *We know what you do and we admire you for it, for surely you see sights that would make the rest of us blanch.*

But I am a fraud, Lily thinks guiltily, for I ran away. I am not what they think I am.

As the train pulls out of Liverpool Street station, she wonders just why it was that she agreed – offered – to do this. After a few moments' thought the answer comes to her.

Because of her grandparents and her beloved Aunt Eliza, who, with firmness, clear moral values and a great deal of quiet love, brought her up after her father's death and her mother's defection to the lover by whom she was already pregnant when Lily's father died. All three of those remarkable people believed you should face your fears. Look your devils in the eye and shame them into submission. Lily has rarely had such a large and frightening devil as the one that sent her racing home from India, and facing up to it – him – is hard. Oh, more than hard. But she is going to do it. She *is* doing it.

She makes her tense body relax, settling back in her seat. She looks out at the crowded, busy mass of London's terraces, tenements and slums, and after a while shades of black, grey and brown give way to leafless trees, bare fields, winding lanes and the occasional beautiful aspect of frost-hard ground white beneath winter sunshine.

Quietly, steadily, Lily prepares herself for what is to come.

She leaves the mainline train at Cambridge and, crossing the platform, waits for the branch-line connection that will take her to the nearest village to Shardlowes School. Miss Long has promised that she will be met there with pony and trap.

The second journey is quite short. The train stops, the porter calls out the name of the station, Lily climbs down. It is a pretty little station, well kept, white-painted half-barrels set along the side of the platform which will be filled with flowers in a milder season.

A porter takes her suitcase. He has a friendly face and not many teeth, and looks as if he is not as strong as Lily herself. 'No, I can manage, thank you—' she begins.

But he holds on tight. 'Nothing's too good for one of you Swans, miss,' he says. 'You the new nurse for Shardlowes?'

'I am.'

'Come this way, then, the trap's waiting outside.'

The driver turns as he hears their approaching footsteps. He is a youngster, still some years off twenty, with a smiling face under a large flat cap, which he takes off in a courteous gesture as he jumps down to take Lily's suitcase and help her up.

'You all right there, miss?' he enquires as Lily settles herself on the narrow bench seat.

'Perfectly, thank you,' she replies.

'I'm Eddy,' the youth says.

'Leonora Henry,' Lily says. It is the first time she has uttered the name to anybody except Felix and Tamáz, and they don't count because they know it is a pretence.

'Nurse Henry, yes, that's right, it's what Miss Long said, who I was to look out for.'

'You have found her,' Lily says with a smile. Eddy, who happens to be glancing at her at that moment, responds with a huge grin.

The exchange seems to have calmed his garrulous nervousness, and now, clicking softly to the bay between the shafts so that the horse breaks into a smart trot, Lily can sense him relax.

They follow the road the short distance from the station into the village, rounding a sharp right-hand bend as a church looms up on the left. They take a right turn, a left, and Lily has an impression of yellowish-grey brick houses, thatched roofs, a pub, a small village shop. Then the houses thin out and they turn left on to a smaller lane. In the distance, over to the right, Lily spots a building of grey brick and red stone, forbidding, dominant, with a large and grandiose porch and wings extending to the rear.

Her heart sinks. It is the school, it must be, and it is stern and threatening and she really doesn't want to go there but—

'That's not it, miss,' Eddy says quietly, apparently noticing the direction of her glance. 'That's the – well, no need to mention it, but you don't want to go there. The school's up ahead, between here and the Cherry Hinton road, and we're almost there!' He almost sings the last few words.

He sounds, Lily thinks, as if he is trying to reassure her by talking so brightly.

She feels a sense of foreboding. She conjures up Aunt Eliza's heartening presence.

They round a shallow bend. Lily sees the figure of a woman in a dark-blue gabardine coat striding along in the direction of the station. She is tall with a masculine bearing, an unflattering felt hat squashed low on her head. She has an empty wicker basket over one arm. She looks up as the trap goes past, and Lily has an impression of light eyes, looking intently at her.

Now Eddy turns the horse in through black wrought-iron gates to the right and they trot up a curving drive running through winter-bare trees to emerge on to a wide gravelled semicircle. A house rises up behind the semicircle. It is built of the same yellowish-grey stone and a flight of steps leads up to the porticoed door. A large bay window juts forward to the right of the door, a square tower to the left, and on either side the building rambles away, its architecture giving the impression that wings and extensions have been added here and there over the years as need dictated.

Eddy has brought the horse to a halt at the foot of the steps and now he jumps down and hurries round to give her a hand. He picks up her suitcase from the back of the trap and as they reach the steps a bright voice calls, 'Miss Henry! Welcome to Shardlowes School.'

Lily looks up to see Georgiana Long beaming down at her. She takes her case from Eddy, murmurs her thanks and walks up the steps.

Not by the smallest wink, tic or nod does Miss Long indicate that there is more behind this encounter than a school teacher greeting the new nurse who has just been engaged. She wrests the case out of Lily's hand and says, 'Forgive me if I go ahead. I shall lead the way to your room, and perhaps you would like to refresh yourself before meeting Miss Carmichael?'

'I would,' Lily agrees.

Miss Long nods in satisfaction and limps her stuttering walk across the wide hall and up the left-hand side of a double stair-case that curves out and comes back to unite with the opposite flight to form a landing. She sets off down the landing to the right, and Lily has an impression of a series of solid oak doors amid the dark panelling. They go through a heavy door to the left and up a second flight of stairs, and at once the light is brighter. Then they set out along a narrow landing with a sloping ceiling on the left, windows at regular intervals admitting the thin winter sunshine. Doors open to the right, widely spaced and suggesting large rooms. Miss Long says, 'These are the dormitories for Senior School, Alice, Louise and Helena' – Lily recognizes the names of three of the Queen's daughters – 'six girls in each, and their classrooms are on the floor beneath. Junior School have both their classrooms and their dormitories up ahead in New Wing.'

They come to a corner, and she points to her left. 'That is New Wing,' she says. 'Junior girls sleep up to eight to a dormitory and we have Red, Blue and Green.'

You couldn't accuse whoever named the junior dormitories of having too vivid an imagination, Lily thinks.

Miss Long is hurrying on ahead, leaving the corridors of dormitories and taking a turn to the right. It leads into a wide passage with a window at the far end and five doors open off it.

'This is New Sanatorium Block – the San – and here is Matron's suite,' she says softly, indicating the first door on the right, 'bedroom and sitting room. Matron's not here just now – she has gone into Cambridge for supplies – or else I'd introduce you. Over here on the opposite side we have Sick Bay' – the first door on the left – 'the treatment room and the bathroom.' She opens each door and Lily has a glimpse inside. The sick bay has six beds, all perfectly made up with crisp white sheets and brown wool blankets, and there is a smell of bleach. The treatment room has a table, two chairs and an examination couch, and all of one wall is made up of cupboards, many with sturdy locks. The bathroom is large, chilly and spotless, the water closet in a small walled-off cubicle.

'And here is your room.' Miss Long opens the final door and steps back to let Lily precede her into the room. There is a single bed, made up like those in the sick bay but with a deep blue blanket. There is a small cupboard in the corner, a dressing table with an oval swivel mirror in a frame, a narrow chair with a padded seat, a pretty little fireplace, a washstand with ewer, bowl and slop bucket beneath, a bedside table with a drawer and a chamber pot cupboard. The walls are papered in a blue and green flowered pattern and the curtains are dark blue.

'It is charming,' Lily says, genuinely pleased.

'We have moved Nurse Evans's belongings out so as to give you space,' Miss Long says.

'Oh! Is that all right?'

'She has few personal items and she won't mind,' Miss Long says. 'Besides, it appears she took most of her possessions with her. She was an army nurse for many years and learned to live simply.' She stands in the middle of the pleasant room, looking round. 'Now I think that's everything . . .'

Lily takes her suitcase and puts it on the little fold-up wooden rack designed for that purpose; no nurse ever puts a case on a bed. Miss Long nods her approval. 'That goes under the bed when you have finished with it.' She points to the rack. 'I will leave you to settle yourself in. Come down when you have done so – can you remember the way back to Main Stairs? – and take the door to the left of the entrance. Miss Carmichael awaits you there with what I am sure will be a welcome cup of coffee.'

Having probably even fewer personal effects than the absent and minimally minded Nurse Evans, Lily unpacks in five minutes. She uses the bathroom, washing the smuts of the journey from her hands and face. Then, not giving herself time to feel nervous, she heads off down two flights of stairs and prepares to meet the headmistress of Shardlowes.

She taps on the door of the room to the left of the entrance and a low-pitched voice calls, 'Come in.'

Lily obeys.

The room is warm, a fire going strongly in the wide hearth. Before it is a long settee, on either side of which is a pair of wing chairs, one of them occupied. On a table behind the settee is a tray bearing a pot of coffee, milk jug, sugar bowl and two bone-china cups and saucers.

There is time for no more than a cursory survey, for the chair's occupant has risen to her feet and is advancing towards Lily, her hand outstretched and a faint smile on her pale face.

'Welcome, Miss Henry. I am Arabella Carmichael,' she says,

taking Lily's hand and limply shaking it; hers is long, slightly moist and, despite the warmth of the room, cold.

'Thank you,' Lily responds. 'How do you do, Miss Carmichael?'

'Sit down' – Miss Carmichael indicates the wing chair on the other side of the hearth – 'and I will pour coffee. Milk and sugar?'

'Just milk, please.'

The coffee is excellent, and made with hot milk.

'Now, let me run through a few matters with you, Nurse,' Miss Carmichael says, re-seating herself in her chair. Lily, noticing the alteration from Miss Henry to Nurse, acknowledges this as the moment she changes from a guest to an employee.

'Miss Long has explained about Nurse Evans's mother, I believe?'

'She has.'

Miss Carmichael looks disapproving. 'It was very sudden. Nurse Evans said she must go at once since her mother was gravely ill, dying, apparently' – she sounds as if she suspects this is an exaggeration to ensure that Nurse Evans's request could not be refused – 'and we had little choice in the matter. It is to our great good fortune, Nurse Henry, that Miss Long's friend knows you, vouches for you and was aware that you were in search of a position.' The faint smile appears again, and Lily wonders if this is the best Miss Carmichael can do.

'My good fortune too, Miss Carmichael,' she says politely.

Miss Carmichael inclines her head, as if such praise is no more than Shardlowes School's – and her – due.

She embarks on a brief description of the layout of Lily's new domain and her duties, but since Lily has already been shown the dormitories and the sick bay, and her knowledge of how to look after girls is undoubtedly vastly greater than Miss Carmichael's, she contents herself with nodding occasionally while she studies the headmistress of Shardlowes School.

Arabella Carmichael is tall, slim, elegant, beautiful in a chilly way and probably in her mid- to late thirties. She sits upright in her wing chair, her back perfectly straight. She is dressed in pale grey: a well-cut skirt and a little fitted jacket that buttons up to a high neck. Her hair is very fair and drawn back into an elaborate bun, her eyes so pale that it is difficult to detect if they are blue, green or grey. She picks up her cup with the most delicate of finger-and-thumb grips on its slender handle, and replaces it carefully dead centre in the saucer. Whenever she has taken a sip, she puts a folded, lace-edged, immaculate white handkerchief to her lips. She radiates self-discipline and authority, appears to be totally without humour and, to judge by her dismissive remarks about Nurse Evans's sick mother, not over-endowed with compassion.

If Lily and Felix are right about Miss Long's secret feelings for her headmistress, Lily can see how they could have arisen, for Miss Carmichael is a fine-looking woman who has achieved success in her profession.

Lily, however, dislikes her.

Miss Carmichael's words are interrupted by a tap on the door. It opens before the headmistress can say 'Come in', and with a fleeting expression of irritation, Miss Carmichael consults the pretty little gold watch pinned to her breast.

'Time has flown and it is later than I thought,' she murmurs, eyeing the newcomer with a frown. Then, looking at Lily, she says, 'Nurse Henry, let me present Miss Ann Dickinson, known to us all as Miss Dickie, who is Head of Junior School.'

Lily gets to her feet to greet the newcomer.

Ann Dickinson is twenty years older than Miss Carmichael, if not more. Her thin gunmetal grey hair is pulled fiercely back into a tight little knot, her face is pouchy, her eyes are intensely dark brown, very small and deeply set, with folds of fat around them and crumpled eyelids. As she holds out her hand to Lily, she is smiling; a sort of twinkly expression that draws her thin lips out into a straight line and bunches her cheeks up beneath her eyes, so that the latter all but disappear. She is dressed in a dark grey skirt and a white blouse with a soft round collar, a small cameo brooch concealing the top button.

Lily's immediate impression is that the smile, the bunched-up cheeks and the twinkle are artificial and that Miss Dickie's true nature is very different.

Telling herself not to be so hasty and judgemental, she grasps Miss Dickie's hand and, in response to the polite words of welcome, says, 'Thank you. I am very pleased to be here.'

She should perhaps have added something about being sure she was going to be very happy at Shardlowes, but it would be a huge lie so she doesn't.

Lily resumes her seat as Miss Dickie perches on the very edge of the settee and describes the composition and the running of Junior School. Just as Lily is wondering how many more times she is to be told about the arrangement of the dormitories, a gong sounds in the hall. Miss Carmichael interrupts Miss Dickie and says, 'That is the gong for First Luncheon, which is for Junior School, so we must excuse Miss Dickie while she goes to supervise.' The older woman gets up, gives the headmistress a brief nod and leaves the room. 'Most of the staff attend Second Luncheon,' she goes on, 'as indeed I hope you will *today*, Nurse Henry.'

There is a definite emphasis on *today*.

Deciding she is not to be cowed, Lily says, 'And on other days?'

'Meals for Matron and Matron's Assistant are taken in Matron's sitting room, brought up by the kitchen staff.'

'I see.' Lily is careful to keep her expression neutral, although she is relieved that meals will not habitually be taken under the pale, cold eyes of Arabella Carmichael.

'As soon as we have eaten' – Miss Carmichael rises, giving the clear impression that the interview is over – 'I suggest, Nurse, that you return to your room and change into the uniform that you will find folded and ready for you in the wardrobe.'

Lily hesitates. What would the real assistant matron do? Meekly comply, or assert a little independence of mind?'

Lily sighs inwardly, for she understands that whatever a real assistant would do is not relevant.

'Thank you, Miss Carmichael, but that will not be necessary,' she hears herself say. 'I am already in my nursing uniform, as no doubt you have observed.' She indicates the beautifully fitting black gown with its row of tiny buttons and starched white collar. 'As you will also see, I was trained by St Walburga's Nursing Service.' She points to the tiny gold letters on her pin. 'After luncheon I shall put on my headdress and apron, so that the pupils and the remainder of the staff will recognize me for what I am.'

Miss Carmichael's marble-pale face is expressionless. Lily believes she can sense the conflict raging within the sparse breast. Is she to put this uppity new arrival in her place, or is it preferable to yield? The school is in dire need of a matron's assistant, and in every other respect Lily – Nurse Leonora Henry – fits the bill.

'Very well, Nurse,' Miss Carmichael says eventually.

This time she doesn't even bother with the faint smile.

As Lily watches her tidy the cups and saucers on the tray, she has the sudden suspicion – no, stronger than that, she *knows* – that Miss Carmichael has no idea her new assistant matron is anything other than she purports to be.

The secret of Lily's true purpose here is a secret known only to herself and Georgiana Long.

In that moment of realization, Lily isn't sure if to be relieved or profoundly troubled.

FIVE

N umber 3, Hob's Court feels very empty.

It is Tuesday morning, the day after Lily's departure. Felix has made himself a cup of tea and checked yet again that Lily has locked the door to the passage at the rear of the house and the door to the shed. After prowling restlessly around the ground floor for some time, he sits down at his desk, flipping through the pages of his notebook. He is waiting for Violetta to provide information on the MacKilliver brothers or Freddie Fanshawe-Turnbull, preferably all three, and also hoping that Marm will turn up more details on the Band of Angels and their establishments.

For the time being Felix has nothing to do, for the Bureau's recent cases have all been resolved. Not that any of them were either taxing or interesting, Felix thinks morosely, and nor did they even earn much.

He feels the mood of dejection deepen.

Because he knows what its true cause is and doesn't want to think about it, he closes his eyes and goes back over everything he has learned about Shardlowes School and the Band of Angels. He imagines he heard Georgiana Long's light voice, speaking of the missing girls . . .

. . . and comes up with something challenging and interesting that he can work on without the absent and temporarily unreachable Lily. Something, moreover, which will involve all his resourcefulness and get him out of the office into the bargain. He puts his notebook and pencil in his inside pocket, bundles himself into his outdoor clothes, then lets himself out of 3, Hob's Court and hurries away in the direction of Victoria Station.

He marches east along the Embankment, turning up to the left just before the hospital. He calls at Kinver Street, where he swiftly packs a small overnight bag, leaving a note

for Marm to say he's going to Brighton and may be away for
a day or two.

Despite the cold, he is too hot when he reaches Victoria
Station, for he has walked fast. He unbuttons his heavy coat
as he strides to the ticket booth, then, following the clerk's
laconic pointing hand, heads for the right platform. The
locomotive is building up steam, about to leave; the barrier
clangs shut immediately after Felix has gone through. He
hurries past the extravagantly comfortable Pullman coaches to
the second-class accommodation further along, and swings up
into a half-empty carriage. He nods a greeting to the other
passengers – a vicar and his steely-eyed wife, a young man
with a battered suitcase and a shiny suit, an elderly woman
knitting something in violent purple – and sits down just as
the train jerks into movement.

By good fortune, none of the others has wanted to take the
seat nearest the window facing forward, Felix's favourite. His
small bag stowed on the rack above, his coat, scarf, hat and
gloves rolled up beside it, he settles back with a private sigh
of delight. He loves train journeys. He has perhaps an hour
and a half to enjoy and he intends to make the very most
of it.

The train pulls into the station.

Felix looks up in faint surprise as the clergyman courteously
asks him to move his feet so that he and his wife may disembark. Muttering an apology, Felix obliges. Despite his intentions,
halfway through the journey his thoughts had turned to what
he was going to do when he arrived, and for the last three-
quarters of an hour he has been thinking hard and writing
notes. He retrieves his bag, puts on his coat and jumps down
after the clergyman. Depositing his bag in the left-luggage
office, he heads out into the brilliant light and intensely cold
air of Brighton.

He knows the town rather well.

In an earlier phase of his life he was the companion, secre-
tary and general assistant of a widowed French countess some
sixteen years his senior. He was also her lover; a state of affairs
greatly to their mutual satisfaction and enjoyed honestly and

openly by both. Solange Devaux-Moncontour had a decrepit old pile of an ancestral home in rural Brittany and a seaside house in Dinard, but she loved to travel – she loved to travel with Felix particularly – and one glorious summer she had taken a small apartment in the heart of Regency Brighton.

Quite a lot of Felix's forty-five minutes of musing on the train had in fact been taken up with cheerful and erotic memories of Solange, if he is honest with himself.

His knowledge of the town comes in handy now because he knows where the office of the largest-circulation local newspaper is located and walks straight to it.

A plump and harassed middle-aged woman with a pencil stuck in her tidy bun – 'I'm Kitty, want some help?' – sits him down in a corner of the outer office and sends a lad to fetch back numbers for the previous autumn. Such is Felix's manner that she doesn't seem to mind this interruption into her busy day and even offers him a cup of tea.

He consults his notes, verifying what he has already committed to memory. Miss Long said that the girl who ran away with the travelling salesman was in Brighton *a few months ago, in the autumn,* and so Felix commences his search in the previous September. He works steadily and patiently, and presently realizes he is into the third week of October. Then the article he is looking for jumps out at him from page five: *Seaside Shenanigans* cries the headline, expanded in the sub-heading by *Haberdashery Salesman's Saucy Jaunt Ends in Tears.*

Felix reads the article.

A travelling haberdashery salesman was forced to leave his lodgings on Thursday morning because he was unable to pay his bill. Mr Wilfred Anderson, aged thirty-two and believed to hail from East Anglia, had been presented with the account for his first week in the lodging house in Everly Street by Mrs Ethel Shove, his landlady, she having become suspicious because, although claiming to be in the town to work, Mr Anderson rarely seemed to leave his room. Furthermore, Mrs Shove had begun to entertain grave suspicions that the young lady who accompanied

Mr Anderson was not, as stated, his wife: 'She was no more than sixteen or seventeen,' Mrs Shove confided to our reporter, 'and there was a good deal too much laughter and merriment coming from the room for them to be anything other than a honeymoon couple, if indeed they were wed, yet Mr Anderson had told me he was there on business.'

Felix reflects that Mrs Shove has a somewhat jaundiced view of marriage if she believes that laughter and merriment end with the termination of the honeymoon. Perhaps Mr Shove is a serious sort of fellow, he thinks.

He also wonders how much the unmarried state of her guests was bothering Mrs Shove *before* she began to entertain doubts as to Mr Anderson's ability to pay the bill.

He reads on.

Mrs Shove was reported to be in some distress as she recalled how her attempts to extract payment from Mr Anderson resulted in a rapidly escalating argument:

'There were words bandied about that I do not like to repeat,' she said, 'and the young lady joined in, calling me a word I never expected to hear from the mouth of a gently raised girl.' Mr Anderson was finally obliged to admit that he could not pay his account in full, offering to give Mrs Shove all he had whilst only retaining sufficient to purchase his rail fare back to Norwich, upon which his female companion cried loudly, 'And what about me?' to which Mr Anderson allegedly replied, 'I'm broke because of you and I have no more to spend on you.'

Mrs Shove related how the young lady asked if she could give her the money to return to the small village near Cambridge whence she had come; Mrs Shove gained the impression that she had been employed in a select girls' school, perhaps as a maid or in the kitchen. Mrs Shove, reluctant to admit to her kind-hearted and charitable generosity, eventually said that she had acquiesced to the request.

Felix smiles to himself, reflecting that the price of a rail fare was little enough to pay in return for such a juicy story that she must have known would be much enjoyed by the inhabitants of Brighton and do a great deal to publicize her establishment.

He reads through the remainder of the article, making one or two brief notes, and is about to close the newspaper when the plump woman comes over to his corner and, with a smile, observes, 'I see you're reading the Saucy Salesman story. Headline catch your eye and distract you, did it?'

'No,' he replies. Instinct tells him that honesty will pay with this sturdy woman, whose expression suggests she has seen it all and is rarely surprised by anything. 'It's the very matter I came here to find out about.'

She perches a generous hip on the edge of his desk, gives him an assessing look and says, 'Then you're talking to the right person.'

He opens the paper again: the article is accredited to *Our Reporter On the Spot, K. Kingston*. K, he thinks. And her name is Kitty. 'You?'

'Me,' she agrees, 'or, if we are to be as grammatically correct as our editor would like, I.' He raises his eyebrows in silent query. '"Reporter on the Spot" is a little inaccurate,' Kitty continues, 'since the spot I habitually occupy is right here, but the editor usually asks me to write the piece when there is what he calls female interest. Which suits me well, actually, since I'm given the domestic crimes and the very occasional intra-familial murders, the salacious goings-on like this one' – she indicates the article – 'and the performances on the pier and in the music hall, whilst my male equivalents are dispatched to cover council meetings, planning issues, government directives and the rest of the dry-as-dust matters that fill our pages. They do the black and white,' she concludes with a grin, 'I do the colour.'

'I'd say you had the better part of the deal,' Felix remarks.

The grin widens. 'Me too.' She glances round, peering into the corridor outside the office. 'Now I'll call the boy to make you and me some more tea, and while we drink it you can tell me why you've sought out this story.'

*   *   *

'So, with nothing for me to do on the case until I hear from other people,' Felix concludes after a further cup and a half of very good tea and some ten minutes' conversation, 'I decided to investigate the one lead I do have.'

Kitty Kingston gives him a long, assessing look. They are now sitting in her office, the door closed, but Felix has not let the intimate setting, nor Kitty's intelligent grey eyes, seduce him into giving away very much of the story. He has merely told her that the school from which the runaway girl fled is anxious for an explanation as to how she ended up in a Brighton boarding house with a haberdashery salesman. He is careful not to correct the misapprehension that she was a maid and not a pupil. What he says is true in essence, for hadn't Georgiana Long said the girl was 'unwilling to give a full account of how she got there'? It is a natural concomitant to conclude that Shardlowes would be keen to know.

Then abruptly Kitty begins to speak.

'Apparently she was a very pretty girl,' she said. 'Good figure, wavy fair hair, deep blue eyes, with that look of demure docility that fools so many men who are too busy ogling the bosom, the tiny waist and the rounded hips and forget to look properly. She was astute, that young lady, knew full well how to employ her looks and her charms to achieve her own ends.' Then, while Felix is digesting that, she adds, 'Do you know her name? She called herself Mrs Anderson, and her salesman referred to her as Bonnie.'

Felix thinks quickly, working out whether there is any reason to withhold this fact. He shoots a glance at Kitty, who is looking straight at him.

He takes a gamble, acting largely on instinct. 'Esme Sullivan.'

'Thank you,' Kitty murmurs. 'I thought you'd be able to tell me. And while we, or rather you, are putting the cards on the table, I take it she was a pupil and not a maid?' He hesitates. 'Oh, come on, Mr Wilbraham!' Kitty says impatiently. 'Maids don't talk as if they have a plum in their mouth and stare down their pretty little noses at ordinary mortals as if they are barely worthy of notice.'

'She was a pupil,' Felix confirms.

Kitty leans back in her chair. 'In return for your frankness,

I will tell you what I know. When the landlady made it clear that—'

'Mrs Shove,' Felix puts in, pronouncing it as if it were the synonym for *push*.

Kitty laughs. 'Show-va,' she corrects. 'Apparently it's of Dutch origin. Whether that's true or not I wouldn't like to say, but Mrs Shove is far too refined to let anyone get away with *Shove*.' This time she repeats Felix's version. 'As I was saying, she challenged Wilfred Anderson regarding the bill, they began to argue, the girl joined in and Ethel Shove chucked them out. The girl widened her eyes and probably managed a tear or two and asked Mrs Shove for the fare back to East Anglia, and Mrs Shove eventually gave it to her.'

'That would be her "kind-hearted and charitable generosity",' Felix supplies.

Kitty grins. 'Well, it made a cosy end to the piece,' she says. 'In truth, Ethel Shove never gives anything to anybody unless she is somehow to profit by it, and in this instance, she wanted to make sure she emerged as not only the innocent victim but one with the decency and the Christian charity to help a young woman in distress. And if that young woman was indeed in distress,' she adds softly, 'then I'm the Queen's granddaughter.'

'And she – Esme Sullivan, also known as Bonnie Anderson – definitely asked for the fare back to Shardlowes?'

'Not specifically. According to Mrs Shove, she said she'd have to go by train to Cambridge and the branch line out to the village where Shardlowes School is situated.'

Felix is surprised that Esme should have mentioned the school by name. 'She definitely identified the school?'

Kitty looks at the large clock on the wall, then back at Felix. 'Got an hour or so to spare?'

'I have.

'Then come with me and we'll go straight to the horse's mouth.'

Ethel Shove's guest house is in a narrow little back street quite a long way behind Madeira Square. The house, like its neighbours, has seen better days, although the step has been swept and the window glass is largely free of seagull splatter.

Kitty Kingston marches up to the maroon-painted door and bangs the glossy brass knocker a few times. The door is quickly opened, revealing a thin woman dressed in black who holds herself so erect that she gives the impression of a pencil. Her sparse silver hair is twisted into a tiny topknot and her light-brown eyes are suspicious. 'Yes?' she says curtly, then, recognizing Kitty, the frown turns into a rather artificial smile. 'Oh, Miss Kingston!' she says. 'Have you come back for more details?'

'Yes, Mrs Shove. Shall we come in?' Kitty is doing so even as she says the words. 'Better not to speak where the neighbours can hear us, eh?'

'Yes, yes, of course . . .' Ethel Shove indicates a door on the left of the hall, and Felix follows Kitty into a room so overfilled with furniture that weaving a way across the richly patterned carpet is something of a challenge. He knocks into a sideboard and a little table, and although ornaments tinkle alarmingly, nothing breaks or falls. He lurches towards an upright chair and gratefully sits down, Kitty settles herself on a chaise longue and Ethel Shove hovers just inside the door.

'How did you know where the girl calling herself Mrs Anderson was bound?' Kitty asks without preamble.

'She was going back to the school,' Mrs Shove says. 'Shardlowes School.'

'She told you that? She actually mentioned the name?'

Mrs Shove begins to nod in affirmation but then abruptly stops. 'No!' she says, eyes rounding in surprise. 'No, now I come to think of it, she didn't.'

'So how did you know?' Kitty persists.

'I saw a luggage label,' Mrs Shove says. 'Isn't that extraordinary? I had quite forgotten – it must be the drama of it all. No, she didn't mention the actual place. When she asked me to give her the fare home, she just said she had to return to where she had come from and it was a village just outside Cambridge. But as *he*' – she cannot bring herself to mention Wilfred Anderson by name – 'was carrying her suitcase down the stairs, he banged it against my wallpaper and I told him to be more careful, and he sort of *thrust* it at me as if it was a weapon!' She is affronted all over again, her sallow face reddening unattractively. 'Nearly caused a mishap too, because she was just ahead of him on the stairs and the suitcase caught her shoulder and he had to grab her arm hard to stop her falling.'

'And that was when you noticed the label?' Kitty prompts.

'Yes! Well, not a label, not exactly' – she closes her eyes, the better to picture the memory – 'a chalk mark, like something a porter or a luggage-van guard might make, and it said, *For Shardlowes School.* Just *s, c, h* and half an *o*, then a smudge,' she elucidates, 'but not many other words begin with *scho*, do they?'

'Schloss?' Felix supplies.

Both women give him a long-suffering look. 'That's *s-c-h-l-o*,' Kitty says crushingly. Turning back to Mrs Shove, she says, 'And you very generously gave her the sum she said she needed to return to this village?'

'I did.' Mrs Shove looks, if it is possible, even more self-congratulatory.

'And you are sure that's where she was going?'

'Well, I didn't follow her to the railway station and watch her purchase a ticket!' Mrs Shove snaps. Then, her face falling in dismay, at last she says in a very different voice, 'What's the matter? Did she not arrive back at the school?'

And together Kitty and Felix say, 'No.'

'I think,' Felix says when he and Kitty are once out on the street and walking briskly back towards the seafront, 'that I shall see what I can find out at the station.'

'After three months?' Kitty says. 'You'll be lucky.'

'Not quite three months,' Felix says pedantically, 'and railway stations are staffed by men, many of them young and all of them, probably, with an eye for a pretty girl travelling on her own.'

Kitty accedes to the wisdom of this. 'Well, I wish you success,' she says. They have come to the junction where the way back to the newspaper office branches off to the right. She stops and holds out her hand. Felix shakes it. Then, reaching inside his coat pocket, he extracts a business card and gives it to her.

'World's End Bureau, 3, Hob's Court, Chelsea, private enquiry

agency, proprietor L.G. Raynor,' she reads aloud. She looks up, eyes narrowed. 'Thought you said your name was Wilbraham?'
'I did.'
She grins. 'So allowing me to assume you were the boss of the outfit was misleading?'
He returns the smile, waving a vague hand in apology. 'Yes.'
Then suddenly her face straightens. 'World's End Bureau,' she whispers. 'You solved the Albertina Stibbins case!'
'Yes,' Felix says again.
Kitty gives a low whistle. 'Good grief,' she mutters.
Then with a nod and an appreciative lift of the eyebrows, she turns and strides away.

Felix speaks to a number of the employees of the London, Brighton and South Coast Railway, including two ticket-office clerks, a junior station master and three porters, before he finds what he is looking for. An elderly man with a stoop leans on the handles of his porter's barrow and, in answer to Felix's question, says with a reminiscent smile and a gleam in his rheumy old eyes that yes, he does remember such a young lady.
'Will you tell me about her?' Felix asks urgently. He is amazed at his good fortune, secretly having been as sceptical as Kitty concerning his chances.
The old man glances over his shoulder at a station master with highly polished buttons and a look of self-importance and mutters, 'Not now. I knock off at six. Buy me a pint of stout in the Buck and then I will.'
Felix agrees, slips sixpence into the old man's hand as a gesture of good will and walks away. He checks the times of evening trains to London – there are several, which is welcome news as he will be able to return tonight – and looks around outside the station for a pub called the Buck. It is in a dirty little back street, and he memorizes the location.
He glances at his pocket watch. He has nearly four hours to fill. He hasn't yet eaten and the sea air has made him ravenous, so he decides to spend at least two of them on a long lunch in a restaurant with a view over the promenade and the sea.
He has, he tells himself, earned it.

* * *

The late lunch, in the restaurant of a seafront hotel, is as fine as he anticipated except that he manages to draw it out for even longer than two hours. Then he accepts the offer of a cup of coffee in the lounge with an attractive lady resident, although manages to resist her rather obvious unspoken invitation to continue their encounter upstairs in her room. The sea air, he thinks as finally he leaves, sharpens appetites other than for food.

He walks for a mile along the promenade, then back again. It is colder than ever, and as soon as he stops his fast pace he feels the rising wind trying to blast a way inside his layers of clothing. He has a cup of tea in a pleasant little cafe, then, ten minutes before the appointed time, returns to the Buck.

He is sitting at a small table with a pint of bitter before him when the elderly porter comes in. Felix rises, crosses to the bar and returns with a glass of almost black stout.

'It was back in October, near the end of the month,' the porter begins, a moustache of cream foam enlarging his own magnificent facial adornment, 'and I know that for a fact because it was the wife's birthday and I needed to get off sharpish as her sister was coming round. Anyway, this young girl – lovely she was, pretty as a picture – has a man with her – older, she's maybe eighteen, maybe a bit younger, he's in his thirties, I'll wager – and they're arguing, he's trying to persuade her to do something she doesn't want to and she says, *No, no, I have to get back, I've got the money and I'm buying a ticket to London and I'm going on to Cambridge and you can't stop me!* Then he says something else, but he's talking softly, see, and I can't hear him, and she pushes him away and marches off to the ticket booth and leans in to mutter to the clerk, he hands her a ticket and she pays the money. Then the man says, *At least let me see you to the platform* and she says, *No, go away, leave me, you've done enough*, only she doesn't say it like she's grateful but like she's bloody furious with him, pardon the language.'

'Of course.' Felix is agog. 'Go on.'

'Anyway, the man, he gives up and storms off, and after a moment she hurries after him and stands at the entrance peering out, and I'm thinking to myself she's checking he's really gone.

Me, I'm feeling sorry for her by now, being as how she looks very young, and she's alone, and it's getting late, so I go up to her and says, "Porter, miss?" and she turns these beautiful big blue eyes on me and breathes, "Oh, *thank* you!", like it's a huge relief to have some help, which even at the time I think is a bit artificial since she's just carried her own case to the entrance and back with no apparent effort, but anyway, like I said, I'm sorry for her, so I put her little case on my barrow and set off towards the platform for the London train.' He leans closer, eyes narrowing, and, lowering his voice to a hoarse whisper, says, 'But then guess what she says?'

Felix has a very good idea what it was: the refusal to allow the man to purchase the ticket, the soft muttered words to the ticket clerk, the checking to make sure her companion had gone, all indicate the same thing. But, not wanting to spoil the old boy's moment, he whispers back, 'No! What?'

The porter sits back again. 'Wasn't really going to London, was she?'

'Good Lord!' Felix exclaims.

'No, she wasn't,' the old porter says, nodding.

'So which platform did she tell you to take her to?'

The old man draws out the moment. Then eventually he says, 'The one for the west-bound train.'

'And you checked, of course, with your colleague in the ticket booth as to her destination?'

'Course I did.' The porter grins. 'She was bound for Portsmouth.'

SIX

Lily's first full day as assistant matron at Shardlowes School begins early on Tuesday morning with a peremptory knock on her door. As she calls out 'Come in', the door is pushed open to reveal a broad, fat figure in a heavy dressing gown, her grey hair in pins and curl papers, her big, florid face shiny and cross-looking, standing on the landing.

Lily is glad that this unexpected visitor has not found her in bed and waking muzzily and untidily from deep sleep, but seated before the dressing table in her wrap, having already slipped along to the lavatory and fetched the jug of hot water with which she has just finished washing.

'Nurse Henry, I assume,' the fat woman says.

Of course, Lily thinks. She waits.

'I am Matron,' the large woman says, in the tones of one announcing a far grander title. 'I had a bugger of a day yesterday, the suppliers let me down *again* and I missed my train, which meant I had to wait almost half an hour for Eddy to fetch me, and as a result I have taken chill and shall stay in bed today.'

'A wise precaution,' Lily murmurs.

Matron looks at her intently, frowning slightly. 'Yes, well.' She sniffs wetly, as if to prove the point about having taken chill. 'You're a Swan, or so I'm told.'

'I am,' Lily confirms.

'And you refuse to wear our uniform, preferring your own,' Matron ploughs on, and to Lily's ears she sounds as if she hasn't decided whether to be resentful or admiring. Lily makes no comment.

'Well, there's not likely to be much to do today,' Matron continues. 'Several of Blue are down with a cold, none of them sufficiently unwell to be off lessons, and there's a nasty cough in Helena. Then there's a sprained ankle from last Saturday's hockey match, and that's about it. You can busy yourself tidying the sick-bay cupboard, Evans'll have left it in the usual chaos,

I have no doubt of that.' She scowls, sneezes explosively and with no attempt to smother it with her handkerchief, turns and begins to close the door. At the last moment another thought strikes her and she opens it again. 'The little Dunbar-Lea child will probably come creeping and crawling to you for something or other but don't you have any truck with her, she's a malingerer if ever I saw one.' A fierce scowl distorts Matron's heavy brow. 'The wretched girl's been pestering me with some problem concerning her *mother*, if you please, set off by a visit her parents made last September. Goodness, the child's lucky to have *had* a visit, it's more than most of them get, and now this nonsense.' Matron shakes her head at the folly of it. 'Miss Dickie needs to take a firm hand with the girl. Me, I usually find that a large dose of castor oil sorts her out.' With a nod of satisfaction at her own sagacity, Matron shuts the door – slams it, in fact – and Lily is alone.

She gets up and goes to the wardrobe, taking out her black uniform gown with its stiff white collar. Putting it on feels as if she is dressing herself in calm confidence. She brushes her hair, drawing it back into its bun, puts on her starched white apron and then fastens the wide band of stiff white cloth around her head, attaching it securely around the bun as she used to do every morning at this time. Then she unfolds the black veil of a fully qualified SWNS nurse and pins it to the white band.

At last she looks at herself in the looking glass.

Her heart seems to arrest for an instant, then beats very quickly for a few seconds before resuming its steady rhythm.

'Enough,' she says aloud, more shaken than she will admit.

She turns away, makes her bed with economical efficiency, checks to see that all is neat and tidy and leaves the room.

It is early still: more than an hour until the girls will clatter down to the refectory for breakfast. But Lily will not be idle and allow entry to everything she is trying not to think about. She lets herself quietly into the sick bay and performs an assessment of its state of tidiness. There is room for improvement, and she makes a mental note of how she will go about it.

She notices a kettle, teapot, caddy, biscuit barrel, cups and saucers on a small shelf in the corner, as well as a small spirit stove. She slips along the landing to fill the kettle and then makes a pot of tea. She pours out a cup, puts two biscuits in the saucer and puts it on a tray, together with sugar bowl and spoon, and carries the tray along to Matron's room. She taps very softly, in case Matron has gone back to sleep, but there is another of the tremendous sneezes and Matron calls croakily and crossly, 'What is it *now*?', as if this is the fourth or fifth time Lily has bothered her rather than the first.

'I thought a cup of tea might be welcome,' Lily says, going in and putting the little tray down on the crowded bedside table; Matron, she reflects, is a fine one to accuse other people of chaos, her own room being a fusty-smelling jumble of draped garments, knick-knacks, photographs in frames (mostly of a fat spaniel) and too much furniture.

But Matron is looking at her from the piled pillows and the tumbled bedclothes with a look of affection.

'D'you know, Nurse,' she says, 'this is the first cup of tea anyone's brought to my bed since – oh, good God, since for ever, probably.'

Lily smiles. 'Sugar?'

'Three.'

Matron sips at the tea, eyeing Lily over the cup. 'Got your day planned?'

'Yes.' Lily folds her hands over her apron, keeping them still as a SWNS nurse is taught. 'I have yet to familiarize myself with the morning routine so I intend to visit the dormitories, where I'll check on the state of the colds in Blue, the cough in Helena and the sprained ankle in – actually, Matron, I don't believe you told me which dormitory that was.'

'No, I didn't.' Matron is looking at her approvingly. 'Louise. And it's Eunice Carter, who's a big girl, pale blonde hair, good hockey player although resents being put in goal so frequently. It's her size, see, she blocks balls so easily and—'

'Thank you,' Lily interrupts smoothly. 'Now, may I fetch you another cup of tea before I go?'

Another assessing look, this time with narrowed eyes. Matron assents to the second cup – 'And a handful of those biscuits too' – and then Lily backs out of the stuffy, slightly malodorous room and firmly closes the door.

*   *   *

A bell rings out loudly and for some time as Lily strides along the corridor where the junior dormitories are located. She approaches the middle one, Blue, and quietly lets herself in.

Seven beds are arranged within. Their occupants are reluctantly waking up in obedience to the bell's insistence. An older girl stands inside the door, eyeing the seven smaller girls. Lily observes that one little girl has the long, glossy black hair and dark skin of India, another has a deformity of some sort of the right hand, and a third is grossly overweight; this last child is wheezing and puffing as she bends to retrieve some item from under her bed. The girls are dragging on heavy black stockings, navy blue shin-length gowns and white pinafores; the older girl – a monitor or prefect – wears a full-length navy skirt and a white high-buttoned blouse, a blue sash over her blouse from right shoulder to left hip. Lily deduces from her watchful gaze and the smaller girls' clear awe that the sash is a badge of office.

All is calm, all is quiet.

The older girl, sensing Lily's presence, turns.

'I am Nurse Henry, assistant matron,' Lily says.

The girl – she is about fifteen, brown hair in a long braid down her back, rather dour expression – says politely, 'Good morning, Nurse Henry,' eyebrows raised in faint enquiry.

'I understand some of the girls in Blue have a cold,' Lily says softly. 'I have come to ensure they are fit for lessons.'

The monitor's expression gives away her surprise, revealing to Lily that such a visit is unusual. But she is too well-mannered to question a member of staff. She calls out three names and three girls of about eight or nine step forward, one hopping as she puts on a stocking, all three faces wearing similar expressions of apprehension. Lily asks one or two questions, putting a hand to one damp forehead, but the girls all say they don't feel too bad and the one with the damp forehead – it is the black-haired child – says it's not the sweat of fever, she's just washed her face.

Lily turns back to the monitor. 'Thank you . . .?'

'Sudie Brown-Caldicot, Helena dormitory, monitor for Blue dormitory,' the girl supplies smartly.

'Thank you, Sudie. Good morning, girls,' she says to the dormitory in general as she turns to go.

'Good morning, Nurse,' eight voices respond.

Lily walks on to the seniors' corridor and finds the three doors marked Alice, Helena and Louise. Here the older girls supervise themselves, calmly following an efficient routine. The girl with the cough in Helena says she has slept well, and Lily tells her to come to the sick bay for some cough syrup if necessary. The big blonde in Louise is limping quite badly, and Lily instructs her to report to her after breakfast.

A second bell clangs out as Lily leaves Louise dormitory, and there is the sound of some three dozen pairs of booted feet as the girls march along the corridors and down the stairs to breakfast.

Lily waits until the sounds are a distant rumble, then takes a moment to peer into each of the six dormitories. Beds are made, nightgowns are stowed under pillows, damp towels and flannels hung on the wooden racks beside the washstands.

She walks back to the sick bay, reflecting on her first impressions. She feels uneasy. Despite the good manners and the highly efficient morning routine, there is something out of kilter up here in these chilly corridors. She is striding on, deep in thought, when suddenly the temperature drops abruptly and all at once she is very cold. Immediately following this sensation comes a memory – far too vivid a memory – of her misgivings about this place. Not only mine, she thinks, for Felix felt them too.

She stops, sensing the atmosphere around her.

She can hear a hum of distant voices, a faint clatter of cutlery, a door closing. Normal sounds. The cold feeling has gone.

Nevertheless, she puts her hand to her bosom and feels for the little glass bottle she wears next to her skin. It is a gift from Tamáz and it is a protective amulet. It has already saved her life once, and she'd had no intention of coming to Shardlowes without it.

Better to be safe than sorry.

Back in her room, she discovers that breakfast has been left for her on a tray. Tea, porridge, poached eggs on toast, all well-cooked, and if the tea and the food are a little cold, that is nobody's fault but hers since whoever brought the tray must have expected to find her in her room.

She discovers she is very hungry and eats every scrap.

The morning passes swiftly. She treats the sprained ankle, and the big blonde called Eunice Carter copes with the discomfort of her injury with stoicism worthy of a good sportswoman. She looks briefly mutinous when Lily orders no games for this week at least, but Shardlowes' discipline comes into play again and she accepts the ban without comment, thanking Nurse as she limps away.

Lily spends the remainder of the morning sorting out the sick bay. She imposes her own order on the cupboards and shelves, wondering if Nurse Evans will manage to find anything on her return to duty and deciding she doesn't much care.

She looks in on Matron a couple of times. On the first occasion Matron is deeply asleep and stertorously snoring; on the second she is sitting up and peevishly asking Lily if it is lunch time. It is, and Lily takes her own meal in to eat with Matron. The conversation is illuminating; Matron accepts Lily's remarks about the excellent standard of discipline in the school as if she herself had instigated it, only admitting in response to Lily's questions that it's Miss Dickie who is really responsible, adding, 'She gets them young, see, and she has her own methods.'

It is only afterwards, remembering, that Lily feels that sense of chill again and understands that the words are open to a sinister interpretation.

It is mid-afternoon. Lily is back in the sick bay, having taken advantage of a quiet hour to go for a walk. It is bitterly cold outside; she has been forcibly reminded that she is in the Fens.

She is putting away some fresh supplies that have been delivered during her absence – bandages, sanitary towels, flannels – when there is a timid little tap on the door.

'Come in!' She turns expectantly.

The door opens slowly and the top half of a face appears in the gap. It is that of a child not yet on the cusp of womanhood; eleven or twelve. Soft light-brown hair is centrally parted above a broad, pale forehead, and the large eyes are china-blue.

'Come *right* in,' Lily says with a smile.

The eyes crease up as the child returns the smile. She opens the door fully and steps into the room.

The hair, the eyes and the smooth white skin are where beauty stops. Beneath the little button of a nose there is a deep, dark, puckered scar that once split the upper lip, now drawn up to reveal the teeth, giving an unfortunate, rabbit-like appearance.

Hare lip, Lily thinks automatically, probably repaired soon after birth and not well.

As if that were not enough, as the child advances towards Lily it becomes clear that she has a limp that is even more disabling than Miss Long's. Looking down, Lily sees that the right leg is considerably shorter than the left, a condition only partially alleviated by a huge corrective boot with a heavily built-up sole.

'Good afternoon,' Lily says. 'Who are you?'

'Marigold Jane Dunbar-Lea,' the child responds. The g of Marigold and, even more so, the d and b of Dunbar are mispronounced. In her head Lily hears the voice of the tutor in one of her SWNS lectures: *The cleft-palate deformity means that only an imperfect seal is made in the mouth and the necessary pressure for certain letters and diphthongs cannot build up.*

'Well, Marigold, sit down here' – Lily pushes forward a wooden stool – 'and tell me what I can do for you.'

Slowly Marigold sits down, eyes fixed on Lily. 'You're not going to . . .' – *y're hot hoing ho* – she begins, then firmly shuts her mouth.

'Not going to what?' Lily asks gently.

Marigold shrugs. 'Matron and Nurse Evans usually send me away.'

'I shall not do that.'

'You—' Then, surprise flooding the little face, 'You can understand me, and we've only just met!' *Han. Het.*

Lily nods. 'I have to listen very carefully,' she admits, 'but yes, I can understand you.

Marigold's expression suggests this is something of a miracle. 'But—' *Hut.*

'Now,' Lily says briskly, 'are you hurt? Have you a pain?' Are you malingering, as Matron says you tend to?

'I have a pain here.' Marigold points to her belly. 'We had boiled bacon and butter beans with parsley sauce for luncheon – I expect you did too, Nurse – and I had two helpings, and now my tummy feels very full and it hurts.'

'Butter beans often make you feel bloated,' Lily says. 'May I feel your tummy?' Marigold nods. Lily feels distension, hard under her hand. 'I think it will pass,' she says after a moment, 'but in the meantime I shall give you some peppermint mixture, which is good for the digestion, and suggest that you gently rub your tummy like this.' She puts her hand on her own belly, slowly making firm circles around her navel. Marigold copies the gesture. 'If you are still in pain at bedtime,' Lily goes on, 'come to see me and I shall prepare a hot water bottle.'

She doses Marigold with a large spoonful of peppermint mixture, and the girl jumps off the stool and heads towards the door, calling her thanks over her shoulder.

'You're in a hurry to get away!' Lily responds with a smile.

Marigold turns, grinning. 'Yes. I'm making my escape before you fetch the castor oil bottle.'

She stumbles out, closing the door, and Lily listens to the sound of her uneven gait fading along the passage.

She has the distinct impression that Marigold's bright eyes and keen intelligence have just been sounding her out.

With supper eaten in her room, the tray collected and no further duties for the day, Lily is tempted to ease off her boots and stretch out on her bed. She has done all she can to settle into Shardlowes and learn its routine. She ought to be tired, for it has been a long and challenging day; instead she feels restless. She paces to and fro across the small room, but the restricted space does not allow her to vent her nervous energy. If only there were a clear and obvious cause for anxiety, she thinks, then I could tackle it and decide what to do. But there isn't.

It is a moment when, were she back in Chelsea, she would have talked the day's events over with Felix. He would have been the perfect ally just now, for hadn't he too felt that strange, sinister sense of something wrong when Miss Long had finished explaining herself to them?

But Felix is a long way away. She could send him a letter; fully intends to do so, in fact, and they have arranged that she will write to him as F. Wilbraham at the Kinver Street apartment, so that if by mischance anyone were to see the letter in her hand as she went to post it, neither address nor addressee will give anything away. 'Felicia is my late brother's widow,' she would say.

As yet there is nothing, other than these vague fears and suspicions, to write . . .

Irritated with herself, she winds a long scarf round her neck and picks up her weatherproof cloak. Quietly letting herself out of her room, she makes her way soft-footed along the dormitory corridor, down the first flight of stairs and then, turning away from the majestic main staircase leading down to the entrance hall, descends to the ground floor down a more modest servants' stair that she discovered this afternoon. The rear hall has a door that opens on to the side of the building, unlocked, and from there she follows a paved path round to the semicircle of gravelled drive at the front.

She keeps to the edge, under the sparse shadow of the trees, where the gravel is too thin to make much of a crunch. She strides out fast, movement easing her troubled spirit. The drive is longer than she remembers, and she doesn't recall the trees having a sufficiently thick network of branches to make such darkness . . .

She walks faster, cross with herself for falling prey to her own imaginings. Nevertheless, when the black barrier of the gates looms up ahead, she can't help but be flooded with relief.

'Stupid,' she mutters. 'Stupid, fanciful woman.'

The gates are firmly shut, and there is a length of chain holding them together fastened with a sturdy padlock. Lily leans against the left-hand one, gloved hands round the icy-cold bars. Is the world locked out or am I locked in? she wonders.

Stop that.

She stands for a few moments looking out at the sleeping landscape. One or two lights shine very faintly away to the left, where the last houses of the village peter out. Distantly she hears a train whistle, mournful somehow in the loneliness of the night.

Angry with herself for her inability to control her mood, she turns and walks smartly back up the drive towards the house.

As she rounds the shallow bend just before the semicircle opens out, a terrible sound rips through the air.

It is a howl: a long-drawn-out, agonized howl, full of fear, full of pain, full of despair. Lily's heart seems to stop, then commences a rapid drumming. The hairs on the back of her neck rise up. Sweat breaks out on the palms of her cold hands.

The howl comes again, louder now, closer . . .

And then sense and logic reassert themselves.

Not a demon escaped from hell, not a fire-breathing black devil dog.

She knows this sound: she heard it once before in India when a condemned man, driven to murder by disease and the chaos in his own mind, had escaped from his cell. The army did not like their soldiers to evade justice and every possible step was taken to hunt down the fugitive and bring him back for his hanging.

They had sent the bloodhounds after him.

And that is what this awful sound is.

Lily waits until her heart has slowed to close to its normal beat. She straightens her back, squares her shoulders and marches on, around the semicircle and towards the path leading round to the side door.

Where, rounding the blind corner, she bumps hard into someone coming the other way.

Afterwards, she is proud of herself for biting back the scream. Just now, she is so scared that she is trembling.

She is gathering herself, preparing a query delivered with calm eloquence, when the other person holds up an object in their hand, makes a swift movement and, as the lantern's shutter is opened, light floods out.

'It is late for being out of doors, Nurse?' a woman's voice says, rising at the end into a question.

Lily stares down into the pale face of Miss Dickie. 'I might say the same to you, Miss Dickie,' she replies coolly.

'*I* have been to check that the main gates are closed.' Miss Dickie's plump cheeks rise towards the pouches beneath her intense dark eyes as she does her version of a smile: the one that involves only her mouth and the pads of fat on her face.

And she has just told Lily a lie, for wherever she's been, it's not to the gates.

'I see.' Lily can hear the unspoken question *And where have you been?* as if it is being shouted aloud, but she will not explain herself. Easing past Miss Dickie's sturdy figure, she says easily, 'Too cold for lurking outside,' and starts off towards the side door.

Instantly angry with herself all over again, as Miss Dickie says, 'It is a disturbing sound, is it not?'

Fool, *fool*, Lily berates herself. Nobody possessing the faculty of hearing could have missed that ghastly howl – even as the thought flies through her head it comes again – so how could she have been such an idiot as to refrain from mentioning it?

'Yes, indeed,' she says, stopping and turning back to Miss Dickie. 'An escaped prisoner, I imagine, and they are tracking him with dogs.'

'Bloodhounds, yes,' Miss Dickie agrees.

'I shall wish you goodnight, Miss Dickie, and—'

'They are not, however, on the scent of a prisoner,' Miss Dickie presses on, as if she hadn't heard the interruption. 'Well, a prisoner of a sort, I suppose.' The face-crumpling false smile again, this time accompanied by a humourless little laugh. 'Do you not know, Nurse Henry?'

Hating having been backed into this position of weakness, Lily has no choice but to say coldly, 'Know what?'

Miss Dickie leans closer. She smells of carbolic soap with an under note of old sweat. 'Our neighbours over there!' she hisses, pointing her free hand away to the right.

And Lily remembers the looming, forbidding building she passed on the way here. The one she thought must be the school, only for Eddy to correct her, saying, *You don't want to go there.*

'What is it?' she mutters, even as the answer springs into her head.

Miss Dickie nods slowly. 'You do know, don't you?' she murmurs. She pauses. Then she says, 'It is the lunatic asylum.'

SEVEN

F elix stands irresolute outside Brighton station.
He very much wants to leap on to a train to Portsmouth
and hope that his luck will hold; that he'll encounter another
porter, or ticket collector, or a lad selling newspapers, who will
remember the pretty young woman on her own who arrived at
the station at the end of October. He is like the keenest of
hounds with the strong scent of a wily fox in his nose, and he
very nearly yields to the temptation to pursue his quarry.

But reason asserts itself. Feeling that in some unfathomable
way he is letting himself down, he fetches his redundant
overnight bag from the left-luggage office and heads to the
platform for the London train.

Portsmouth is a big place, he tells himself as the train puffs
off towards the South Downs. His compartment is empty, and
he has a suspicion that he might have muttered the words aloud.
In addition, who is to say that it was Esme Sullivan's final
destination? Felix has a vague idea that Portsmouth is where
several regional railway companies coincide, and quite possibly
Esme was planning to change trains and head on towards
Somerset, Devon or Cornwall, or up into Wales.

All of which is very reasonable and sensible, and none of
which can do much to stop the feeling that he has just taken
a wrong step.

The Kinver Street apartment is empty when Felix arrives home.
Marm has obviously found his note, and now beside it is
another one: *Good luck, you dirty devil, and I trust she's worth
the price of the room. Will be away myself for a night or two
so you'll probably return before me, hence this note.* At the
bottom he has added enigmatically, *May well have turned up
something to interest you . . .*

Felix grins at the suggestive remark, then mutters a soft curse
when he reads the final words. 'And naturally you're not going

to leave me even the smallest hint as to what that something might be, are you, Marm?' he says aloud.

Surprised at how much he misses the landlord who is fast becoming a good friend, Felix makes himself a scratch supper, pours a generous few fingers of whisky and settles down in front of the fire to his solitary evening.

The following morning he is at 3, Hob's Court precisely on time. To his surprise, he can hear someone in the back of the house and for a heart-lifting moment he thinks it's Lily.

But then he hears a racking, phlegmy cough. Mrs Clapper's face appears in the kitchen doorway and she holds up a stern hand. 'Don't you come any closer!' she says in the sort of tones a lion tamer might employ to deter an agitated lion. 'I'm only here for as long as it takes me to put the kitchen and the scullery to rights and I don't want *you* catching Clapper's bad bronicles as well.' The angry resentment in her voice eloquently expresses how she feels about having been infected herself. 'Where's Miss Lily?' she adds accusingly, as if Felix might have stashed her away in a cupboard.

'She's gone to Cambridgeshire on a job,' he says mildly. 'I'm very sorry you are unwell, Mrs Clapper, and I'm sure Miss Lily would not expect you to come to work if you're feeling—'

'*I'm not unwell!*' Mrs Clapper yells in defiance of what she has just said, and the untruth is further demonstrated by a bout of harsh coughing that leaves her pale and breathless. Felix strides forward, takes her by the arm and sits her down on the kitchen's one seat, a rickety and uncomfortable stool, and, ignoring her protests, he puts water on to boil and makes her a cup of tea. Very aware of her narrowed, critical eyes on him as he does so, he judges it is a mark of how ill she really is that she does not try to stop him.

He looks around as he waits for the tea to brew. Mrs Clapper must have been there for quite some time, he thinks, for the kitchen and scullery are restored to perfect cleanliness and order, and he doesn't need to go out to the lavatory to know that the same will apply there.

Mrs Clapper sips her tea. Both of them wait while she assesses its quality.

'Not bad,' she says, looking up at Felix, and for the very first time in their acquaintance, he detects the faint suggestion of a smile.

Capitalizing on this minuscule lowering of her defences, he says, 'You've done a grand job, Mrs Clapper. Now, please, go home and try to rest' – she gives a disbelieving snort at his naivety, as if to say, *What? Me, rest, with Clapper and his bronicles to see to?* but he plunges on regardless – 'and Miss Lily and I will look forward to seeing you back here once you are well.'

'I'm not—' she begins.

'You're not unwell, yes, I know, you said. But, honestly, Mrs C' – she looks at him suspiciously but makes no comment at the new abbreviation – 'Miss Lily is away, as I told you, and so is the Little Ballerina, and—'

'Huh! *Her!*' Mrs Clapper's sparse eyebrows descend in a ferocious scowl of disapproval.

'—and I'll be out and about more than I'm here, so really there's no more for you to do now that you've completed your excellent tidying and cleaning job.' Felix waves his arm to demonstrate the shining kitchen.

'But—' Mrs Clapper's protest begins and peters out, and Felix can hear that her heart isn't really in it.

'Go home,' he says. Gently he takes her empty cup from her hands. The fingers are bent with arthritis, and he feels a sudden surge of compassion. Turning away so that she will not read it in his face – she would *hate* it – he adds brightly, 'The sooner you're on the mend, the sooner we'll have you back!'

She gets off the stool, fetches her hat, coat, muffler and the old string bag she always carries, and he sees her to the door. She heads off down the steps without speaking, but just as he is about to close the door she turns, looks straight at him and says gruffly, 'You're not quite as bad as I thought.'

As she shuffles away, he is smiling broadly. It is a long time since he has received such a valuable compliment.

He sits in the outer office, debating whether it is worth lighting a fire. The small kitchen range is going; Mrs Clapper has managed to find time to do some baking in between bouts of cleaning and coughing, and Felix can smell hot pastry and ginger. He wanders back into the kitchen and pours a cup of tea.

He faces the fact that he doesn't know what to get on with. Has he anything *to* get on with?

He perches on the uncomfortable stool and extracts his notebook from his pocket. He reads swiftly through his notes, coming to the unwelcome conclusion that in every area of investigation he is waiting to hear from somebody else and cannot act in any meaningful way until he does.

'Bugger,' he mutters aloud.

He finishes his tea and washes up the cup and saucer. Mrs Clapper's baking is cooling on wire trays and the heat from the range is lessening. Concluding that no purpose will be served by his remaining in the house, and that it would be a waste of money to squander coal on a fire, he puts on his outdoor clothes and is about to set off back to Kinver Street when the door knocker sounds through the silent house.

He answers the knock and the telegram boy hands him an envelope. Ripping it open, he sees it is from Violetta. He says softly, 'Oh, *good!*' then, looking up at the lad, adds, 'No reply, thanks,' and steps inside, closing the door firmly so the boy realizes there isn't a tip in the offing.

He re-reads the telegram. *Have news re you know who. Will be at the Tom late tonight. Come and join me. V.*

First Marm, now Violetta, thinks Felix.

Wondering how he's going to fill the empty hours that stretch out ahead, he stuffs the telegram in an inside pocket and, checking he has locked the door, sets out along Hob's Court and down on to the Embankment.

He half hopes Marm will return before he leaves for the Peeping Tom, but he is disappointed. Resisting the urge to speculate yet again just what it is that Marm has found out, he sets out for the music hall and queues to buy his ticket as the large open space in front of the stage begins to fill up. He knows which box Violetta habitually uses, and makes his way to it. He pulls a couple of the red-velvet-covered chairs to the front of the box and sits leaning his elbows on the rail, staring out at the mêlée below. He holds out no expectation whatsoever that there is a sophisticated and intellectually challenging evening of entertainment ahead, for he knows from past experience that the Tom has probably set the all-time low level for bawdiness, smuttiness, double entendres and downright filth, but he doesn't mind.

Presently he hears the door open and turns to see Violetta entering the box. She is dressed in a low-cut, tight-fitting gown in royal-blue silk, a corsage of flowers at the bosom, and she is in the process of lowering a heavy fur-lined cloak from her beautiful, smooth white shoulders. She smiles at him, her face lovely in the soft light, and she looks every inch the grand lady. Gracefully seating herself in the chair he pulls back for her, she shatters the illusion by saying, 'Bloody hell, it's cold outside, and my audience were a miserable bunch tonight. Get the bubbly ordered, there's a good lad, and we'll get pissed as farts and let the world go hang.'

As Felix sticks his head round the door to put in the order for the champagne, he reflects that it probably isn't the moment to remind Violetta that she's summoned him here because she has something to tell him. Moreover, that this moment won't arrive until she's sunk at least a glass of champagne and probably more.

At Shardlowes School, Lily embarks on what is to be a disturbing day.

The morning begins in a similar manner to yesterday, with a cup of tea taken to Matron. She is still in bed, seemingly determined to make the very most of her cold and let Lily do the day's work, which suits Lily admirably since it leaves her free to pursue her own path.

Today she selects another of the six dormitories for her early morning visit, and quietly opens the door to Red, the first of Junior School. The eight beds are all occupied and the girls range from a very small child of no more than four to a couple of girls of around eight years. The four-year-old has a wall eye and a very runny nose, and when she speaks it is clear that she has a problem with her adenoids. An older girl stands watching and she introduces herself as Rhoda Albercourt, Louise dormitory. She is a sturdy girl, pasty-faced with the furious red stigmata of acne across her forehead and cheeks. She is courteous and unfazed by Lily's appearance in Red dormitory, and Lily surmises that news of yesterday's appearance in Blue has spread.

Since nobody in Red requires the services of the assistant matron – well, the child with adenoids would benefit greatly from medical attention, but it is beyond the scope of the Shardlowes sick bay – Lily goes on down the corridor to Green dormitory. Here the girls are older, and two – a girl with slanting eyes and gypsy features and another exquisite Indian girl – look as if they are approaching womanhood. Lily spots Marigold Dunbar-Lea, in the act of struggling into the built-up boot. She gives Lily a wide grin, stretching the ugly scar that bisects her upper lip, and Lily smiles back.

'Kathleen Richmond, Helena, monitor of Green dormitory,' smiles the round-faced redhead standing just inside the door. 'Good morning, Nurse Henry. All present and correct.' She waves an arm to indicate the seven beds, six of which are occupied. The seventh is neatly made up and clearly has not been slept in. 'Well, except for poor Cora,' Kathleen Richmond adds in a soft whisper that is just for Lily's ears. 'Nearly two weeks now, and not a word.'

Lily turns to look into the kindly brown eyes and reads genuine distress. 'Cora?' she repeats.

'Oh, of course, I don't suppose you know,' whispers Kathleen. 'Cora Naughton-Smythe went missing after hockey practice the Friday before last.' Her lower lip trembles. 'She's only *eleven*!' So much do the words distress her that they are more mouthed than spoken.

'Yes,' Lily says. 'I did know, in fact, although not the girl's name. And there was another one too, I believe?'

Kathleen nods vigorously. 'Isa Hatcher, yes, back in December, she's a Senior and she's in Alice.' She leans closer, her mouth right by Lily's ear. 'Esme and I didn't think they were—'

Lily becomes aware that the door behind her has just opened quietly. Spinning round, she sees Miss Dickie standing right at her shoulder, considerably too close for comfort. She stares at Lily for a heartbeat, her eyes cold, then the face-crinkling smile appears and she says, 'Sensible of you to familiarize yourself with your charges, Nurse. No cases for you here, however.' She steps back, a clear invitation for Lily to take herself off, and Lily has no option but to do so.

'Good day, Kathleen,' she says cheerfully to the redhead, now blushing with the awkwardness of the moment, 'and thank you for introducing me to Green dormitory.'

Relief at having been given an excuse for being found deep in conversation with the new assistant matron floods Kathleen's face, and she nods vigorously. 'Thank you, Nurse!' she gasps.

And, her outer calm masking a fast-beating heart, Lily walks away.

Esme and I, she thinks as she returns to her room and her breakfast. Esme Sullivan, the runaway. Were Esme and Kathleen in the same dormitory? Lily wonders if there is a way she can find out, and, as she turns into the sick-bay corridor she thinks of one. Before she can ask herself if it is wise she is knocking on Matron's door.

'Sorry to disturb you again, Matron,' she says briskly, 'but I have now visited all three of the Junior dormitories and I would like to have a list of the girls in each, and in the senior dormitories, with their medical history, if such a thing exists?'

'Of course it does!' Matron bridles, not an easy feat when slumped in bed. 'There's a ledger – a big, thick book bound in brown leather – and it records all the girls' names and details of their general health, their problems and complaints. It ought to be on the shelf above the little table in the treatment room, but that fool Evans has probably left it in the last place she was looking at it, which could be anywhere because she's careless and simply will *not* abide by my rules and—'

Lily, recognizing a rant when she hears one starting up, quickly interrupts. 'Thank you, Matron, please don't disturb yourself' – Matron is starting to roll around like a hippopotamus in mud, probably in preparation for getting out of bed – 'I'm sure I shall find it.'

She leaves the fusty room, closing the door firmly behind her. She is aware of the cacophony of feet as the girls hurry down to breakfast in answer to the bell's loud summons, and reckons she has a good half an hour before anyone comes to

interrupt her. She lets herself into the treatment room and begins
her search.

The ledger is not on its accustomed shelf – Lily is quite
sure she would have spotted it by now if it had been – and it
takes her almost a quarter of an hour of rummaging before
it turns up beneath the boards that form the floor of the little
cupboard where the sanitary napkins are kept. Nurse Evans
had perhaps been recording the issue of napkins to a girl, if
such things are recorded, but then why put the ledger *under*
the floor? An aberration, perhaps, while she was distracted by
anxiety over her mother?

But then all thoughts of what Nurse Evans might or might
not have been thinking are driven from Lily's mind, for she
has opened the big ledger and discovered it to be the very item
she would have prayed to have access to, for not only does it
list the present occupants of the six dormitories; it also covers
the last four and a half school years.

And, as Lily begins to turn the ledger's pages, she understands that it must have been hidden in the bottom of the
cupboard – by someone in a hurry, perhaps – precisely so that
the temporary assistant matron will not get a sight of it. Not
by Matron, since it is she who has just innocently made Lily
aware of it. Then by whom? Who dashed into the treatment
room between Nurse Evans's departure and Lily's arrival and
found that hiding place?

Lily turns to the first page of the ledger. It lists each dormitory's occupants at the start of the September term in 1876.
She starts to read.

The first discovery is that the ledger records the details and the
health of Shardlowes staff as well as that of the girls. Not Miss
Carmichael or Miss Dickie, but everyone else from teachers to
maids and kitchen staff. Lily comes across Georgiana Long,
forcing herself to skim over the details of the English mistress's
minor complaints, although she can't help noticing that Miss
Long's limp is, as she had suspected, because of a club foot.
(She also notes that Miss Long only joined the school a little
over a year ago, replacing an earlier English teacher called
Genevieve Swanson.) She finds the record for Mademoiselle

Clemence Launidel: she has already noticed the French teacher, who is young, pretty other than the absence of chin, fussy about her appearance and snooty, and who suffers from periodic headaches so severe as to necessitate bed rest in a darkened room with cold flannels for her forehead and generous doses of laudanum. There are only three other members of the teaching staff, other than Miss Carmichael and Miss Dickie: Miss Mallard must be the white-haired, elderly and prickly history teacher who, judging by the ledger, has not had a day's illness in four and a half years, and Miss Smithson, then, is the plump middle-aged woman with the shawls, the veils, the flyaway hair escaping from the grey bun and the perpetual air of being flustered and a little late, who teaches art and music. The last teacher is Geraldine Blytheway, known to her colleagues and her pupils alike as Miss Gerry, who is responsible for all physical activities from hockey to country dancing as well as an activity referred to as comportment. She is a strapping young woman with an Eton crop and a manly stride who dresses in a severe flannel skirt and a white shirt with a collar and tie. Other than frequent embrocation rubs administered by the assistant matron, Miss Gerry appears to enjoy excellent health.

Lily turns to the lists of pupils.

Immediately she appreciates why a relatively small community like Shardlowes School requires both a matron and an assistant matron, for this section of the ledger is crammed with words in small handwriting neatly entered beside many of the names. Lily recalls Miss Long's remarks about the halt and the lame, and understands.

Beside some names she notices small symbols; some sort of discreet code, perhaps, to indicate when a girl is in a delicate state of health? Lily has come across such overly sensitive measures throughout her nursing career, and while she understands the reason for them – menstruation is simply not a matter for discussion, even among girls and women – nevertheless she is frustrated by this attitude.

She reads on.

Presently she notices other symbols, some repeated quite regularly, others more haphazard in their distribution. She tries and fails to spot a pattern.

She recognizes the repetition of names allocated year by year to different dormitories as girls progress up through the school. Louise dormitory is clearly for the oldest girls, and the last place where their names appear; Red is for the youngest. Sometimes names disappear at the end of a school year rather than appearing in the next dormitory up.

Lily stares at one particular symbol that appears perhaps four or five times in total. She thinks she has seen it before. She wonders what it means.

She flips on through the ledger to the pages recording the current population of Shardlowes School. She reads the seven names in Green. One of them is Marigold Dunbar-Lea; another is Cora Naughton-Smythe. Nobody has erased or even put a pencil line through Cora's name; do they believe she will come back?

How can they all be so calm? Lily, looking up from the ledger, is suddenly filled with a powerful emotion that at first seems like anger: amazed, flabbergasted anger. Here she sits in this elegant establishment with its well-behaved pupils, its cool and restrained headmistress, its decorum, its polite good manners, yet beneath the smooth surface a horror has happened, for one girl has run away and two more are missing.

One of them is only eleven years old.

Lily trembles as anger gives way to something else and from out of nowhere she experiences a sweeping dread that sends a cold blade up her back and forces her to stifle a gasp of dismay.

And she cries silently, *Why don't they DO something? Why don't they try to find them, uncover what's happened to them?*

It is as if something within her answers her own question, for a quiet voice seems to say, *That is why you are here.*

She sits perfectly still, letting the powerful sensations run their course. Anger probably will not help, and paralysing dread most certainly won't.

She begins to feel calmer.

She goes back to the ledger, turning to the seniors. Six girls aged between thirteen and fourteen in Alice dormitory, although one of them, thirteen-year-old Isa Hatcher, is no longer there. Lily feels the power of her anger resurge, but she controls it.

As with Cora, there is no indication beside Isa's name that she has gone. Lily notes in passing that she is one of the three girls in Alice not to have commenced menstruation, for the little *Ma* symbol that Lily understands to mean *menarche* is not there. She counts five girls aged fifteen to sixteen in Helena, including the two monitors Sudie Brown-Caldicot and Kathleen Richmond. One name has a pencilled line through it: that of Esme Sullivan. So she and Kathleen were indeed in the same dormitory . . .

There are six girls of seventeen or eighteen in Louise, including the hockey player Eunice Carter and the monitor Rhoda Albercourt. Among the names are several denoting foreign nationality, and Lily recalls what Georgiana Long said about girls from abroad.

The big ledger provides a conscientious account of every illness, injury, physical malfunction and disability, and Lily is impressed with the diligence of whoever is responsible; at least two women, judging by the different handwriting styles. Lily thinks of Georgiana Long saying, *Many girls are sent to Shardlowes School because their families and society at large have little or no use for them.* Some of the reasons she gave for these girls' presence at Shardlowes do not show up in a medical record; Lily thinks of what the little teacher said about those who were too clever or not clever enough; those who constituted one or two daughters too many for a struggling father to manage a dowry. Other conditions, however, are revealed: a girl of nine who is deaf; an eleven-year-old who has fits and is thought to be mentally subnormal; Marigold Dunbar-Lea with her cleft palate and her malformed leg; a girl of seventeen who has calipers; Lily studies the record of sores and abrasions.

Lily sits perfectly still, totally focused.

When it dawns on her that there are quiet footsteps approaching along the passage, it is almost too late to put the ledger back in its hiding place, rearrange the pile of napkins and rags, softly close the cupboard door and return to her seat. Trying to control her breathing, she reaches for the big box of assorted bandages set aside for tidying – she cannot be caught doing nothing – and, with an expression of polite enquiry, looks up as the door opens and her visitor comes in.

Miss Dickie's hard little eyes stare down at her.

'May I help you, Miss Dickie?' Lily says calmly.

Miss Dickie says nothing for a moment. Then, the transparent smile appearing for a moment, she says, 'It is not an urgent matter, Nurse Henry, but Miss Gerry wonders whether Eunice Carter's ankle will be recovered in time for hockey practice on Friday.'

Lily forces a smile. 'I treated Eunice yesterday, Miss Dickie, and ordered no games at least until next week. If her attendance at hockey practice is really important enough for you to come to enquire about it' – she hopes her scepticism is not detectable in her voice – 'then please tell Miss Gerry that I will examine the ankle again on Friday morning and let her know.'

Miss Dickie bows her head in a curt little nod, turns smartly and takes her leave.

And Lily thinks, Eunice Carter's ankle indeed! That old woman was snooping, and very nearly discovered me studying the one thing she undoubtedly hopes will remain hidden from me.

The shiver of unease comes again, this time with sufficient power to make Lily feel slightly sick.

The morning passes quickly, for Lily is kept busy. When she takes yet another cup of tea in to Matron, Matron asks – quite politely – if she'll catch up with the mending if she has nothing better to do, and Lily readily agrees. She sits quietly sewing ragged sheet hems and torn pillowcases, and on her own initiative does a sides-to-middle on a sheet whose central section is almost worn through.

In the latter part of the morning a ten-year-old called Jessie Killick is brought to the sick bay from a singing class by a highly flustered Miss Smithson. The blood from the child's copious nosebleed has stained both her own white pinafore and not a few of Miss Smithson's many garments.

'We were in the middle of "Abide with Me"!' Miss Smithson exclaims, and the indignant expression she shoots at Jessie Killick suggests it is an extra abomination for the bleeding to have begun during a sacred song.

Jessie, it becomes apparent, is not a child to be cowed,

especially by a near-hysterical spinster clad in far too may flyaway layers of fine wool and chiffon. 'I *loathe* "Abide with Me"!' she hisses from behind the large blood-soaked handkerchief. 'It's stupid and it makes the soppy girls cry, but it doesn't make *me* cry!' The look she shoots at Lily out of furious brown eyes sees to say, *It takes much more than a song do that*, and Lily can't help but think she's probably right.

Seeing that Miss Smithson is gathering herself to issue some emotion-laden reprimand in response to Jessie's sacrilege, Lily steps in. Taking Jessie by the shoulder, she walks her over to the little stool beside the work bench and sits her down, saying over her shoulder in a tone of clear dismissal, 'Thank you, Miss Smithson, that will be all. I will care for Jessie now.'

Miss Smithson's ineffectual little mouth gapes open. Suddenly looking down at herself, she gives a little gasp of horror. 'Oh, my goodness gracious, *look* at me!' she exclaims. 'I'm *drowned* in the wretched child's blood!'

Jessie looks at Lily over the bloody handkerchief and Lily can tell from her eyes that she's grinning maliciously.

'It really isn't all that much,' Lily says firmly to Miss Smithson. 'I suggest you remove the few affected garments and drop them in at the laundry on your way back to your class.' She places a clear emphasis on the last seven words, wanting to remind Miss Smithson of her responsibilities and, in addition, get rid of her.

Miss Smithson is fussing about with her shawl and a couple of scarves, but, perhaps recognizing a stronger will – a surely not uncommon occurrence – obediently she turns for the door. 'I shall have to find another shawl – my violet crocheted one, I believe, will match my ensemble . . .' Her voice trails away as she wanders off down the passage.

Simultaneously Jessie and Lily begin to laugh.

'Enough,' Lily says after a moment. 'Now, young lady, let me see what you have done to yourself.'

For the next few minutes she is busy with cold water, pads of lint and a compress, which she instructs Jessie to hold firmly over the bridge of her nose. Presently it is clear that the bleeding has stopped, and Jessie jumps down from her stool with a cheerful, 'Thank you, Nurse!'

'Just wait a minute before you dash off, Jessie, because—'

'Oh, I have no intention of dashing off,' Jessie replies disarmingly. 'It's ages before the bell – we'd only just begin the lesson when my nosebleed started – and if I return to class Miss Smithson will make *such* a fuss.'

Lily studies her silently. Jessie stares innocently back. 'The best thing for sudden blood loss is a cup of hot, sweet tea,' Lily says.

'And a biscuit or two is efficacious, or so I have heard,' Jessie says hopefully.

Lily grins. 'Hop back up on your stool, Jessie, and I shall see what I can do.'

'You're much nicer than Nurse Evans,' Jessie declares as they each begin on a second biscuit (Lily makes a mental note to replenish the supply somehow; what with the present incursion and the depredations due to keeping Matron sweet and safely tucked up in bed, the biscuit barrel is half empty). 'But then,' Jessie adds thoughtfully, 'Nurse Evans doesn't like it here.'

'Does she not?' Lily enquires, affecting only mild interest.

Jessie shakes her head until a warning hand on her arm from Lily ('Nosebleed!' Lily mutters) stops her. 'No. Me, Harriet and Charlotte – they're my special friends – and the rest in the dorm think she's *scared*.' Her brown eyes widen as she says the word.

'Nurses don't get scared, or if they do they are trained not to show it,' Lily says firmly.

'Well, I can see *you* don't get scared,' Jessie amends, 'but she's not like you. She's frightened of Miss Dickie and as for Miss Carmichael, goodness, we've seen Nurse Evans cower behind a door so she didn't even have to say good *morning* to Miss Carmichael!'

'I dare say she had her reasons,' Lily remarks, trying to look as if she is discouraging gossip while in fact doing the precise opposite.

'She did! She *did*!' Jessie's voice is squeaky with excitement. 'It was at the end of last term, just after the huge upset over the storytelling, and—'

'Storytelling?'

'Oh, of course, you weren't here.' Jessie leans close to whisper. 'The girls in Alice were all very worried about Isa Hatcher going missing – especially since it wasn't very long since Esme Sullivan in Helena went, though she was quite a lot older – and they kept asking what was being done to find her and the staff and the bigger girls just said everything was all right, she was undoubtedly safe and well, but *nobody* believed them and the Alice girls started making up ghost stories and horror stories about the Black Dog of the Fens and how he'd been heard howling and then a stooping figure in a dark cloak came in the night and in the morning Isa wasn't there, and—' She stops abruptly, the flow of words cut off by a sound that might have been a gulp or a suppressed sob.

Lily takes her hand. 'And somebody overheard and reported the girls, and they got into trouble?'

Jessie nods. 'Dorcas Williamson and Zubaida Maloof mainly got punished because they were the chief storytellers. Zubaida's from Cairo – that's in Egypt,' she adds helpfully, 'and she put in all sorts of bits about dead mummies rising from their tombs and walking abroad, not that it seemed very likely in the middle of the Fens, but it made a good tale. Anyway, the two of them had detentions and no puddings for a week and I think they both got their hands caned although nobody actually *said*, and the rest of Alice dorm just got lines and extra prep.'

'So how did Nurse Evans come into it?' Lily asks.

Jessie leans close again. 'We think she must have gone to Miss Dickie and said she thought the girls in Alice weren't making it up, well not all of it, but obviously the bit about the mummy they were, because she'd seen or heard things too. Then Miss Dickie must have told Miss Carmichael, and Myfanwy – Myfanwy Price, she's in my dormy – just happened to be in the corridor outside Miss Carmichael's room and she heard Miss Carmichael yelling, and honestly she *never* yells, she never even raises her *voice* – and then Nurse Evans came out and she was weeping and her nose was running and her eyes were all red, and after that she just hid away up here and hardly anybody saw her unless they came to the San specially to look for her.'

Lily is thinking so intently that at first she doesn't realize

Jessie has stopped talking. When she does, she looks up to see the child's anxious eyes on her.

'And now Cora Naughton-Smythe has gone missing and the storytelling has started again?' she suggests gently.

'It never really stopped,' Jessie whispers. 'We've all just got better at not being caught.'

Lily studies her, observing the courage in the child that is making her fight to overcome her fear.

'It is distressing to have seen your school-fellows go missing,' she says after a moment. 'Perhaps it is even more upsetting when the adults tell you everything is all right when you sense that it is not.'

Jessie mutters something that sounds horribly like, *We all know something's going on.*

Lily puts her arm round the girl's shoulders and gives her a brief, bracing hug. 'Go back to your lesson now,' she says. 'It must be almost time for the bell.'

Jessie jumps down. As she opens the door to leave she turns back to look at Lily. 'You're going to help, aren't you?' she says very softly.

And equally softly, putting her finger to her lips in the age-old gesture that says *don't tell*, Lily replies, 'Yes.'

EIGHT

'Oh, I never seem to tire of Mister Magically Magical and his tricks!' Violetta gasps, wiping tears of laughter from her eyes. 'The things he gets away with! I thought I'd die laughing when he extracted the egg from that woman's backside!'

At the Peeping Tom it is the interval, Felix and Violetta are two glasses apiece into the champagne and Violetta is mellow; so mellow, in fact, that she is sitting sideways in her chair and leaning comfortably against Felix as if they have been familiar with each other's bodies for years. Not that he minds – far from it, for he feels just the same and there is something about Violetta that reminds him fondly of Solange – but he hopes the alcohol and the merriment haven't yet obliterated whatever it was she planned to tell him tonight.

He is just wondering how to phrase a gentle reminder when, as if she reads his mind, she sits up a little straighter and, lowering her voice, says, 'Now, much as I'm enjoying your vulgar laughter and your delightfully muscular body, young Felix, these delights are *not* what we're here for!' She smacks him lightly, right at the top of his leg, and he feels a definite twinge of arousal. Another twinge of arousal, in fact, for she has been having quite a powerful effect on him all evening.

'If that's for my benefit,' he murmurs, right in her ear, 'then a little higher, please.'

She emits a smutty guffaw. 'Now, now!' she says reprovingly. 'You were asking about the MacKilliver twins' – all at once she is businesslike – 'and I said I'd see what I could find out.'

'Yes,' he agrees.

'Well, I had a word with my old friend Freddie Fanshawe-Turnbull – you know, Old Turnip-Head, who we were talking about last time?'

'Yes,' he repeats, trying not to add, *of course I do!*

'It was after my evening's performance and we were all in

the Café Royal, and he was even more deeply in his cups than usual, so I took my chance and made sure I sat next to him, flattered him a little and stroked his whiskers – like I told you, I'm far too old for his tastes but he was on his own and any port in a storm – and I said very casually that I hadn't seen much of the twins of late and how were they? He's always been easily led, has Freddie – that's half his trouble, really – and it didn't take much to have him reminiscing and repeating tasty bits of gossip, and I prompted him here and there, and before long we were almost back as far as the nursery and how poor old Cameron's obsession with cosseting, cuddling and comforting his dollies made his father apoplectic and was the reason for far too many beatings with the hairbrush bare-bummed over Nanny's knee, which no doubt added spice to the whole thing and sent him rushing straight back to his dolls to earn himself some more.'

'Good grief,' Felix mutters. When he has managed to get the image out of his head, he says, 'Was it just the two of them, Cameron and Mortimer, or were there other siblings?'

'I asked Freddie that, and he said there were at least two and probably three more children born subsequently, but Mama MacKilliver was rather delicate after giving birth to the twins and none of the infants survived, although one, a little girl, lived for a few months.' Perhaps sensing Felix's reaction, she adds, 'It happens, Felix. Procreation is a perilous business, fraught with drama, pain and danger.'

'I know,' he replies. He wonders if the boy Cameron's fascination with caring so tenderly for his dolls was because he had been an unwilling witness to his mother's travails in the marital bedroom as she struggled fruitlessly to provide further children. To her grief, perhaps, when her babies died. *But what do I know?* he asks himself.

'Anyway,' Violetta resumes after a few moments, 'it appears Cameron's been absent from London for quite some time now.'

'Up in Scotland, presumably, hidden away at the ancient pile on the Moray Firth,' Felix comments.

'Findhorn Hall, yes,' Violetta agrees. 'Only – listen, this is interesting – Freddie says he and Mortimer went up for a spot of fishing back in the autumn, and Mortimer was fully expecting to find Cameron pottering about in his velvet slippers and his Turkish cap like he usually does, but he wasn't there.'

Felix is struggling to see why this is interesting. 'He's an adult, wealthy, independent,' he says shortly.

Violetta shoots him a look. 'So you'd think,' she agrees enigmatically.

'But?' he prompts.

'Well, you see, the thing about poor old Cameron is that he needs a bit of watching,' she says. 'He's usually at Findhorn Hall with the resident staff, or down in London with Mortimer keeping an eye, or having one of his periodic spells being treated by doctors who understand men like him, or he's off staying with some old childhood friend he's still close to. That's what Freddie says, anyway, and I reckon he ought to know.' She falls silent, absently gulping another half-glass of champagne.

Felix is still at a loss to understand why she's telling him this; why she deemed it sufficiently important to have suggested this meeting at the Tom, why even now she is leaning into him again and automatically he has put his arm round her, drawing her closer, feeling her welcoming warm flesh and smelling her delicious gardenia perfume . . .

And as they turn their faces towards each other and begin, inevitably, to kiss, he thinks he probably has his answer.

He wakes on Thursday morning with a thick head and a smile of happy reminiscence on his face. Violetta's ever-obliging coachman had been waiting for them outside the Peeping Tom when they staggered out, entwined in each other, and he took them on a meandering drive while they fell upon each other in the cosy darkness within, removed just enough garments to get at each other and consummated their fierce mutual attraction in approximately five very satisfactory minutes. ('Gorgeous, my poppet,' Violetta had panted as they fell apart, 'only next time, let's make it last a little longer, eh?')

Now, turning on to his back and wincing slightly as a pain stabs through his temples, Felix reflects with deep contentment on the promise of next time. Violetta, he is well aware, has a man in her life – the steadfast, powerful and hopefully tolerant Billy – and his own relationship with her is unlikely to amount to more than a repeat or two (or maybe more) of what happened last night, and that is absolutely fine by him.

He has closed his eyes and is reliving the moment when one of Violeta's gorgeous breasts spilled out of her corset and into his waiting hand when his door is opened, Marm's face appears and he says softly, 'I come bearing a cup of tea, which I trust will ease your alcohol-induced headache. May I enter?'

Hastily bunching up the bedclothes over his groin, Felix replies, 'Yes, please do.'

Marm perches on the end of the bed, hands Felix a cup and saucer and, after an arched glance towards the middle of the bed, takes a sip of his own tea. 'Did you find my note?' he asks.

'Your note . . . Yes!' Memory floods back, pushing eroticism aside. 'You said you might have something interesting for me.'

'Indeed,' Marm agrees, 'and now, with the passage of a further twenty-four hours – in which my endeavours on your behalf have not been my sole preoccupation, you understand – *might have* has become something a little more definite.' He looks at Felix, his clever blue eyes bright in his dissipated face. He wears an odd expression; he looks . . . reluctant, is the best Felix can come up with. 'Want to hear it?' Marm asks quietly.

Felix nods.

'Esme Sullivan, runaway schoolgirl, turned up in Brighton,' Marm begins, taking a notebook out of his pocket and thumbing through to the right page. 'You were off on her trail, and—'

'I found it, or at least I discovered where it led,' Felix interrupts. 'She managed to extract her fare back to Shardlowes from the landlady of the Brighton boarding house, but she didn't return to the school.'

Now Marm is looking very grave. 'Where did she go?'

'Portsmouth.'

Marm mutters something that sounds like, *Oh, no.* 'You're quite sure?' he says aloud. All the usual levity has gone from his voice.

'Yes, reasonably sure. Why?'

'It's probably not the girl – after all there's no name, no identity . . .' Marm mutters. Then he says, the words coming out like bullets, 'What did Esme look like?'

Felix brings to mind Kitty Kingston's description. 'Sixteen, seventeen years old, very pretty, fine figure with a good bosom and a small waist, wavy fair hair, deep blue eyes.'

There is silence in the room. Felix has an idea that he knows what it forebodes. 'Tell me?' he asks quietly.

'Sorry, sorry.' Marm shakes his head. 'Not fair to keep you in suspense.' He takes a deep breath, then reaches in his pocket again and takes out a newspaper cutting. 'I made contact with a chap I know in Chichester, and I have nobody in the area who is anywhere near as good as Douglas Blackmore. He checked the local newspapers to see if your missing girl had come to the attention of any of his fellow journalists. He sent me this.' He hands over the cutting. 'It's probably not her!' he adds, repeating himself, his voice distressed.

Felix unfolds the piece of paper and begins to read.

WHO IS THE GIRL IN THE WATER? yells the headline, and underneath the sub-heading continues: *Body of the Solent Siren still unidentified after more than two weeks and police baffled.*

The by-line informs him that the piece was written by someone called Michael Nicholls, reporter on a Portsmouth newspaper, and it was filed in the middle of December.

He reads on.

> She was washed up on Southsea beach, coming to rest beneath the new pier. She was young, she was surely beautiful once, her long fair hair glossy, her unsullied flesh white and smooth and her eyes brilliant before the sea altered her. Somebody must be missing her, but with no clue on her naked, splayed, sea-battered body to indicate who she was or where she came from, this poor grieving soul must wonder in vain what has become of her, aware that the worst may have happened but hoping and praying that their beloved daughter, sister or wife has merely run away and will return in her own good time. But she will not, our mystery Solent mermaid, for the sea has taken her and the sea does not give back.

'Oh, God,' Felix murmurs.

Silence falls once more.

'There's no certainty that this poor girl is your missing Esme,' Marm says presently. 'Michael Nicholls's emotive prose contains not a few inaccuracies – the mermaids of legend can swim and breathe under water, so to call a victim of drowning a mermaid is absurd. And the sea *did* give back in her case; she was washed up under Southsea Pier in Portsmouth.'

Felix isn't really listening. He is wondering how he can verify the dead girl's identity; whether the police are still working on the case.

Marm – a man of rare sensitivity, Felix reflects – must have been aware of the direction his friend's thoughts would take. 'We cannot know just how hard the police tried before they decided they were baffled and gave up,' he says gently. 'There are probably corpses washing up on the Solent all the time, and I'm sure the police in a bustling place like Portsmouth, with more than its share of randy sailors, unscrupulous merchants and all manner of other troublemakers, have better things to do with their time.'

'Do you think it's worth a visit?' Felix asks.

For the first time Marm smiles. It is only a faint smile. 'What I think doesn't matter,' he replies, 'since I'm quite sure you'll go anyway.'

By mid-morning Felix is on a train from Waterloo to Portsmouth.

Before he left Kinver Street he wrote a swift letter to Lily, which he posted on the way to the station. Writing in what he hoped looked like a feminine hand to Nurse L. Henry, Shardlowes School, he tried to couch what he had to tell Lily in terms that would be informative yet not arouse suspicion if the letter were to fall into the hands of the curious. He pondered over a readily comprehensible substitute for Marm and came up with Mariella.

> My dearest Leonora,
>   I trust the air of the Fens is not proving a trial, and that your new post is suiting you. I write in haste, dear sister-in-law, to let you know that I shall be away from home for a few days although dear Mariella has

undertaken to forward my mail as soon as I provide an address. I am in need of some sea air, my dear, and therefore to the coast I am bound, with a brand-new mystery novel in my luggage, the enclosed puzzle within which I plan to solve before my return. I have read as far as the heroine's flight to Portsmouth, and thence I shall follow her, there being nothing, in my experience, quite like being in the very place where a story is set for enhancing one's enjoyment!

With fondest regards from your loving sister-in-law Felicia

Now, sitting in the half-empty compartment, he wonders how soon the letter will land in Lily's hands. There is a great deal more he would say to her were she present beside him, although since so much is speculation, perhaps it is just as well he has been confined to that brief, stilted message.

With an effort, he turns his thoughts away from Lily and, taking his notebook from his pocket, goes through his pages of notes on Esme Sullivan. He finds himself silently praying, *Please don't let the corpse be hers*, recognizing even as he does so that if it's not hers it will be that of some other unfortunate young woman.

It is, he reflects as he has done so many times before, a cruel world.

Marm has provided the address of the newspaper for which Michael Nicholls writes. The office is in Southsea, and as Felix walks he finds his pace increasing, both because Portsmouth is even colder than London and also because he is distressed at what he may be about to find out.

He is also angry. With whoever put a girl's body in the water, with the wickedness of people, with Michael Nicholls for that lurid piece of writing. And when he bursts into the newspaper's office and is pointed in the direction of the journalist in question, it is the young man's misfortune to be the only object of Felix's fury who happens to be standing right in front of him.

Felix has Marm's cutting ready in his hand. 'I want to talk

to you about *this*,' he says loudly, brandishing it in Michael Nicholls's face. He is a pallid, pasty young man with receding hair and round shoulders, several inches shorter than the tall Felix and not a few pounds lighter.

'Er . . .' he hedges, fumbling for his glasses and putting them on before peering at the cutting – damn, thinks Felix, I can't hit him if he's wearing glasses – then as the small print leaps into focus, says with a grin, 'Ah, yes, the Solent Siren! Good one, eh? Came up with it myself.'

Felix doesn't answer straight away, instead nudging Michael Nicholls back into his little box of an office, closing the door and leaning against it.

'You also called her a mermaid, which is inaccurate for a victim of drowning.'

'Who says she drowned?' Nicholls says with a touch of belligerence. 'I do not believe *I* did,' he adds pedantically.

'How did she die, then?' Felix flashes back, and he makes an involuntary move in Nicholls's direction.

He flinches and mutters anxiously, 'Steady on! You a relative, then?'

'Since the young woman's body has not been identified, or hadn't when you wrote your . . . *piece*' – he spits out the innocuous word, investing it with heavy scorn – 'how can I possibly say?'

Nicholls studies him, eyes narrowed behind the thick lenses of his spectacles. 'But you've got someone gone missing. Stands to reason,' he adds, 'else why are you here?'

Felix breathes in and out once or twice, still struggling with the urge to do violence. Then he says, and to his satisfaction he sounds quite calm, 'I *am* looking for a missing young woman, yes.' Deliberately he stops, waiting for Nicholls to fill the silence.

'Sister? Wife?' he says, and he can't quite disguise his eagerness.

You'd like that, wouldn't you? Felix thinks. You'd like to write your *piece* for tomorrow's paper, that the grieving relative sought you out because of your article; that, purely thanks to you, he found out at last what happened to his lost loved one.

'Has anything been discovered concerning the victim?' he says instead of answering the question. 'How she died, for example, since you seem to be implying she didn't drown? Or some clue to her identity, perhaps through a personal object found close by?'

Nicholls looks as if he'd love to answer in the affirmative but after a moment he shakes his head. 'Not that I've heard. Mind,' he adds ruefully, scratching his thinning hair, 'the police wouldn't tell me even if they did find out something.'

'Still furious with you over *police baffled*?' Felix suggests.

The grin widens. 'Something like that.' He meets Felix's eyes. 'Look, I'm sorry if that poor girl meant something to you.' He is still fishing, Felix thinks, and he doesn't respond. 'Believe it or not, I did feel sorry for her, she was that pretty,' Nicholls says with a sigh.

'You felt sorry for her,' Felix replies softly. 'Because she was pretty? God knows what you'd have come up with if she'd been old and ugly, eh?'

'Now look here,' Nicholls begins, 'I have my job to do and that job is providing the public with information, and I do it conscientiously and to the best of my ability and I—'

Felix has heard enough. He leans in close – Nicholls flinches again – and murmurs, 'Fuck you.'

Then he strides out through the door and shuts it gently behind him.

His anger has cooled by the time he reaches the sea front and he is already regretting having been so aggressive. He clambers down on to the beach. The new pier juts proudly out into the sea like a pointing finger, and Felix stares morosely up at it and wishes it was a warm summer's day and he had time and inclination for frivolity.

He picks up a handful of pebbles and starts trying to spin them, but the sea is rough and the best he can manage is three bounces. Presently he becomes aware that someone has come up to stand beside him.

'Sea's too restless,' says a cracked old voice.

Turning, Felix sees an old man in a heavy coat, a sou'wester pulled down low over his eyes, a beard covering the remainder of the flesh on his face. 'Yes,' he agrees.

He turns back, sensing the old man's narrowed blue eyes on him.

'Visitor?' the man says presently.

'Yes,' Felix says again.

Another pause. Then: 'It was over there they found her.'

Now Felix turns to face the old man so quickly that he feels his neck crack. 'What? How did you know that's why I'm—' He stops himself before the admission is out.

The old face is smiling sadly. 'For one, not many folks venture on to the beach when it's as cold as today. For another, you look pensive. For a third, you're the latest in a very long line, son, although there haven't been so many recently. Interest wanes, and there's always another sensation to feed the prurient appetites of the masses.'

Felix, feeling vaguely that he might just have been insulted, reaches into an inner pocket for a World's End Bureau card. 'I'm investigating a missing girl,' he says. 'I heard about the body that was found here and I wondered if it could be her.'

The old man studies the card for some time. 'You this Raynor fellow?'

'This Raynor fellow is in fact a woman. I'm Felix Wilbraham.' He removes his right glove and holds out his hand.

The old man takes it in a hard grip. 'Walter Nelson,' he responds.

'Good name for a sailor,' Felix remarks. He has spotted the base of an anchor tattooed on the man's forearm.

'Now nobody's ever pointed that out before,' Walter Nelson says with a poker face.

'Sorry.'

There is a brief pause. Then Walter Nelson says, 'There's a place up there where they do a decent pot of tea and a tasty toast and dripping slice. If you'd like to treat me, I'll tell you what I know.' He leans closer and Felix catches a strong smell of alcohol. 'A darn sight more than I told either the police or that blasted reporter, but then I didn't take to them.'

Does that mean he's taken to me? Felix wonders silently as he follows the old man up the beach and across the road to the tea room. If so, it is surely something of a mixed blessing . . .

* * *

'Beginning of November, it was,' Walter Nelson says, having satisfied the worst of his hunger and thirst with a mug and a half of very dark brown tea and a thick slice of toast and dripping, liberally salted. 'We'd had a spell of sunny weather back end of October, then November came in with a shout and there was a series of bad storms driven in on the south-westerlies, and the eastward-bound Channel flood down round the bottom of that out there' – he waves the hand holding the last corner of his toast in the direction of the Isle of Wight – 'was piling water up the East Solent, so the tides here along the shoreline had to be seen to be believed, specially when the moon was around the full.' He shakes his head, pale blue eyes wide with wonder at nature in the raw.

'Some wild nights, then,' Felix observes.

The wrinkled face cracks into a hundred wrinkles as the old man grins. 'Aye, I've had my share of them,' he says with a chuckle.

'A girl in every port?'

'Aye. You'll know the toast: "To wives and sweethearts, and may they never meet".'

They share a moment's reflection. Walter Nelson, Felix guesses, is thinking back to the days of his prime; Felix is wondering how soon he can introduce the subject he's here to find out about.

Walter, however, pre-empts him. 'It was very early one morning,' he says presently in an altogether different tone. 'I don't sleep so much nowadays, specially when I've put back a few, and this particular day I was up around dawn, walking along above the high water watching the sun come up. Clouds had cleared, see, and although the wind was still strong at my back, I knew it'd be a fine day.' He stops, looking down at his dirty hands folded on the table top. 'She was in the water from her knees down, up under the pier like I showed you. She'd have been deposited there at high water, and the tide was falling by then.' He pauses, takes a wobbly breath and then continues. 'Now I've seen sights I'd far rather wipe from my memory, only I've not yet found a way, but that girl, that poor little girl . . .' He shakes his head.

'Little girl?' Felix asks softly.

'Well, she was – er, she was maybe sixteen, seventeen and a woman in body.' For all his sailor's talk of wild nights, to Felix's surprise Walter Nelson blushes slightly. 'I couldn't help but look, see, because I needed to check if there was any life left in her. I knew there wasn't any hope, really, soon as I set eyes on her, but I had to make sure.'

He is staring hard at Felix now, as if desperate for his understanding.

'Of course,' Felix says.

'Well, she was dead as dead,' Walter says matter-of-factly. 'She'd taken a battering in the water, and some sea creature had taken one of her eyes' – he gulps and wipes a hand across his mouth – 'but the other one was open, and looking up at me, and blue like the eyes of my little sister's china-faced doll.'

'Do you think she drowned?' Felix asks.

Walter gives him an assessing look. 'I can't answer that,' he says. 'Like I say, there were marks of violence on her, but she'd been in the sea with a storm raging, and there's no violence on God's earth like the power of the sea.' He goes on staring at Felix, who senses there is something more.

'Go on,' he says neutrally.

Walter leans forward, his voice dropping to a mutter. 'Now I've told nobody else this, mark you, because, like I said earlier, I didn't take to the police and saw no reason I should do their work for them.' Felix suspects Walter has had his share of rough encounters with the forces of law and order over the years. 'And as for that rat-faced reporter . . . Did you *see* what he wrote about that poor girl's flesh and her naked body?'

'I did.'

'Dirty sod ought to be flogged,' mutters Walter. 'I knew it, soon as he came sniffing round asking me for my story. I recognize the type. *I* didn't tell him she was naked, and I didn't utter a word about pretty blue eyes and splayed limbs. It must have been one of the mutton-shunters.'

'One of the police?'

'That's what I said.'

'So what was it you didn't tell them?'

There is a very long pause. Walter stares down at his empty plate, pushing toast crumbs into a neat little mountain. Then he says, and Felix can detect the reluctance, 'She had a long strand of that lovely fair hair wrapped around her neck, and I couldn't bear it, I felt it was hurting her still, choking her, for all I knew full well she was dead. So I knelt down beside her and said a prayer, like the padre used to do when we lost a shipmate at sea, and while I did that I looked down into her pretty face, and that wide eye was criss-crossed with red lines and little red spots, and I know, because I once had to give evidence about the death of a whore in Port Said, that this means someone's been burked.'

'Burked?' Felix isn't familiar with the word.

'Asphyxiated. Face covered with a blanket. Like Burke and Hare did,' Walter says succinctly.

'Ah. But the police must have seen this too,' Felix says. Didn't police surgeons look at dead bodies?

Walter shrugs. 'Maybe. Probably. If they bothered to look, that is,' he adds in a low, disapproving mumble.

'Could those red marks not result from drowning?' Felix persists. 'You die from lack of air when you drown, surely, so in a way it's like being suffocated?'

Walter shrugs again. 'Dunno,' he mutters. He shoots Felix a quick glance. 'I'm only telling you what I saw.'

'And I'm very grateful,' Felix says. He hesitates, not wanting to cause offence, then thinks, offence be buggered, and reaches inside his pocket. Extracting a couple of coins, he slides them across and places them under the rim of Walter's empty plate. 'Raise a glass to that poor young woman,' he murmurs, and, quick as a flash, a dirty hand shoots out and the coins vanish.

'So perhaps,' Felix speculates aloud, 'she was dead when she was put in the water. Somewhere along Portsmouth's long shoreline and not necessarily here at Southsea, if like you say there was a storm?' He looks up at Walter.

Walter smiles grimly. 'Not necessarily anywhere in Portsmouth either,' he says. 'Even when there isn't a storm, and no more than a strong sea running, there's funny old currents out there, what with the Solent and the way the Island sits like a rock in a stream.'

'So – so you're saying she could have been swept along from anywhere? From Brighton, say?' But no, he thinks instantly,

Esme Sullivan – if this girl was she – had left Brighton and come to Portsmouth.

Walter Nelson is shaking his head. 'Not Brighton, no, nor anywhere east of here. Use your wits, lad! I told you there was a south-westerly blowing, and objects don't get borne along against the run of wind and sea!'

'But anywhere west of here?'

Walter just stares at him.

When finally he speaks, it isn't to answer Felix's question. Instead he says, very quietly, 'One last thing.'

'Yes?' Felix says.

'I covered her with my coat, see, while I waited for someone else to come along,' Walter whispers. 'Seemed only decent. And I couldn't help but notice the bruises.'

'Bruises? From the sea, like you said earlier and—'

'*No.*' The single word is harsh. 'Five little oval bruises, on the top of her arm, like a big hand had caught hold of her and squeezed tight.'

A chill floods through Felix.

And he hears Ethel Shove's voice in his head.

Nearly caused a mishap, because she was just ahead of him on the stairs and the suitcase caught her shoulder and he had to grab her arm to stop her falling.

Oh, dear God, he thinks. I have found Esme Sullivan.

NINE

On Thursday, two communications arrive for Nurse Leonora Henry. The first is a letter from her sister-in-law Felicia, which arrives by the noon post. Lily reads it with avid interest, interpreting the words to reveal that Felix has hared off to Portsmouth in the footsteps of Esme Sullivan.

She spends a busy hour or two with a succession of girls appearing in the sick bay. The weather is even colder today, there has been a sharp overnight frost, and many girls have developed sniffles, aches and pains and, in one case, a troubling cough. Three girls have slipped on the ice and hurt themselves. Lily very much wants some time alone to think about what Felix might or might not be in the very act of discovering in Portsmouth, but she is fully occupied.

Then in the early afternoon there is a telegram.

Continuing with the subterfuge of the mystery novel and its resolution, 'Felicia' writes: *Finished novel and know what became of her. Poor girl drowned and washed up Southsea beach. Still puzzling out full plot details. Felicia.*

Lily sits perfectly still, the telegram spread out on her lap.

So Esme Sullivan is dead.

She wonders how Felix can be so certain, but then she realizes first, that he would not have sent the message unless he was, and second, that she trusts him and believes him.

That poor, poor girl.

Lily understands now that she has been telling herself that Esme will be found; that whatever mission took her from Brighton to Portsmouth was fulfilled, that any day now she will return in triumph to Shardlowes and reveal why she left and what she has achieved.

It is not to be, Lily thinks sadly, instead there has been a tragedy, and—

But another thought interrupts that one.

Whatever mission took her from Brighton . . .

Suddenly Lily sits up very straight.

What if the same mission took her *to* Brighton in the first place, because Brighton is on the south coast and it was there that Esme wanted to go? What if the travelling salesman was a means to an end and not an end in himself?

Lily sinks back again. No, she tells herself, I must not let myself be carried away by speculation. Esme was bored with school, hungry for excitement, and carried away by the thrill of a handsome face – always assuming Wilfred Anderson was handsome – and the chance of an adventure. Of a week in Brighton posing as a wife, with all that it entailed.

So why, Lily wonders, did Esme travel on to Portsmouth when the days with her travelling salesman ended so abruptly?

Her thoughts fly round inside her head until she cannot determine which suspicions are likely or even possible and which are no more than extravagant speculations.

The sick bay is quiet. Matron, having got out of bed for an hour this morning, has exhausted herself with the effort and is now fast asleep; Lily suspects she is running a temperature.

And out of nowhere the thought bursts into Lily's head: *I must write to Felix*, simultaneously hoping that Felicia has done as she said she would and provided her friend Mariella with her address in Portsmouth. There is nothing she can do about that; without giving it another thought, she finds her leather writing case, her pen and her little ink well and, sitting down at the small table in the treatment room facing the open door so that she will not be taken by surprise, she begins to write, systematically recording everything that has happened and a great deal of what she has been thinking ever since arriving at Shardlowes.

Writing to Felix isn't the same as talking to him, naturally, since he is making no contribution, but nevertheless, as Lily folds the five closely written pages and seals the envelope, her mind is suddenly a great deal clearer. One or two conclusions that she has tentatively drawn appear to have been wrong, and she needs to think them through again. First, however, she must put her letter in the post; it is a little after two o'clock, and if she hurries, it will very likely be delivered to Kinver Street this evening and be on its way to Felix in the morning.

*   *   *

Striding back across the hall on her return from the post box at the end of the drive, she spots Georgiana Long halfway up the stairs, Miss Dickie a few steps ahead. Miss Long turns and catches Lily's eye, a smile beginning on her round face. I need to talk to you, Lily thinks, and, eyes still on Miss Long's, she inclines her head a couple of times in the direction of the sick bay, silently urging Miss Long to understand the message. Almost imperceptibly Miss Long nods, then hurries on up the stairs after her companion.

Not wanting to be engaged in conversation by Miss Dickie just now (or indeed ever), Lily ducks out of sight and returns to the sick bay via the servants' quarters and the back stairs.

She looks in on Matron, whose forehead is slightly sweaty above flushed cheeks. Lily reaches down her hand for the softest of touches, and Matron feels hot. Resolving to return presently to check again, Lily crosses to the treatment room and extracts the ledger from its hiding place. She sits down at the little table and opens it, no longer worried that Miss Dickie, or anyone else for that matter, will sneak up on her and demand an explanation.

Because, although virtually everything else remains a mystery, Lily now knows who hid the ledger.

It wasn't Miss Dickie. She is sure of this for two reasons: first, if Miss Dickie had hidden the ledger she would have selected a hiding place within her own area of Shardlowes in order to keep an eye on it; and second, because in all likelihood the deputy headmistress doesn't even know the space beneath the bottom shelf in the supplies cupboard exists.

Miss Dickie may not even know the ledger exists, come to that.

It is almost certain that one of the sick bay staff hid it, and since Lily has ruled out Matron, who alerted her to the ledger's existence, then it can only have been Nurse Evans. Following that line of reasoning, Lily has concluded that Nurse Evans must have suspected something, or discovered something, or even verified something, immediately before she was called away so abruptly to tend her ailing mother, and that, not wanting anybody else to do the same, hid the ledger before she left. And in that case—

No.

Now, sitting with the book open in front of her, Lily looks up wide-eyed as another realization strikes her.

Once again she hears Jessie Killick's clear young voice.

Nurse Evans doesn't like it here.

Me and the rest in the dorm think she's scared.

And Georgiana Long's voice, when she showed Lily into the room that had been Nurse Evans's.

She has few personal items and it appears she took most of them with her.

Lily knows with total certainty that Nurse Evans is not coming back. And she wonders urgently *why*.

Abruptly getting to her feet, Lily slips out of the treatment room and into her own room – Nurse Evans's room – embarking on a swift and surely futile search for anything belonging to her predecessor that might reveal the address of her parental home in North Wales – a book, a luggage label – but there is nothing. She returns to the treatment room and the ledger. Will Matron have the address? Miss Carmichael surely will, but Lily can hardly approach her. Briefly she considers asking Miss Long to try to find it but dismisses the idea, for if anyone were to surprise Miss Long in her search and demand to know what she was up to, it is doubtful that the little English teacher would have the aplomb to come up with a plausible explanation.

Can Lily think of an excuse for asking Matron for it?

Just now, however, Matron is fast asleep and not very well.

Lily returns to the ledger, her notebook, pen and ink to hand, and begins to record the symbols that appear beside the girls' names, their frequency and which girls are involved. There must be a key to the code . . . impatiently she flips ahead through the blank pages. And, as two pages towards the back are loosened by her actions, a letter slips out. Picking it up, Lily discovers it's not a letter, just an empty envelope, and it has been used as a book mark. For there, on the pages between which the envelope has been placed, is the list of symbols and their meaning.

But before Lily studies it, she examines the envelope. An uneducated hand has written *Nurse Evans, Sick Bay, Shardlowes School*, and the name of the village. Flicking it over, she sees the sender's name and address on the reverse: *George Latter, 27 Chark Street, Shadwell, London E.* Whoever George Latter is – friend, lover, fiancé – he certainly isn't Nurse Evans's dying mother. But – and Lily's hopes revive as suddenly as they were dashed – if he has been writing to her (and judging by the envelope, writing is something of a challenge), then might he not be privy to her reasons for abandoning her post at Shardlowes?

Lily folds the envelope and tucks it away in her writing case. As soon as Felix gets in touch and she knows where he is, she'll pass the Shadwell address on to him and he can go and ask.

She sits for a good half-minute reining in her impatience and her frustration, for she wants to talk to Felix *now* and she can't, then turns to the symbols and makes a note of their meaning. Most refer to medical states and conditions, both temporary (chills, coughs and colds, injuries of various severity, menstru-ation-related complaints) and permanent (lameness, impairment in sight and hearing, proneness to nervous debility, problems with learning, problems with personal hygiene, severe acne, obesity, failure to thrive). Then she returns to the list of names.

She realizes that the strange little mark that she thought she recognized, and that appears at most five times, is not included in the key.

She studies it again and once again there is that sense that it is familiar. It is like a lotus flower, just opening, and a line has been drawn diagonally across it. She is reminded of the lotus flowers of the Buddhist faith . . .

. . . and into her mind comes the one word *India.*

The imaginary wooden door inside her head that she keeps tightly shut on every sound, sight, smell and memory of India shudders a little, but she pushes against it.

And, summoning all her mental strength, puts the mystery of that little symbol right to the back of her mind.

She has extracted all that she can from the ledger for now and it is back in its hiding place when she hears an uneven tread out in the corridor and Georgiana Long's face peers round the door. She looks anxious and she whispers, 'I don't think anybody saw me but I can't be sure – oh, dear, I'm afraid I'm not very good at subterfuge, and—'

Lily gets up, ushers her into the treatment room and closes the door. 'No need for subterfuge, Miss Long, for surely school staff are at liberty to consult Matron or her assistant just as pupils are?'

'Yes, yes, of course,' Miss Long replies, 'but there is nothing wrong with me save for this beastly foot of mine.' She gives the ugly built-up boot a resentful scowl.

'Then shall we say, if anyone is so insensitive as to enquire, that you have come to consult me because you are experiencing discomfort?'

Miss Long looks at her balefully. 'I suffer perpetual discomfort, Nurse, although I am indeed in a little more pain than usual today, having stupidly turned my foot over on the path outside when taking my class for a brief breath of air before luncheon.' She looks mutinous. 'That *wretched* Miss Blytheway, she will insist on daily exercise, even when staying within and keeping warm is surely by far the more sensible choice, and—' She breaks off, and Lily can sense her distress.

She is not surprised at it. In addition to discomfort and pain, Lily has recently seen for herself how some of the girls take a malicious delight in mocking the little English teacher, stumbling along in her wake in imitation of her awkward, ugly gait and stifling their giggles. She also saw Miss Dickie watching them, a strange expression on her face, and afterwards drawing them aside to administer a brief lecture on 'poor Miss Long' and how it was not kind to mock another's misfortune, all the while her small, deep, eyes glittering with something that looked very like the patronizing and malicious triumph of the able-bodied over those who are not so lucky.

Lily really does not like Miss Dickie.

She says kindly to Miss Long, 'Is there anything I can do to help?'

Miss Long gives her a wry smile. 'I have a club foot, Nurse, which turns at an unnatural angle away from the ankle. I was put in a wrench as an infant, although my distress at the resultant pain disturbed my parents more than my twisted foot. It is too late now, I fear, for any remedial measures, and my boot is

adequate.' The last few words are spoken with dignified firmness and Lily understands that the matter is closed. 'Now, you
wished to speak to me?'

'Yes,' Lily says. 'This is my fourth day at Shardlowes and
it is high time you and I met in private.' Miss Long opens
her mouth to speak but Lily forestalls her. 'Before you ask,
I have nothing definite to reveal. I strongly suspect, however,
that Nurse Evans discovered something that disturbed her
and that her absence is permanent.'

To her surprise, Miss Long nods. 'I believe so too.'

'I further suspect,' Lily continues, 'that more girls have gone
missing than those you mentioned.' Miss Long doesn't speak.
'You have been here a little over a year, Miss Long, and you
took up your post mid-term. I find myself wondering whether,
like Nurse Evans, the English teacher who preceded you also
uncovered some disturbing facts and this was the reason for
her leaving the school in the middle of term?'

Miss Long is silent for so long that Lily begins to think
she isn't going to answer. But then, with a deep sigh, she says,
'Genevieve Swanson wrote to me. Oh, I know I should have
told you, but I was so keen that you should approach the
situation with unbiased eyes.'

'What did her letter say?' Lily asks, restraining the powerful
urge to yell, *Of course you should have told me!*

'That she was leaving Shardlowes because she was afraid.
Something was happening here that she did not understand, and
a girl she was very fond of – a clever girl, perhaps too clever,
Miss Swanson said – had gone, and when she – Miss Swanson
– enquired, she was *warned off*, was the expression she used,
and told that the girl's guardian had unexpectedly returned to
England and collected her late one evening.'

Lily is thinking very swiftly. There seems to be rather a
lot that Miss Long has omitted to tell her, and the fact that
yet another girl has disappeared from Shardlowes simply
horrifies her.

She waits until she is sure her distress will not be apparent,
then says quietly, 'Miss Swanson didn't believe whoever told
her this?'

'It was Miss Carmichael, and no, she most certainly did not.'

'Have you maintained your correspondence with Miss Swanson?' Lily asks, trying not to let the eagerness show.

A bashful expression crosses Miss Long's open face. 'Well, no. When I say she wrote to me, it would be more precise to say she left me a letter; she hid it in my room, where I found it a few days after my arrival.'

'You have never had any further contact?' Lily hears her own words and realizes she has been too forceful.

Now Miss Long looks worried. 'She had left when I arrived and, as I say, there were no further letters from her, although I did write to the address she put at the top of the page.'

'Do you still have this address?'

'Oh yes! I'll give it to you, but I'm sure she's no longer there. It was a temporary lodging, a hostel, she said, and she was only staying while she found another post, and no doubt she's—'

'Where was it?' Lily interrupts.

'In Cambridge,' Miss Long whispers.

So close, thinks Lily.

'Oh, I can guess what you're thinking!' Miss Long bursts out. Lily shushes her, and she drops her voice to a hiss. 'I *know* you think I'm a coward, that if I was concerned I should have tried to seek her out, but you don't know Shardlowes like I do, like all of us here do!' Her face is flooded with hot blood and her eyes glisten with the tears of distress. 'People here – the teachers, the staff, the older girls, even Junior school, poor little things – are furtive and secretive, and they stand in pairs and in tight private groups, and I hear the whispering between heads bent close together that abruptly ceases when I approach, and all the time there is Miss Dickie, smiling that smile while her little cold eyes watch and at times I feel her hostility like a knife in my side!'

Lily waits while she calms herself. Then she says quietly, 'Miss Long, it is clear to me that rather too many girls have gone missing from Shardlowes School.'

And Miss Long looks at her out of swimming brown eyes and says miserably, 'I know.'

Early on Friday morning there is a letter for Nurse Henry addressed in Felix's disguised handwriting. Receiving it in the entrance hall from the monitor who hands out the post, it takes most of Lily's self-control not to tear the envelope open immediately.

She walks with an outward show of calm back to the sick bay, shuts the door of her room firmly behind her and, leaning against it, reads what Felix has to say.

Still in the guise of the sister-in-law, Felix writes:

> Having concluded my mystery story and the weather on the south coast turning to the inclement, I decided yesterday afternoon to return home to Kinver Street, where your lengthy, informative and interesting letter awaited me. I am pleased to hear that your new post suits you so well, dearest Leonora, and that the staff and pupils alike are agreeable. Another communication was also waiting for me at Kinver Street, containing the disturbing tidings that Great-Aunt Dill has broken her wrist and Great-Uncle Hector is having difficulties managing; this latter will surprise you as little as it does me, dear, knowing as we both do that, despite the household's very well-trained servants, Hector is always put out of sorts by even the most minor of emergencies. Accordingly I plan to travel up to Thetford today, and it would be most delightful were you able to meet me for tea in Cambridge, where I can very easily enjoy a short pause between trains. Let us meet at our favourite place, and seek out a suitable establishment in which to take refreshment. I shall await you there from three o'clock unless I hear to the contrary.
>
> Your loving sister-in-law Felicia

For a panicky moment Lily can't for the life of her recall what he can mean by *our favourite place*, then remembers a conversation they once had about churches and how they agreed that King's College Chapel was the one they liked best.

Flooded with relief because she will be talking to him so soon, Lily lays her plans.

*   *   *

A short time later Lily knocks at the door of Miss Carmichael's room. The girls are still down in Hall finishing breakfast, and Lily hopes the headmistress is a quick eater and already back at her desk.

'Come in,' calls a low-pitched voice.

She is.

Lily enters and walks smartly up to the desk. Hands folded over her stomach, standing straight in her severe and elegant SWNS uniform, headdress framing her determined face, green eyes intent behind the small round spectacles, she has no idea how formidable she looks.

Miss Carmichael's quick look of surprise, just as quickly wiped away, suggests she is impressed. 'Nurse Henry,' she says. 'What is it?'

'I am concerned about Matron,' Lily says with perfect truthfulness. 'Her cold is worse, congestion is settling in her chest and she has a troublesome cough. The supplies cupboard in the treatment room is reasonably well stocked, but I have my own methods and there are items I require. I shall undoubtedly have several girls to see this morning, but I plan to go into Cambridge after an early lunch and locate a pharmacy.' She has made up her mind not to ask Miss Carmichael's permission. Acquiring the appropriate medicaments is purely a professional matter – Lily's profession of nurse and not Miss Carmichael's of headmistress – so permission is neither necessary nor relevant.

Miss Carmichael's very slightly raised eyebrows suggest she has noticed but is not going to argue. 'Of course, Nurse,' she says. 'There is a train from the local station at a quarter to two, and I will instruct Eddy to be ready with the trap at five and twenty past one.' There is an almost discernible pause. 'If that suits?'

'Very well, thank you, Miss Carmichael.'

Lily has turned smartly and is heading for the door, but Miss Carmichael says, 'Oh, Nurse?'

Lily looks back over her shoulder. 'Yes?'

'How are you settling in? I have been remiss, for I ought to have asked before, but I have been fully occupied with – er, with other matters.'

With searching for missing girls? Lily wonders. 'Quite well,
thank you,' she says coolly.

'You find the sick bay satisfactory?

'Adequate, Miss Carmichael. Now, if you will excuse me,
girls will be arriving to see me.'

Miss Carmichael inclines her head in a regal gesture and Lily
strides away.

There are indeed girls waiting. Three stand outside the treatment room, one has already installed herself and is perched
on the edge of the examination couch.

'Come off there, please,' Lily says as she closes the door. 'There
is a fresh white sheet spread out and you are crumpling it.'

'Oh!' The girl looks surprised, but does as she's told, standing
up smartly. She is one of the Seniors, seventeen or eighteen,
and her light brown hair is braided and wound around her head
in a coronet, with a little fringe of curls over her high forehead
like that made fashionable by the Princess of Wales. She has
a perfect hourglass figure and, were it not for the red nose and
the rheumy eyes, she would be as lovely, if not more so, than
Alexandra. 'Minna Fanshawe, Louise dormitory,' she says in
answer to Lily's look of enquiry.

'What can I do for you, Minna?' Lily asks.

Minna Fanshawe's symptoms – runny nose, headache, aches
and pains, lethargy – are repeated not only by the three girls
waiting to follow her into the treatment room, but by all the
others who come to the sick bay that morning. The cold is
running like fire through the school, and Lily makes a mental
note to acquire as many medications as she can carry back to
Shardlowes.

She looks in on Matron for the third time that day just before
lunch. Matron is propped up on several pillows. She wants to
lie down but Lily has told her in the sort of voice that brooks
no disagreement that phlegm on the chest isn't dispersed
when the patient is lying down, and Matron has grudgingly
accepted the truth of this. Despite sitting up, she has still slept
away most of the morning, but now she is awake.

Lily hands her a mug of hot water with lemon, honey and

ginger, and while her patient sips at it, informs her of the planned excursion to Cambridge.

Matron grunts. 'Very wise,' she croaks. She nods towards a plain, functional desk beneath the window. 'Cash box is in there. Take what you want but make sure you put it in the book.'

Lily obeys, extracting what she thinks she will need and then entering in the appropriate place the date, the amount and the purpose of the money. So deeply is she back in her nurse's identity that she begins to sign her real name, remembering only as she writes the L for Lily Raynor and changing it to Leonora Henry. After her signature, she adds, as she has done so many times in the past, *Sister, SWNS.*

She is kept busy until the moment it is time to go downstairs to find Eddy and the trap. She wouldn't have had a moment to change from her uniform into her civilian clothes, but it hasn't even occurred to her to do so.

Eddy greets her cheerfully and on the short journey to the station they talk about the weather – snow is threatening as the day goes on – and the outbreak of colds in the school. 'When d'you want meeting, miss?' he says as he pulls up. 'There's one gets in just after four, another at quarter to five, then the next at five thirty.'

'Oh – no earlier than a quarter to five, please Eddy,' she replies. She wonders if that will give her enough time. 'Although—'

Eddy understands. 'Not to worry if you're not on it, miss,' he says with a grin. 'They're roughly every three-quarters of an hour and I'll wait for the next one.' He leans down confidingly to her and says, 'I'm pals with Bert Gotobed, him as carries the bags and that, and he'll let me sit by his fire and take a cup of tea.' His right eyelid drops like a shutter in an exaggerated wink.

'Oh, good,' she murmurs back. 'I won't tell!' she adds with a smile.

He tips his cap, whistles to the pony and they trot briskly away.

Felix arrives in Cambridge far too early for the three o'clock rendezvous and at eleven, he is standing in the market square wondering how to fill the next four hours.

He has been suffering from extreme restlessness ever since Walter Nelson's description of the dead body washed up on Southsea beach revealed that it was that of Esme Sullivan. To begin with, this sense of urgency worked in his favour, for it sent him hurrying to the police station, demanding to be told everything they knew about the corpse. Despite Walter's scathing doubts about whether or not they looked properly, Felix was confident they would be able to tell him *something*.

He was wrong.

The starchy young constable who deigned to speak to him – and who studied his World's End Bureau card as if it were a lewd photograph – said dismissively that it was not uncommon for street girls to end up in the water, what with the company they kept and the alcohol they consumed, and when Felix asked angrily how he could be so sure the dead girl had been that sort of woman, had shrugged and said in a superior tone that made Felix want to punch him, 'This is a port, sir. What do you expect?'

Fuming, Felix took himself off before he gave in to the temptation. It was just the same as it was in London, he thought as he strode angrily back to the station. Street girls, whores, prostitutes, whatever you chose to call them, were plentiful and cheap, and when they came to a violent end, it was their own fault for leading the life they did.

There being no point in remaining in Portsmouth, he took the next train back to London and didn't even begin to brighten up until, arriving back at Kinver Street, Marm greeted him with the welcome news that there was a letter from Lily.

Now, stamping his feet against the cold in Cambridge's market square, he realizes that his early departure might have been a mistake, for Lily could only have received his reply this morning and he hadn't given her sufficient time to send a telegram saying she would not be able to be at the rendezvous.

'She'll be there,' he mutters aloud. 'I know she will.'

After a desultory wander through the colleges, a brisk walk along the river – beginning to freeze over – a steak and kidney pie and a pint of excellent beer in a pub with a roaring fire, he sets off for King's College soon after two o'clock. Entering through the South Door, he sits down in a row of pews in the nave, in front of the impressive rood screen. The sound of choristers floats through from the choir stalls, and someone is softly playing the organ. It is very peaceful, and for the first time in days Felix feels himself relax. He looks up at the extraordinary beauty of the fan vaulting. Time passes, and, still looking up at the roof, he is in the middle of wondering how such perfection was achieved four hundred years ago when he hears a voice say softly in his ear, 'That is quite enough of craning your neck, or you will suffer for it later.'

Lowering his head and spinning round far too swiftly, he sees Lily seating herself beside him.

He is taken aback by the rush of happiness that floods him. Hoping she hasn't noticed, he says, 'You're early.'

'I am,' she agrees.

He risks another glance. She is dressed in her nurse's uniform, and over the high-collared black gown she wears a thick knee-length coat. Her hair is severely bound in its bun and largely hidden by the wide-brimmed bonnet.

'You look . . .' he begins.

'Like a nurse?' She raises an eyebrow as he nods. He wants to add that she now looks much more like a nurse than when she left the World's End Bureau four days ago, but he is not sure how she would receive the remark.

'I *am* a nurse,' she murmurs. Then, briskly, 'Felix, I haven't got endless time, and there's an address here in Cambridge I want us to check, so let's quickly tell each other all that we have found out.' He begins to make a comment but she interrupts. 'Yes, I know I wrote to you at length, but for one thing I've found the address of someone who I'm sure is associated with Nurse Evans, and if I *tell* you everything as well, I'm sure there will be nuances and subtleties I omitted. I'll go first.'

And as he listens to her succinctly describing the school, the staff, the girls, the sense of unease, the fear, the ledger with its lists of pupils and its symbols, he reflects that she is indeed a nurse; that something in this job that she has undertaken – with some reluctance, as he recalls – has taken her back to that former stage of her life.

He is not quite sure whether he feels quite the same about Nurse Raynor – Nurse Henry – as he did about the Lily who set up the World's End Bureau. But as he listens to her outlining her suspicions, he is very willing to wait and see.

'So you think both the English teacher and the assistant matron who preceded you have gone for good?' he says when she has finished.

'Genevieve Swanson has definitely gone,' she replies. 'Gone and been replaced by our Miss Long, who to the best of my knowledge is a permanent member of staff and not engaged on a temporary basis as I am.'

'You want me to check this?' He holds out the envelope on which is written a name and an address in Shadwell. She nods. 'And you know of somewhere here in Cambridge where this English teacher stayed?'

'I do.' She glances at the notebook open on her lap. 'It's on the other side of Christ's Pieces. Not far.' She meets his eyes again. 'Your turn.'

It doesn't take as long for him to describe his recent activities. When he explains how he can be certain that the dead body is that of Esme Sullivan, her face drops in sorrow.

'I truly believed she was alive and safe,' she whispers. 'I had convinced myself she left Shardlowes with her travelling salesman because for some reason she needed to get to the south coast, and allowing herself to travel under Walter Anderson's care – as his wife in fact – was a price she was prepared to pay.' Reflecting on the high jinks and the laughter that Mrs Shove reported hearing from the couple's room, Felix silently adds, *Rather more than prepared.* 'And I honestly thought,' Lily goes on, 'that she – Esme – was the sort of girl to have the intelligence, the initiative and the courage to achieve what she set out to do, and that in her own time she would turn up.'

'Yes I know,' Felix says gently. 'I thought that too.'

'You too believe she left Shardlowes to do some specific task?'

He shrugs. 'I'm not sure. But *you* do, and you're usually right.'

For the first time since she sat down beside him, Lily smiles.

TEN

The hostel where Genevieve Swanson stayed between leaving Shardlowes and taking up her next post proves to be a house in an elegant terrace that forms one side of a square of similar terraces, some ten minutes' walk from King's Parade. A small garden separates the yellow front door from the pavement, and fresh-looking white net curtains hang at the window beside the door. The letter box and door knocker shine with recent buffing, as does the discreet brass plaque to the right of the door on which is written *Causeway Gardens Hostel for Professional Women*.

Lily glances at Felix, who nods, and knocks. They have arranged that she will do the talking, and as the door opens to reveal a tall, well-built woman of perhaps fifty with abundant white-streaked hair, severely dressed in dark grey but with a friendly smile, Lily says, 'I wonder if you can help me? I am looking for a Miss Genevieve Swanson, who I believe lodged here briefly a little over a year ago, and—'

But the woman's expression alters as Lily says the name, and now she interrupts. 'Is the young man with you?'

'Yes, he's—'

'Then come in, both of you. Quickly now, the heat is escaping!'

She ushers them along a hall, past a closed door on the left, through a door across the passage and in through a second one on the left. Lily and Felix find themselves in a pleasant room furnished with a chaise longue, several wing-backed chairs and a large, square table surrounded with upright wooden chairs with leather seats. There is a soft mauve mohair shawl on the chaise longue, a tapestry bag with knitting needles sticking out of it on the table beside some neatly stacked books, a row of well-tended saintpaulia on the windowsill and a pleasant aroma of lavender.

The large woman pulls out two chairs. 'Please sit down,' she

says. 'I was making a pot of tea. You'll take a cup, and a slice
of Madeira cake? Good, good. I am Eileen Woodfall and I am
warden of the hostel.'

Lily risks a swift glance at Felix as their hostess disappears
into the kitchen, but he is looking straight ahead, a suitably
bland expression on his face. She is struck by how very
masculine he seems, in what is so obviously an all-female
establishment.

Presently Miss Woodfall returns bearing a huge wooden tray.
Felix leaps up to take it from her, but with a quick, dismissive
shake of the head which seems to say he is only a man and
cannot be trusted with such a task, she puts it down on the
table and deftly sets out the contents. When they all have a full
cup and an enormous slice of what looks and smells like a very
good cake, she says, 'I have frequently asked myself when
someone would come asking about poor Miss Swanson.'

'*Poor* Miss Swanson?' Lily has spoken too sharply and she
smiles at Miss Woodfall to try to mitigate the aggressive words.

Miss Woodfall looks from one to the other of them, her eyes
settling on Lily. 'Before I continue, perhaps you would do me
the courtesy of explaining who you are and what is your interest
in Genevieve Swanson?' It is phrased and spoken as a question
but it has the force of a command.

Once again Lily catches Felix's eye and she thinks he nods
very faintly. The truth, then, she thinks.

'My name is Lily Raynor and I am an SWNS nurse, as no
doubt you will have deduced from my uniform, and presently
engaged in that capacity. However, I am also the proprietor of
a private enquiry agency, and my associate Felix Wilbraham'
– she indicates Felix – 'and I have been engaged on a delicate
matter in an establishment near here.'

Miss Woodfall sips her tea and pats her lips with a fawn
linen napkin. 'Thank you for your honesty,' she says, adding
quietly, 'what there was of it. Oh, I don't blame you for your
reticence,' she hurries on, 'for undoubtedly discretion is an
important part of an enquiry agent's job.'

Lily doesn't speak. Miss Woodfall goes on looking at her
intently, as if trying to assess her trustworthiness. Then abruptly
she says, 'Genevieve Swanson is dead.'

'*Dead?*' Lily and Felix repeat the word in chorus.

'I am afraid so, yes,' Miss Woodfall says, her face sombre. She sighs deeply, then goes on with clear reluctance, 'I suppose I had better tell you the whole story.'

'We would be grateful,' Lily says.

Miss Woodfall tops up the teacups while she gathers her thoughts. Then she says, 'Miss Swanson arrived on a chilly autumn night in some distress. She had a small suitcase with her and told me that her trunk had been left at the station. I had a room, although it was in fact only available because Miss Swanson said she would not be staying long, and she took up residence there and then.'

'She was in distress, you said?' Lily asks.

'Oh, indeed so,' Miss Woodfall confirms. 'She had clearly been weeping, and I was in no doubt that something had frightened her. I reassured her that she was perfectly safe here at Causeway Gardens Hostel, for our stout front door is *always* locked and bolted at night, and our handyman lives close by and is available for emergencies of all kinds.'

'What had frightened her?' Felix asks politely, and Lily guesses he, like her, very much wants their hostess to get on with her tale.

'Well, I didn't know straight away, Mr Wilbraham, but the next evening I prevailed upon Miss Swanson to join me in a cup of cocoa with a drop of brandy to hearten it, and really, I think she was only too pleased to share her anxieties, for almost immediately she told me she had recently left her post as teacher of English in a prestigious girls' school because of something she was not prepared to divulge, and that she was now feeling very guilty indeed because the teacher who would be taking her place could have no idea of what was going on and she feared for her safety. She said she had left a note for her with a warning, but she truly felt she should have done more.' Miss Woodfall looks anxious. 'I *do* hope you are not here because another English teacher has gone running off in distress into the night?'

'Miss Swanson's successor is perfectly well and still at the school,' Lily reassures her. She pauses. 'In fact it was she who engaged us to investigate this – er, this mysterious business at the school, and I believe I can reassure you that she is fully aware of the need for caution.'

Miss Woodfall looks relieved.

'How did Miss Swanson die?' Felix asks, and Miss Woodfall gives a small shudder at the bluntness of the question.

'Of course, you'd want to know,' she murmurs. 'Well, Mr Wilbraham, I am afraid I cannot tell you. I know of her demise because the police came here asking if any of her belongings, specifically a diary, notebooks, papers, that sort of thing, had been left here – they had not, for she packed her small case and took it with her when she left, although of course I cannot speak for the trunk at the station – and when I demanded to know why they were asking, they told me her body had been found beside a railway line.'

Lily begins to express her horror at this, but Felix overrides her: 'Which line?' Turning to glare at him, she notices that his face is pale and suddenly gaunt with distress.

Miss Woodfall too, it seems, understands that his abruptness is caused by anxiety. 'It was near Havant, on the LB and SCR,' she says.

'London, Brighton and South Coast railway,' Felix says. Then, his hazel eyes on Lily's, he says very quietly, 'She was following the same trail as Esme Sullivan.'

There is a stunned silence in the warm, welcoming room. It is broken by the clock on the mantelshelf melodiously striking the first quarter. With a gasp, Lily looks at it and sees that it is a quarter past four. The train that Eddy is to meet will be leaving Cambridge station in about twenty minutes, and it is a long walk to the station, and she will be lucky if she makes the next one.

She gets to her feet. 'I am afraid I must go, Miss Woodfall,' she says. 'I am sorry we have to hurry away, even more sorry that we have resurrected such distressing memories.'

Miss Woodfall also stands up. 'I regret being the bearer of bad news,' she replies.

Felix is already halfway to the front door, having apparently picked up on Lily's urgency. They leave the hostel in a flurry of hasty goodbyes and Lily strides off down the pavement, heading back towards the centre of the town.

'It's probably quicker if we go down that road,' pants Felix beside her, pointing to the left.

'Yes, perhaps, but I have to find a pharmacy. There is a list of items I must purchase – we have a nasty cold and chesty cough infecting the school and I lack the ingredients I need to prepare my preferred remedies.'

Felix nods and increases his pace.

They find a pharmacy in a curving little street off the marketplace and Lily reads out her list to the quietly efficient young man behind the counter. As he packs the pots, bottles and powders into two neat brown-paper packages – 'They're heavy, so I'll do one for each hand,' the young man says – she feels Felix's eyes on her and looks up. 'What?' she says quietly.

He has a strange look on his face. It is half admiring, half wistful. 'You,' he replies.

'Me?'

'Yes. You've changed,' he goes on, lowering his voice further. The pharmacist shoots them an interested glance, then returns to his packing.

'Explain.'

'You—' He pauses, starts again. 'When you left Chelsea you were the proprietor of the Bureau; efficient, courageous, good at your job. Now you're no longer that – well, no longer primarily that.' He pauses again, and she believes she knows what's coming. 'You're a nurse again,' he says, the words barely audible, 'and it's not just because you're wearing the uniform.'

She nods slowly. 'Yes,' she says. 'I know. There are people at the school who are quite seriously unwell – Matron, for example, and one of the youngest girls is already running a temperature – and I can make them feel better. Before you say it' – for he looks as if he's about to speak – 'I know it's not what I'm meant to be doing there, but you must understand that I can't help it. I'm a fully trained nurse and I can't just stand by. Be assured,' she adds sternly, 'the one job does *not* preclude the other.'

He grins at her sudden vehemence, pretending to back away in fear. 'I didn't think it did.' He looks down at her. 'But—'

'But?' she demands when he stops.

'I hope the private enquiry agent hasn't gone for good,' he blurts out, 'because I really liked her.'

Lily feels her mouth drop open. '*No!*' she says. 'Oh, no, I'm sure I—'

'Your parcels are ready,' the pharmacist says. 'I've made carrying handles in the string – will you manage, Nurse?'

Felix strides over to the counter and picks up both parcels as if they contain feathers. 'She won't have to manage,' he says firmly. 'Come along, Nurse.'

At the station Lily has about twenty minutes to wait for her train. Felix has a ticket for the London train, which is pulling into the station as they arrive; he and Lily are red in the face and out of breath, and Lily presses her hand to the stitch in her side. But he lets the train go without him in order to have a little longer with her. 'They are quite frequent,' he assures her, although he has no idea if this is true.

They stand together on her side of the platform. He places the packages carefully on the ground at her feet. 'Will you manage them at the other end?' he asks.

'Oh, yes. Eddy will be waiting with the trap.'

'Eddy?'

'He's young, cheerful, friendly, and—'

'And sweet on you?'

She gives him a steely glance. 'Don't be absurd.'

He wonders why they are standing there making small talk. It appears the same thought has crossed her mind, for she says suddenly, 'How soon can you check on the Shadwell address?'

He reaches into his inside pocket to reassure himself that the envelope she gave him in the chapel is still there. It is superfluous, really, since he has copied the address into his notebook, but he senses the envelope itself is somehow important to Lily. 'I'll go this evening, soon as I'm back in London and before I go home to Kinver Street,' he says.

Her face falls. 'But it's Shadwell. It's not a very—' She stops abruptly.

He grins. 'Not a very safe place after dark, were you going to say? Yes, I know, Lily. I'm familiar with the area.'

'*Are* you?'

'Remember when we first met and you raised an eyebrow at one of my middle names?'

'Felix Parsifal Derek McIvie Wilbraham.' She smiles. 'I remember.'

'As I believe I told you, Derek comes from my grandfather Derek Smith, tinker, scrap-metal dealer, originally of Essex and latterly of East London,' he says. 'Before his wife made him move to somewhere more salubrious and socially acceptable, he lived in Limehouse, which you probably don't know is very close to Shadwell.'

'You used to *visit* him there?' She sounds amazed.

'No, they'd moved away long before I was born. But he sensed I wasn't as shocked by his roots – which are my roots too – as everyone else, and when I was little, before I was packed off to school, he used to sneak me away and take me round his old haunts.' It had been their secret, his and Granddaddy's, and the memories are highly colourful and very precious.

She is still looking worriedly at him. 'But you will be careful?'

He smiles. 'Yes, Lily. I'll be careful. I promise.'

There is the toot of a train whistle, and they both turn to see Lily's train approaching. He bends down to pick up her parcels, about to hand them to her. Before he lets go of the strings, he says, 'And you too, Nurse Henry.'

'*What?*' she demands, almost crossly, although he is quite sure she knows what he means.

'You be careful too,' he says urgently. 'A woman and a girl have died, your predecessor fled, at least two more girls have gone missing, and the link between them all is the very place where you are currently employed as assistant matron. We know, or strongly suspect, that both Esme Sullivan and Genevieve Swanson were pursuing their own investigations into whatever was disturbing them, and one was found dead in Southsea, the other by the railway line near Havant.' He has been speaking too forcefully; he reads it in her face. 'I know you have to carry on with your probing, Lily, because that's what you're there to do, that's the business of the Bureau, that's what Georgiana Long is paying you for.' He pauses, takes a breath. Then he says, at not much above a whisper,

'But I would find it hard to bear if yours was the next death I had to investigate.'

The train has come to a steaming, noisy halt, and doors are opening up and down its length. He hands her into a carriage, at last relinquishing her parcels. She looks pale, and although he is quite sure his last words are the reason for this, nevertheless he does not regret them. She needs to be reminded she's not invincible, he tells himself, and if that is what it took, then it is well done.

Nevertheless, her expression as she leans out of the window to say goodbye touches his heart.

'Keep me informed,' he says.

'You do the same,' she replies.

They are still staring at each other as the train gathers itself and pulls away.

It is late and fully dark before Felix's train deposits him at Liverpool Street Station. He takes a succession of trams and buses and finally hops off some way along the Commercial Road, taking a turn down to the right towards the river into the docks and aiming for Shadwell Basin. He has no idea where Chark Street is and so goes into a pub, where he has a pint of good beer and a doorstop of bread with cheese and pickle – he is ravenous, and it seems longer than half a day since the pie in the Cambridge pub – and asks the landlord for directions.

The landlord looks at him dubiously. 'You come down in the world, then?' he enquires. Felix raises his eyebrows. 'I mean to say, nicely dressed gent such as yourself having business somewhere like that?'

'My business is personal,' Felix says.

The landlord shrugs. 'Suit yourself.' But clearly he hasn't taken offence, because he proceeds to give Felix careful instructions, drawing a neat map on a page in the open notebook Felix has put before him. 'There, you can't miss it,' he says as he finishes his sketch.

Felix smiles. 'That's what people always say.'

But the landlord is right, and Felix finds Chark Street without making one wrong turning.

It is more of a yard than a street, for at some time probably quite recently a vast wall has been built across it, forming the landward boundary of a dock basin. Twin rows of single-storey houses run either side of the street, the stone pavers of which are in an advanced state of disrepair. There is an iron pump in the middle of the road, and all the doors are firmly closed, the windows shuttered.

Felix makes his way along to number 27 and taps on the door. There is no reply, but he thinks he has heard movement within. He taps again and calls out very softly, 'Mr Latter? Mr George Latter?'

So abruptly that it makes him jump, the door is wrenched open about a hand's breath and a voice says in a harsh whisper, 'Not so loud!'

'Are you George Latter?' Felix repeats.

'Who wants to know?'

Felix has a World's End Bureau card ready and he pokes it through the gap. 'What the hell's this?' the rough voice demands.

'My card,' Felix replies. 'Will you let me in?'

No response.

Reluctantly he takes the envelope out of his pocket. He holds it up so that the man within can see it but keeps a tight grip on it. Not tight enough; there is a muffled grunt and a huge hand grabs it, ripping it so that Felix is left clutching only the corner.

Nothing happens for a few seconds, then the door is opened more fully and the same enormous hand grasps Felix by the coat lapels and pulls him inside, slamming and bolting the door. In the dim light of a single candle and a low-wicked lantern set on a rickety table, Felix sees a vast man of well over six foot, six foot six perhaps, with a face carved of granite by not a very good sculptor and the shoulders of a stevedore.

'I'm George Latter,' he says in a soft voice that is far more threatening than the grunt or the harsh whisper. 'Where did you get this?'

'It was found in the sick-bay ledger in a girls' school just outside Cambridge,' Felix replies. The huge man exudes danger and menace, and Felix is picking this up – you wouldn't be in

your right mind if you didn't, he thinks – but as yet he feels
no sense of imminent threat.

'And?' the man says aggressively.

Felix realizes that he is not going to give anything away until
Felix offers more of an explanation. Since it seems to be a
moment when only the truth will do, he crosses his fingers for
luck and says, 'The Bureau has been asked to investigate the
disappearance of girls from Shardlowes School. My associate
is at the school, acting as assistant matron, and she was told
that her predecessor, Nurse Evans, had been forced to take leave
unexpectedly to care for her ailing mother in North Wales. My
associate has uncovered reasons to suspect this is not true; that
Nurse Evans, having found out something that deeply disturbed
her, used the sick mother as an excuse and has left for good.'

There is a very long silence, heavy with the sense that the
next few moments could go one of two ways, and Felix feels
the danger now. Then with a deep sigh that makes the candle
flame flicker and all but go out, the big man pulls forward a
couple of cheap wooden chairs and says, 'Sit down. I'll put
a brew on.'

Felix sinks down onto the chair with legs that suddenly feel
weak. It's fatigue, he tells himself, it's not at all because I was
fully expecting to receive a huge, angry fist in my face.

Presently the man returns from the dark alcove into which
he disappeared, bearing two enamel mugs of tea so dark that
it could dye wood and sweet enough to rot teeth at a touch.
But it is exactly what Felix needs and he sips at it, blowing
on it to cool it so he can get it down.

The man is smiling, teeth shining in the heavy beard. 'Sorry
if I scared you.'

Felix nods. There doesn't seem to be anything to say.

'You're right,' the man goes on after a moment. 'She wasn't
just disturbed, she was terrified. Feared for her life. She'd heard
the howling again, see, and that always meant danger.'

'Howling?' Felix asks.

But it is as if the big man hasn't heard. 'George Latter,' he
says, pointing a thumb like the head of a hammer at his chest.
'And you're this L.G. Raynor fellow?'

Not for the first time, Felix explains.

'Carrie Evans is my half-sister,' George Latter goes on. 'Same mother, my father died when I was little and my mother married Thomas Evans and they had Carrie. We've always been close,' he says fondly, 'I've no quarrel with my stepfather, and Carrie's a good girl, one of the best.'

'So when she began to be concerned about what was happening at Shardlowes, she got in touch with you because you were much nearer than the family in North Wales?' Belatedly, for he should have asked this first, he says, 'I trust your mother is holding her own?'

There is a deep rumbling sound as George Latter laughs. 'Carrie's and my mother isn't ill, Mr Wilbraham, and there hasn't been any of the family in North Wales since Noah was a lad in short breeches. My grandfather couldn't stand the piety, see, and the constant bloody hymn singing, and he moved here to Shadwell back in the fifties and brought his kin with him.'

Looking round the room, which although clean and tidy is within a building and on a street that have definitely seen better days, Felix is wondering how to ask diplomatically how a girl from a place like this managed to rise to the post of assistant matron at a school such as Shardlowes. George Latter, who has probably noticed his eyes roaming over the worn rug, the meagre fire and the paint peeling from the woodwork, says with a hint of annoyance, 'We don't *live* here, Mr Wilbraham. It was once my auntie Bertha's house, who took to drink, but we've kept it on as a – well, never mind that, it has nothing to do with Carrie's trouble and it's none of your business.'

Felix, remembering his grandfather Derek's tales, has a fair idea what use men working on the London docks might have for a shabby old house in a forgotten street, but wisely keeps his silence.

'No, no, we don't live here,' George repeats. 'But I call in regularly and it's come in handy as an address, because Carrie, she was afraid someone would see who she was writing to and come looking, and although I've no fear for my own safety, I've a wife and little ones to think about and I'm not at home all the working day, and half into the night often as not too.'

'I understand,' Felix says, sounding calm even while he is

thinking with dismay that whatever dark threat lies hidden at
Shardlowes must be grave indeed for a man like Latter to take
such measures . . .

Then, as he is struck by an even worse thought, he says
urgently, 'Is Carrie all right? She's not—'

George leans forward and slaps a huge hand on Felix's knee.
'She's safe, Mr Wilbraham. She knew when it was time to flee
and she has kinfolk to rely on. No harm has come to her, and
it won't while George Latter walks the earth.'

It is the first reassuring news Felix has heard all day.

ELEVEN

E ddy is on the platform as Lily disembarks from the train and jumps forwards to take her parcels. He waves aside her apologies for keeping him waiting and merely says, 'Get what you wanted, did you, miss? Good, that's right!' proceeding to whistle cheerfully all the way back to Shardlowes.

Hurrying up the steps to the door, Lily's mind is already running ahead to how she will prepare the remedies she requires, what proportions to use, whether there will be a large enough bowl to set up a steam inhalation using the camphor, juniper, menthol and peppermint oils she has just acquired. She reflects that Felix was right: the nurse in her has come to the fore and since she got off the train she hasn't given a single thought to the true reason she is at Shardlowes.

The girls are going into tea in Hall as she hurries across to the stairs and she spots Miss Blytheway, who has a huge white handkerchief to her face and is blowing her nose vigorously. Two Seniors are with her, one of whom Lily recognizes as Rhoda Albercourt, monitor of Red dormitory. She too is sniffing, and the tip of her nose is red.

'*Wretched* cold!' Miss Blytheway greets Lily, glaring at her as if it is her fault that so many are falling victim to it.

'I am about to make up some remedies that I trust will alleviate the symptoms,' Lily replies coolly. 'Perhaps, Miss Blytheway, you would be good enough to announce at tea that I shall be in the treatment room from now until bedtime, and any girl or member of staff who needs my help shall have it.'

Miss Blytheway nods and says a grudging, 'Very well, thanks,' and she and the two girls march away.

Lily puts down her parcels in the treatment room, takes off her hat and coat and puts on her veil and apron. Then she goes in to see Matron, whose scarlet cheeks and laboured breathing are not good signs. Lily wakes her from her doze, plumps up the pillows and sits her up, gives her some water and then says,

'I shall make something that will help, Matron. Try to stay awake while I prepare it.'

Back in the treatment room she sets a large pan of water on to heat. She has several remedies to work on, including horse-radish cough syrup and a mustard poultice for Matron's chest. While the water comes to the boil, she unpacks her purchases, sorts them and finds places for them on the shelves, setting aside the box of cough jujubes and removing a couple to take to Matron.

For the next half-hour she works swiftly and efficiently. By the time the first group of girls come tapping on the door, Matron's poultice is in place and she has been dosed with two large spoonfuls of ipecacuanha, and already reports that the tightness in her chest is easing.

Lily sees ten girls and three members of staff. None of the latter is Miss Carmichael or Miss Dickie. Either the women are immune to cold germs or, if not, they choose to treat them-selves rather than come in need to the temporary assistant matron. None of those who do present themselves is yet sufficiently unwell to be removed to the sick bay, and Lily loses count of the number of times she says bracingly, 'It is only a cold. Have a good night's sleep, and although you will feel worse in the morning, your symptoms will ease once you are up and about.'

Most of the girls look sceptical but, as Lily well knows, this is the way with colds. Nevertheless, once her last patient has left she goes into the small ward next door to the treatment room and makes sure all six beds are ready for possible occupation.

It is now after eight o'clock and the school is quiet. Juniors will be in their dormitories, Seniors enjoying the last hour before they too go to bed. Lily tidies the treatment room, thinking what a great pleasure it will be to take her boots off and sit down, and as the demands of her nursing role fade, the far more alarming matter of what is happening at Shardlowes crowds into her mind.

Two people are dead, she knows for certain that two girls are missing and she strongly suspects there are more. Have they, like poor Esme and Miss Swanson, delved too deep and brought retribution on themselves? Is this what Isa Hatcher and Cora Naughton-Smythe did? But poor little Cora is only eleven: what threat could she possibly have been to whoever wants so desperately to guard Shardlowes's secret that they will throw a woman off a train and drown a seventeen-year-old girl? Always assuming, of course, that both deaths were not simply terrible accidents, and—

There is a very soft tap at the door. Startled, not to say annoyed, for she badly needs some quiet time to order the tumult of her thoughts, Lily opens it to reveal Marigold Dunbar-Lea standing outside.

'You should be in bed,' Lily says. 'Have you caught the school cold too?'

Marigold shakes her head, the light brown curls swinging. 'I don't get colds.' *Hon't het holds.* 'But my boot has been rubbing and my foot hurts.' *Hoot, heen.*

Quickly tuning in to Marigold's particular mode of enunciation, Lily says, 'Come and sit up on the couch, and I shall see what I can do.'

Obediently Marigold clambers up and is already unlacing the built-up boot on her right foot as Lily joins her. The boot drops to the floor with a loud thump. Marigold's right leg is normally formed as far as the knee, but below it there is a mere three or four inches of shin before a twisted, distorted foot forms the termination of the limb, and the leg is perhaps six or seven inches shorter than the left one. Lily takes the foot in her hands, gently turning it this way and that, observing the places where the brutally heavy boot rubs so that hard pads of protective skin have formed. One of these pads is reddened and swollen at the edge, and it has wept a little blood.

'Yes, that does look sore,' Lily says calmly. 'I shall bathe it and rub on some emollient cream, and then I shall pad the foot while the rubbed place gets better.'

Marigold watches with interest while Lily prepares what she requires, and submits to the treatment in stoical silence, although she cannot help the involuntary flinching.

'I am sorry, this must hurt rather,' Lily says.

'I'm used to it,' Marigold says. 'I've had people poking and prodding and mauling me ever since I can remember, but fortunately they did the operation on my face when I was too small to understand what was happening.' Hare-lip repair was usually done soon after birth, Lily reflects. Whoever had operated on Marigold hadn't managed a very good job. 'It was done in India, where I was born,' Marigold adds. 'I'm meant to have a second operation here when I'm older, but I'm still waiting and I don't know how much older I have to *be* because they won't say and when I write to Mama and ask, she seems to have forgotten about her promise and that's just *typical* because she doesn't bother to answer *any* of the things I write about and she never *ever* responds when I mention the little games we used to play.'

Marigold sounds cross, but Lily hears real hurt underneath the truculent words. 'That must be disappointing,' she says mildly. She has bathed the foot and is now mixing drops of rosewater and lavender into the moisturizing, soothing cream whose recipe is her own invention.

'There's Claud, too,' Marigold mutters.

'Claud?'

'Claud's a tiger, a sleeping tiger, and he's a jade statue and *very* valuable. Mama didn't often have time to put me to bed but when she did, it was wonderful because she'd smell so sweet and be dressed in one of her lovely rustling silk gowns and we'd play our game with Claud which I loved *so much*, and Mama would bring him in from the mantelshelf in the drawing room and say, *Look, here's Claud*, and she'd press his cool, hard, green stone muzzle against my nose, and then she'd say, *He is looking for his princess, for he is a prince in disguise and must find her and keep her close, for when the little girl grows into a beautiful woman, a kiss from her on the top of Claud's head will turn him back into a prince, they will marry and live happily ever after!* And I was always half excited and half fearful because Claud had a *very* severe expression and although he had his eyes closed I was perfectly sure he was watching me, and it was a frightening thing to kiss a tiger. And Mama would see that I was scared and she'd say, *Not yet, my darling, Claud will not be ready for his princess's kiss until she is sixteen years old and that is a long time away!* And, oh, Nurse, it's not so very long now because I am eleven already and I shall very soon be twelve, but when I ask Mama in my letters whether Claud is getting ready for the kiss she's forgotten, or doesn't want to play any more, and she *never* answers! And last year when—' But she does not go on.

A fat tear rolls down Marigold's face and Lily's hearts twists in sympathy. But what can she say to comfort the girl? She can't say bracingly that she's sure it won't be long before Marigold's parents come home on leave and everything will be all right because she has no idea if this is true.

She thinks and then says, 'It is often the way, Marigold, that when we are away from our home and our loved ones, we think they have forgotten all about us.' Memory stirs, and she recalls a time in India when she was at her lowest and no letters had come from her grandparents and Aunt Eliza, and she had all but drowned in self-pity as she told herself they didn't care any more, that she was truly out of sight and out of mind. And of course it wasn't true, for love does not die because of distance.

Marigold is looking interested. She wipes away the tear with an impatient gesture and says, 'You were sent away when you were small too?'

'Not when I was small, no, but when I qualified as a nurse I went to India.'

Marigold's face lights up. 'Oh, where? We used to live in Lucknow, did you go there?'

'I did, yes, but I was posted to a place right up in the foothills of the mountains.'

Marigold sighs. 'I'm told it's beautiful there, and cool in summer.'

'It is,' Lily agrees.

There is a brief pause, then Marigold says, 'I'm rather concerned – well, *very* concerned – because when Mama—' But she does not go on.

Lily wonders if to encourage her, but the child's face is set and closed; whatever is causing her anxiety, she is not ready to share it.

'Now,' Lily says briskly, 'I am going to administer this cream.'

For some time neither of them speaks. Marigold, having held herself stiffly as Lily began in expectation of pain, begins to relax. Presently she says, 'You have a very gentle touch and your face does not slide downwards in disapproval.'

'Thank you,' Lily says.

'In fact,' – *n hact* – Marigold goes on, 'you are a much better nurse than . . .' She leaves the comment unfinished, but an exaggerated jerk of her chin towards Matron's room is explanation enough.

'I liked being a nurse,' Lily says very softly, and to hear herself say the words comes as a surprise, for she has buried her India memories deep.

'But you're still a nurse. Aren't you?' Marigold sounds understandably mystified.

'Oh, yes, of course I am!' Lily says hastily. 'I meant I liked nursing in India.' Until that dreadful event happened, the unimaginably awful *Incident*, she adds silently.

'You would have been the best, and I should know,' Marigold says gently.

'That form of nursing is no longer my chosen profession.' The chilly response sounds oppressively stiff.

Marigold's large, clear blue eyes are intent on her. She says simply, 'Why?'

And Lily shakes her head, for she can provide no answer.

It is very late, utterly silent and profoundly dark, and in her bedroom Lily sits on a hard chair before the partly open window. The night air is bitingly cold and damp, smelling of the Fens; smelling of dark, slithering things.

She wonders where *that* thought came from.

Why? Marigold said.

Why.

Why is nursing no longer your chosen profession?

You would have been the best, and I should know.

And over the past days, while Lily has been so deeply and fully engaged in caring for Matron and the girls and staff members who are affected with this debilitating cold, she has been a nurse again and it has become her profession once more; being a private enquiry agent is presently coming a rather poor second.

Why?

For the first time in almost two years, Lily braces herself to look at that question.

She sighs, reluctance that verges on abhorrence flooding her mind. She does not *want* to go back, even in the safety of her little room and the privacy of her own thoughts. She banged the door so tightly on what happened to her in India – on *The Incident* – that not even the smallest glimmer of that brilliant southern light shows around the edges or through the keyhole.

She shuts her eyes.

She distracts herself, wasting a few moments conjuring up in her mind's eye a stout wooden door with elaborate iron hinges and latch. Heavy bolts are shot home at the top and bottom and she turns a huge old key in the lock.

But then suddenly she obliterates the image.

'Stop it,' she says softly out loud. 'Stop shutting it away.'

After all this time she cannot quite believe this is happening.

Is she really going to open the door and go back inside her memories?

She waits.

An image of the small town floats behind her closed eyes. The strong, unadorned walls of the military compound. The beauty of the ancient buildings in the civilian section. The river running in its deep cleft separating the two halves of the settlement. The trees, the flowers. And, soaring up in the most dramatic of backdrops, the mountains that form the Roof of the World.

In her mind Lily is already back there.

She opens the stout door and walks into her own past.

When Lily Raynor completed her five years' training with St Walburga's Nursing Service – the nuns and the nurses alike known universally as Swans – she was qualified as a battlefield nurse and a midwife. The convergence of two such different areas of medicine was because not a few of the soldiers of the British army serving far from home took their wives and their families with them. Lily was posted to the small barracks town of Pescha, in the far north-east of India, and her first reaction on climbing down from the train was awe at the majesty of her surroundings.

Pescha was a beautiful spot. It had been a small kingdom
for centuries before its monarch had regretfully accepted the
protection of the British Raj, and it had earned a reputation
as a place to go when one was sick, weary, sad or simply
exhausted from the sheer effort of living in the heat, the dirt
and the endless, ceaseless, hurrying, urgent crowds of
humanity in the vast lands to the south. The capital city was
an oasis of verdant lawns, fountains, trees, flowers, some
exquisite old buildings and a brash palace. The surrounding
countryside ranged from the long, deep valley that wound
through the heart of the country to the graceful curves of the
cool foothills and the soaring peaks of the Himalayas to the
north, where India bordered Bhutan. The people were pros-
perous, by the standards of the subcontinent; not wealthy
(except for their royal family, who were ridiculously rich),
but not many people starved to death. The climate wasn't too
bad: summers could be hot, especially in the south of the
country and down in the valley, and winters occasionally
brutal, but the opinion of the Europeans who lived there was
that it could be a lot worse.

The necessity for an army barracks had arisen because of
border strife. Other covetous eyes had lighted upon Pescha, and
neighbouring lords and princes wanted her rich and fertile lands,
which supported the cultivation of rice, tea, timber and opium.
The British army's presence issued the polite reminder that
Pescha belonged to the Pescharese, and that rampaging invaders
were not welcome. The British were the British, however, and
managed to turn the situation to their advantage: empire-builders
are not known for their philanthropy.

It was not until several weeks after her arrival that Lily saw
anything of the country outside the hospital where she spent
her days (and sometimes her nights) and the curtained-off cell
in the big dormitory that was her own little piece of privacy.
Nurses and nuns worked side by side but slept apart, and the
nuns' dormitory was behind a firmly closed door.

The hospital was made up of four long, low buildings around
a central courtyard. All the senior SWNS nurses were nuns; no
matter how good at her job, no lay nurse ever rose to a position
of superiority over a nun. On arrival Lily was still a junior

nurse; by working harder than she had ever worked, she gained her promotion to senior within a year.

The work was varied and it took her out of the hospital and into the distant places where injured or sick soldiers needed medical treatment. North-East India opened up before her eyes as the hard-working little locomotives pulled the medical train up impossible gradients and over rickety trestles high above valleys so deep that it was impossible to see the bottom. In the outlying stations the work was tough and often bloody: she learned to assist a doctor lopping off a man's mangled lower leg without wincing, to extract hideous parasites from pale English flesh without revulsion, to hold a young soldier's hand as he died in agony crying for his mother and keep back her own tears.

If she ever thought about the future it was in vague terms; she imagined doing precisely what she was doing, perhaps one day becoming a senior sister in charge of a whole wing . . .

But then everything changed.

No.

No, no, NO!

Lily's voice screams inside her head, her eyes fly open and she finds herself back in her room in the school in the cold Fens. She has gone back into the past as far as she dared and it is enough. She cannot go further.

But she suspects that this is a crucial moment; a pivotal time in her whole life. That it is now or never.

And she knows she must.

Early in 1879, Lily was sent to assist the army doctor carrying out the health checks on the girls in the chakla. Lily knew about the chaklas, or she thought she did. As she was instructed in her new role, she realized the depth of her ignorance.

The troops of the British army in India were men with the usual male appetites, and, other than the minority whose wives and children were with them, they were single and on six-year placements. It was unrealistic to pretend they would not require the services of prostitutes. The women were procured from the villages; whether by choice or under duress was not made clear.

'Many of these women are near-starving,' said the stern-faced nun giving the lecture, 'and use their bodies in order to survive.'

The army needed its fighting men to be fit. Once in the chakla, the women were examined regularly for signs of disease. Those found with symptoms were sent to the lock hospitals. For the three weeks of their treatment, the women were regularly examined internally.

It was a practical necessity, Lily told herself as she scribbled in her notebook, keeping up with the instructing nun's swift words. Nevertheless, her woman's soul rebelled at the thought of regular internal examinations.

But then the impassive voice of the nun went on to speak of the Contagious Diseases Act.

'In order to ensure a healthy supply of prostitutes,' she said, her face utterly expressionless, 'the law states that all women discovered in the vicinity of army barracks must be detained and examined, and—'

Lily raised her hand and heard herself speak.

'I beg your pardon, Sister, but when you say women, do you mean prostitutes?'

The dark eyes turned to stare at her. 'I mean precisely what I say, Nurse,' she said.

'But – what if a woman has innocent business and is no more a prostitute than—' She had been about to say *than you or I*, but managed to bite back the words.

The nun regarded her silently for a few moments. Then, without answering Lily's stammered question – indeed, with no comment whatsoever – she resumed her lecture.

When Lily entered the medical officer's building adjoining the barracks on the first morning of her new posting, she had convinced herself that the Contagious Diseases Act was there as a sort of safety net; that women were not really grabbed and forcibly examined for no more reason than proximity to the soldiers' quarters.

She was wrong.

The first thing that truly shocked her was how young the women were. Most of them weren't even women: the oldest were perhaps eighteen but the youngest looked barely into puberty.

She endured more than a week of biting back her revulsion and the furious, angry words she longed to utter: 'Treat them with dignity! Be gentle! They are human beings, not animals!'

And then Manda came into the clinic.

Manda was sixteen, frightened, sad and grieving, apparently numb to the indignities perpetrated upon her. Her looks were European, the lustrous dark hair accompanied by pale skin and blue eyes. As Lily tended her – she had open sores that needed treatment morning, noon and evening – Manda gradually broke her silence. At first it was no more than a whispered 'Thank you' when Lily apologized for the pain of the treatment. Then a few muttered words when Lily asked why she was weeping. And, bit by bit, Manda's terrible story emerged.

She had been engaged as the personal maid and companion to the wife of a colonel. She believed that her pale looks had led her to this privileged post, and she was deeply grateful, determined to work hard and give the colonel's wife no cause for complaint.

But then the colonel's junior officer saw Manda. Dazzled by her beauty, he began to court her; perhaps he even fell in love with her. There was talk of marriage, but then someone – in all likelihood the colonel's snob of a wife – managed to impart to the young adjutant that there was 'something a little bit dubious' in Manda's background . . . she might *look* like a European, but apparently there was an Indian grandmother . . .

So the adjutant abandoned the idea of marriage. Manda adored him, so it seemed a pity not to capitalize on that. For a couple of months he bedded her, and then one night when she slipped away to their usual meeting place, he wasn't there.

Shocked, uncomprehending, Manda tried desperately to seek him out. What has happened? she longed to ask. What have I done? She began to haunt the adjutant and, embarrassed, the butt of ribald jokes from his fellow officers, he did not know what to do.

Until an older and more experienced officer told him.

Following the older man's instructions, the young adjutant went to the authorities. He implied Manda was a whore, that she had fallen for him and he'd had her, and now she imagined some sort of attachment between them and would not leave him alone. Manda was promptly taken to the lock hospital and examined. She was found to be free of any of the most prevalent diseases but she had some sores on her vulva that required treatment: contrary to her fond belief, she had not been the sole recipient of the young adjutant's attentions. Utterly bemused, unable to accept that her beautiful loving soldier had told the medical men that she was a whore, Manda retreated into herself.

'Manda is a pretty name,' Lily said one day in a hopeless attempt to raise a smile. 'Is it short for Amanda?'

The girl shook her head. 'No. It is a Hindi name, and it means important.'

Important.

Looking at the girl, fighting to keep the pity from her eyes, Lily thought how ironic that was.

Manda's treatment came to an end. She expected to be sent back to the colonel's house, but the colonel's wife was having none of it. So Manda was sent to the mahaldarni – the madam – who looked her up and down, gave a curt nod and admitted her to the chakla.

Lily, certain there had been a mistake, a misunderstanding, hurried to beg an interview with her chilly, detached superior. Lily was dismissed, her protest waved away.

Some of the nurses and nuns took her aside. 'It is what happens,' one of the senior nuns told her quietly. 'What has been done to your young patient is deeply wrong, but it has the tacit approval of the military authorities and it is backed by the law.'

The army needed to keep its soldiers happy, Lily thought, blind with fury, and to be kept happy the men had to have access to sex. The women with whom they had sex had to be healthy, or else the men would become unfit for work.

Simple. Ruthlessly logical.

But Lily could not let the matter rest.

Finally she was taken aside by the senior army medical officer for the Pescha region.

She heard his firm, fast footsteps coming up behind her in a deserted corridor of the hospital. 'You are making a nuisance of yourself, Nurse Raynor,' he said in glassy public-school accents. 'I must ask you to desist.'

'But Manda isn't—' Lily began.

Then the senior medical man grasped her upper arm, holding it in a painfully tight grip. He leaned down, his mouth against her ear, and hissed, 'I am informed that you have been trying to gain admission to the chakla to see your young friend.'

'Yes indeed, for I am deeply worried about her and I—'

His grip tightened. He didn't like being interrupted.

'To reach the chakla, one must pass close by the barracks,' he said musingly. 'Right by the soldiers' quarters!' he added in feigned wonder, as if it had only just occurred to him. Then, leaning close again, he said, 'If you are seen there again, Nurse, it will be assumed that you are there for the purpose of soliciting, and I am sure you do not need me to tell you what will happen next.'

She almost fainted.

Her legs shook and it seemed as if her knees could no longer hold her up.

No, he didn't need to tell her, for she had seen it for herself – oh, far, far too often! – and she knew.

Arrest. Detention. The rough hands of two or more men stripping her, putting her on the table, her legs in stirrups and the terrible 'steel rape' as the speculum was thrust into her.

Some women fought; Lily had seen them and silently applauded their courage, although resistance led to greater brutality and she had seen a young girl receive a severe injury to her spine.

Would she be brave enough? Would she cry out her innocence? Would it do any good if she did?

The senior medical man released her arm and she slumped against the wall. Her heart was thumping in dread, she could hardly breathe, she wanted to be sick.

He stared down at her, a supercilious smile crossing his handsome face.

Then, slowly, he nodded. Then he walked away.

He knew, just as she did, that she would not protest any more.

*　　*　　*

She could not bear to stay.

She endured a sleepless night, then another, and on the morning of the third day she sought an interview with her superior and said that sickness in the family necessitated her immediate return to England.

She was not allowed to go straight away. She endured two and a half weeks of working under the disapproving, disappointed eyes of nuns and nurses who thought the job was too much for her, that she was giving it up because she couldn't stand the strain of long days, very hard work and little sleep.

She did not dare to tell them the truth.

She lived those days in terror of the senior medical man carrying out his threat. He seemed to appear before her all the time, that same sardonic smile on his face, that expression in the pale blue eyes that seemed to say, *Where's your brave stance now, Nurse? Not so easy to protest on behalf of others when you face the same thing yourself, is it?*

She wouldn't have denied the accusation even if she could. For he was absolutely right.

She endured the long journey home, the endless succession of trains and the troopship, eyes turned inwards so that she saw nothing. Nothing but her own deep shame – sometimes in her nightmares the terrible procedure with which the senior medical officer threatened her had already happened, *was* happening, and she woke screaming and sweating – and her cowardice. Back in England, reeling under the additional blow of discovering her adored Aunt Eliza had died while she was on her way home, she took the necessary steps to end her nursing career.

She was numb with anguish, heavy-hearted, grieving for her aunt. Grieving for the life she had loved.

And she had absolutely no idea what on earth she was going to do next.

It is long after midnight. Lily, cold, unmoving as stone, still sits beside her window.

I have done it, she thinks, and she is shaky and slightly nauseous. I have opened the door, gone back into my past, faced the horror I fled from.

She doesn't know if she is relieved or regretful. She doesn't know *how* she feels; it is too soon.

Slowly she stands up, straightening her stiff muscles. She goes to the bathroom, undresses, puts on her nightdress, turns back the bedclothes. The actions are automatic and she hardly knows what she does.

She lies in bed in the darkness. She is exhausted, both body and mind desperately in need of sleep.

But she doesn't think it will come easily.

If at all.

TWELVE

Back at Kinver Street, Felix finds Marm in his chair by the fire, glass of whisky in his hand, and he responds gratefully to his friend's invitation to join him.

'It is late and you smell of the great outdoors, so I deduce you have—' Marm begins, but Felix interrupts. His mind is so full of what he has discovered that he has little room for anything else and barely registers Marm's words.

'I need you to contact your friend in Chichester again,' he says, taking a huge mouthful of whisky that burns pleasantly as it encounters his tongue and throat.

'Douglas Blackmore?'

'Yes. The Southsea man he put us on to – Michael Nicholls, the one who wrote the piece about the body under the pier – was useless, but I accept that's not your friend Blackmore's fault.'

'Good of you,' murmurs Marm. 'What is it you want me to ask him?'

'Whether he can dig up anything about the death of a woman found near Havant on the LB & SCR a year ago last autumn.'

Marm sits perfectly still, frowning slightly, staring into the fire. Felix might have suspected he hadn't heard or was ignoring the question, but he has lived with Marm for long enough to recognize his thinking face. Marm, it appears, is capable of going inside himself and rummaging around in the great reference library in his head until he comes to the very item he requires. Sometimes the retrieval is swift; sometimes, as now, it takes a little longer.

Then Marm puts down his glass, holds up his hand with the forefinger raised and says, 'Wait there.'

He goes through into his own room and to the big old desk beneath the window. He delves into a drawer, then, with a soft sound of impatience – 'Of course, *over* a year ago,' he mutters

– moves to a tall filing cabinet. He flips quickly through files, then, with a satisfied 'A-*ha!*', comes back to the fireplace.

He indicates the thick file he has brought back with him. 'My Lost Women file,' he says.

Yes. Felix ought to have thought of this, for he is fully aware of its existence.

For Marmaduke Smithers is a crusader on behalf of women who suffer suspicious deaths; specifically, poor women, unimportant women, prostitutes; any woman whose demise has not, in Marm's opinion, been treated with sufficient seriousness by the investigating authorities. He has been angry for a long time and, the very first time Felix met him, complained furiously that his editors constantly cut his articles about such women and deleted all the speculation and tub-thumping because it wasn't what readers wanted to hear about. Since the case last year that was the cause of that initial meeting, however, public interest has been roused and the public conscience pricked, and Marm's pieces have of late been in some demand.

He has kept his Lost Women file faithfully for years, adding cuttings and notes of his own speculations on each woman's fate, and quite often since moving into Kinver Street, Felix's final image as he retires for the night is of Marm sitting by the last of the fire, intent on the newest case in his file.

For there are always new cases.

'Here it is,' Marm says softly. 'Havant and the railway line rang a bell. Knew I'd seen or heard something about that one.' He takes a sip of whisky, his eyes flipping rapidly from side to side as he reads the cutting and his own notes. 'The body was that of a woman in early middle age and the incident occurred when you said, back in the late autumn before last. She was modestly dressed in good-quality but far from new clothes, reasonably well fed and in adequate health if a little on the thin side, according to the post-mortem.' Marm looks up at Felix. 'She wasn't a prostitute, there were no signs of violence or ill-usage that could not be explained by the fall from the train, so I filed it but did not pursue it.'

'She was a school teacher,' Felix says quietly.

Marm gives him a sharp look. 'I can't fight for all of them,' he says curtly. 'Besides, the coroner's verdict was accidental

death. They think she might have believed the train was stopping at Havant whereas it went straight on. It was late, not
many passengers and nobody was waiting, and the driver
decided to risk it.'

'She was an intelligent woman!' Felix protests. 'She surely
understood that you don't alight from a moving train!
Besides, if that had been the case she'd have been found at
Havant, not – how many miles did you say it was down the
track?'

'Two and a half,' Marm admits with obvious reluctance,
glancing back at the cutting. 'But she could have been dragged!'

He is sounding heated now, and Felix realizes his distress is
due to guilt. But he's right, Felix thinks, he can't save everyone,
and he does as much as any man could for the causes he does
espouse. The poor bugger looks exhausted, and he has a nasty
cough.

Filled with affection for his friend, he says, 'I'm sorry, Marm.
I know you can't pursue every instance of a woman's death
that could be murder but was probably an accident.'

Marm huffs a bit but seems to have recovered his equanimity.
Then he says, 'Who was she?' and Felix tells him.

'How did they identify her?' he mutters.

'*Did* they?' Felix asks, then, immediately answering his own
question, 'Yes, of course they did, because someone went to
the hostel in Cambridge asking about her belongings.'

Marm has gone back to the cutting again. 'Ah, yes, I see.
She had a little purse hidden away in an inside pocket,' he
says. 'Her name had been written carefully in ink, and there
was a small amount of money, her train ticket and a piece of
paper with the address of the hostel neatly printed in what is
described as a lady's hand.' He turns his gaze to the fire. 'Hmm.'
He sounds thoughtful.

'What are you thinking?' Felix demands.

'I'm wondering,' Marm says slowly, 'what happened to her
possessions. She'd have had a handbag at least, and possibly a
valise as well.'

'But there's no mention of them?'

'Not only is there no mention but the coroner remarks upon
the lack,' Marm replies. 'Says it's a shabby sort of thing, when

a woman dies in such a dreadful accident and someone sees fit to steal her belongings. The police searched the line, you see, and the train, but found nothing.'

'If she was killed,' Felix says, the thought developing even as he speaks, 'then wouldn't the perpetrator make quite sure there would be no way of identifying her? He'd have taken the handbag and valise because they'd have been easy to spot, but he must have missed the little purse.'

And Marm, looking at him with the light of battle kindled in his eyes, says, 'Yes.'

On Saturday morning Felix is at 3, Hob's Court soon after half-past eight. He is only too aware that in Lily's absence it is up to him to keep the Bureau running, and that three days have now passed since his brief visit on Wednesday.

There is a promising amount of post, some of it still where it fell from the postman's hands on the mat just inside the door, some of it placed on Felix's desk, undoubtedly by Mrs Clapper. Ripping open the half-dozen envelopes, Felix is happy to find a cheque from a satisfied but dilatory client who should have settled up two months ago and a thank-you letter from the fiancé of the jealous young woman who accused him of running an opium den. (*She broke off the engagement*, the letter says, *told me all the hullaballoo was too much for her nerves, which was rich since it was her started it* – except that you did really by kissing her sister under the mistletoe, Felix thinks – *and I'm now courting her sister, who is a great deal easier-going and hence this letter.*) The remaining items are publicity circulars, which Felix chucks in the waste-paper basket. He puts the cheque aside for paying into the bank later, files the thank-you letter in the appropriate place and then wanders through into Lily's inner sanctum.

On her desk is a folded sheet of paper addressed in a firm hand to Miss Lily, the writing heavily underlined, as is the PRIVATE in block capitals in the top left corner.

Felix suspects it is from Mrs Clapper, and his instinct is to respect her request for privacy and leave the note for Lily on her return. But then he reasons that the Bureau is his respon- sibility just now, that Mrs Clapper's communication may be urgent, that it could even be to do with a new client, and that such speculations are pointless anyway since he knows full well he's going to unfold the paper and see what Mrs Clapper has to say.

It is just as well he does.

> Miss Lily I do not like to bother you with this and I know the Boorow is your business and it is not my place to interfeer but when Persons of a certain Type come knocking on the door demanding to see Mr Felix and won't take no for an answer when told he is not here and I do not know when he will be and then tell me I have to give out his address when I know full well that is not allowed well it is TOO MUCH and I feel I must say something specially seeing as there was a smell of alcohol and also flowery perfume and she was dressed in evening clothes seemingly well I have to speak my mind hoping you will understand yours faithfully B Clapper Mrs.

Mrs Clapper's handwriting is that of the school girl she was several decades ago, round, clear but largely unformed and she has no use for commas. Felix speculates on what B might stand for . . . Beryl? Bertha? Bernadette? Bianca? He grins at the unlikeliness of Bianca, but you never know, and—

Then, furious with himself for his time-wasting and his inattention, he realizes who this perfume-and-alcohol-smelling visitor dressed in what looked to Mrs Clapper like evening clothes must have been.

When was the visit?

He scans the letter again, searching for a date, and there it is at the top of the page: Thursday noon.

The day before yesterday.

Felix replaces the folded page exactly where he found it, collects the cheque from his own desk, throws himself into his outdoor clothes and runs out of the office.

He stops only to pay in the cheque and then takes a tram to the West End. Only when he is trundling along the King's Road does it occur to him that Violetta is not a morning person and it is still not ten o'clock. He curses under his breath for a good half-minute, then works out a plan of action. He knows where she is performing at present, having met her outside the Aphrodite Theatre only last Monday, and so he will go there first. It's Saturday, he reassures himself, and there is certain to be a matinée performance, so Violetta will surely arrive at the theatre in good time and maybe even around noon, which is only a little over two hours away.

He is right and there is a matinée today.

He is wrong about Violetta arriving in good time; or possibly his idea of what constitutes good time differs significantly from hers. He goes for a cup of coffee to fill in the time until midday, stands outside the theatre for an hour watching the comings and goings, becomes so cold that he cannot feel his hands or feet and returns to the small eating house for a hasty bowl of soup with bread and cheese, all the while peering out of the window at the stage door, and he is back at his post outside when Violetta finally turns up at ten to two for the half-past two performance.

'Felix, come in, I want to talk to you!' she calls out over her shoulder, gliding elegantly up the steps to the door. She exchanges a few muttered words with the heavily built man in the cubicle just inside, indicating Felix and presumably saying it's all right to let him in, then sweeps off down a dark and dank little corridor smelling of very old sweat and, strangely, also carnations and curry, turns left and right as she weaves a way through a maze of passages until finally she flings open the door of a small room with a table and chair set before a large mirror, a sofa covered with cushions and a thick blanket and a rack on which there are several brightly coloured outfits which Felix guesses are Violetta's costumes.

'Sit,' she says, pointing to the sofa, 'we'll have to talk while I prepare. *Maudie!*' The last word is yelled so loudly that Felix's ears ring, and before the echoes die a small woman dressed entirely in shades of brown comes scurrying in, clean towels and what looks like a voluminous white petticoat over her arm. She notices Felix on the sofa but then totally ignores him – perhaps she is used to strange men in Violetta's dressing room

– and proceeds to set out potions in pots of various sizes and a jam jar stuck with make-up brushes.

'I came to see you,' Violetta says, a note of accusation in her tone. 'You weren't there.'

'No, I'm sorry, I had leads to follow up on the coast and then a meeting with Lily.'

'She's all right?' Violetta's huge and beautiful brown eyes meet his in her mirror.

'Yes, she's quite all right.' He manages to quell the instant of fear he feels. 'What did you want to see me about?'

Again she meets his eyes, this time sliding her own in a sideways glance at her dresser. 'Oh, it'll keep till later. If you have time, you could watch the performance, and then you can take me out to tea afterwards.'

He says courteously, 'There's nothing I'd like more.'

He would have said if asked that spending close on two hours sitting in a crowded theatre watching a lurid melodrama (about an abandoned woman searching for her lost daughter, taken from her in infancy by her husband who, unbeknownst to the woman, was secretly a Russian prince who needed a daughter to offer in marriage as a pawn to further his own ambitions) was the last thing he would either want or enjoy. But he had reckoned without Violetta da Rosa's skill as an actress, her luminous beauty and her enduring sexual appeal, despite the growing tally of her years, for virtually every man in the audience, most definitely including him.

He joins in the enthusiastic applause, and Violetta is brought back to the stage for three curtain calls, modestly bowing and wiping a surreptitious tear from her eye as she nods and smiles. 'You dear, *dear* people,' she exclaims with apparent spontaneity over the limelights, 'how very welcome you make me feel!'

'We love you, Violetta!' a man shouts, and the cry is taken up all round the theatre. Several bouquets are thrown on to the stage, and with grace Violetta picks them up, pressing some roses to her face with an expression of delight. 'They're mine!' yells a man two rows in front of Felix, turning round to those sitting nearby with a triumphant expression, as if the audience's darling having selected his flowers for close attention somehow marks him out as someone special.

The applause fades away as it becomes clear Violetta is not going to return a fourth time, and presently the theatre begins to empty until Felix is sitting there alone. He is about to go and see if Violetta is ready to leave when he hears hurried footsteps from behind him and, turning, sees her approaching. 'Come on, I want my tea, I'm spitting feathers,' she says, and, standing up, he offers his arm and escorts her out of the theatre and on to the street.

'Now, I've been asking questions on your behalf,' Violetta says as soon as they are seated in the discreet and charming little tea room she has brought him to and she has ordered tea and cakes, 'so get out your notebook and your little silver pencil and listen.'

'Questions about what?' he says, obeying.

She leans closer and says very quietly, 'The MacKilliver twins, or, to be precise, Cameron MacKilliver.'

'Go on.' He suspects that she has something good for him; there is a strong sense of excitement thrumming through her.

'I've been talking to Old Turnip-Head – Freddie – again. It was at a party on Wednesday night, after the show, and—'

'It was lucky you bumped into him,' Felix interrupts.

She sends him a scathing look. 'Luck had nothing to do with it, young Felix,' she says. 'I made sure he'd be there. The party was thrown by a good friend of mine and I suggested she invite Turnip-Head and she said good idea because he's on his own at present and she always has a pretty protégée or two around in need of a rich benefactor.'

It is his turn to give her a meaningful look, but she shrugs. 'Oh, come on, you know how it works,' she says sharply. 'Men like Freddie Fanshawe-Turnbull prey on lovely girls young enough to be their daughters or granddaughters – although Freddie's not nearly as bad as some, he doesn't lust after children – so why shouldn't the girls get something out of it?'

'That wasn't what I meant, I—' But Felix isn't sure he can explain his sudden sense of revulsion. In fact it seems to be the very ways of the world that dismay him and that is far too big a topic for a teatime conversation. Besides his companion has important information for him. 'Sorry. Please, go on.'

'I cornered Freddie and we embarked on one of those long, rambling chats that people who've known each other for years enjoy, catching up with what they've been up to, exchanging news of mutual friends, and I made sure to keep his glass topped up. By the time I steered us round to the MacKillivers, it seemed like a natural next step in the conversation and he didn't suspect a thing when I pressed him.'

'What do you mean, pressed him?'

'About Cameron. Mortimer's the twin who is Freddie's chum – they've been friends for years, and as I told you before, Freddie regularly goes up to Findhorn Hall for shooting and fishing – and being so close to the one implies knowledge of the other. Cameron shuts himself away at Findhorn Hall but he also—'

'He also goes to stay with an old schoolfellow. Yes, you told me that before too.'

She gives a nod of approval. 'Glad to know you were paying attention. It was that very friend I was pumping Freddie about, and it appears that this man's family's estate was close by Findhorn Hall and the two of them, him and Cameron, spent much of their early childhood on boyish larks together and renewed the adventures each time they came home for the school holidays. It sounds from what Freddie said as though they were both misfits – as I mentioned before, Cameron was odd from the start – so in all likelihood they suited each other well.'

Felix is interested, but he cannot see the relevance of Cameron MacKilliver's boyhood to the missing girls and the two dead women. Except, of course – and he recognizes that it is an important and surely significant exception – that Cameron is a member of the Band of Angels, who are patrons of Shardlowes School. He returns his full attention to Violetta.

And he sees instantly that, astute woman that she is, she has noticed the moment's absence. 'It *is* relevant, trust me,' she says softly.

He smiles. 'Sorry. Please, continue.'

'From what Freddie was saying – or *muttering*, because he was well into his cups by this time and he'd lowered his voice as well, which you'll understand in a moment – it sounds as if there have been incidents up near the MacKilliver ancestral home.' She pauses – she is an actress after all, Felix reminds himself – then says, 'Whispers concerning young girls. Rumours of people being paid to keep quiet.' She taps a finger to the side of her nose.

'*What?*' Felix hisses. 'Recently? But surely this should be reported and—'

'*Hush!*' she hisses back, the short syllable accompanied by a dig in the ribs from her sharp elbow. 'No, of *course* not recently – this was years ago, and Freddie said it was all muttered tales and rumours spread behind the closed door of village hovels. He says there was no truth in them, or if there was it amounted to no more than a pair of randy young lads pushing themselves too far on village girls.'

'So why are you telling me?' he demands crossly.

She glances to left and right, but the people at nearby tables are intent on their own conversations, and the noise level is in any case too loud for easy eavesdropping. 'Because there's something wrong with Cameron,' she whispers. 'The other place he goes when he's not at Findhorn Hall is to see a doctor, who—'

'A doctor who understands men like him.' The memory of her voice speaking those words sounds clear in his head. 'Yes. What did you mean by that? What sort of doctor?'

'One for the mentally ill,' she says quietly. 'The place where poor old Cameron is sent when his madness overcomes him is a lunatic asylum.'

'Good grief,' Felix whispers back, fighting his fear and revulsion. In common, he suspects, with almost everyone else, he has a horror of mental illness.

Violetta glances at him. 'Treatment has advanced of late,' she says coolly. 'It's not naked idiots fighting their chains in their filthy cells for the Sunday entertainment of gawping visitors like the Bedlam of old, you know.' Her tone is harsh.

'No, I suppose not,' he agrees, although in truth he has no idea what goes on behind an asylum's forbidding walls. Then, his curiosity overcoming him, he asks, 'What's the matter with him?'

'Freddie's not sure,' she replies, calmer again now. 'I told you how he – Cameron – used to play with dolls?' Felix nods. 'Well, Freddie reckons something in Cameron stopped at that age – when he was obsessed by his dollies – and that it's to do with losing the little baby sister.'

'And being an unwilling witness to his mother's childbearing and grief,' Felix murmurs.

Violetta looks at him in surprise. 'Yes,' she agrees. She raises her eyebrows in a silent question.

'It's what I thought when you told me before,' he replies. 'If Cameron was close to his mother, he'd be sad for her and probably very frightened, yet not understand why she was in such profound distress.' Then abruptly he adds, 'But hundreds – thousands – of children go through the same experiences and they don't all turn into lunatics.'

'Cameron's not a lunatic in the strict sense of the word,' she corrects him, 'because his moods are not dependent on the moon.'

'You know what I mean,' he grumbles.

She sighs. 'I do. From what Freddie knows – which isn't much, but I suspect Mortimer confides in him when it all becomes too much to bear alone – Cameron descends into a state where he believes he has to *save* people. At such times he sees growing up as some sort of expulsion from the child-hood paradise, and he becomes very agitated and distressed, crying out that he's been singled out to save them, to keep them from the horrors and the perils that await in the adult world.'

'He has never married, has he?'

'No.' She smiles sadly. 'I very much doubt he has even kissed a woman in a sexual way since those putative boyhood fumblings – if indeed there was any truth in the rumours – nor even held a pretty white hand.'

'But he's not—' Felix hesitates.

She looks at him again. 'No. Not that either, although there has always been talk about—' Abruptly she shuts her mouth.

'About Mortimer?' Felix suggests. 'But you said he'd been married?'

She gives him look that says eloquently that he is being naive and, judging by the way she turns her head away and does not

speak, he thinks he's guessed right and that Mortimer MacKilliver
is rumoured to prefer his own sex.

Breaking quite a long silence, Felix says, 'My instincts
tell me that the nature of Cameron MacKilliver's state of mind
– of his sickness – must be connected to what is going on at
Shardlowes School.'

Violetta nods. 'I feel the same way. But how *can* it be?'
she adds. 'It's not as if the Band of Angels have anything to
do with the schools they help to fund, other than stumping up
the money. Cameron has probably never been to Shardlowes
in his life, nor any of the other schools, and it's doubtful he
even attends the Band's meetings unless he really has to. In
fact,' she concludes, 'other than increasingly rare visits
here to London, spells in the asylum and going to stay with
his old boyhood friend, he doesn't engage in life outside
Findhorn Hall at all.' She turns to Felix, the frustration evident
in her face.

Felix nods absently. He is thinking hard, and the conclusion
to which he is rapidly arriving is not welcome at all for it
involves going away again, and considerably further than to
the south coast, at the very time when, for some reason he's
not sure he wants to explore, his concerns for Lily's safety are
rapidly multiplying.

She's in a sedate girls' boarding school, he tells himself,
what harm can she possibly come to?

She's there for a purpose and she's good at her job, the other
part of his mind replies, *which means she'll be asking questions,
trying to find things out, and a girl and a woman have already
been killed for doing just that.*

*But Lily is neither a seventeen-year-old girl nor a frightened
middle-aged spinster English teacher*, he protests. *She is astute,
she knows how to be careful, she—*

She almost died in the course of your last major case, the
relentless voice in his head says, and it is loud in its triumph.

He feels a soft, warm hand take hold of his and squeeze it.
'You're worried about her, aren't you?' Violetta says softly.
'That boss of yours?'

'Yes.' There's no point denying it as Violetta seems able to
read his thoughts.

'Then get on with doing what you have to do,' Violetta says firmly, 'but not before you warn her.'

'Warn her of what?' he asks helplessly. 'I don't *know!*'

She nods her understanding. 'Just tell her to take more care?' she suggests. 'Say she's putting herself in danger by making enquiries?'

'She knows that already,' he says.

'Tell her again,' Violetta says relentlessly. 'It's your duty, young Felix.' Her velvety brown eyes on him are compassionate. She adds softly, 'You'll never forgive yourself if anything happens to her.'

Afternoon is turning to evening when he emerges from the tea room: alone, for Violetta understands his sudden urgency and sends him on his way with an admirable lack of fuss, shooing him out and saying she'll see to the bill.

He makes his way as fast as he can back to Chelsea. But his destination is not the World's End Bureau's office and he runs straight past the end of Hob's Court and down to the river.

He's not sure the object of his flying mission will be there; not even sure how to go about finding him. But it's vital he does, so as his racing feet thunder along the towpath he says a silent prayer. The prayer is not answered as definitely as he'd have liked, but he is able to leave a message, and the man who undertakes to deliver it appears calmly confident that he will find the intended recipient in the fairly near future.

Felix wishes fiercely (and for reasons he really doesn't want to think about) that he didn't have to be doing this; that he could carry out the task himself. But he knows it will take too long; that giving in and doing what he so much wants to do will mean a long delay, and some deep instinct tells him there is no time for delay. Besides, what would be his excuse for turning up? He would risk revealing the truth, and she would be furious . . .

Felix races back the way he has come, calls briefly at Kinver Street and within not much over an hour he is on the night train departing from King's Cross.

THIRTEEN

ily is heavy-eyed on Saturday morning, still shaken by the trauma of returning to her past and what happened there. It is not solely the horror with which she was threatened, she reflects miserably as she washes and dresses, but also her shame, for in her panic and fear she thought only to save herself and she ran away.

She cannot bear to think what has happened to the exquisitely beautiful Manda.

She goes through the first of her morning duties with barely half the required attention, only pulled back to herself when Matron rebukes her sharply for almost dropping the tea tray, not having put it down on to Matron's crowded little bedside table with enough care.

'Not sickening too, are you?' Matron demands, pausing to cough. 'Can't have you abed too, Nurse, so you'd better not be.'

'I am well, Matron,' Lily replies.

Matron is still staring at her, eyes narrowed critically. 'You don't look it,' she remarks.

That has nothing to do with sickening for a cold, Lily thinks. 'How are you today, Matron?' she says, deflecting Matron's attention from herself.

'I thought I was better, but this cough still troubles me,' Matron replies. Lily, close to her as she straightens the bedclothes, can hear the phlegm bubbling in Matron's chest.

'I will bring another bowl of hot water and inhalant,' Lily says.

It will help to ease the congestion, she thinks. At least she hopes so, for if not Matron may well develop pneumonia, and then—

Don't think about that, she tells herself sternly. *Not yet.*

She spends a busy morning treating a steady stream of girls with cold symptoms, but none is as unwell as Matron.

Just before lunch she is surprised to receive a visit from Miss Carmichael.

'I apologize for not having come to see you before, Nurse,' the headmistress says, her eyes sweeping round the treatment room as if hunting for signs of laziness or neglect. Lily, who has just finished tidying and knows the room is immaculate, stands with her hands folded, waiting to see what Miss Carmichael wants.

'You have had a busy week,' she says presently. 'The school does not usually have so many patients for our Matron and her assistant to treat.'

'I prefer to be busy,' Lily replies.

Miss Carmichael nods. 'Quite.' Then, barely pausing for breath, she goes on, 'I do not know if you are aware of this, for tomorrow is the first Sunday you will be spending with us, but it is customary for Matron's assistant to attend church with the school before seeing to any patients who cannot wait until Monday. We take seriously the Lord's admonition to keep holy the Sabbath Day.' She gives a little nod of self-congratulation. 'However, after luncheon it is also our custom to take a short time for ourselves, and accordingly you may have the afternoon off.' She is looking at Lily as if expecting her to sink to her knees in gratitude, but Lily refrains, simply nodding her understanding.

'Should you wish to leave School,' Miss Carmichael goes on, 'Eddy and the trap are at your disposal, allowing of course for any arrangements already made with him by myself and Miss Dickie and the teaching staff.'

'Of course,' Lily echoes faintly.

Miss Carmichael sends her a cold look, then turns and walks stiffly off down the passage.

Saturday afternoon passes slowly and Lily reflects on the perversity of life: just when she would like to be rushed off her feet so she doesn't have time to think, she has nothing to do.

The day is very cold, but the sun is shining and so she sets out for a walk. Several girls are out in the grounds, playing a hectic game on a broad lawn under Miss Blytheway's supervision, and there is a lot of laughter. Noticing a little pavilion set further along the path, Lily strolls up to it.

She is not the only occupant: Marigold Dunbar-Lea is sitting inside, legs tucked under her, a thick cloak pulled tightly around her, its hood covering her bright hair, and snuggled under a heavy woollen rug.

'I cannot run and join in, Nurse,' she greets Lily, 'but I do like to watch.'

'What is the game?' Lily asks, sitting down beside her.

'It's called Wave-me-Free, and you have to go and hide, and when the person who is the Catcher catches you, you have to go to that tree' – she points to a magnificent oak tree, the width of its vast trunk suggesting great age – 'until one of the other Hiders comes out of hiding and waves to you, and then you can go and hide again too, only of course the Hider waving to you mustn't be seen by the Catcher or they have to stand by the tree. See?'

'Yes.' Lily watches the girls out on the lawn, who are red-cheeked and panting, shrieking and laughing as they pop out of the bushes and the shrubbery, trying to wave before they are seen. Miss Blytheway is dashing around and laughing as enthusiastically as any of her pupils, and Lily admires her for making the daily exercise such fun.

Presently she turns to Marigold. 'How is your foot today?'

'Better, thank you Nurse,' Marigold replies. 'The cream you used really helped, and as you told me, I put more on this morning.' She grins. 'The other girls wanted some because they all love the scent!'

'I'm pleased,' Lily says. She adds tentatively, 'Is Green Dormitory a pleasant place?' *And are you happy in it?* is what she really wants to know.

'Oh, yes!' Marigold says fervently. 'We comfort and reassure each other when we get scared, and we all look after Chandra because she's Indian and she gets very homesick, so we try to cheer her up and give her things from our tuck boxes if we have stuff to spare and we let her read out huge extracts from the long letters her mother sends her, only they're in her own language and she's not very good at quick translation so it gets a bit tedious actually, and we care about each other, we're like a group of sisters.'

When we get scared.

Now why, Lily wonders uneasily, do these young girls get scared?

It is something she must think about, for these words come as no surprise.

Marigold's mention of correspondence from home reminds Lily of what Marigold said about letters from her own mother, and how she failed to respond to Marigold's specific questions. There had been something about a jade tiger called Claud . . .

'I expect you all receive letters and parcels,' she says.

Marigold shrugs. 'A few,' she admits grudgingly. Then, her voice slightly brighter, 'I'm not sure who she is, but there's someone who leaves things for me with the kitchen maid. Food parcels, with things like Victoria sponges and rock cakes. They're not much good but it's nice of her. I think she knows my family,' she adds offhandedly.

'That must make you feel special. Does it not?' she prompts when Marigold doesn't reply.

Marigold is picking at a frayed edge of the blanket and merely nods.

Lily recalls Marigold's behaviour yesterday. She is wondering how to encourage her to talk about whatever is worrying her when abruptly Marigold bursts out, 'They came to England, Father and Mother!'

'They – but I thought it was a long time since you had seen them?' But then she has a sudden memory of Matron mentioning a visit in the previous September.

'I *know*, I wanted to tell you because I knew that's what you thought, and you've been very kind to me and it felt bad to let you believe an untruth, but I— Oh, Nurse, it's *awful*, and I know I've probably got in a muddle and I've misunderstood and I'm being stupid – people *always* think I'm stupid because of how I talk and how I walk, but I'm not, I'm *not*, and—'

She pauses for breath, and Lily reaches for her hand. Taking advantage of the temporary cessation of Marigold's distressed outpourings, she says quietly, '*I* don't think you are anything of the sort, Marigold. I think you are a particularly intelligent and astute girl, and I am quite sure someone as clever as you knows what astute means.'

'Yes,' Marigold mutters. She sniffs, and wipes her nose on her woolly glove.

'Now that we have established that,' Lily goes on, 'I shall add that I perceive you are distressed, that something has happened that disturbs you, and that you are wondering whether this something is real or in your imagination. If it is the latter, then you will feel foolish mentioning it. If the former, you will feel guilty if you do not share it with someone who may be able to help.'

Marigold is looking at her wide-eyed. 'How did you *know*?' she breathes. 'That's *exactly* how I feel!'

Lily smiles modestly. 'Experience,' she replies. Then, still holding Marigold's hand, she says, 'You can tell me if you like, although of course you don't have to.'

Marigold shoots her a swift glance. 'I've been wanting to tell you ever since I met you. I felt you were – that you would—' She stops, her cheeks reddening in embarrassment.

Lily gives her a moment to recover her composure.

Then Lily says calmly, 'Sometimes just speaking our worries to another person helps us to see them for what they really are.'

Marigold is silent for some time. Then she says in a rush, 'They came to England, Daddy and Mother, last autumn. I have three younger brothers, Roger, Raymond and Rafe, and a little sister called Rosemary but she's still a baby. Roger was seven last year and it was time he went to a good preparatory school' – Lily hears the voice of a parent in the child's words – 'and they brought him to England to go to Daddy's old school, and when they'd done that they came here to see me, but it was a *very* short visit indeed although that *truly* wasn't their fault as they had to hurry to catch their boat and I'm sure they'd have liked it to have been longer and Daddy said it was a shame it was so brief and it would have been simply marvellous if it could have been longer because we haven't seen each other since I was sent away from India when I was nearly four to come here to be treated for my leg and my lip and everything and – and—' But her tears are overcoming her and she cannot go on.

Lily lets go of the small hand and instead puts her arm round Marigold, drawing her close. Responding instantly to the gesture, Marigold turns into Lily's chest and buries her face, her body shaking with her sobs.

Presently Lily says, 'It is so painful, and I understand, and indeed it is a pity that they could not have spared more time, but sadly ships sail when *they* want to and not when—'

But Marigold is struggling to sit up, pushing tear-damp hair out of her eyes, staring up at Lily with an expression of deep distress.

'Oh, but you don't *understand*!' she cries wildly.

'Then tell me,' Lily says quietly.

Marigold gulps a couple of times. 'Do you remember, yesterday I said about Mother not responding to things I said?'

'I do. She didn't answer when you referred to Claud and when he was going to kiss you.'

'That was just a silly, babyish game,' Marigold says dismissively. 'But it's what it *means* that's important! Oh, oh, don't you see?'

'I—'

But Marigold is into her stride now. 'She doesn't respond when I try to play the Claud game with her in our letters just like she never responds to everything else, to all the little things I remember from when I was very small, and they think I don't realize, they think I'm just being silly like they're always saying I am, and childish, and that I can't possibly remember so clearly from back then because I was only an infant and far too young to understand, and now they think I can't possibly have noticed, not in a million billion years, because I'm *stupid*' – she spits out the hated word – 'and I don't count.'

Feeling a chill around her heart, Lily says very softly, 'What do they think you haven't noticed, Marigold?'

For some moments Marigold sits staring up at her, as if even now, having gone so far, she can't quite bring herself to reveal what it is that is distressing her so profoundly. But then she straightens up, squares her small shoulders and says, 'I do not believe that woman is my mother.'

After a couple of changes of train, Felix is finally ejected onto the small platform of a minute station far out in the lonely chill

of the north somewhere between Forres and Nairn, early on
Sunday morning. The air is biting, the sky high above is pale
blue and mist partially obscures the landscape. He has spent a
long and uncomfortable night, he has managed at most an
hour and a half of sleep, he is stiff and very hungry and he is
wondering why on earth he is here and what exactly he hopes
to achieve.

A wizened, shrivelled clerk takes his ticket, and Felix wonders
if he always looks like that or if he has been shrunk by the
intense cold. In answer to Felix's query concerning Findhorn
Hall, he stares blankly and silently for some moments before
jerking his head to the right. Then he disappears back inside
his booth and slams the door. Felix hears the sound of a bolt
being shot.

Reflecting on his warm and open-hearted welcome to
Scotland, he pulls his scarf up over his nose and mouth – the
air feels like ice – and trudges on his way.

In the Sabbath quiet he heads off down the narrow little
lane, which is hardly more than a track, its surface compacted
mud with two deep, parallel indentations where wheels run.
There is sea to his right and before him the line of a stream or
small river snaking its way down from the higher ground inland.
An enormous house looms up out of the sea fret ahead and to
the right, and as he draws nearer he makes out a stone wall
high enough that not even a tall man could see over it, in a fine
state of repair. The track converges with the line of the wall,
and presently he comes to a pair of strong iron gates.

Beside the right-hand gatepost there is a letter box – this
house is obviously important enough to have its own – and set
into the same gatepost is a neat rectangle of slate into which
is incised *Findhorn Hall.*

The gates are locked. Felix peers through the bars and sees
a well-tended drive leading to the semicircular opening in
front of the huge house, which is a monstrosity in dark stone
with towers and turrets, battlements and buttresses. There is
a carriage porch in the middle of the front wall, and Felix can
just make out a pair of stout doors, black-painted and banded
with iron.

Smoke issues from several of the chimneys and muffled

sounds of early morning activity carry on the still air, the sharp edges dulled in the mist. Clearly there is somebody at home . . .

He waits, uncertain. There is a heavy black-painted iron bell pull beside the gates, which would undoubtedly summon someone to see who he is and what he wants. But what will he say in reply? *I'm a private investigator and I'm here to ask exactly what sort of madness affects Cameron MacKilliver and what significance, if any, there is to the fact that he and his brother are members of the Band of Angels and the Band of Angels support a girls' school in the Fens where girls have gone missing and two women have been killed?*

Any manservant worth the cost of his employ, Felix reflects, would refuse him entry at best and give him a good kicking for his temerity at worst.

He hears the sound of a pony and trap, and someone is whistling cheerfully. Turning, he watches as a red-faced man, well wrapped up and wearing a huge knitted hat, pulls up the pony, jumps down and unloads a crate of groceries.

'Good morning!' Felix says, mildly surprised that there is a delivery on a Sunday. The inhabitants of Findhorn Hall must be good customers. 'Are you going in?'

The man laughs shortly. 'Not me. The dogs will be out. I leave the deliveries here' – he indicates a low wooden platform beside the gates – 'and someone comes out for them.'

'Dogs?' Felix echoes.

'Aye. Couple of wolfhounds and a mastiff.'

'They don't like visitors, then?'

The man gives him a slightly suspicious look. 'They like those they invite well enough, but that's the reason they don't welcome the *un*invited ones,' he explains after a moment. Leaning closer, he says, 'Lords and dukes and the like, you understand. Even royalty, on occasion. Good fishing, and the moorland's fine for deer and grouse.' He climbs back on to the trap. 'No guests just now, and the brothers are from home,' he adds, jerking his thumb at the crate he has just deposited. 'I'd be leaving three or four times that much if they were in residence.' He eyes Felix uncertainly for a further moment, then says, 'You could ask up at Covesea Abbey, up the road there.'

He points. 'Someone might help you, the Stirlings and the MacKillivers being long acquainted.'

Then he slaps the reins on the pony's backside and they trot away.

Felix is still staring up at Findhorn Hall. The idea of a houseful of servants in a house where the masters are absent is tantalizing, but Felix has no excuse for demanding entry and asking intrusive questions and he knows he'd receive short shrift. Berating himself for coming so far on nothing more than an impulse, he sets off down the track towards the stone bridge he can see ahead where it crosses the river.

From the summit of the bridge's hump he spots another house, to his left and inland from the small clutch of dwellings that huddle round a little harbour over to the right. This too is a sizeable building, set in open parkland into which the surrounding moorland is making steady encroachments, and he assumes it is Covesea Abbey. Home of the Stirling family . . . The name is familiar, and he knows he has heard it recently. He decides to let his mind work away on puzzling out where this was without any conscious help from him, and carries on walking. Coming to a bifurcation in the track, he follows the delivery man's advice, takes the left-hand fork and heads towards the big house.

He can see even from a hundred yards away that this house has not been cared for in the way that Findhorn Hall has. Approaching, he wonders if anything at all in the way of maintenance has been done for years. The drive is full of stringy grass and weeds, and there are deep potholes filled with half-frozen puddles. The house is infested with ivy, there is a hole in the roof, and the few visible patches of stonework are darkly stained where water from leaking gutters has penetrated. Gates lie open between the remnants of what was once a fence and one is almost off its hinges.

There is a rotting wooden board hanging from the right-hand gate. Felix makes out most of the letters of *Covesea Abbey*.

The building is too dilapidated, and its outlines too fudged by ivy, to detect if it really was once an abbey, or whether a newer construction was erected after the demise of the religious foundation. Encouraged by the wide-open gates, hoping the delivery man was right and someone here really will help, Felix walks on determinedly to the battered old front door.

There is no bell pull here, only a heavy iron knocker that has all but seized up. Felix manages to raise it, creating a shower of rust, and he bangs it down on the ancient wood a couple of times. He waits, listening, and presently hears brisk footsteps. The door is opened – the creak it makes rises to a high-pitched sound that pains the ears – and a man stares out at him. He is in late middle age, lean, with the ruddy tan of a life spent outdoors, and dressed in heavy tweeds.

'Mr – er, Mr Stirling?' Felix asks.

The man gives a short, harsh laugh that contains absolutely no humour. 'No *Mister* Stirling here for more than half a century,' he replies. 'What do you want?'

'I planned to call at Findhorn Hall, but I'm told neither of the MacKilliver twins are there, and—'

'Doubt they'd have let you in even if they were,' the man interrupts. 'Not royal or a government minister, are you?'

'No,' Felix admits.

'Then they'd have no time for you.' The man is assessing him, the lively blue eyes keen and not entirely unfriendly. 'Not that the fact diminishes you in my view, I might add.' He is still staring, clearly coming to a decision. Abruptly he opens the door more widely to the accompaniment of another ear-flinching screech and says, 'The kettle's on the hob. You look half frozen so you'd better come away in.'

Felix, who can no longer feel his feet and is sure several dewdrops have been falling off the end of his icy nose, gratefully accepts.

'Angus Leckie,' the lean man says, holding out a ham of a hand. Felix shakes it, then obeys the curt nod and sits down in a chair beside the range.

'Felix Wilbraham.' He removes a World's End Bureau card from his inside pocket.

Angus Leckie interrupts his tea-making, holding the card at arm's length. 'A private investigation bureau,' he murmurs. 'And you're looking to talk to the MacKillivers?'

Felix, sensing both a stirring of interest and a possible ally

– the remark about royalty and government ministers is definitely encouraging – grins and says, 'I'd rather talk *about* them than *to* them.'

Angus Leckie gives a guffaw and his stern face relaxes. 'Then you have washed up at the right place, for the Stirlings and the MacKillivers have ties of friendship that go back a long way, and—'

'Stirlings!' Felix exclaims. He has suddenly remembered why the name is familiar: Stirling's is the London club of which the Band of Angels are all members and where they meet.

'Stirling, aye, that's right, that's the family name.' Angus Leckie looks puzzled and more than a little irritated.

'Sorry, please go on,' Felix says.

But his interruption seems to have acted as a warning to Angus, who doesn't meet his eyes as he pours out two large mugs of tea. He puts one down beside Felix, then opens a cupboard and takes out a bottle of whisky, adding a generous slug to his own mug and raising his eyebrows enquiringly at Felix, who nods.

After they have both taken several thoughtful sips, Felix ventures, 'You live alone here?'

Angus grunts. 'No. I caretake, if that is the word. I come in several mornings a week – including on the Sabbath, when I've a mind to do something other than go to the service at the kirk – when I light the range, I make sure the roof hasn't fallen in, I sweep up the dead birds and the vermin that have found a way in and cannot get out again.' He sighs deeply. 'I lodge with my widowed sister down by the harbour, and I would not live here at Covesea if they paid me twice the pittance they do. When they remember,' he adds bitterly.

'You must—' Felix begins.

'I was gillie here, you understand,' Angus goes on, not apparently having noticed, 'years back, when Miss Adeline's husband William Featherwood looked after the land, and since he went I perform the same role for the MacKilliver estate, pandering to the rich whenever they deign to favour us by a mass slaughter of our wildlife.' He takes another mouthful of tea, grimaces and adds a further generous slug of whisky.

Felix wonders if this is his first mug of whisky-laced tea and rather doubts it. Thinking carefully, reckoning he has just one chance to get his companion to open up and keen to give the right prompt, he says after a moment, 'You said just now there hasn't been a Mr Stirling for some time. No male heirs?'

'No there are not!' Angus replies. 'Old Hector Stirling married a beauty, but he should have gone for a breeder and not a fragile little flower like her. Or that's what my auntie used to say, and she *knew*, you see, because she was housekeeper here at Covesea and not a lot passed her by.' His eyes slide out of focus as he stares back into the past.

Felix sends up a silent prayer of gratitude for having been provided with a natural and garrulous gossip, and one, moreover, who appears to have a deep-seated grudge against his employers.

'So the fragile little flower didn't produce a son?' he ventures after a moment.

'Well, the first-born was a girl, and they named her Adeline. There *were* sons but they did not survive.' Angus adopts a suitably mournful expression, shaking his head sadly. He shoots Felix a shrewd glance. 'There's my granny in her little cottage by the quay, producing a baby regular as the turn of the year and all twelve of them survive, while Madam lives up here with the likes of my aunt to wait on her every need and she manages but the two, Miss Adeline and the last-born. She's still alive,' he adds laconically.

Felix judges by his expression that he expects some sort of reaction to this. Impatient and barely listening, he murmurs, 'Really?' He is cross with himself, deeply regretting having come here, for it's the MacKillivers he needs to know about, not these Stirlings. But then the two families were close, and there is this odd fact that the Band of Angels's London club is called Stirling's . . . Hoping this is relevant, Felix makes himself pay attention.

And over the next quarter of an hour he learns rather a lot about the last surviving Stirling.

Her name was Hortensia, she was headstrong, decidedly odd and, according to Angus's great-aunt, she sensed her parents' longing for a son. 'But it was too late for that,' Angus says, 'for Madam was worn out and announced she wanted her own bedroom with a lock on the door.'

Felix notices how Angus Leckie's eyes sparkle with salacious malice as he relates that juicy detail.

'So young Hortensia, she gives them the next best thing and becomes a tomboy,' Angus continues, 'climbing trees, making catapults, tormenting cats and stealing food from the kitchens, and nobody can stop her playing with the boys, and she was far more courageous and adventurous than the lad who was her best friend.' Angus smiles, his expression softening. 'My aunt was her ally. She admired the little rascal's spirit and many's the time she saved the child from a beating.' He gives a reminiscent sigh. 'When she was eighteen she ran away,' he goes on, 'to London then to Paris, and she lived on a remittance provided by her father.'

'I dare say he was glad to see the back of her,' Felix suggests.

'I dare say you'd be right,' Angus responds.

'What about the older sister?' Felix still can't see how this could be relevant, but nevertheless he asks. 'Was she a rebel tomboy too?'

'Miss Adeline? No, she was a prim little miss, mealy-mouthed and self-righteous, according to Auntie, and prinked herself up prettily when suitors began to call. She married a wealthy local landowner named William Featherwood and . . .'

Angus Leckie's voice drones on – something about this Adeline having a son named Leonard, but Felix's attention is wandering. Fatigue is combining with whisky on a virtually empty stomach, the battered old range is pumping out a surprising amount of heat, his eyelids are drooping and he is wondering what on earth he is doing here, listening to this tedious old man rambling on and on about people Felix has never heard of and in whom he has no interest. I came to find out about the MacKilliver twins, he thinks, and it seems I've failed.

He has had a wasted journey.

He wonders how soon he can leave.

Angus is still in full flow, droning on about how this Leonard Featherwood became a diplomat and settled in the French capital, how he married and had a daughter . . .

Felix dozes.

He is woken by Angus pouring more whisky into his mug.

The old man seems to have forgotten about his guest. For the past quarter of an hour has been talking to himself.

'The family name is Stirling,' Felix says in the momentary lull, 'and I understand that the MacKilliver twins belong to a London club of the same name, so I'm wondering if—'

But Angus hasn't heard.

'Like I said, they called the child Mary,' he says. 'Beautiful little angel she was, and everybody loved her, and when she was only a year old she was brought here to the Abbey to spend the summer with her grandmother. Miss Adeline had been widowed and was lonely and sad, and it wasn't wise for a child of a year old to endure the heat of a Paris summer.'

Something has entered Angus's tone; something that, despite himself, makes Felix compelled to sit up and pay attention.

'What happened?' he asks.

'Cholera happened,' Angus says succinctly. 'Oh, not here – no need for that fearful face! It was in the filth and the furious summer heat of Paris.' Angus spits out the name of the City of Light as if that beautiful, sophisticated city was the worst London slum. 'The epidemic took the rich and the poor alike, and rumour had it that it crept into Leonard Featherwood's household via some maid who'd picked up the deadly sickness visiting her kin. Wiped her out, and Leonard and his wife too.'

Drawn into the tale, Felix says, 'What happened to Mary?'

'Mary was saved.' Angus rolls pious eyes up to the ceiling, as if thanking heaven for God's mercy. If he can see heaven in that filthy mess of dust-laden cobwebs, Felix reflects, suppressing a whisky-heated belch, he deserves a round of applause. 'Poor little child was not old enough to understand what she had lost. Miss Adeline didn't have much truck with infants but she did her duty, none can deny it.' He looks as if he'd quite like to.

'The child was luckier than many,' Felix says.

Angus nods in agreement. 'Aye, that she was. She was happy here with her grandmother Adeline, and the mistress grew fond of the lass.' He sits back in his chair, rubbing his hands over his face as if giving it a vigorous wash. Then, looking at Felix once more, he says, 'She was never the same, the old mistress, when young Mary married and was swept off to India – Lucknow, or some such outlandish place full of foreigners.' He waves a dismissive hand, wiping out the entire subcontinent at a stroke.

'Did she not approve of Mary's choice?'

'No,' Angus replies. 'Then Mary had her little girl out there, so the mistress couldn't chuck it under the chin and bestow a silver mug.' He smiles, but there is little humour in it. 'Then of course she *did* meet the child, because she was brought here to the Abbey by that beanpole of a nursemaid with the peculiar name, and it was for the mistress to sort out the problem, and she wrote to Miss Hortensia and she came up with an answer. Then she – the mistress – took ill and died, and I reckon she was missing the child – she was Mary's daughter when all said and done, even if she lacked her mother's beauty and grace – and she . . . and she . . .' Angus's eyes turn to Felix and he is clearly confused. 'What was I saying?' His words are slurring badly now, and the effects of a large intake of whisky appear to be catching up with him.

Felix edges forward on his uncomfortable chair, preparing to stand up and quietly slip away. Angus is staring round at the dirty, dilapidated room, a frown on his face. 'It's all going to ruin since the old mistress died,' he says mournfully. 'Nobody cares, nobody comes here any more, there's only Miss Hortensia and she's far, far away in the south on that little island and she won't come back.'

Little island.

Felix's heartbeat races as something he hadn't thought of before suddenly strikes him.

'She said as much when mistress wrote to consult her about a school for the child, she said she'd not set foot up here in the Abbey and there was no shaking her, even though the mistress told her she was ailing and . . .'

But Felix has stopped listening.

FOURTEEN

L ily goes to church on Sunday. She wears her SWNS uniform, leaving off the apron and exchanging her nurse's veil for the black bonnet. She is so firmly in the role of assistant matron that it does not occur to her to wear anything else.

She walks to church in the obedient two-by-two crocodile of Shardlowes pupils and staff, and her companion is Miss Blytheway. While the chatty games mistress comprehensively explains the rules of Wave-me-Free, Lily notices a figure lurking beside the churchyard wall and identifies the tall, rangy woman in navy gabardine she spotted when she first arrived at Shardlowes. The woman is intent on Marigold Dunbar-Lea.

The service is not too long, the hymn singing is excellent and led by an enthusiastic choir under a choirmaster who extracts the best from his group of villagers, and Lily is quite sorry when it is over.

Back at the school there is a telegram waiting for her but on ripping it open she discovers that it is not, as she expects, from Felix. It is very brief – a time, a place, two initials – and, Lily hopes, would reveal very little to anybody but her.

She can barely eat her lunch for the combination of excitement and fear. Why is he here? What has happened? And if it's so important, why can't Felix come in person?

She sets out from the school just after two o'clock. Too early for the rendezvous, but she dare not risk someone coming to seek her out and demanding her attention; preventing her from getting away from the school.

She walks, follows a circuitous route, past a couple of pubs, the bars empty now and their doors firmly closed. She walks into the churchyard half an hour early, but he is there.

He is under the bare branches of an oak tree, leaning against the trunk. He is almost precisely as she holds him in her memory, the top hat he always wears pulled low over his eyes.

In deference to the bitter weather, however, he wears a heavy, high-collared black overcoat over his shirt, breeches and waistcoat.

There is no river or canal close by, nor any waterway that could carry any craft larger than a rowing boat, and it is the first time she has seen him not in the vicinity of *The Dawning of the Day*. For a second or two this makes him seem strange, unknown, but then her perception changes and she sees him in a different light. And she understands that he is not really out of his element at all, so at home is he here in this Cambridgeshire churchyard, and she remembers that his ancestors right back up the paternal line were all Fensmen.

He steps towards her, dark blue eyes intent on her face. 'You are safe, cushla? Not harmed?' he asks softly.

'Yes.'

He looks relieved. 'I am glad that the telegram reached you. It was not intercepted?'

'No, I do not believe so.'

He nods. 'I stopped to send it on the way up to Bishop's Stortford.'

'Is that where you left your boat?'

'Yes. It is where the navigation ends. I came on by train.' He looks at her, eyebrows raised, and she realizes he hasn't seen her in her SWNS uniform before. He smiles, but makes no comment.

'Why are you here?' she breathes, the words barely audible, for she still can hardly believe it.

'Shall we walk?' He holds out his arm and she takes it. They leave the churchyard by a small gate at the rear, emerging on to a quiet lane. There is nobody about; nobody to see them.

'I had a message from your associate,' he says as they pass a field gate and the lane narrows. 'It was imperative that he contact you, but he could not spare the time to come himself.'

'So . . . so he looked for you and asked you to come instead?' It is all but incredible. Does Felix know about the boat basin and the master of *The Dawning of the Day*? He must do, but even as Lily understands this, she hopes Felix does not know *all* about Tamáz Edey . . .

'He came to the basin and I was not there, but another boatman knew where I was and undertook to take the letter to me.'

'Where were you?'

'Limehouse Basin. I had just returned there.'

He does not say where he returned from and Lily doesn't ask. Her mind is full of Felix, who in his need knew to seek out Tamáz; knew that, where she is involved – more especially, where her safety is involved (and she remembers what his first words to her just now were) – Tamáz will not fail.

'What is the message?' she whispers.

Tamáz reaches inside his coat and withdraws a folded piece of paper. Her name is written on it – just *Lily* – in Felix's hand. She knows without even thinking about it that Tamáz will not have read the note. Hastily she unfolds it, her eyes flying along the lines of writing.

> There is danger at the school for pupils, for staff and I have no doubt for you as well and perhaps more than anyone else because you are there to expose secrets that must be kept hidden. I cannot be specific yet but I feel such a sense of fear for you. I am on my way north to try to discover what lies behind this business and I am so sorry but I do not have the time to seek you out in person, so I am entrusting this warning to somebody I know you trust, as I find I do too.

It is signed simply *F*.

She looks up at Tamáz. 'He trusts you,' she murmurs.

He grins.

'He's worried about me, he says there's a secret and it's dangerous, and—'

'Yes,' he interrupts. 'I have been aware for some time now that you are in peril, and I was planning to find you even before this.' He touches the letter.

'Felix says he's gone north, where presumably he thinks he'll find answers, and—'

'He is doing what he must,' Tamáz says, once again interrupting, 'but the more imperative thing was to warn you.' He lets the words hang in the cold air for a moment, and Lily

wants to defend Felix, to protest that he *has* warned her, he's
sent Tamáz in his stead, but, meeting his level stare, she realizes
there is no need.

'You just said you were already aware I was in danger,' she
says, his words finally penetrating. A shudder of fear shakes
her, for she realizes that she already knew this.

'You are,' he says. They are right out in the country now,
the village left behind and the lane no more than a cart track.
Tamáz pauses and looks around, over the empty fields and the
winter-quiet hedgerows. 'I have been here before. It used to be
a fair and honest place, its waters clear and clean, its moorings
safe and reliable.'

'Its waters . . . but there's no water here, not even a stream.'
He does not speak. 'Is there?'

He sighs. 'It changes, cushla.' He raises his eyes again, and
this time his glance ranges right out in a wide arc across the
surrounding lands. 'Once everything here was water, and
the Fens stretched from here to the coast, but then the
Dutchmen came and brought their particular skills, and they
built dykes, and they drained the marshes and sent the water
back to the sea, so that now we have lost the wide spaces
through which we once roamed in our clever boats and our
little craft that could slide up the smallest creek.' He stops, and
she senses that he is far in the past and bringing himself only
with difficulty back to the present.

Again she recalls his ancestors. And she wonders just how
far back their occupation of the Fenlands goes . . . Surreptitiously
she looks at him, this strange friend of hers with whom
the friendship itself is slightly odd. Not for the first time, she
reflects that there is so much about him that is unknown, for
he is deep.

But one thing she does know is that she trusts him.

'So it is not a fair and honest place any more,' she says
briskly. Mystical musings are all very well, but she has a job
to do.

'No,' he agrees as they walk on. For some time he is silent,
as if assembling his thoughts. Then he speaks. 'Many who
live in the village and the surrounding countryside are like
me – not a few are my kin – and they know this place as I

do because the old tales and traditions are passed down through the generations. Those who belong here understand the land and the waters that flow beneath it, for their families would not have endured into the present if they had not learned how to survive here. But now there is a new fear, and people live under its shadow.'

'You – do you mean the asylum?' The thought springs into her mind and she utters it without thinking. 'Yes, I've been warned about it.'

She hears Eddy's voice again. *You don't want to go there.*

Tamáz starts to speak, stops, then says, 'The lunatic asylum evokes dread because those on the outside do not know what happens within. Yet in itself it is not a fearsome place, for the staff are enlightened and patients are treated with kindness, only restrained when it is for their own safety.' He looks at her. 'And that of others,' he adds.

'I heard the bloodhounds,' she whispers. 'Someone said that a patient had escaped, and they sent the dogs to hunt him down. *Very* enlightened,' she adds bitterly.

'The dogs find the trail,' Tamáz says. 'If they succeed in locating the runaway, which usually happens unless he has outside help, they stand guard until the asylum staff arrive to take him back.'

'But they *howl*.' Remembering the sound, she shivers.

'They bay, cushla. It's what they do when they are following the scent.'

She is seduced by his words, by his voice, for this strange man has captivated her. But she must resist.

'So the patients are kindly treated, the bloodhounds don't harm them and life in the asylum is sweetness and light,' she says. 'Why, then, is this place full of fear?'

He doesn't answer for some time. Then he says, 'Lily, the folk legends are right, for there *are* evil things that dwell here in the ancient Fenland, and the modern way of life that has covered up the old ways is little more than a superficial skin.' He shoots a swift glance at her and mutters, 'It is why I have been concerned for your safety. I *know* this place and ever since I knew where you were going, I—' He stops. After a moment, he continues. 'When evil comes here – comes to the

asylum in the form of a deeply troubled patient, for example
– then the malignant forces that are always present are
aware, and they come to seek it out, and they reinforce it and
make it far stronger. And—'

It is her turn to interrupt. 'Then why on earth build a lunatic
asylum here?'

He looks at her, and she reads the answer in his face. He
nods as if to recognize the fact, but then speaks anyway. 'Because
they don't know.'

'You could tell them!'

He looks down at himself, and with a gesture of his hand
indicates his tall, powerful frame, his beard, his long hair and
his distinctive, idiosyncratic style of dress. She is used to him,
and has always taken him as himself, as Tamáz, but now she
understands what he is implying.

'They wouldn't believe you,' she whispers, and he nods.

They walk on. The track passes through a thin copse, the naked
trees like skeletal limbs clawing up at the grey sky. Presently he
says, 'There are rumours of a man, wealthy, powerful and gravely
disturbed, for whom no treatment has much effect.'

Treatment. The word conjures up worrying images. 'What
do they do to him?' she whispers.

'I cannot say, cushla, for these are rumours, as I said, and
not likely to be reliable. But—' He pauses. 'There is evil here.'

'What sort of evil?'

He pauses, and she knows he is reluctant to tell her. She
also knows he will, for he has come all this way to warn her,
to make her aware she must be careful. Moreover, he has
just made it quite plain that it's not just Felix who is worried
about her.

'The rumours say he creeps out under cover of darkness with
a big sack and steals children.' He meets her eyes. 'Girl
children.'

'*Girls . . .*' The single horrified word shoots out of her mouth,
and then she is turning, breaking into a run, flying as fast as
she can back to Shardlowes School to tell them, to warn them,
to lock and bar doors, to close gates and thread them through
with chains and an iron padlock.

She feels the thump of his feet on the ground as he races

after her, and then his large hands take hold of her shoulders and he stops her as easily as if she herself were a child. 'Wait,' he says, and he isn't even out of breath.

She bends over, her stays cutting into her as her ribs try to expand to admit air. 'But they have to be told!' she yells at him, face right up against his. 'They've got to keep the girls safe, they must be warned so that they *know* and—'

He has turned her so that she is leaning against him and now he wraps his arms round her, holding her so close that she can feel his heartbeat. His coat and waistcoat have fallen open to the icy air, yet he is warm.

He says, 'Cushla, they already know.'

Aghast, she breaks away so that she can stare at him. 'They *know*? But they can't, they—'

'Of course they do,' he says gently. 'The school has existed for many years, and so has the asylum. You have only been here a week, and already you have heard the hounds. How could they not know?'

'But the man, the dangerous lunatic with the sack who hunts girls, what about him? Do they know about *him*? *Do* they?'

She is shouting now, beside herself, desperate to get away, to tell someone, to protect, to take those innocent girls into her care and keep them safe, and here he is holding her so tightly that she cannot escape.

Still he holds her. 'Those are but rumours,' he says quietly. 'If you were to go to the asylum and demand to know if they are true, the doctors and the staff would deny them, explain that such a thing is not possible, make you feel like an ignorant country fool for believing the stories.'

'But they *are* true?' she asks, quietly now.

And he shrugs.

Suddenly exhausted, she leans into him. 'What shall I do?' she whispers. 'What *can* I do?' For if Tamáz is to believed – and she does believe him for he does not lie – then this man, this horror who stalks by night, is rich and powerful, and such men are protected from the consequences of their excesses by a network of the similarly privileged who look after their own.

Even if they are dangerous and like to steal young girls.

He is stroking her back, firmly, rhythmically, just as she has observed him soothe the old black and white horse who pulls his boat. She is similarly soothed, for his power is quiet but compelling.

'You ask what you should do,' he says presently. 'Watch, be vigilant, be careful.'

'There must be more!'

'There is *not*,' he says very firmly, 'because those within the school who know what is going on will be always alert for people who ask questions, who spy, who try to uncover what must remain covered.'

'But why should they *want* to keep it covered?' she cries.

He looks steadily at her. 'Because the instinct to safeguard the interests of the rich and powerful outweighs the duty of protection of young girls who nobody wants.'

She gasps in distress, mouth open to protest at his brutal words, but then she thinks, He's right. Oh, dear Lord, he's right.

'A teacher and a nurse have both left abruptly,' she says after a moment. 'The nurse was my predecessor and said she was going to looking after her sick mother, but I don't think she's coming back.' I think she's probably dead, she adds silently, and in a moment of weakness she wishes she could say to him, *Take me with you when you leave, let me come aboard* The Dawning of the Day *and I will stay with you and be safe.*

But she doesn't.

She moves slightly, about to straighten up, wrench herself from him, set out back to the school. He understands, and just as she turns away he reaches up a hand and lays his fingertips very lightly on her cheek.

They are back in the churchyard and very soon they will separate. She holds on to the moment.

She is about to speak the words of farewell when his head goes up and he steps beneath the dark shelter of a huge yew tree, pulling her with him. They stand, utterly silent, unmoving, and she hears brisk little footsteps on the road beyond the churchyard wall.

A figure comes into view, erect, striding briskly, hands folded over a small book; a prayer book? But the figure does not come into the churchyard . . .

She – it is a woman – gives the impression of purpose, of busyness, but there is something furtive about her, and once or twice she looks around, a frown replacing the bland expression.

Tamáz breathes right into her ear, 'That woman is dangerous.'

'How can you be sure? Do you know her?' she breathes back.

'I do not know her but I do not need to,' he replies. 'Lily, these places are the home lands of my forefathers, and although the waterways are filled in and the encroaching land is inhabited by others, we remember, and the water down beneath us remembers, and I recognize what she is.'

'She— then she is one of your people?'

'It is not why I say she is dangerous, but yes, her ancestors were of Fenland blood.' He gives her a penetrating look.

'Just like yours, but *you're* not dangerous!'

He grins and says softly, 'Oh, cushla, you know better than that.' Then, his face straightening, he adds, 'All groups include good and bad, and Fenland people are no exception.' He nods towards the woman in the road. 'She is dangerous in a sly and secretive way, and I read it in her as if it was written in words. Keep her at a distance, and if you must pass her, neither engage her in conversation nor meet her eyes.'

Lily stares after the departing figure.

So I am not to talk to her nor even look at her, she thinks.

Which will not be easy, for the small upright bustling figure even now heading back towards Shardlowes School is Miss Dickie.

Lily and Tamáz bid each other a slightly formal farewell. She has not revealed that she has recognized the small upright figure, and he has picked up her slight withdrawal. She knows these things in her soul, without having to work them out, and she is saddened. He turns to walk away, and she thinks of him striding back to the station, waiting for a train down to Bishop's Stortford – and on a Sunday the limited service is hardly likely to supply a train at the very moment he wants one – and the long hours that will undoubtedly pass before he is aboard *The Dawning of the Day*. She steps towards him and he turns back, a slightly quizzical expression on his face. She wants to hold him, for their earlier embrace is a warm and vivid memory, but the mood has changed and now there is a sense of formality between them, so that she does not feel she can touch him. These thoughts flash through her head in an instant.

She says with admirable calm, 'Thank you very much for bringing the message, and for your counsel.'

He nods. 'I am glad to have helped.' Then he dips his head in a sort of bow, turns and walks away, to be swallowed up in moments by the misty gloom of late afternoon.

She watches the empty space where he was standing, fighting the strong urge to run after him.

Then she leaves the churchyard and heads back to the school.

FIFTEEN

Shardlowes is still when Lily quietly enters through the servants' door and slips up the stairs to the sanatorium block. She takes off her cloak and bonnet and puts on her apron and veil. It is gone five o'clock; she was with Tamáz for longer than she thought. She goes into the treatment room, checking that she has sufficient supplies of the cough syrups, throat lozenges and inhalants that the girls suffering miserably from their colds will undoubtedly come to ask for between now and bedtime.

Then she goes across to Matron's room and taps softly on the door. Immediately Matron calls, 'Come in!', and Lily has the brief impression that she sounds brighter.

This impression is underlined by Matron's appearance, for she is sitting up in bed and a book lies open on the bedclothes. She is wearing a crocheted bed jacket in a particularly violent shade of mauve, and there is a very faint colour in her plump cheeks that is not the flush of fever.

Lily finds herself smiling. 'You look better,' she says warmly.

Matron nods. 'I feel better.' She gives Lily a long, assessing look, then her face softens slightly and she gives a curt nod. 'You've looked after me quite well,' she says gruffly, and Lily can tell it takes some effort to issue even this grudging compliment. 'Thought I might be in for a bout of pneumonia' – so did I, thinks Lily – 'but we've kept that devil at bay.' She pauses. 'Well, I suppose *you* have,' she amends, and now the effort causes her to squirm a little.

'You have a strong constitution, Matron,' Lily says, stepping forward to straighten the rumpled bedclothes and help Matron plump the pillows, 'and your own good sense told you to stay right where you were until you felt your strength begin to return.'

'I'm not out of the woods yet, not by any means,' Matron

says very firmly, just in case Lily has any idea of taking it easy
now that her superior is recovering.

'Of course not, you'll have to continue the bed rest for several
days after your temperature has returned to normal, and—'

'A week at least, I always say,' Matron interrupts.

'—and there is no reason to hurry, for our only cases just
now are colds and none of the sufferers seem too unwell.'

'Don't tempt providence!' Matron says reprovingly.

Lily smiles. 'Are you hungry? Shall I ask the kitchen to send
you up something tasty for supper?'

Matron's little eyes gleam. 'Yes. Sunday evening's usually
cold slices from the roast with salad, but I want something hot,
so tell them I want bubble and squeak – there's bound to be
leftover vegetables – and a helping of the teatime trifle. A big
one!' she adds as Lily sets off to pass on the order.

It is getting late. Ten o'clock has struck on the church clock,
the melodious sounds carrying on the cold, still air. Lily crosses
to her window, looking out at the night. She is uneasy but does
not know why. She raises the lower section on its sash, leaning
out and looking over to where the bulk of the asylum looms
up in the darkness. She thinks about everything Tamáz told her;
about a madman with a sack; about fear spreading through a
Fenland village built on land that holds ancient memories.

It was sufficiently alarming in daylight, with Tamáz's warm,
strong presence beside her, but now, in the silent night, alone,
it is far more than that.

She reaches up to draw down the window, for the air is dank
and chill. But she hears, or thinks she hears, voices; soft whispers, and a palpable sense of tension . . .

She leans out again, glad that she had extinguished her lamp
before going to the window so that there is no light to give her
away and reveal that she is listening. One voice is Miss Dickie's:
she has a tight little mouth which does not move much as she
talks, giving her words a clipped and sibilant quality that is
unmistakable. The other is a man's.

Lily edges further out over the windowsill, straining to hear.
The only men to be found in or around Shardlowes are Eddy
and a general handyman who sees to the boilers and tends the

grounds, but this man is not a servant. The voice is that of an educated, sophisticated man, moreover one in a position of authority over Miss Dickie.

For it sounds as if he is telling her to do something she does not want to do.

'But I must insist!' he says, and the staccato words are suddenly loud, demanding, instantly followed by a '*Sssssh!*' from Miss Dickie.

'You have no choice but to comply,' he repeats in a soft, reasonable tone. 'You *know* this, Ann.' He pauses, then in an even quieter voice he adds, 'For one thing, there is the money. I believe I am right in saying that you and Salt have become accustomed to it?' Miss Dickie mutters something inaudible. 'I thought so,' the man murmurs. 'And I need hardly remind you that now is not the time, my dear, for words spoken out of turn, for the Prince is on the very point of accepting the invitation, and nothing must stand in the way of the Angels achieving what has been their aim for so long.' There is more, but the voices are softer and Lily cannot make the words out.

And presently she hears firm footsteps pacing away down the path, and then the quiet closing of a door.

She shuts the window. The room has become very cold, and she draws the heavy curtains, crossing to the little fireplace to put a couple of small logs on the glowing embers. She fetches her shawl, wrapping it tightly around her, but the shivering is more from apprehension than cold.

She knows that something is about to happen, although she has no idea what . . .

She does not go to bed, instead making herself as comfortable as she can in her chair, determined to stay awake, to hear the first warning signs of whatever it is that will happen this night.

She is shaken out of a half-doze by a sound she has heard before: the baying of bloodhounds. She leaps up, confounded by sleep and her head swimming, rushes to the window, forces up the lower pane, leans out, straining her ears.

Nothing.

She leans out further, but the night is quiet and still, very cold but with no sign of anything out of the ordinary.

Did I imagine it? she wonders. Did I dream it, the sound put
into my sleeping mind by what Tamáz and I talked of?

She shakes her head as if the action will somehow clear her
ears and enable her to hear the hounds again.

Still nothing.

She is tempted to return to her chair. Tempted, even, to
undress and go to bed, to sleep soundly until the bright morning
comes. She resists, instead lighting her lamp and quietly letting
herself out of her room. I will walk along the corridors where
the dormitories are, she tells herself, Alice, Louise, Helena,
Red, Blue and Green, and I will reassure myself that all is well,
the girls asleep and safe in their beds just as they should be.

She pauses only to exchange her soft slippers for her strong
boots, for the left one has a sheath sewn into the seam in which
she keeps a very sharp boning knife. Then she gathers her
courage and sets off.

All is calm in the passage where the senior girls have their
dormitories, the night so quiet that she can make out soft
snores from Louise and the sound of someone turning over
in her sleep in Helena. She proceeds to the juniors' section,
walking quietly but quickly, turning the corner and entering
the dark corridor . . .

. . . and suddenly she is falling, the lamp flying out of her
hand, and in the second before she hits her head very hard she
has time to think in terror, The lamp! Oh dear God, the lamp!
Fire!

Then blackness takes her.

Felix is on the night train. He is cold and his back aches, but
these bodily discomforts fade in his agony of anxiety for Lily.

The previous day was one of enlightenment, via the garrulous,
embittered, scandal-loving Angus Leckie, until the bottle of
Scotch was almost empty and alcohol finally overcame him.

But then he mumbled that comment about a little island.

Felix left him where he lay, his conscience forcing him to
make sure the range was stoked up, tuck a blanket round Angus
and alter the angle of his head to prevent his neck seizing up.
It was the company that had made him go on drinking, Felix
reflected fairly as he closed the door and set off for the track,

so it was only right. The thundering hangover would be more than enough to cope with without a chill and a stiff neck as well.

He had marched as fast as he could to the little station, where his frustration was increased tenfold on learning from the time-table posted up beside the firmly locked door that the next train was not until mid-afternoon. It was not yet midday, so he had some three and a half hours to wait.

As he stood pacing to and fro on the track outside the station, however, his friend the delivery man came along. Taking pity on him – 'It's a sparse train service up here, y'see sir, particularly on the Sabbath, but reliable for all that, and the afternoon train will be on time, you mark my words' – he went on to offer Felix a bite to eat if he'd a mind to it, to pass the time.

Felix had clambered up on the cart almost before the delivery man had stopped speaking.

Now he sits on the train, staring out into the blackness of the night. He is not sure where he is. His journey is made up of complicated changes, its completion in any sort of decent time far too dependent on each successive train being as punctual as the first one.

So far, so good, he tells himself.

At midnight he is standing on the platform in Edinburgh station waiting for the London train. There has been a cow on the line and it is late.

Felix curses every cow ever born.

Lily, Lily, he thinks.

He has tried not to let his anxiety overcome him, and this has proved relatively easy all the time he's been moving and making his slow but steady way towards her. Now, though, held up by a daft bloody cow which has somehow escaped from a field that a stupid careless farmer failed adequately to fence, he is pacing up and down Edinburgh station and his mind is filling with images of Lily in danger, Lily on the trail of the truth and pushing, pushing to uncover it, Lily arousing the attention – the enmity – of someone who would very much rather she didn't . . .

He makes himself stop there.

It will do no good to wind himself up into fury and there is surely no need for despair.

Not yet.

'I do not know the whole truth myself,' he mutters to himself, still pacing. An elderly man sitting on a bench gives him an alarmed look, and Felix flashes what he hopes is a reassuring smile.

I know more of the story now, thanks to Angus Leckie, he continues, restraining himself to thinking rather than muttering, but there are still gaps; places where I have guessed, and may well have guessed erroneously.

He sends up a quiet prayer that he is wrong about Lily being in desperate and imminent peril, but he doesn't think he is. Because she's *there*, at Shardlowes School, and she's not a woman to walk away from a tantalizing secret . . .

There is a loud whistle and a huge cloud of steam; the scent of sulphur, the rumble of great wheels driven by huge cranks, and then a rattle of carriages as the London train, calling at Berwick, Newcastle, York, Lincoln, Peterborough and, most crucially for Felix, Cambridge, draws up alongside the platform.

Lily is dreaming of India. Images of warmth, of rain in such volume as she had never suspected could exist, of gorgeous silks on beautiful, dark women; of a horror that came out of the shadows straight for her, of a little girl saying, *She is not my mother* . . . She gasps, for she is in pain, and tries to turn away from the light, and someone puts a large hand on her shoulder in a gentle touch and whispers very softly, 'Leonora, wake up, we must go.'

She struggles up through what feel like layers of that same gauzy silk she has just been dreaming of, brushing them away from her face. 'My head hurts,' she moans. Perhaps the person waking her up is Matron, and she's come to give her something to stop the pain. 'Is that you, Matron?' she mutters. But no, Matron is in bed and can't get up until a week after her temperature has returned to normal, she said so herself.

Whoever it is shakes her, not at all roughly but it is enough to send darts of agony through her head.

She tries to remember what happened . . . yes . . . it's coming back . . .

She had been at the corner of the two corridors where the senior and junior dormitories were. She fell and was terrified because of the lantern in her hand, desperately afraid it would shatter, the oil would spill and the whole wing would go up in a deadly blaze. But there is no smell of smoke, and the pain in her head is not the agony of burned flesh.

So what happened next? She forces herself to think, *think*.

She remembers coming to, and finding herself lying in a huddle against the corridor wall. There was blood streaming down her forehead; a lot of blood, and straight away she realized she'd hit it hard against the sharp corner where the two walls meet. She was also in pain from some wound on the back of her head, and her left shin was throbbing, although just then as she lay on the ground, the bleeding was the urgent injury.

Then suddenly somebody was there, someone who emanated such a sense of tension and anxiety that it seemed to permeate the air like a tangible thing. This someone was swooping down to crouch beside her, urging her to sit up, to stand, telling her quietly but firmly that she must move away from the dormitory corridors so as not to disturb the girls, ushering her along, hurrying her, making her walk far more quickly than she wanted to . . . *who was it?*

Lily screws up her eyes, trying to see the image.

It was Miss Dickie.

And then, very determinedly, Miss Dickie had helped Lily, only half conscious, to the treatment room – Lily remembers that sibilant voice hissing, 'To the sick bay, Nurse Henry, for you require medical attention' – and she must have summoned Matron from her bed because suddenly she was there in her nightgown and flowing robe, tending the wound on Lily's head with quick, skilful hands and tutting as she did so about being woken up at all hours and people not being careful enough as they went wandering around after dark and *why* they had to do so was a mystery to her.

'She tripped on that worn patch in the drugget.'

It was Miss Dickie's voice making the statement, her tone one of utter conviction.

'She must have caught her toe,' Miss Dickie went on, 'and it caused her to fall headlong and hit her head on the corner.'

Lily, in a great deal of pain, confused, feeling more than a little nauseous, allowed herself to be helped into her nightgown and into bed.

Now, as she tries to recall the sequence of events, she clearly remembers thinking – perhaps saying too – that something wasn't right . . . But then Matron gave her a soporific which she suspects contained rather a lot of laudanum, and as the pain blessedly began to ease, she fell helplessly and deeply asleep.

But now 'Wake up, Leonora!' says that voice again, and this time the hand that shakes her is a little more forceful.

Very slowly and carefully, apprehensive of the pain that will probably follow, she opens her eyes.

The first thing she realizes is that it is morning – well, after sunrise, anyway, for a soft, misty light penetrates the room.

The second thing she realizes is that Felix is bending over her. Seeing that she is looking at him, hastily he puts his mouth right against her ear and says softly and urgently, 'You must get up as quickly as you can, dress and come with me.'

She lifts her head about an inch from the pillow, feels a stab of pain and lowers it again. 'But I—'

'You *must*,' he repeats. 'I'm sorry, but there is no choice.'

He steps away from the bed, still watching her, and very slowly she sits up. She is very dizzy, and feels so sick that instinctively she looks around for a bucket. There is one beside the bed, and she vomits into it, the action sending fresh waves of agony through her head. Is it concussion, her professional self wonders, or the aftereffects of that large dose of laudanum?

Felix is looking at her anxiously.

'It's all right,' she manages. She waves a feeble hand. 'Wait outside.'

Still drowsy, she sits there on the bed until he's left the room, then stands up and, holding on to the bedstead, crosses to the washstand, pours cold water into the bowl and washes sketchily, splashing cool water on her face and her sore eyes. Her fingers feel the bandage that Matron must have wound around her forehead, and she is careful not to wet it. Moving very slowly, she dresses, and recent habit, distress and pain make her reach

automatically for her SWNS uniform. The black bonnet with
its deep brim does quite a good job of concealing her bandage,
and she is grateful for the thick cloak, for she can't stop
shivering. She stoops to pick up her small bag – her head throbs
violently in protest – and leaves the room.

'Dear Leonora, there you are!' Felix exclaims loudly. Miss
Long is standing in the passage looking very worried – and
also as if she very much wants to speak to Lily – and Matron
is just behind her, dressing gown tightly fastened over her
nightgown, muttering about concussion requiring the patient to
rest quietly in bed, not go gallivanting off into the early morning,
even if there *are* sick relations needing attention. Felix ignores
Matron, murmurs, 'Thank you, but not just now if you please,'
to Miss Long, and hurries forward to help Lily. She leans against
him, more grateful than she can say for his strong support. She
catches Miss Long's eye and takes in her agonized expression,
and Miss Long mouths something . . . Frowning, Lily thinks it
is *Look in your little bag!*

But, 'Come along now, Leonora dear,' Felix is saying very
firmly, 'I will help you and make absolutely sure you do not
fall on the stairs. The pony and trap are waiting, and we shall
soon be on our way.'

His arm is around her waist, tightly, urging her along, and
Lily has no option but to go with him. Carefully they descend
to the hall.

Miss Carmichael stands beside the door, her face very pale
and with dark circles around her eyes. Her expression is severe
and Lily senses that she is extremely worried about something.
She also looks angry, but she is trying to cover these emotions
with a not very convincing expression of sympathy.

'First Nurse Evans's mother, and now your little brother,
Nurse Henry,' she says rather tartly. 'I should perhaps specify
in future that the post of assistant matron is only open to a
woman with no dependants to whom she feels she must rush
when they fall ill.'

So that is the story Felix has told, Lily thinks. I have an
imaginary little brother and he is unwell, and being a nurse,
the family has sent for me.

She tries to make her brain work. 'He has been sickly since

birth, Miss Carmichael,' she says with just the right amount of reproof in her voice, 'and it has always been I who have tended him, for he loves and trusts me and responds best to my care.'

Miss Carmichael mutters something that could well be an expression of hope for a swift recovery, but could equally well be an admonition for her assistant matron to return to her post as soon as she can. She nods a curt farewell, and just as she is closing the heavy front door, Lily thinks she sees Miss Dickie hurrying towards her, as pale as Miss Carmichael and her mouth working with some strong emotion.

Something has happened, and Lily does not think it is merely the matter of the assistant matron taking a tumble and then being fetched to go and care for her sickly little brother. Her head is bursting, she does not begin to understand, and it hurts too much to try to puzzle it all out.

Felix hurries her down the steps to the waiting trap, and Eddy stares at her with fascinated amazement. 'Coo, Nurse, you don't half look pale!' he says. 'Sure you should be out of bed?'

Quite sure I shouldn't, she thinks, but all she says is, 'Thank you, Eddy, drive on, if you please.'

'Sorry about the imaginary little brother,' Felix mutters as Eddy flicks his whip over the pony's rump and they move off. 'It's the best I could think of in a hurry.'

'But I don't understand—' she whispers back.

Felix frowns, shaking his head. He indicates Eddy. 'Later,' he mouths.

The trap bumps and rattles its way along the track and Lily tries to hold herself as still as she can, for every jolt sends a stab of pain through her head. The wound on her forehead smarts with a sharp sort of pain, but there is something else . . . She raises a surreptitious hand to the back of her head, sliding her fingers up beneath the back of her bonnet, and finds a lump like the rounded end of an egg. Even this soft, tentative touch hurts like the devil, and she suppresses a cry. Felix must have felt her start – the trap seat is narrow and they sit pressed close together – and looks at her enquiringly.

Just as he did, she mouths, 'Later.'

Eddy pulls the pony up in front of the station, jumping down to help his passengers, and Felix hurries Lily inside, barely giving her time to thank Eddy and say goodbye. She wants to find a seat, but the benches set along the platform are all occupied. She feels herself sway, and Felix puts an arm round her. The look on his face suggests he's going to select some hapless man or youth and demand they give up their seat for a lady who is feeling faint, but before he can do so, to her great relief there is the toot of a train whistle. A black-smoke-puffing locomotive appears around the bend and comes clanking into the station.

Felix finds a half-empty carriage and they sit down next to each other. But this is not the time for confidences, for several people crowd in after them and soon every seat is taken. Lily cannot control her need to know, however, and mutters angrily to him as the train pulls away, 'Why have you come for me? I was—'

'You were in danger and you'd just been hurt,' he hisses back, 'and I had absolutely no choice.'

Danger.

You are in danger.

And she remembers Tamáz's anxious face, and how his first words to her were: *You are safe, cushla? Not harmed?*

She recalls how Felix was so concerned for her that he went hunting for Tamáz to ask him to bring that message.

She remembers the alarming, horrible legend that Tamáz recounted. She thinks of missing girls, of secrets, of an atmosphere of fear, of staff who chose to leave a good, secure job rather than stay at Shardlowes.

She recalls the many moments when she has felt afraid. Oh, more than afraid; when she has felt cold dread that seemed to snake right up her spine.

And she thinks perhaps they are right, Felix and Tamáz, and she is indeed in danger.

SIXTEEN

The rattle and the rhythm of the train are soothing. Lily slips into a light doze, the conversations around her floating through her mind and sometimes making her smile. She is very aware of Felix and she can *feel* his impatience to speak to her like a physical presence beside her. The seat is narrow for the six people who sit along it, and she is tight against Felix's shoulder and arm, so close that she can feel the heavy muscles moving as he restlessly shifts, the urgency in him making it impossible to sit still. Lily wishes he would, however; he'd be a far more comfortable bolster if he did . . .

She must have slept, for suddenly the train is pulling into a soaring London station and someone is yelling loudly. 'Liverpool Street! All change, end of the line, ladies and gents, Liverpool Street!'

Felix takes her arm and they hurry outside, where he shoves his way to the front of the queue for hansom cabs and soon they are being swept away across the city, over the river and into another station. Lily, bemused, half asleep, in truth not feeling at all well, thinks it must be Waterloo, but she has no idea why they are there or where they are going. 'I thought we were going home,' she says to Felix as he hurries her up the steps, and he turns to give her a swift glance that seems to say, *I'm sorry.*

They are at the ticket booth and he is buying tickets, and although she sees him speaking to the clerk she cannot hear what he says. Then another platform, and a long train awaits them, its locomotive already puffing and panting in its haste to be on its way.

This time they have a carriage to themselves. Lily sinks gratefully into a corner seat and closes her eyes, wanting more than anything she has ever wanted to sleep, *sleep*, until the world rights itself and she understands again, until she stops hurting so much. She glances at Felix, perceives that he is struggling with conflicting desires – she detects he's desperate to tell her something but can see she's suffering and badly needs rest – then she closes her eyes and falls deeply asleep.

She wakes and immediately knows she's better. Not perfect yet, for her head still hurts and she feels a little queasy, but the most important thing is that the awful confusion has gone. She can now recall with complete clarity not only everything that's happened recently but also her own conclusions, unproven though they are.

The train is standing at a long platform and Felix has gone.

She peers out and spots the station sign: PETERSFIELD. It's not a lot of help as she isn't sure where Petersfield is. A few people are still filtering out through the ticket barrier and there is nobody on the platform, by which she deduces that the train has been stationary for long enough that everyone wishing to board has done so.

She spots a small refreshment stall at the end of the platform, and Felix is hurrying away from it. The guard blows his whistle, green flag in his hand, and she opens the carriage door for Felix to jump inside as the train begins to move.

'And I haven't spilled a drop,' he says, handing her a mug of tea.

She takes it and sips greedily, for hot tea is the very thing she wants just now. 'Don't you have to give the mug back?'

'Strictly speaking I do, but I explained to the chap that my companion was unwell, and he said it was all right to hand it in at the stall on the next station.'

She nods and goes on sipping. The tea is delicious.

He is eyeing her intently, and she suppresses a smile. He is so obviously itching to ask if she's all right, if at long last they can *talk*, and out of pure devilment she keeps him waiting a few moments longer. Then she says, 'I was already feeling better, probably from the sleep, but the tea has done the trick. Who goes first?'

He slumps in his seat, relief evident in his whole body. 'You,' he says. 'I want to know how you got hurt.'

She collects her thoughts, mentally checks through the various hurts and begins. 'I met Tamáz – and thank you very much for sending him to come and find me – and he told me the Fen around the village is a perilous place and that there are many ancient tales and a dark rumour about a man with a sack who takes children, and he warned me that Miss Dickie – the assistant head, remember?' He nods. 'She's dangerous. Tamáz said he could see it in her because she's of the same ancestry as him' – Felix, she notes, looks a little sceptical – 'but I already knew I had to watch her. That night – last night?' He nods. 'I was back in my room and I heard voices, Miss Dickie's and a man's, and they were saying something about the Prince, or maybe *a* prince, being about to accept an invitation and nothing must happen to prevent that, and I had the feeling that she was unhappy, or unwilling, and he was coercing her. Then I heard footsteps going away and the servants' door closing, and I sensed very strongly that something was badly wrong, that something was about to happen, and I tried to stay awake, sitting in the chair by the window, but I fell asleep and I woke up to hear the bloodhounds baying from the asylum and I decided to see that all was well in the girls' dormitories. I had checked the seniors and was just turning into the corridor where the three junior dormitories are when I fell and hit the front of my head' – she indicates the bandage – 'and I bled a lot. I think I knocked myself out briefly, and then Miss Dickie was helping me up and urging me to come away from the dormitories so as not to disturb the girls. Matron looked after and gave me something to make me sleep, and the next thing I knew was you, waking me up.'

'Sorry,' he says. 'Really, truly, I'm so sorry. But I had to. I'll explain, but finish your tale first. How did they explain your fall?'

'Miss Dickie told Matron I'd caught my foot in the worn patch of drugget.'

He looks at her, eyebrows raised. '*Is* there a worn patch of drugget?'

'Yes, there are several, but I wouldn't have said there was one where I fell.' Before he can comment she goes on, 'And in addition, consider these two factors: as well as the cut on my forehead, I have a huge and rather sore bump on the back

of my head, and there is also this.' Nobody has entered the
carriage at the various stops since Waterloo and it is empty
except for the two of them, so she raises her skirt and unlaces
her boot to reveal her left shin. 'You can't see it properly through
the stocking, but can you make out an indentation?'

He is looking decidedly embarrassed. 'Er—'

She tuts in impatience. 'Oh, really Felix, it's an ankle. Oh,
all right, a lower leg, but there's no need to be coy. Here.' She
grabs his hand and puts his fingers on the deep dent in her shin.
'Feel it now?'

'Yes.' He has already withdrawn his fingers and is sitting
primly upright, hands folded in his lap like a spinster aunt. She
tries to suppress a laugh and fails, and reluctantly he laughs
with her. 'That must hurt,' he says.

'It did. It does.'

'Trip wire?'

'I imagine so, yes.'

'But why was it there and who put it there?'

'I've been thinking about it, and it has to be Miss Dickie.
And she must have hit me on the back of the head, because it's
physically impossible to fall and bang your head simultaneously
at the front *and* the back.'

'But how did she know someone would be snooping about
outside the dormitories?'

'One answer is that she's been wary of me from the start.
Another is that the trip wire wasn't specifically for me, but for
anyone who was where they weren't meant to be.'

'And why weren't they meant to be there?' he asks. 'Why
was Miss Dickie being so careful? Why was it she who turned
up to tend you when you fell?'

'And why was she so determined to get me right away from
the dormitories? I sensed even at the time that she was tense
with anxiety, and it certainly wasn't out of concern for me.'

They look at each other, and she reads the same profound
suspicion in his eyes that is tearing through her.

And at last, and perhaps far too late, she recalls Miss Long's
agonized face and her pretty mouth shaping the words *Look in
your little bag*.

'*Oh!*' she gasps.

She drags at the strings that hold the bag closed, sticks her hand inside, frantically feels around—

—and there is a piece of paper, folded very small.

She extracts it, tearing the corner, unfolds it, spreads it out, and with Felix leaning against her reading over her shoulder, sees written in Georgiana's neat hand the chilling message: *Another girl missing in the night; from Green Dormitory and rumour has it that it is Marigold Dunbar-Lea.*

In the first horrified instant, what Lily notices most is that even in an extremity of anxiety, Miss Long has used a semi-colon.

Felix says into the shocked silence, 'Do you know this girl?'

'Yes.' The single word is almost a sob. 'Oh, why didn't I stop to listen to Miss Long? I should have—'

But he interrupts, quite forcefully. 'Lily, what difference would it have made?' he demands. 'We were already leaving, we've reached this point as quickly as we could, and stopping to hear what Georgiana Long had to tell you would have only served to delay us, besides which she obviously didn't want to talk openly in front of that fierce-looking matron, which was why she put the note in your bag.'

'I suppose you're right . . .'

'I *am* right.'

But suddenly she sits up very straight and says, 'Where are we? Why are we here? Where are we going?' She can hear the panic in her voice and is cross with herself for her weakness.

He seems to understand, for he touches her hand, and his is warm. 'What would you like first?' he says with a smile, but it's a rhetorical question because already he is answering. 'This train is taking us to Portsmouth, we're somewhere in Hampshire and I think we'll reach our destination in half an hour or so. We're going there because of what I discovered in Scotland.'

'Scotland?' He nods. 'You've been to *Scotland*?'

'I have. To be precise, to the Moray Firth, where the MacKilliver brothers have their ancestral home.'

'The MacKilliver brothers who are founder members of the Band of Angels who fund Shardlowes School?'

'Those are the ones. Their estate is called Findhorn Hall, and next to it is a very dilapidated place that is owned by the Stirling family.'

He is looking at her expectantly, and she realizes she is meant to perceive some significance in this fact. She shakes her head. 'Sorry.'

'Well, you're still recovering,' he says charitably. 'Stirling's is the name of the London club where the Band of Angels meet.'

'So it is!' she breathes. 'Go on.'

'I met an informative, resentful and indiscreet man who looks after the Stirling house – it's called Covesea Abbey, and it has seen better days – and he was angry about having to care for a place the owners don't give a fig about and where they rarely, if ever, bother to visit, and that combined with most of a bottle of whisky led to him telling me a lot that I'm sure he'll now be regretting. If he remembers.'

'And what he told you is linked to Shardlowes School?'

He sighs heavily. 'I am very afraid it is.'

'Tell me.'

He looks at her. 'It's not good,' he warns.

'Felix, I already *know* it's not good,' she says sharply.

She closes her eyes as he begins to speak.

Presently she opens her eyes again and turns to him.

'You still have not explained why we are going to Portsmouth. Yes I *know* it's where Esme Sullivan went,' she goes on before he can interrupt, 'so I presume that she discovered the same link to the town that you did – perhaps she overheard something – and—'

'It's also where Miss Long's predecessor Genevieve Swanson was going,' he says darkly, 'or at least it's fair to assume so since she fell from the Portsmouth train.'

'So she found out too,' Lily whispers. 'But why? Why were they going there, and why are we?'

He looks at her for a moment and she thinks he looks uncertain.

'Because I'm fairly sure I know where the missing girls are being taken.'

'You – but why didn't you say so straight away?' She is half out of her seat. 'We have to get there, we need to look for them, to find Marigold before—' But she can't even think about that, never mind put it into words.

Felix takes her hands and gently but firmly sits her down again. 'We *are* going there, Lily, as fast as we can.' She starts to protest but he doesn't let her speak. 'I learned from the caretaker at Covesea Abbey that the Stirlings have pretty much died out. The old woman had siblings but only one is still alive.' Now the uncertainty is back in his face, and he looks almost furtive . . .

'I made an assumption, Lily,' he says after a brief pause, 'a wrong assumption.' Before she can demand whether his mistake is important and if so if it can be put right, he rushes on. 'Violetta da Rosa told me that Cameron MacKilliver suffers from periodic bouts of insanity, that he is a recluse and shuts himself away at Findhorn Hall, that from time to time he is treated by doctors who specialize in cases such as his, and that the only other time he leaves his ancestral home is when he goes to stay with an old childhood friend.'

'I don't see how—' she begins.

'Please, Lily, let me finish!' he pleads, and she nods. 'I took *childhood friend* to mean *school friend*, and I thought this old friend was a man. Then when I learned from Angus Leckie – that's the name of the caretaker – that the last surviving Stirling is a woman called Hortensia, I didn't connect her with Cameron and I was barely listening.'

'Surely—' But she can see he hasn't finished. 'Sorry.'

'Lily, everything Angus said about Hortensia Stirling couldn't have been *more* relevant. Every small detail becomes *absolutely* relevant when you understand that Hortensia Stirling and Cameron MacKilliver were playmates from when they were very young, and have remained close friends to this day.'

'It's – he goes to stay with a *woman*?' All that Lily has learned concerning Cameron MacKilliver surely makes this extremely unlikely, but Felix is nodding.

'Yes, that's exactly what he does.' He smiles grimly. 'But it is most certainly not a sexual relationship.'

'How do you know?'

'Because neither of them is – er, is like most people,' he says delicately. 'Cameron, according to a friend of Violetta's who

knows him quite well, has always been odd, and this friend
reckons something went amiss in Cameron's early years, perhaps
to do with witnessing his mother's travails in the childbed
and the trauma of losing babies and infants. Anyway, Cameron
liked to play with dolls and he never developed the usual interest
in women. He has never married and has no children, and in
all likelihood has never – er, hasn't—'

'Has never had sexual intercourse,' Lily supplies.

'Quite.'

'So did he and this Hortensia Stirling play with their dolls
together?'

'No, far from it, because according to Angus and his tittle-
tattle, Hortensia knew her parents would have preferred a son
and became a tomboy. She was headstrong and brave, and I
imagine she and Cameron each turned into the other, if you see
what I mean, and—'

'She was the boy and he was the girl,' Lily suggests.

'Yes. They would have gone their separate ways in time,
although during the years when Cameron was sent away to
school no doubt they always resumed their closeness during the
holidays.'

Lily is thinking very hard. It is not easy, for it makes her
head ache and she is aware that her mind is not operating
with its usual fluidity. It is taking her longer than it usually
does to form connections and to make sense of all that Felix
is telling her.

But it is with some confidence that she breaks her silence by
saying, 'She bought a house in Portsmouth, didn't she?'

Felix mimes applause. 'Very nearly. She lives in Ventnor, on
the Isle of Wight.'

'The Isle of Wight . . . That's the other side of the Solent,
isn't it? You take a ferry from Portsmouth?'

'It is and you do. I think – I'm reasonably sure – that it's
where Cameron MacKilliver will be.' The doubt has crept back
into his expression. 'That his old friend Hortensia's house is
where he goes when he needs to creep away.' He makes a
violent gesture. 'If I'm right, that is, and that it is indeed he
who is behind the disappearances, and I haven't got the whole
thing wrong and we're haring off in completely the wrong

direction and all the time he's hidden himself in some ruin of a barn in deepest rural Cambridgeshire and that poor little child is—'

But, 'Stop,' Lily says very forcefully, putting a firm hand on his. 'Felix, we are where we are because you have very good reason for bringing us here. Would it have been better to stay at Shardlowes or return to Hob's Court, worrying ourselves silly over what was the most sensible thing to do? Isn't it far, far wiser to use all the available information, arrive at a logically deduced conclusion and have the courage to act upon it?' He doesn't reply, so she says urgently, 'It is, Felix, it *is*, and that's what we're doing!'

He raises anguished eyes to hers. 'What if I'm wrong?'

Several possible replies run through her head. In the end she just says, 'I don't believe you are.'

SEVENTEEN

The train puffs and pants at the end of its run, which is the station at Portsmouth harbour, and Felix and Lily hurry along the platform to emerge into a stiff breeze off the Solent.

'Look, over there,' Lily says anxiously, pointing, 'there's a sign saying ferries to the Isle of Wight and one's just tying up so if we hurry we can—'

But Felix moves swiftly to stand right in front of her, blocking her way, and he knows he's far too big for her to shift. He looks down into her pale face, the bandage just visible under the sheltering brim of her nurse's black bonnet. Deliberately he cuts off the thought of what she has been through over the last twelve hours. 'When did you last eat?' he asks sternly.

'Oh—' She shakes her head impatiently and winces with pain. 'Er – yesterday. I had cheese on toast in the evening.'

'Just as I thought,' he says. 'I'm starving, even though I had breakfast of a sort on the train from the north, so before we do anything else we're going to fortify ourselves with good food and, with any luck, strong drink.'

He sees every step in her inner struggle, but thankfully her nurse's good sense wins and she nods curtly.

'Very well, then,' she says with obvious reluctance, 'but we must be *extremely* quick and I'm not at all sure strong drink's a good idea.' She gives him a stern look.

'I wasn't serious about the drink.'

'Oh.'

It is perhaps twenty minutes later, they have each wolfed down two rather solid cold beef sandwiches with horseradish sauce and a slice of Victoria sponge and drunk a large mug of tea, and, trying not very successfully to suppress a burp, Felix is elbowing a way through the crowds on the pier to where a ferry is preparing to leave. The man on the barrier starts to give the usual lecture about last-minute arrivals not only risking their own safety but delaying the departure and causing inconvenience to other passengers, but Felix glares at him and mutters, 'Criminal investigation, very urgent,' and the man subsides, contenting himself with yelling, 'Well, don't do it again!' after their departing backs.

The wind is far more evident out on the water and it is carrying spiteful little drops of freezing rain that come in regular flurries, so Felix leads the way into the saloon. But it is very crowded, there is a stink of unwashed clothes and malodorous bodies, at least three men are smoking very strong tobacco in their pipes and somebody has been sick, so they go out again, this time on to the leeward side of the ferry, and stand close together for warmth, leaning against the side of the saloon.

'Do you know exactly where we have to go?' Lily asks, not for the first time.

'I do,' he assures her. Putting rather more confidence than he is feeling into his voice, he continues, 'We disembark at Ryde, then take the train down to Brading, Sandown, Shanklin and round Boniface Down to Ventnor. Or possibly *under* Boniface Down, since I gather there's an impressive tunnel.' He sees her sudden frown – he was half expecting it since he knows full well a detailed itinerary was not what she wanted – and says, 'It's only a dozen miles or so, we'll be there in no time.'

That is pretty much a guess, but her frown has eased, which is the main thing. 'And you know where the house is?'

'Yes.' Felix recalls how, having settled the sleeping Angus Leckie, he had tiptoed through the dank and depressing rooms of Covesea Abbey until he found what appeared to be a study, with about a thousand books slowly mouldering on the shelves, a strong smell of mice and a huge roll-top desk, its lid halfway open, in which he had found what he sought: a leather-bound mould-covered address book. 'I have the location and it'll be easy to find, the address is The Esplanade.'

She nods again. She starts to speak, hesitates, then whispers, 'And if it's true that it really is Marigold – well, whoever it is, naturally – do you think she'll still . . .' But she doesn't go on.

He knows exactly what she was going to say. He reaches out for her hand, but does not comment.

And in silence they watch as the Isle of Wight steadily draws closer.

The journey down to Ventnor might indeed have been not much over a dozen miles, but the train takes a long time over its stops and starts, and minutes turn into an hour, an hour and a quarter. They dive into the Boniface tunnel and the dark underworld takes them in, great billows of sooty, smelly smoke sneaking in through the tiny opening at the top of the carriage window.

Then they are in Ventnor, and Felix grabs Lily's arm as they hurry out of the station.

He is putting on an act for her, for in truth he has no idea of the geography of the town and his earlier confident assurance is starting to look a little thin.

But in fact locating the house is easy.

They stride through the little town and all at once a gap appears between two buildings; a narrow, twisting road leading downwards . . . to the sea. They turn to the left, to the right, left again, and there on the right is the most extraordinary house. It is perhaps four or five storeys high, it has gables and turrets, and it is set against the rocky cliff face that rises up behind it, so that the first floor at the front is the ground floor at the rear. The sturdy front door with its iron knocker in the shape of a dragon is down at the lowest level, beneath an ornate and showy porch, but Felix notices that a path leads up to the back of the house, ascending a short flight of stone steps before ending in a gate giving on to what looks like a little garden. A low door is set in the side of the house.

So there is, then, he observes silently, another access to the upper floors.

He and Lily race on down the steep road, cross over and stride over the little forecourt to the door. He raises the dragon knocker, bangs it hard once, twice, three times. After a pause of perhaps ten seconds that feels very much longer, the door opens and an elderly man, stooped and grey and dressed all in black, says creakily, 'Yes?'

Felix is about to speak, but Lily forestalls him. Holding out one of the World's End Bureau cards, which the old man holds at arm's length to read, she says with quiet authority, 'I am Lily Raynor, proprietor of the Bureau, and this is my associate Felix Wilbraham. We are here on a matter of extreme urgency and we must speak to Miss Hortensia Stirling.'

The old man is beginning to shake his head even as she is talking. 'Oh, dear lady, I'm afraid you will have to come back tomorrow, or even the day after,' he says with the utmost courtesy, 'for the Mistress does not like to be taken by surprise, and in any case she always rests in the afternoon and could not possibly see you *now*.' His rheumy, pale blue eyes widen in dismay at the very idea.

'I do not believe you can have understood,' Lily says icily. 'A matter of extreme urgency, I repeat, and any delay, even of a few minutes, could mean the difference between life and death.'

'Life and death?' he repeats, clearly horrified. 'Somebody is in danger? Oh, dear me, dear, dear me, I cannot think how this could involve the Mistress, truly I cannot, and—'

'Perhaps you should ask her if she is willing to see us?' Felix interrupts gently.

The old man turns to him. 'Do you think I should disturb her?' he whispers. 'Will she not be angry?'

How should I know? Felix thinks, but wisely he just smiles and says, 'Well, yes, I think you should.'

The elderly butler, if that is what he is, is just starting to turn and shuffle away when there is the sound of a door being opened – quite forcefully, so that it bangs back against the wall – and a loud voice full of the haughty confidence of the wealthy and powerful who have never had to work for their living comes booming down the hall: 'What is it, Murchison? What's all this noise?'

'I am very sorry, ma'am,' the old man says, hurrying towards the source of the voice and trying to bow at the same time, 'but these people are investigators – from London!' he adds, as if it were the most amazing element of Lily and Felix's arrival, 'and they are – they say they need to—'

Slowly the woman advances along the hall from the deep

gloom of the house's interior. She brushes the old man aside
and emerges into the light from the open door.

Felix feels Lily go tense beside him, and he suspects she is
suppressing a gasp. He feels exactly the same, for the figure
before them is extraordinary.

Hortensia Stirling is perhaps in her mid-sixties. She is a tall
woman and holds herself very straight. She has broad shoulders
narrowing to boyish hips, her body shape very apparent because
of the garments she is wearing: a thigh-length tunic in some
sort of soft, shimmery silk in brilliant crimson patterned with
mauve and yellow swirls over slim-fitting leggings that taper
to her narrow ankles. On her large feet she wears scarlet leather
slippers whose turned-up toes each have a small and melodious
bell on the tip.

Her face is like a mask.

Her iron-grey hair is worn short, club-cut to jaw level, apparently by someone wielding a pair of garden shears. It is parted
at the side, swept across her broad forehead and held in place
by a jewelled clip in the form of a butterfly and set with red,
blue and predominantly white gems which, from the way they
are catching the meagre daylight and sparkling so brightly, must
undoubtedly be precious stones.

Her eyes are pale grey and set beneath very straight dark
brows. Her nose is like an arrow pointing down her face, her
mouth is thin and wide, her chin prominent and, just now, stuck
out towards her visitors in a not very welcoming manner. 'What
do you want?' she barks.

'I have given your manservant a card,' Lily says with what
Felix thinks is considerable sang-froid. She looks at the old
man, who jumps and instantly holds out the card to his mistress.
She snatches it, reads it in an instant, and straight away some
inner strength seems to go out of her.

She leans against the wall, her eyelids fluttering. She mutters,
'I always knew someone would come, some day.' Then she
straightens up, fixes her chilly gaze on Lily and Felix and says,
'You had better come in. Murchison, bring tea.'

Without another glance at any of them, entirely confident
that all three of them will do exactly as she has ordered,
Hortensia Stirling straightens her back and marches down the

hall, through the doorway out of which she has just emerged, turns to her left and leads her visitors into a large room crammed with a ornaments, photographs, portraits and seascapes, silverware and a great deal of furniture. Bay windows look out over the sea, and the fading light spills in. A fire burns in the wide fireplace.

Hortensia Stirling returns to what is clearly her chair, to the right of the fireplace and with little tables either side bearing books, a pair of spectacles, several cups, a dirty glass and a bottle of whisky. She subsides into the chair with a sigh, wrapping the turquoise mohair shawl draped across it over her legs.

'Sit,' she commands.

Felix pulls out a dining chair from the dusty walnut table for Lily and, when she is seated, sits down beside her. He can feel her desperate impatience coming off her like a physical force, but it seems she knows as well as he does that if they hurry this old woman, if they try to take control, she will clam up and they will get nowhere.

Hortensia looks at Felix, then at Lily. 'You're the boss?' she asks sharply.

'I am,' Lily agrees.

'Good for you,' Hortensia growls. Then, almost in the same breath, 'You've come for him, haven't you?' A sound like a sob breaks out of her, quickly suppressed as she presses a large handkerchief to her face.

'We believe your old friend Cameron MacKilliver may be here, yes,' Lily says, 'and we further believe' – Felix detects she is fighting to control the tremor in her voice – 'that he is probably not alone.'

And very slowly Hortensia nods.

Felix feels Lily gather herself to leap up and he grabs her. '*I know!*' he hisses as she glares down at him, 'I know we have to hurry, but if we don't go about this the right way she'll have us thrown out of her house, he'll have time to get away and then there'll be no stopping him!'

Hortensia has been watching them, an unreadable expression on her strong face. 'In fact there is no hurry,' she says as Lily sits down again.

'No hurry . . .' Lily repeats. 'Oh, dear God, you mean—'

'The child is still alive,' Hortensia says calmly. 'Deeply asleep and quite unharmed. He *loves* them, d'you see, he really loves them. Cares for them with such tenderness, for he believes it is his mission to save them.'

'Save them from what?' Felix asks, cold with horror.

Hortensia looks at him. 'From womanhood,' she replies simply.

'But – how?' Lily whispers. 'He cannot stop the process, for it is a natural occurrence.'

Hortensia stares at her, possibly only now taking in how she is dressed. 'You're a nurse,' she says. 'One of those what d'you call them, St Walburga's.'

'St Walburga's Nursing Service, known, from the initials, as Swans,' Lily says.

'Yes. Them.' Hortensia digests this. 'You'll know, then.'

Felix catches Lily's frown, and guesses she is as puzzled by this enigmatic remark as he is.

Then Lily leans forward and says calmly but firmly, 'Miss Stirling, the child we believe to be in Cameron MacKilliver's keeping is a pupil at the school where I am assistant matron, and she has of late been in my care. I am extremely anxious about her and I am not altogether reassured by what you have just said, and accordingly I would now like you either to take me to her or to tell me how to find her.'

Lily stands up, squaring her shoulders, and in her stalwart posture Felix reads the authority of a woman trained to care for others, to save lives, to make difficult decisions with speed; a woman used to giving orders and to having those orders obeyed.

For a moment it seems to him that Lily and Hortensia are battling each other; that bright swords made of light clash and strain as each tries to dominate the other. He blinks a couple of times and the images vanish. Good grief, he thinks, I'm more tired than I thought.

And meekly Hortensia Stirling says, 'Back into the hall, take the stairs, then go right and along to the end of the landing, up the next flight and it's the little door to the left. It opens on to a spiral stair leading up into the turret, and that's where he has his set of rooms. That's where he takes them and looks after them so lovingly.'

Lily nods a curt acknowledgement, turns and strides away.

Felix is on his feet. 'Is Miss Raynor in danger?' he demands forcefully.

Hortensia waves a hand. 'No, no, he'll pull up a chair for her and offer her a cup of tea and a scone.'

Felix is still looming over her. 'If she comes to any harm—'

'She won't.' Hortensia cuts him off.

'I should go with her,' Felix mutters, looking at the door through which Lily has just left.

Hortensia tuts in impatience. 'No you should *not*,' she says, barking out the words. 'You are a man, a large, tall and strong-looking man, and if you go blundering in up there, pushing your way into a delicate state of affairs which I am certain that cool-headed nurse will manage perfectly well alone, you will only distress poor Cameron, and *then* there might well be harm done.' She glares at him. 'Young man, I *know* Cameron. We've been close since we were small children, and I understand him. I'm probably the only person in the world who does,' she adds in a murmur, and her head droops. Then, looking up at him again, she says curtly, 'Oh, sit down, do!'

Reluctantly Felix obeys. 'Your old friend has taken two children,' Felix says baldly. 'Three, in fact. Girl children, before they begin to mature. He takes them from the school and—'

'A school which, like all of them, should send up prayers of gratitude each and every day for the Band of Angels!' Hortensia cries, face working with anger. 'Do you *know* about the Band of Angels?' She doesn't let him answer. 'The membership is made up of *very* important men,' she goes on, 'men who have great wealth and influence, who feel a true compulsion to do the good works they do, across so many spheres of life.' She shakes her head, brows drawn into a frown. 'I cannot say that I sympathize with this compulsion, but they are men of the world and undoubtedly understand its ways better than I.' Suddenly she glares at Felix. 'Nothing must be allowed to hinder them. *Nothing.*'

'There has been mention of a prince who is considering joining the Band of Angels,' Felix says. 'Do I take it he is one of ours?'

Hortensia's pale eyes meet his and she neither agrees nor disagrees, which Felix takes to mean *yes he is.*

'And obviously such a man would very quickly change his mind if he knew about Cameron's little ways?'

'Obviously.' Her voice is cold.

'So another child has to be sacrificed,' he murmurs.

'Well she won't be *now*,' Hortensia replies tartly, 'with that Amazon of a nurse on her way up to the turret set.'

Felix sends up a silent prayer that she is right.

'And so, because Cameron MacKilliver is a member of the Band and he and his twin are major benefactors,' Felix resumes, 'the school's headmistress turns a blind eye when girls go missing.'

Hortensia stares coldly at him. After a moment she gives a faint shrug. 'They are but girls, and unwanted for the most part,' she says.

Felix cannot believe what he has just heard. '*Unwanted?*' he echoes. 'And so they don't matter? They are unimportant, and can be sacrificed?'

She shrugs again. 'There are always too many girls.'

He has no words to express his outrage. 'But – but—'

'But, but, but,' she repeats, a cruel smile on her face. 'Are you a goat, young man?' She leans towards him, all at once intent. 'Face the truth, if you are brave enough!' she hisses. 'These girls are redundant. Foundling, orphans, surplus daughters, dependent females for whom husbands must one day be sought and paid for. The world can perfectly well do without a handful of them.'

She leans back in her chair, nodding, smiling a satisfied, supercilious smile, clearly confident that she has nullified every last one of Felix's objections.

Looking at her, he realizes that no words could penetrate her certainty.

In the sudden cessation of conversation he realizes that he has forgotten all about Lily.

Now he strains his ears, but can hear nothing: no raised voices, no sounds of disturbance. He concludes, feeling slightly guilty, that all is well.

For he very much wants to go on talking to Hortensia Stirling.

'Cameron is treated at the asylum in the village, isn't he?'

For the first time the arrogant, aggressive expression falters. She frowns, her brow creasing in puzzlement. 'In the village . . .' she repeats, and mutters something else which Felix doesn't catch. 'I do not know the whereabouts of the asylum,' she says aloud, the confidence of lifelong privilege in her haughty tones, 'and, indeed, I do not care to. I am aware that from time to time Cameron goes there, but it is a *purely* voluntary arrangement.' She lays heavy emphasis on the word.

For some reason he does not understand, Felix senses it is important to pursue the question of the asylum.

But, taking his second false step in as many minutes, he says, 'You claim that the girls who have been taken are unimportant. Redundant, was the word you used.' She nods curtly in acknowledgement, straight eyebrows raised as if to say, *And what of it?*

'Perhaps you are unaware, but an English teacher at the school also went missing,' he says, deliberately keeping his tone calm and unemotional. 'Miss Genevieve Swanson.'

'Was that her name?' Hortensia asks indifferently. 'I did not know. She suspected, or so I am led to believe, and she was on her way here.'

'And there was also a pupil from the senior school, Esme Sullivan,' Felix goes on in the same level tone. 'Her body was washed up on Southsea Beach.'

'Yes, yes, it would be,' Hortensia says indifferently. 'I expect she ended up in the sea. Out there.' She jerks her head towards the beach below the house. 'It happens, sometimes, that a body is swept up in the currents around the Island and washes up on the mainland.'

Felix, revolted at the ruthlessness of her utter indifference, opens his mouth to protest but she hasn't finished.

She leans forward and whispers, 'Mortimer found out. He found out about both of them, the woman and the girl. I do not know how, for I do not confide in him nor he in me. I've always disliked him, arrogant little boy that he was, and he's grown into an equally arrogant man and a deeply unpleasant one too, and Cameron is afraid of him. Mortimer tormented him when they were small, d'you see, and poor dear Cameron has never forgotten. Well, you don't, do you? The horrors of childhood may be buried deep but they do not go away. Yes,' she adds thoughtfully after a moment, 'Mortimer will have carried out the clearing-up, just as he always does.'

'Mortimer MacKilliver takes what action he deems necessary to cover up what his twin brother does, so as to save both Cameron and the reputation of the Band of Angels,' Felix says very softly.

And, as if it is perfectly reasonable and only to be expected, Hortensia says brightly, 'Yes! Quite so.'

Felix's mouth has gone dry and it is a moment before he can speak. When he can he says calmly, striving to keep his tone even, 'Miss Stirling, just how long has your friend Cameron been a regular visitor here?'

He fervently hopes she will understand what it is he is really asking her.

She docs.

Her head spins round to face him and for the briefest of moments there is true, deep anguish in her old eyes.

She knows, Felix thinks in a flash of understanding. She is perfectly well aware that what Cameron does – is allowed to do – is nothing less than monstrous. But it is easier to look the other way and shut her mind to the horror.

But then she masks the distress and her face resumes its haughty lines.

'How long?' she repeats. 'Oh, let me see now . . . He's always come to see me, from when I first purchased this house years and years ago, although back then it was but infrequently.' She frowns, and he senses she is very relieved to have this question to ponder, distracting her as it surely must from far darker thoughts. 'Then . . . yes, *yes*, it was not long after the Band of Angels became involved with that school near Cambridge that Cameron began to come more frequently, and to stay for longer.' She shoots Felix a swift glance in which he reads shiftiness, not to say guilt. 'I remember the occasion well, because it was just before the one and only time my elder sister Adeline wrote a proper letter to me.' Hortensia leans towards him again, and a hand like an eagle's claw and heavy with rings reaches out. 'Adeline had a problem, d'you see, for her great-granddaughter had just been brought home from India and her parents – Adeline's granddaughter Mary and her husband Roddy – seemed to expect Adeline to find somewhere suitable. Adeline!' she exclaims with a throaty laugh. 'Of all people, my sister Adeline, who really did not have a maternal bone in her body!' The smile fades and she looks reflective. 'She loved Mary, though.' Slowly she shakes her head. 'It was truly astounding, and nobody ever fathomed it out, but it seemed there was some quality Mary had – innocence, purity, kindness, perhaps simply *goodness* – that penetrated Adenine's hard crust. She truly loved Mary, and it damaged her deeply when she insisted on marrying Roderick Dunbar-Lea and going back to India with him.'

Something is clamouring for Felix's attention but he ignores it. Has no option, for Hortensia is in full flow and not to be stopped.

'She was canny, though, Adeline,' she says confidingly. 'She'd been caring for Mary since the child's parents died and she knew the girl was naive and needed someone to watch out for her interests.'

'So she—' Felix begins.

'Mary was her sole heir,' Hortensia says, speaking over him, 'and Adeline was an astute woman who understood the ways of the world. She was wary of the dangers posed by unscrupulous suitors, who could ensnare the innocent Mary and sweep her off her feet.' She looks at Felix. 'So what do you think she did?'

'Why not tell me?'

'Adeline instructed her lawyer to make absolutely sure that Mary could not inherit until she was twenty-five.' She nods in approval. 'She hoped Mary would have lost the stars in her eyes by then and seen Roddy for what he was.' A frown clouds her brow. 'I hope she was right . . .'

It is time, Felix thinks, to steer her back.

'You were speaking of a great-granddaughter, and what Adeline did about her,' Felix prompts softly, although he already knows.

'Hm? What?' With some difficulty Hortensia brings herself back into the present. 'Oh . . . there were problems, health difficulties – the child had had an operation but it hadn't gone

well, and she was a funny-looking little thing. Didn't walk
properly – something amiss with one leg.' Her eyes turn inwards
again. 'Odd, how nature works. Roddy was a very handsome
man and as for Mary, she was nothing less than beautiful.
For that golden couple to produce such a child was the worst
luck. Of course, the little cripple's appearance was the reason
she was shipped home to Adeline with that tediously devoted
nursemaid.'

She looks up at Felix again, apparently recalling the question.
'As to what Adeline *did*, she wrote to me with the problem,
and I came up with the solution.' She preens herself.

Felix has the strange sensation that the truth is appearing
beneath a rapidly clearing layer of cloud. 'And what did you
suggest?' he asks quietly.

'Well, Cameron had only recently been to visit – I just *told*
you that! – and he'd been full of this school in Cambridgeshire
to which he and the Band of Angels were being so very
generous, and he described how they took girls from a
very young age and how most of them became permanent
boarders, and I thought, my goodness, the very thing for
Adeline's great-granddaughter! Naturally I said as much to
Cameron, and he said it sounded as if the school was absolutely
right for the child, so I wrote to Adeline and in next to no time
the child was off her hands and happy as could be, I have no
doubt, at this school . . .' She frowns deeply for a moment and
then shouts triumphantly, 'Shardlowes! I knew I'd remember!
Shardlowes School, in a village just outside Cambridge!'

And Felix, chilly with dread, thinks, a village with an asylum
where Cameron MacKilliver is a regular in-patient.

As if Hortensia's recovery of an elusive memory is sparking
off one of his own, all at once he knows why the name
Dunbar-Lea is familiar. He lunges for the chair where Lily was
sitting and scoops up the little bag she has left on the floor
beneath it. Hortensia's scandalized expression as she watches
him wrest it open and thrust his big male hand inside would
be funny in any other circumstances, but in this awful moment
he has room for no thought but Miss Long's letter . . .

. . . and its fateful words.

He looks up, straight into Hortensia's worried face.

'Is the child's name Marigold?' he demands, the words emerging with such urgent anxiety that she flinches.

'Yes!' she cries, her expression turning rapidly from amazement that he should know to a horrified realization of what this might mean.

But Felix has no time for her now.

For it has just occurred to him that it is rather a long time since Lily went upstairs.

EIGHTEEN

With fear swiftly rising to horror at what she will find, Lily is stealthily climbing up through the tall house with its many levels and tucked-away rooms. Up to the second floor, and here is the little door that opens on to the spiral stair. Fighting to control her shaking legs, she climbs to the top. One hand reaches for the little glass bottle on its chain, hidden under her clothes. She bends under a low lintel, emerging into a set of rooms at the very top of the house, several doors opening off the main room. Windows overlook the sea.

A large man dressed in dark coat and trousers stands with his back to her, peering round the partly drawn curtains to the lively sea below. Hearing her footsteps, he turns round, his forefinger to his lips.

'Quietly now,' he says softly, smiling sweetly. 'We must not wake her.'

'Very well,' Lily replies, keeping her voice low.

He stands beaming at her, apparently not fazed by her presence. He is broad, his belly pushes the costly but stained and dirty fabric of his waistcoat into a dome, and his legs look too thin to hold up his bulk. His shirt is none too clean. He has a shock of white hair which stands up like a halo around his head. He is clean-shaven, and the flesh of his plump face is as pink and shiny as if Nanny has just given it a good scrub. His eyes are round and blue, and they are full of childlike trust.

Presently he says, 'Have you come to take her away?'

Lily recognizes the voice. She thinks she has heard it before, in the darkness beneath her window at Shardlowes. Not sure how to answer, she says, 'For now I just want to make sure she is all right. I'm a nurse, you see.'

'Yes, yes, yes, of course you are, I see your uniform!' Cameron claps his hands. 'Now I understand.' He turns, trotting across to the open door into a second room. 'There she is,' he mouths, pointing.

Lily sees a very small bed made of white-painted wood with railings like those of a cot, although it is larger than a cot. The foot end is painted in soft pastel colours: an image of lambs playing in a flowery meadow. There is a fluffy pink wool blanket neatly folded on the side rail.

'She was too hot, so I took off the top cover,' Cameron whispers right behind her, making her jump and then shudder in dread at his nearness. 'You must assess whether a child is warm enough by touching the back of the neck, not the forehead as so many people do. But I expect you know that already.' She turns and he is smiling at her, his eyes wide.

She makes herself turn her back on him. She *must*.

She bends over the cot.

Marigold lies deeply asleep, her soft light brown hair spread over the little white pillow in its frilled, lace-edged pillow case; across one corner the word *Baby* is embroidered in chain-stitched pink silk. Glancing at the small table beside the little bed, Lily spots a large bottle of laudanum, a flask of water, a spoon and a pretty little silver mug. Marigold lies on her side, one arm and shoulder out from the light covering bedclothes. She is dressed in a pink nightgown with short sleeves and a yoke from which the generously gathered fabric hangs.

'I shall cut her hair and put on her bonnet presently,' Cameron whispers, and Lily sees he has in his hand a baby's bonnet in white cotton, large enough for a girl's head.

Lily hesitates.

She does not know this alarmingly strange man; she has no idea what he will do if she tries to thwart him.

But she cannot allow him to cut poor little Marigold's hair.

Cannot allow him, in fact, any further access to her helpless body.

She thinks for quite a long time – Cameron has turned away and is looking down at the sea again, humming to himself; it sounds like 'Baa Baa, Black Sheep' – and she feels no threat from him.

For now.

She makes up her mind.

She puts her plan, such as it is, into action.

Drawing herself up straight, assuming her full authority as the trained and experienced nurse that she is, she says softly, 'Cameron? Is it all right if I call you Cameron?'

He spins round to look at her. 'Of course, for it is my name!' he says with a smile.

'Thank you. *My* name is Lily.'

'Lily! Very pretty.'

'Cameron,' she says while he stands there beaming at her, 'I do not believe that this little girl belongs here with you, although I know how much you want to take care of her.'

He nods with the wild, uncontrolled action of an enthusiastic child. 'I do, yes I *do* want to care for her!' he agrees. 'She doesn't *belong* here?' Now he is frowning, and Lily senses the very edge of danger.

Silently saying, *I'm sorry, dear Marigold, I'm so sorry*, Lily draws back the bedclothes. 'She is imperfect, you see' – she points to the sad little inward-turning foot – 'and to make her perfect she needs professional attention of the sort that I do not believe you can provide. Although I know you would if you could!' she adds as Cameron's scowl deepens into something worse.

He does not speak.

'And there is her lip, and the cleft inside her mouth.' Lily touches Marigold's upper lip and very gently opens her mouth. She does not respond, and Lily suspects he has given her a large dose of the laudanum. 'Both these issues can be corrected, but it is a skilful task and she will need the very best of care.'

'She has to stay here,' Cameron states firmly. 'She must be with me, for I have to stop her growing up.'

'I can help,' Lily says, trying to sound calm and matter-of-fact as if she has conversations like this every day. 'The operations on her foot and on her mouth will simply make her prettier.'

Now he begins to look doubtful. 'Will they?'

'Yes.' She is praying now, praying very hard, and she has gradually moved so that she stands between Cameron and the unconscious Marigold.

'But I know how to stop it, you know,' Cameron says in a sing-song voice that is the most frightening of all. 'I love these little ones, you see, Nurse, and it is up to me to keep them in their childhood innocence, for otherwise they grow, they turn into *women*' – the word is a barely audible whisper, and he seems to shy away from it as if it terrifies him – 'and I know what happens then for I have seen it, and it is terrible, the agony, the blood, the pain, the grief, and I cannot, I *must* not, let it happen to my wee ones.'

Lily faces him. She gathers her courage and stares into his mad eyes. 'I shall take her and I shall look after her,' she says calmly.

He is still staring at her, his eyes so wide that there is white all round the blue irises.

Slowly, steadily, she turns away and reaches down into the cot. She puts an arm beneath Marigold's shoulders, another under her thighs, and starts to lift. Marigold is heavy, though, heavier than she looks, and Lily falters. She moves the arm under the child's thighs a little and tries again.

And then there is a whooshing sound; as if something large is flying through the air. Lily spins round, and her astonishment at what she sees causes the muscles in her arms and back to respond so that Marigold's inert weight falls back into the cot.

She is trying to look in two directions simultaneously, because she cannot believe what she is seeing.

Cameron MacKilliver is standing in front of her and behind her.

But there is no time to puzzle it out, no time to think at all in the two or three seconds that pass as the something large continues its flight. Then the heavy china jug crashes against the back of her head and she slumps down onto the dusty-smelling carpet.

Lily opens her eyes.

She is sitting on the floor, propped up against a velvet-covered chair. Her head hurts.

She looks up.

Cameron MacKilliver stands before her, exactly where he was standing before, and happily there is only one of him now. She says croakily, 'What happened?'

'The weight of the child was too much for you,' he replies. 'You lost your footing and you fell.'

This does not tally with her own idea of what has just happened, but she does not say so. Her vision is muzzy, and she blinks a few times.

She can see him more clearly now and what she sees confuses her. It is the same man, yet he is not the same . . . The coat and trousers are of very similar dark, good cloth, yet they seem fresher and they fit him better; the white shirt is clean.

'What is it?' he asks. His face is sweating, he is twitchy and tense, and as if that were not enough, his voice has changed . . .

'You—' she begins.

His expression darkens. 'Yes?' he murmurs. Even the one word sounds ominous.

Lily glances up at the cot. Marigold is stirring; she moans softly, and her exposed arm twitches.

'I must see to the child,' Lily says, and with difficulty she raises herself up, stage by laborious stage, until she is standing. She hopes he cannot detect that her legs are shaking.

She leans over Marigold, touching her very gently on the forehead. She is clammy and hot, and as Lily puts her fingers on the child's wrist she detects a racing pulse.

'Marigold needs help,' she says very calmly. 'She has been given rather a lot of laudanum, and now she must be allowed to wake up and—'

He makes a gesture of hopelessness. 'Laudanum,' he repeats. 'It is so hard to judge aright, and that has been the perpetual problem. At first they have to be kept sedated, for otherwise they become distressed, and something has to be done to stop their sobbing.'

Lily feels a chill creep over her.

'Is that how they died?' she asks, keeping her voice as quiet and gentle as she can. 'They cried out, perhaps realizing the danger they were in, and they had to be kept quiet? With more laudanum? With a pillow over the face?' She nods in the direction of the little pillow in the pretty white case embroidered with *Baby*.

'I – he—'

But whatever he was about to say remains unspoken.

There are footsteps on the stairs – loud, heavy footsteps – and a voice is bellowing 'Lily! *Lily!* Are you hurt?'

His sweaty face falls in despair, but in the blink of an eye the expression is replaced by another. He lunges at Lily, one hand in the cot and on Marigold's innocent exposed throat, the other grasping for Lily, tangling in her hair, twisting her somehow so that an all but unbearable pain bursts out in her neck . . .

. . . and then Felix is there.

His eyes widen in horror, he takes in the situation at a glance and hurls himself forward.

But his adversary is ready. He still has hold of Lily but he has abandoned Marigold and he has something in his free hand.

It glitters as its blade catches the light.

Lily screams out a warning but Felix ignores it.

His impetus is such that he probably couldn't stop even if he wanted to, and the bulk of his big body crashes into Lily's captor. He cries out and just as Lily feels she can't stand the agony in her neck a second longer, it is gone.

Nevertheless, there are large black spots floating in front of her eyes. She bends over, letting the blood flood into her head, and after the briefest of time straighten up again.

Her eyes shoot to Felix.

He returns her anguished look and quickly says, 'I'm all right. Not hurt.'

She spins round to look at Marigold, who is asleep once more.

Finally she looks at her assailant, being held down very firmly in a little nursery chair by Felix's superior weight and strength.

And into this frozen tableau the colourful figure of Hortensia Stirling emerges, panting from her hurried climb up the stairs.

She takes in the four figures in the turret room and demands, 'Where's Cameron?'

'There,' Felix says, indicating the man in the chair.

But Hortensia shakes her head, her expression scathing.

'That's not Cameron, it's Mortimer.'

*   *   *

'I shall send for the police,' Felix says firmly.

'*No*,' Mortimer says forcefully. The two men glare at each other. 'I beg you, do not,' Mortimer goes on more calmly. He looks at Marigold, who is struggling to raise her head and opening and closing her eyes groggily, her expression deeply puzzled. She is holding Lily's hand so tightly that Felix can see Lily wincing.

'No harm has been done,' Mortimer says very softly to Felix.

'Girls have died! Two women have been killed!' Felix speaks in a furious whisper, aware that this is not fit for Marigold's ears.

'Where is the proof?' Mortimer shoots back. 'None will be found, and on that you may safely take my word.'

'But your brother is—'

'My brother is a simple soul,' Mortimer interrupts. 'He is an innocent who does not understand the world. He acted out of love and a desire to save his beloved girls from growing up.' His expression is anguished. 'He could never stand the weeping, it broke his poor heart.'

'And the older girl, Esme Sullivan?'

'She was clever. She traced her missing fellow pupils all the way to Cameron's lair.' He lifts a hand in an elegant gesture, indicating the turret rooms. 'She accused Cameron and began yelling at him, courageous girl that she was, and once again he couldn't stand the noise of her distress; he put his hands on her throat and the next thing he knew, she was dead.' Mortimer pauses. 'I put her body in the sea. And I knew about the English teacher too,' he goes on before Felix can ask. 'I had word from Shardlowes that she was also on the trail and I approached her on the train. There was an altercation and she fell from the carriage.' Briefly he drops his head in his hands. 'I journeyed on to Portsmouth and later returned to find her bag and small valise.'

There is silence in the turret room.

Into it Hortensia asks again, 'Where is Cameron?'

With a sudden, sharp exclamation Felix leaps up and over to the slightly open window.

The body of a large man is lying on the hard ground at the foot of the tower. A great pool of blood surrounds his head.

Mortimer emits one great sob, quickly suppressed. 'He jumped,' he whispers. 'I tried and failed to stop him. Is he dead?'

'I believe so, yes,' says Felix quietly.

Then he turns and his eyes meet Lily's.

And he knows full well she is thinking exactly what he is: Do we believe him? Or did Cameron's identical twin push him to his death?

Relieved of Felix's restraining weight, Mortimer is getting to his feet. Walking towards the door, where Hortensia steps out of the way. They hear his footsteps descending the spiral stair.

Lily says sharply, '*Felix!*'

And, knowing exactly what she wants of him, he says, 'You think I should run after him, apprehend him, get him in an arm lock and march him to the nearest police station? And then what, Lily?'

Even in her distress and pain, she too understands.

Mortimer MacKilliver is a man of wealth, status and influence. Felix has none of those advantages.

If Felix were to blurt out his extraordinary tale and his accusations as he thrust Mortimer at some bemused policeman – aiding an abductor, involvement in a suspicious death on a train, disposing of bodies, the assault on Lily – it is pretty obvious, in the absence of any proof or corroborating evidence, which one of the two of them would end up in the cells.

There is silence in the turret room. Felix has the strange feeling that he can almost see the wildly disturbed air settling again. Lily is bending over Marigold, smoothing the hair from her forehead, speaking softly, her voice and her actions heartbreakingly tender.

Marigold, he thinks. The child's name is Marigold Dunbar-Lea. Perhaps simply because she was an easy target for his accomplices, the final victim of Cameron MacKilliver's misguided and fatal kindness was his old friend's great-grandniece.

Moving so that he is standing right beside Hortensia, he bends down and says very softly, 'Miss Stirling, do you know who this child is?'

*   *   *

Lily suggests that the best, indeed the only thing, is to bundle
Marigold up in warm clothing and take her back to Shardlowes,
and Felix agrees. They cannot leave her here, for, despite
Hortensia's guilt and shame, despite the fact that she now knows
who Marigold is and, horrified at how close she came to death,
is making all sorts of wild promises and saying she'll prove
she means it if only they'll give her a chance, Lily does not
trust her and she senses Felix doesn't either.

'Marigold comes with my associate and me back to the
school, Miss Stirling,' she says. As she watches the old chin
lift and the autocratic expression take shape, Lily adds, 'Once
she has recovered, we shall explain. We'll say that Cameron
was bringing her here to meet you, because you are her great-
grand-aunt and her only relation in England, and that he kept
it a secret in order to surprise her.'

Hortensia sniffs disapprovingly, but after a while gives a
grudging nod.

Leaning towards her, Lily says very quietly, 'That is for
Marigold's benefit, Miss Stirling, to provide an explanation
which hopefully will allay her distress. It is *not* for yours.'

As she sees them out, Lily supporting Marigold and Felix
going on ahead to summon a cab, Hortensia whispers plaintively
to Lily, 'My sister's great-grandchild! Her beloved Mary's
daughter! Must this be goodbye?'

Lily, a stern dismissal on her lips, takes in the genuine regret
and grief in the old eyes. 'It will be up to Marigold,' she says
firmly.

And then, as the cab draws up and Lily begins to help her
charge down the steps, Marigold turns and gives the old woman
a very sweet smile.

Between them Felix and Lily manage to keep Marigold half-
awake as they help her on and off the ferry, but she sleeps away
the train journey to London. As they set out for Cambridge,
however, the resilience of youth is already restoring her and
she has recovered sufficiently to begin telling Lily and Felix
her tale.

'Miss Dickie came to the dormitory in the middle of the
night and told me I was coughing and I mustn't wake the others,

and she said I had to go outside into the corridor to be given some cough mixture. Even while she was making me drink it, I was thinking it was not right because it should have been you, Nurse Henry, because *you* are assistant matron, not Miss Dickie. Then straight away I started to feel strange, muzzy-headed and sleepy, and then Miss Dickie was saying not to worry, everything was all right and she'd look after me, then she, or I think perhaps someone else, a man, put a lovely soft snuggly blanket round me and then I was in a carriage, I think, and there was a hot stone bottle to keep me warm, and a really kind, gentle old man said he had a very special surprise for me and the sooner I went to sleep the sooner I'd find out what it was.'

Lily is watching her closely for signs of distress as she recalls what happened. So far, she does not see any.

'The journey was so long – at least I have a feeling that it was, although in truth I slept a lot, and the old man looked after me so tenderly and frequently asked if I was warm enough.' Marigold looks at them, smiling. 'We went on a boat, and the kindly old man helped me when I stumbled and made someone fetch me a cup of tea, and all the time I knew I ought to be demanding to be told what was happening, where we were going, but he was *so kind*, and I kept falling asleep, and anyway I felt safe with him.' She hesitates. 'I really sensed that he loved me, although I didn't know why he did.'

'I believe he did, Marigold,' Lily says quietly.

Marigold nods. 'Then there was another carriage ride and we went to a big tall house by the sea, and I was so sleepy, and I thought I was being dressed in pretty nightclothes and put in a little bed, but I think it might have been a dream.'

'I expect it was,' Lily smiles.

It is just as well that Marigold should think this; even more fortunate that Lily and Felix got to her when they did. For Hortensia, still in shock at the revelation that the last intended victim of her old friend Cameron MacKilliver was her own great-grandniece, poured out much that she may later regret.

Watching Marigold sitting up straight, turning frequently to look out of the train window and remark with excitement on what she can see, Lily feels cold all over again as she remembers Hortensia's words.

He calms them with sweet drinks laced with laudanum. They are dazed and sleepy and cannot resist. He takes off their clothes, restrains them in the little beds and puts frilly baby bonnets on them to conceal the fact that he has cut off their hair because it is not baby hair, do you see, and it makes them look like women.

The cracked old voice had gone on and on, and it was as if Hortensia had forgotten Felix and Lily; as if she were kneeling in an imaginary confessional.

He keeps them sedated and he puts dummies in their mouths, fastening them behind their heads so that their mouths are stoppered and they cannot cry for help. He is disturbed by their developing bodies and he covers them with napkins. One girl had begun to—

But here Hortensia had shaken her head, for even in her state of shock, some things were too dreadful to recount.

Sooner or later, however, she had continued, *he loses control. The girls become so very scared, you see, they sob, they cry, they try to escape. He drugs them but they wake up. He plays baby games and sings lullabies to soothe them but they will not be soothed, and they grow hysterical and cannot be silenced, and in the end he—*

But she could not bring herself to speak of the end.

Lily wonders where they are, those poor girls, lost girls, outcast girls. She knows the names of two of them – Cora Naughton-Smythe, aged eleven, Isa Hatcher, aged thirteen. She thinks she can guess at the identity of their predecessors, for she believes theirs are the names in the ledger with the strange little symbol beside them.

But Mortimer always cleared up after his brother, and without doubt long habit will have ensured he did it thoroughly. He told them himself that there would be no means of proving what Cameron did: there would *be* no proof, and on that, Mortimer said, they might safely take his word.

Lily is overcome by a wave of depression that is very close to despair. Her job – hers and Felix's job – was to find the missing girls. They have failed, for the girls are dead and, apart from one man who will not tell, nobody knows where their poor bodies are.

Marigold is absorbed in watching a sheepdog herding a flock of sheep, giving an excited commentary on its every clever move. Felix, as if he senses Lily's mood, turns to her.

He meets her eyes, and she can see compassion and sympathy in his face. He says – mouths the words, almost, not wanting Marigolds to hear – 'We saved the last one.'

And the sudden tears blind her as she nods in agreement.

NINETEEN

The station master summons a fly and they are swept through the village and back to Shardlowes. Lily has tried to persuade Felix to return to London; that she and Marigold can perfectly well do this final leg of the journey without him. But he will not hear of it. He has his set expression, and there is no point arguing.

As the asylum looms up in the distance, she acknowledges to herself that she is actually very glad of his company.

They find the school superficially calm but with a constant and barely audible buzz of excited, horrified whispering just below the surface. Miss Carmichael, face as white as chalk, meets them in the hall and a cry of relief bursts out of her as she sees Marigold. Responding to Lily's curt comment that Marigold needs rest, she nods her approval – not that Lily had sought it – to Lily's announcement that she's taking the child straight up to the San and putting her to bed. As Lily helps the exhausted Marigold up the stairs, she hears Felix say quietly to Miss Carmichael, 'I have something to tell you.'

Lily wishes that she could stay and be party to what will follow. But for now she is still assistant matron and her duty is to Marigold.

She had hoped to get the child safely to the sick bay without anybody noticing, but the school is alive with eyes and ears and the upper corridors are lined with avid girls asking questions, demanding explanations, and Lily loses count of the times she says, 'Not now! Marigold needs rest.'

The noise precedes them and Matron is standing outside the treatment room, dressed in her full regalia and with a smile of such warmth and kindness that it takes Lily aback. Matron opens her arms and says calmly, 'Welcome back, Marigold. You must be tired, so bed for you, and cocoa, and a hot water bottle, and anything you would like to eat.'

'Anything? Really and truly?' Marigold perks up. 'And cocoa in bed?'

'Cocoa in bed,' Matron repeats with a chuckle.

Lily relinquishes her hold on the child, who stumbles forward and is caught by Matron. The two women's eyes meet over her head.

'Well done,' Matron says very quietly. 'I shall care for Marigold now.'

Lily knows that this is right, for Matron, restored to full health and efficiency, is in charge here now. Nevertheless, as Marigold is helped into the sick bay's ward, Lily feels such a sense of loss that it momentarily makes her feel faint.

And Marigold turns, looks straight at her and says with the calm maturity of a much older person, 'Thank you for bringing me back, Nurse Henry.'

The door closes and Lily stands alone in the passage.

It is time to relinquish the nurse's role and take up that of the enquiry agent. She is not sure if she is relieved or sorry.

She enters the room off the entrance hall where she first met Miss Carmichael without even a cursory knock. It would not be appropriate, for everything has changed.

Felix and Miss Carmichael sit in chairs either side of the fireplace, and the mood is so tense that Lily thinks she can hear it creaking.

Felix gets to his feet and offers her his chair. 'Miss Carmichael is telling me what has happened,' he says. 'Miss Dickinson has been arrested on a charge of abduction, along with her cousin Abraham Salt, who has been acting as her accomplice. There are unconfirmed rumours that some of the asylum staff have been interviewed.'

Lily glares at Miss Carmichael. 'You finally found out what has been happening in your school and did something about it,' she says coldly.

'I—' Miss Carmichael's mouth goes on opening and closing but no words emerge. She looks on the point of collapse, but Lily finds it hard to feel pity.

'It was not Miss Carmichael who acted, but Miss Long,' Felix says.

'Miss *Long*?' Lily is greatly surprised.

'Yes,' Felix replies. 'She found her courage and went to the police. They knew of this Salt character and his connection with Miss Dickie, and there have been mutterings of some sort of unpleasantness at the asylum and people paid to look the other way.'

'*Unpleasantness!*' Lily cries. 'Is *that* what it was?'

'I know,' Felix murmurs, adding in a hiss, '*Listen*, Lily!' for Miss Carmichael has found her voice and meekly puts her hand up as if asking for permission to speak.

'They – the police' – an expression of deep distaste twists her face, as if she can hardly bear to utter the word – 'said there have never been sufficient grounds for action to be taken, but apparently Miss Long insisted.' She looks as if this was a minor miracle. 'She— I— We are all very—' But, overcome, she shakes her head, unable to go on.

'What of you, Miss Carmichael?' Lily asks coolly. 'Are you still headmistress?'

Felix frowns but Lily feels they have a right to know.

'The Band of Angels have written and they propose that I take – er, that is, I am to go on a short holiday. To the seaside. They will come to the school and make an assessment before a decision is made.' She gulps, her eyes glistening with tears. 'I didn't *know*!' she cries.

Lily looks at her then at Felix. He shakes his head.

'Who will act as headmistress in your absence?' Lily asks.

'Miss Mallard,' Miss Carmichael mutters from behind the handkerchief she is pressing to her face. She removes it and looks straight at Lily. 'I have promoted Miss Long to the position of Head of Junior House,' she says, sitting up a little straighter, 'for I feel she deserves it.'

Quite shortly afterwards, Lily and Felix stand in the hall. He is about to go, and Eddy has been sent for with the trap.

'Either Miss Carmichael truly didn't know what was going on in her school and her only fault was being too willing to dismiss the problem of the missing girls,' Lily mutters, 'or she's desperately covering her tracks.'

'She may well pay for it either way,' Felix replies shortly.

He is, Lily reflects, inclined to be rather more lenient with Miss Carmichael than she is. But then, she thinks, it is not he who has been assistant matron here.

There is a soft tap on the door.

'That'll be Eddy,' Lily says, going to open it.

But it is not Eddy who stands beneath the porch. It is a tall, masculine-looking woman in blue gabardine, gaunt-faced beneath an unflattering hat.

She reaches out a hand in a leather glove and grasps Lily's arm. 'Is she all right?' she asks, and there is deep anxiety in the light-brown eyes.

Lily knows without asking who she means.

'Yes,' she says, putting her hand over the woman's.

The woman sags in relief. Then, straightening her shoulders, she says, 'My name is Dora Tewk, and I must speak to you in private.'

Lily leads the way to the little pavilion beside the lawn where she sat with Marigold. It is cold outside, but Dora Tewk and Felix are dressed for outdoors and Lily has fetched her warm cloak. They sit down, Dora Tewk in the middle, and she begins to speak.

'I am the nurse who had the care of Marigold Dunbar-Lea,' she begins, 'and it was I who brought her home to England. I have a position with a widower academic and his family in Cambridge and I have been keeping an eye on Marigold, bringing her little gifts, for the last nine years.'

There is a short silence. The Felix says, 'You have shown rare devotion, Miss Tewk.'

She shrugs. 'Marigold is a very special child.'

'How did you—' Lily begins, but Dora Tewk turns to her with a smile and says courteously, 'I believe it will be best if I tell my tale in my own way. With your permission?'

'Of course,' Lily says.

'I was trained in London and I went out to India with a major in the Ninth Lancers, his wife and baby son,' Dora Tewk says. 'After only eighteen months, however, my charge died of cholera, along with his mother.' Dora Tewk maintains an expressionless face but she cannot control herself entirely, and tears fill her light-brown eyes before she blinks them away. 'The major was willing to pay my passage back to England but I preferred to stay in Lucknow, and I was re-engaged by Roderick Dunbar-Lea and his wife Mary to look after their little girl, whose name was Marigold.' She smiles. 'That was in February 1869, and Marigold was a week old.'

She looks at Lily. 'You will no doubt know what is wrong with her, for you too have had the care of her. Poor little Marigold was born with a malformed, foreshortened leg, a hare lip and a cleft palate. The lip was dealt with very soon after birth, adequately but not with any degree of skill or consideration for the child's future looks. Her upper lip was left shortened, and she had an unsightly scar. The cleft palate was deemed too tricky to risk an operation by a local man. Roderick would only consider army surgeons, and was probably quite right not to trust them with his little daughter, but had he overcome his prejudices and engaged an Indian doctor, Marigold would have been made whole by the most skilful, careful hands, and life would have turned out very differently.'

There is a pause. Then she says, 'What you will not know – for how could you? – is her father's reaction to his damaged daughter. In short, he found his flawed child an embarrassment. He was, and I am sure still is, a dangerously handsome man and he was married to a beautiful, modest and intelligent woman, yet between them this golden couple produced what in his eyes was a deformed child. He could not bear to watch little Marigold trying to walk, for her malformed leg meant that although she moved about at a fair pace, she was forced to adopt an ungainly waddle. Furthermore, he could not bear to hear her trying to talk, for the fissure in the roof of her mouth means, as no doubt you have observed, that she has great difficulty pronouncing many of the consonants and all of the diphthongs.'

'I learned to understand her very quickly,' Lily says.

Dora Tewk smiles. 'I too, and her mother. Her father, however, lacked the patience and, I believe, the desire.' She frowns. 'And so he decided that Marigold must be removed from his sight and, indeed, from his life. He and Mary would have more children, he was quite sure of that; they would be healthy, whole and, with any luck, some of them would also be male.'

'And so you were commanded to bring Marigold back to England,' Felix says.

Dora Tewk nods. 'Indeed so. I was the obvious choice. That I might have preferred to stay in India was neither here nor there, for there was nobody else suitable and Marigold knew me well after nearly four years in my care.' She adds softly, 'For myself, I loved her – love her still – and could not have borne to abandon her to a stranger.'

'And what happened once you were in England?' Felix asks.

Lily flashes him a look. There is something about him . . . he is eager, straining forward, as if he would draw Miss Tewk's words out of her.

'Marigold was to be put in the care of her great-grandmother, in the hope that the wealthy and well-connected Adeline would find and pay for the appropriate treatment for her. And now' – she raises her chin, as if nerving herself for a difficult task, 'I must explain what had happened before, and why it is vital that you understand.'

'I know something of this,' Felix says softly.

Dora Tewk turns to him in surprise. 'How?' she asks.

There is a pause. Felix looks at Lily, Lily nods, so, at some length, Felix explains.

'And so – so it was your investigations into the fate of these poor girls that led you to find Marigold and bring her safely back?' Miss Tewk asks, looking from Lily to Felix. They nod. 'Then I am deeply in your debt.' She makes a little bow to each of them.

And now, as Dora Tewk picks up her story, Lily listens to the tale of a haughty old woman who had lost her husband and her only son, into whose care was placed an orphaned infant granddaughter for whom her initial dislike changed to grudging tolerance, to liking, finally to love.

'Adeline watched Mary grow into an enchanting but innocent and unworldly young woman and she became fearful, for Mary was her heir and would inherit a small fortune on her death and Adeline was quite sure she would attract the wrong sort of fortune-hungry suitor eager to get his hands on it.'

'So she summoned her solicitor and made quite sure that Mary would not inherit until she was twenty-five and had learned

about the ways of the world and particularly of ruthless, handsome and ambitious men,' Felix supplies.

Dora Tewk looks at him. 'Hortensia?' she asks, and he nods.

'It was a wise precaution,' Dora Tewk continues, 'for Mary
was a warm and generous girl who fell in love easily, and
Adeline had watched as she gave her heart to a succession of
puppies, ponies and stable boys, invariably to have that tender
heart bruised as the object of Mary's love failed to return it.
Adeline was not seriously worried, however, for Mary always
recovered when the next object of adoration came along, and
in this way life jogged along happily enough until the year
Mary turned eighteen.'

'Then what happened?' Lily demands when Dora stops for
breath.

'It was 1866, and Mary fell truly, sincerely and giddily in
love for the first time,' Dora says. 'The young man in question
was Roderick Dunbar-Lea, but everyone called him Roddy, and
he was in the Indian civil service, home on leave. He and Mary
met at a supper party given by a friend of Adeline's. Roddy
needed a wife; a wife, moreover, with good prospects, for
Roddy was a man with grave problems. He was a gambler and
deeply in debt, with no hope of repaying what he owed
and dire consequences if he did not. The trip home was his
final, desperate chance.'

'Did nobody warn Mary?' Lily asks.

'It would have done no good.'

'What about Adeline? Why didn't the friends giving the party
tell her about this Roddy?' she persists.

'Because he kept his problems to himself and masked his
desperation.'

'Yes,' Lily says slowly, 'of course, he would. Go on.'

'Thank you,' Dora says with a certain irony. She is, Lily
observes, a very self-possessed woman. 'Prospects did not come
much better than Mary's, and Roddy set about winning her with
well-disguised and efficient ruthlessness. Despite Adeline's
misgivings – for here in her drawing room beguiling her granddaughter was the very epitome of a dangerous young man –
Roddy and Mary were married in 1867. Watching them prepare
to sail for India, Adeline comforted herself with the thought

that Roddy couldn't get his hands on her money, should she die, until Mary had shed the stars from her eyes and begun to understand precisely what sort of a man she had married.'

'Poor Mary,' Lily murmurs. 'To love him so much, and all the time he wanted her for her money.' She glances at Dora. 'Or did he grow to love her too?'

But Dora just shrugs.

'And then' – she picks up the tale – 'there was Marigold.' She pauses, as if gathering herself. 'I took her to meet Adeline. But Adeline was old and sad by then, frequently confusing Marigold with her mother, and it seemed Roddy and Mary's hopes for Marigold were to be dashed, for it seemed Adeline would do nothing.'

'She wrote to her sister,' Felix says, 'and it was Hortensia who came up with the solution, for her old friend Cameron MacKilliver had connections with a boarding school where they took girls as young as Marigold and where few questions were asked.'

'Yes,' Dora Tewk breathes. 'And so via a ruthless and selfish father, a loving but unworldly and ineffectual mother, an elderly great-grandmother who didn't care any more, her sister and that sister's friendship with a wealthy old man, Marigold ended up at Shardlowes School.'

Presently Lily stirs. 'Marigold believes that the woman who came here last September posing as her mother is no such thing.'

Dora smiles. 'Marigold is a very observant child,' she replies. 'She is quite right.'

Lily smiles. 'I am not at all surprised. Do you know what happened?'

'I believe so, yes,' Dora Tewk says. 'Adeline died in 1872, and as I explained, she had ensured Mary could not inherit until she was twenty-five. But it is my belief that Mary died just *before* the crucial birthday.'

'Your belief?' Felix says sharply. 'You do not know for sure?'

Dora Tewk hesitates. 'Mary was failing fast when I left,' she replies. 'You must understand that I was very close to Mary – it was she who told me the tale I have just related.' She pauses, looking down at her hands in her lap. 'Mary also knew

Roddy kept a mistress. This woman looked very similar to her and her name, oddly, was also Mary: Mary North.'

'So you're saying that Mary died and Roddy substituted his mistress in order that he would get his hands on Adeline's wealth?' Lily asks. Before Dora Tewk can answer she exclaims, 'But how could that possibly happen? Even if the two women resembled each other, someone would notice!'

'There was nobody who *could* notice,' Dora replies. 'Roddy arranged a new posting in Calcutta and his household staff did not go with him. I had already been sent back to England. As far as anyone knew, Roddy's wife was the woman he married in 1867.'

'There are more children,' Lily says. 'Marigold told me she has three younger brothers and a little sister. All of them, no doubt, living handsomely on Adeline's money.'

Dora Tewk is smiling grimly. 'They will not do so for much longer,' she says. 'It is part of the reason I am here.' She looks at Lily. 'I have engaged an enquiry agent of my own, whose contact in India is even now completing his investigations into death records for Lucknow in the last months of 1872 and marriage entries for Calcutta in the same quarter. The process has taken a very long time, but I have recently been informed that it has almost reached a satisfactory conclusion.' She smiles thinly. 'Roddy has not buried his past quite as thoroughly as he believed.'

Lily shoots a glance at Felix and guesses from his expression that he has had the same thought. Hoping she is right in her impression that this plain-speaking woman values honesty, she says, 'Miss Tewk, this enquiry cannot be cheap.'

Dora Tewk turns to her with a wry smile. 'Thank you for your concern, Miss Raynor. You are quite right; it is indeed proving rather costly. However, it is not I who am footing the bill.'

Lily sees from Felix's face that he is already in thrall to this extraordinary woman. 'Who have you persuaded to pay?' he asks bluntly, and Dora Tewk actually laughs.

'I am in contact with the ancient Inverness firm of solicitors who control the Stirling estate; who, I understand, have acted for the family for generations. It appears they already had their

suspicions concerning Roddy Dunbar-Lea and his wife, undoubtedly aroused when Adeline made the final amendment to
her will.'

She pauses, mischief in her light eyes, and Lily and Felix
say together, 'What was it?'

'Apparently Adeline never trusted Roddy and could not
convince herself that Mary would ever stop adoring him. She
arranged her affairs so that Mary only inherited one-third of
her estate. The remainder was put in trust for the children
of Roderick Dunbar-Lea and Mary née Featherwood. As one
would expect from an old and well-respected firm of solicitors,
the money was extremely well managed and the sum has grown
handsomely.'

'And if you are right, then there is only one child of that
union,' Lily says.

'Indeed,' says Dora. 'When Marigold reaches her majority,
she will be a wealthy young woman.'

Lily is frowning, thinking hard. 'But what happens to her
now?' she asks.

Dora seems to understand. 'Her father pays her school fees,
Miss Raynor, and will continue to do so. I do not believe there
will be any legal challenge concerning his subterfuge and his
substitute wife, and consequently no change in the status quo.
Marigold will—'

'Surely she won't stay *here*?' Felix interrupts. 'She'll be far
too frightened, after what's happened!'

Both Lily and Dora turn to him. They exchange a glance,
and it is Lily who says, 'You don't know Marigold.'

TWENTY

Marm Smithers attends the trial of Ann Dickinson and her cousin Abraham Salt. He reports every evening to Felix over the nightly whisky beside the fire at Kinver Street.

It rapidly becomes clear that the two defendants are going to be economical with the truth.

'Those bloody aristocrats in the Band of Angels have *bought* them!' Marm shouts on a night of heavy rain when he and Felix are alone. He is seething with the injustice of it. 'They've found them a very smart barrister who's putting it into the jury's minds that Dickinson and Salt are simple-minded peasants who believed Cameron MacKilliver was paying them so handsomely to facilitate his nocturnal excursion with a little girl because he *needed a bit of excitement!*' He pauses, panting, his thin face flushed. Then he adds, 'They're being paid handsomely now as well, provided they keep their mouths shut about the Band's connection.'

'You *know* that?' demands Felix.

'Yes.' Marm taps the side of his nose. 'Can't tell you how and sadly it's not for publication, but there's no doubt about it. And those aforesaid aristocrats will square their collective conscience and tell themselves Cameron MacKilliver was a mildly eccentric recluse, and they will erase from their memories the unpleasant fact that two women and at least six girls are dead!'

Nobody knows precisely how many girls died at Cameron's hands. Despite extensive searches and enquiries, no trace of any of them has been found.

'And what of Mortimer?' Felix asks.

'Vanished,' Marm replies succinctly.

Felix has suspected as much. 'He'll be like a beetle on its back without the cushioning effects of wealth, privilege and powerful friends that have supported him all his life,' he remarks.

Marm does not answer for a few moments. Then he says, sighing, 'Ah, but it'll be those very same elements that look after him now. He's gone, Felix, and I doubt he'll ever be heard from again.'

Lily has left her post as assistant matron at Shardlowes School. For now Matron is managing alone, but already Lily's replacement has been selected: a middle-aged spinster who has recently returned from Hong Kong and is alone in the world. Miss Carmichael has got her wish, Lily reflects, and found someone totally without needy dependants.

One of Lily's final tasks is to arrange a meeting between Marigold and Dora Tewk. She invites them both to her room in the sick bay and is on the point of leaving them alone when Marigold sends her a pleading glance.

She sits down beside Marigold on the bed and together they face Dora Tewk.

Listening, Lily thinks that Dora could not have improved upon the way she told the story. She is, Lily concludes, a woman of fine moral character tempered with compassion and love, and Lily finds herself hoping very much that Dora will continue to watch over Marigold as she has done for so long.

Perhaps the crucial factor is that Dora does not flinch from the truth; and it *is* the truth, for the Inverness solicitors have confirmed it.

'I *knew* it,' Marigold says passionately when Dora finally stops speaking. 'I *knew* that woman was not my mother!'

But the triumph is brief.

Turning to Dora, she whispers, 'What happened to her?' Her face is taut with grief.

Dora leans forward and takes her hand. 'She was not strong, my dear,' she says gently. 'You probably will not remember, for you were very small, but she was failing fast even as we prepared to leave Lucknow.'

And, thinks Lily, the poor woman's end was probably hastened by losing her adored little daughter. All because a dangerously handsome, feckless and ambitious man could not bear to be in the presence of a flawed child.

Looking at Marigold, who has endured so much in her short

life yet retains a lively interest in the world, a smiling demeanour
and a loving nature, Lily reflects it is Roddy's loss.

Late on the Friday afternoon after Lily's return to Hob's Court,
Georgiana Long comes to settle her bill and brings news. Felix
nips out to the kitchen to make a pot of tea and arrange slices
of Mrs Clapper's Victoria sponge on a plate (Mrs Clapper is
managing two days a week now and today has been baking),
and presently Lily, Miss Long and he are in Lily's office and
settling in for a good chat.

The first news, surprising to Felix but not to Lily, is that
Marigold has announced she wants to stay at Shardlowes.

'As Head of Juniors,' Miss Long states, with only a barely
perceptible puffing-out of the chest, 'I have made it my responsibility to watch her closely, but she does not seem in the least
affected by what *that man*' – she mouths the words – 'did.
It appears he was so kind and gentle that she never even suspected
an ulterior motive. We encourage her in the belief that he was
harmless for, although it is an untruth, it is better for Marigold
to believe it. Miss Tewk agrees, and is adopting the same policy.'

Miss Long's round brown eyes shine as she speaks of Dora
Tewk. Lily wonders if this indicates a transfer of Miss Long's
adoration from Miss Carmichael to a new idol and rather hopes
it does.

'Miss Carmichael has returned from her brief holiday by the
seaside,' Miss Long goes on.

'In sackcloth and ashes and determined to do better?' asks
Felix.

Miss Long shakes her head disapprovingly at his levity but
does not deny it.

'What of Marigold's future?' asks Lily.

'Miss Stirling has announced she wants to be involved in the
child's life,' Miss Long replies. Leaning closer to her audience,
she adds in a whisper, 'We are not at all sure this is wise, but
Marigold is willing to pay her great-grand-aunt a visit provided
Miss Tewk accompanies her.'

'And she will do this?' Felix asks.

Miss Long turns to him. 'She will. She is not going to abandon
the child now.'

'Is Marigold happy?' Lily asks.

'She is indeed, Miss Raynor. Miss Tewk revealed to me that it was in a way a relief to the child to know that her dear mother had died soon after she left for England, for it means that her mother did *not* forget all about her, as she has always feared. Marigold is' – she pauses – 'more *serene* now.'

'I am glad,' Lily says softly.

When Felix has shown Miss Long out and seen her on her way, he returns to the inner sanctum.

'Miss Long is a new woman,' he remarks.

Lily, studying the cheque Miss Long has left on her desk, adds, 'And a businesslike one. This sum is correct to the penny.' She looks up. 'There is a new, fierce spirit in her, and she is determined to do her very best for her girls.'

Felix nods. He looks down at her for a moment. 'Marigold will be all right,' he says.

Lily nods. She doesn't want to meet his eyes because hers are full of tears.

As well as Miss Long's payment there is a very generous cheque from the Inverness solicitors. The accompanying letter, once Felix has translated the convoluted legal language, seems to say that the Stirling estate wishes to make over this large sum in recognizance of the World's End Bureau's actions in saving the life of the last of the Stirlings.

Ann Dickinson and Abraham Salt are found guilty. The jury are not fooled by the former's crinkly faced smile and deem her the more culpable and her sentence is correspondingly longer.

The Band of Angels must have maintained their pressure, for the name of that organization is not mentioned once.

Despite this rather unsatisfactory conclusion to the case, Felix reckons they have cause enough for a modest celebration. He persuades Lily to part with a pound or two from their earnings with which to buy champagne, and they invite Marm Smithers to join them.

Felix suggests that Lily also invite her mysterious boatman.

Felix has not met him; has only seen him in the distance, and
the man looms large in Felix's imagination. He is aware that
Lily has recently slipped away to see him on that boat of his;
the following morning she seemed calmer, as if the distress of
recent events had been put into perspective.

Lily smiles and says no, she doesn't think her friend would
want to come.

The evening is going well. Several toasts are drunk, and Felix's
remark that business is booming is greeted with cheers and a
smug grin from Marm, who has managed to spread the word
that the World's End Bureau played a major role in the arrest
and conviction of Ann Dickinson and her cousin.

He is, however, inclined to be gloomy because the Band of
Angels have escaped without a slur.

'Cheer up, you can't win them all,' Felix says philosophically.

Marm merely shrugs.

Marm has announced it is time to leave, and Felix decides to
go with him. As Marm is struggling into his coat out in the
hall, Felix, more than a little drunk, puts his arm round Lily
and kisses her on the cheek.

It is a chaste kiss, but she frowns at him. 'Is that the action
of an employee towards his boss?' she asks, only half in jest.

He steps back. He is looking at her intently, but then he
smiles. He whispers softly, 'I've seen your ankles. Remember?
On the train to Portsmouth, when you showed me the mark
from the trip wire?'

It is quite clear that she does remember.

She says lightly, 'Only one of them. Look, Marm has managed
to get into his coat at last. Goodnight, Felix.'

He takes the hint and joins Marm by the open front door.
Marm calls out goodnight. Felix turns and looks back at her.

'It was a lovely ankle,' he says, then he slams the door behind
him.

Very late one night the following week, Lily is on her way
to bed when she hears a soft knocking at the front door. She
is already in her nightdress, a thick robe over the top for

warmth, and she knows she is as decently clad as in her daytime attire; apart, that is, for the long flowing fair hair that she has just released from its bun and has not yet tidied into its night-time plait.

She stands in the hall, hesitant.

Whoever is at the door knocks again, more forcefully, and a quiet, well-educated voice says, 'Miss Raynor? I believe you are there? My profuse apologies for the lateness of the hour, but it is imperative I speak to you.'

The letter box flap opens a fraction and a card flutters down on to the mat. Lily picks it up, reads the name . . . and has to lean against the wall for support. When she has recovered, she hurries to open the door.

A tall, well-built, soberly dressed man in his seventies stands outside. Even as the door opens his hat is swept off, revealing collar-length white hair, and he makes a courteous bow.

'Please come in, sir,' Lily squeaks.

He straightens up, and she observes a smile cross the craggy features. He steps inside and she closes the door.

'Are you alone?' he asks.

'Yes. My associate went home some hours ago, my tenant is a ballerina and will not return for some time yet, and it's not one of my housekeeper's days and she doesn't live in.'

She is mentally punching herself for gabbling like an over-excited schoolgirl when a simple *Yes* would have done, but he is nodding and he looks relieved. 'In that case, may we repair to your office, perhaps?'

'Of course.'

She leads him through the outer office and into the inner sanctum, pulling out the chair that Felix usually sits in and wondering, suppressing a giggle, what Felix will say when she tells him tomorrow whose bottom has recently rested on it.

She pokes up the fire, feeds on some more fuel and then takes her own seat behind her desk.

'How may I help you, sir?' she asks, and she is glad to hear how calm she sounds. It is just as well fast-pounding hearts are not audible to others.

Her visitor stares at her for a few moments. He is not smiling now: he could not look more serious. 'I believe I may say with a degree of certainty that the World's End Bureau is aware of the existence of a somewhat secretive philanthropic organization and its role in certain recent events,' he says.

She had a feeling that is why he is here.

There is no point in denying it since undoubtedly he knows the truth, so she just says, 'Yes.'

He nods slowly, and murmurs, 'Oh, dear.'

Lily waits.

After quite a long pause he says, 'If you have been entertaining any thoughts of making this knowledge public – via your associate's journalist friend Marmaduke Smithers, perhaps, whom I do in fact much admire – may I humbly beg you to think again?'

Lily is storing up the remark to repeat to Marm.

Then she says, 'The World's End Bureau constitutes Felix Wilbraham and I, as you probably know.' Of course he does, she thinks. 'We have only briefly discussed the link with the Band of Angels, having been preoccupied with the welfare of the little girl who between us, and thanks mainly to Felix's courage, we saved from almost certain death.'

She hears the echo of her loud voice and for a moment she is horrified that she has spoken to this man in such a forthright, not to say accusatory way. But he is nodding, his expression sad and almost meek, as if he accepts he deserves the castigation.

'You are right to be indignant, not to say furious, if the becoming blush in your cheeks is any guide,' he says, and she recalls his reputation as a devotee of comely women. *And* she is in her nightwear . . .

'Marigold Dunbar-Lea is safe and she has recovered rapidly,' she says in a chilly tone. 'Happily, she has but fuzzy and muddled memories of her days with Cameron MacKilliver. She says he was kind and loving, and she has swallowed Felix's quick fiction that he – Cameron – was taking her to her relation, and that was why she was removed from the school.'

Her visitor nods, and she can see he is about to speak.

But she's not going to let him.

'Marigold survived, but at least two and I am sure not a few more did not,' she says severely. 'In addition, Esme Sullivan died at the hands of Cameron MacKilliver. Even if it was done in a panic because he couldn't stop her yelling at him, it was he who ended her life. And his brother Mortimer pushed poor Genevieve Swanson off a train!'

She is shouting now but she doesn't care. Someone needs to speak for the dead, and right now the role has fallen to her.

He does not say anything for some time. Then, signing deeply, he passes a large hand across his face.

'You are right to be so angry, Miss Raynor, and I admire your passion and your determination to act for those who cannot act for themselves.' A pause, carefully judged. Then: 'If you decide to reveal the involvement of the Band of Angels – as indeed is your right, since it is a fact and cannot be denied, Cameron and Mortimer MacKilliver being founder members – please be aware that it will do harm – a very great deal of harm – to an organization whose unwavering mission is to alleviate poverty and ignorance.' Another pause. 'Particularly in the case of your own sex.'

'I am aware of that,' she replies stiffly, 'but—'

He leans forward, face intent, and for the first time she senses the power in the man.

'*Are* you?' he demands. 'Are you really? The Band are on the very brink of recruiting our most important and influential member, and the benefits he will bring – the sheer wealth, apart from anything else – cannot be exaggerated. His name, however, *cannot* be linked with the recent unpleasantness' – she emits an unbelieving gasp at this but be ignores her – 'and it is my duty to tell you, Miss Raynor, that if you decide to reveal the Band of Angels's involvement, all those members whose reputation is important to them will scatter and flee. Which is,' he adds thoughtfully, 'pretty much all of them.'

'I thought it was a secret organization and nobody knew the identity of the membership?'

He gives her a shrewd glance. 'Miss Raynor, do not be naive.'

Slowly she nods, remembering how easily Felix found out about the Band of Angels; how both Violetta da Rosa and Marm Smithers knew about them and how Marm's knowledge stretched as far as providing a membership list.

She feels the power of his will. He hasn't said any more, but the pressure is steadily mounting.

'What about Miss Dickie and her cousin? They know about the MacKillivers.'

'Neither Ann Dickinson nor Abraham Salt have revealed what they know and nor will they.' His large, mobile mouth turns down. 'There were – ah – incentives.'

It is just as Marm surmised.

'You mean they've been given money to keep their mouths shut?'

He does not answer, but merely bows his head.

Lily is thinking. She and Felix, largely because of Marm's eloquent and powerful words, have pretty much decided not to reveal what they know about the Band of Angels. For Marm has recently discovered that the organization is funding a new push to help street women receive a rudimentary education in the hope that it will help them find work of a different and less dangerous sort. There is talk of the MacKilliver twins' former estate being donated as a residential school for this purpose.

She has one final question.

'What about Mortimer?' she asks softly. 'In addition to his other crimes, it's virtually certain he pushed Cameron out of that window in the turret.' She has tried and tried to recall these crucial few minutes but it is hopeless: there is a deep, dark void in her memory. 'And Mortimer has disappeared.'

Her visitor nods. 'He has,' he agrees. 'He still has friends, Miss Raynor; *good* friends, who understand the trials he has borne through all the long years of trying to control and cover up for his brother and believe he has suffered enough.'

'Enough for two deaths?' she murmurs.

And he will not meet her eyes.

'Mortimer MacKilliver will never be found, Miss Raynor,' he says eventually. 'He has gone far beyond the reach of British justice.'

'You mean he's dead?' she demands.

But he doesn't answer.

Silence falls. Lily's visitor sits perfectly still, but she can sense the impatience for her answer building up.

She says, 'Felix and I will do as you wish, sir.'

He raises his head and stares right at her. 'I have your word?'
'Yes.'
'And you speak for both of you?'
'I do.'
He lets out a long sigh, and she sees his big shoulders slump
in relief.

As she sees him to the door, he turns and says, 'This is not
the first time that I have heard good things of the World's End
Bureau, Miss Raynor, and I very much doubt it will be the last.
Virtue is its own reward, they say, but if I can assist your
fortunes in any way, I shall. Good night.' He has already put
on his hat, and now he doffs it, replaces it and strides away
into the darkness.

A short time later, a key turns in the lock and the door to 3,
Hob's Court is violently thrust open again. The Little Ballerina,
back from her tour and now performing in the West End, irrupts
into the hall, smelly, sweaty, her face heavy with grease and
her cloak grubby and stained.

Lily, still reeling, has not moved out of the hall, but as usual
the Little Ballerina is far too self-absorbed to comment or even,
probably, to notice.

'Big carriage!' she cries excitedly, extending her long,
graceful arms to indicate the size. 'End of road, big black shiny
carriage, pretty white horses just same!'

'Really?' Lily says. Her voice is far from normal but, once
again, it goes unnoticed.

'*Really!*' the Little Ballerina insists. 'Driver in smart clothes
all one colour' – a uniform, Lily assumes – 'and big grand man
getting inside!' She rubs her thumb against her first two fingers
in the universal gesture for money. 'Big grand *rich* man,' she
adds, shooting a sly look at Lily from her narrow black eyes.
'He new client? Come here for you?'

Lily takes a deep breath, making quite sure she will sound
calm, not to say indifferent. Then she says coolly, 'He must
have had business elsewhere. Nobody has called here.'

The Little Ballerina puts on a sulky pout and stomps her way
upstairs to her own rooms. Lily wanders through to the inner
sanctum and makes sure the guard is in front of the fire. She

straightens the chairs, casts a quick look around the room and then she too heads for the stairs.

As she climbs slowly up to bed she is smiling.

She is thinking how fortunate it is that the Little Ballerina is so unobservant; so uninterested in the world outside her own life; so chronically self-obsessed that other people do not penetrate.

Even the prime minister.

For surely, in the whole of London, the Little Ballerina must be one of the few people not to recognize William Ewart Gladstone.